Also by the Author

Non-fiction

Footlights in the Foothills,
Amateur Theatre of Las Vegas and Fort Union,
New Mexico, 1871-1899

Cowboy Reunions of Las Vegas, New Mexico
Writing as Pat Romero

Las Vegas, New Mexico, 1835-1935

PRAIRIE MADNESS

CONSPIRACY AT FORT UNION

EDWINA ROMERO

RANDOM
HORSE
PRESS

First Edition

Prairie Madness
Conspiracy at Fort Union

Copyright ©2008, 2018 by Edwina P. Romero

Publisher: Random Horse Press
PO Box 794
Las Vegas, New Mexico 87701

Editor-In-Chief: Peter Werrenrath
Top Duck Productions
Long Beach, CA 90803

Disclaimer: This novel is a work of fiction. Although some of the characters are inspired by historical figures, most are the author's imaginary creations; furthermore, locations and events, although based on actual places and historical events, are fictional. Apart from historical figures, events and locations, any resemblances between the novel and actual people--living or dead--their circumstances and location are coincidental.

Book and Cover Design by David Pascale

Photo Credits: All photos courtesy of Fort Union National Monument unless otherwise noted

Cover photo: Santa Fe Trail Wagon Ruts

Library of Congress Catalog Control Number: 2015944233

ISBN: 978-0-578-42458-3

Prairie Madness, Conspiracy at Fort Union, is lovingly
dedicated to the strong women who raised me—
Reta, Edna, and Lorraine:
The Keenan sisters.

PRAIRIE MADNESS

CONSPIRACY AT FORT UNION

THE SANTA FE TRAIL

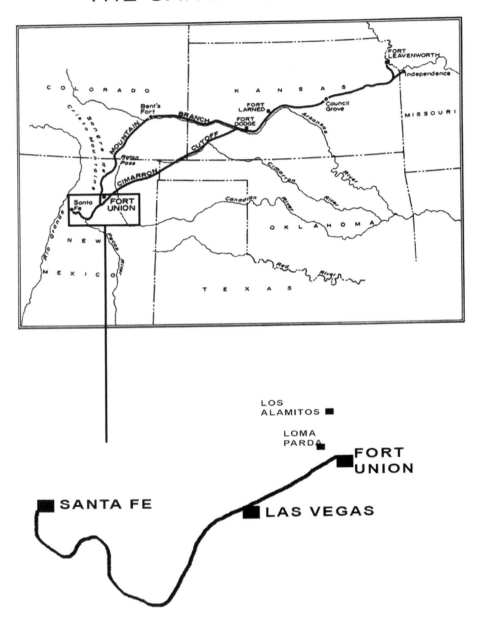

FORT UNION SCHEMATIC

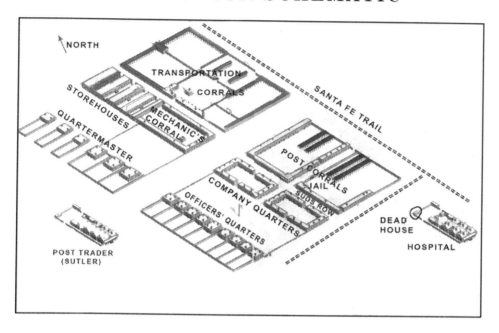

William A. Bell, an English surveyor, visited Fort Union in 1867 and wrote:

"Fort Union is a bustling place; it is the largest military establishment to be found on the plains, and is the supply centre from which the forty or fifty lesser posts scattered all over the country within a radius of 500 miles or more, are supplied with men, horses, munitions of war, and often with everything needed for their support . . . . A large sutler's store must not be forgotten, at which daily sales average 3,000 dollars.* Over 1,000 workmen are here kept constantly employed, building and repairing wagons, gathering in and distributing supplies, making harness, putting up buildings and attending to the long trains of goods and supplies constantly arriving or departing."

* equivalent to $51,000 in 2018

It is a wild wind, a warning wind, a wind cooked up by the Furies. It races around the house, each gust followed by another and another, destruction in its howl—things clatter along the yard, a bucket, a bit of fallen gutter, something heavier, a chimney pot, all swept away in its belly. The sound is at once high and low, signalling two different outcomes.

Edna O'Brien,
House of Splendid Isolation

Dramatic Society to Present Melo-Drama

Regular Correspondent to the Optic. Fort Union, April 14, 1881. The newly erected and charmingly appointed, Fort Union Opera House, will host a production by the Fort Union Dramatic Society of *The Irish Attorney of Ireland, 1770,* a popular melo-drama, starring our own Seán Flannery, formerly of the Comedy Company, at this post.

The Dramatic Society is the most complete dramatic and musical organization this correspondent has seen perform at the Fort. Every attraction is special, every member first-class, and all of the society's offerings thus far have been modest and respectable. The enlisted men of this society reject dramas that deviate in the slightest degree from decency.

Prior to the performance, the 23rd Infantry Band, which most appropriately earned the name of the Best in the West, will play a selection of favorites and march, in formation, from the Parade Ground to the Opera House, located at the Post Trader's Compound.

J. Clooney, Regimental Correspondent

PROLOGUE
In which a body is found

<u>Thursday, April 14, 1881</u>

Clutching the cedar box, slightly smaller than a mailing packet, Porfirio Gonzalez stood behind the counter of his mercantile store and watched Sergeant Seán Flannery swing his crooked leg over the back of his *pinto* mare. Gonzalez smiled and fingered the padlock as he recalled that most of the American soldiers disparaged the paint horses. 'Fit only for Injuns,' he heard more than one private say. Flannery settled into the saddle, stroked the horse's neck, and gently urged her forward. Gonzalez did not imagine that it would be the last time he watched this familiar event unfold. He stared aimlessly as the horse and rider jogged away beneath the mottled shade of the budding cottonwood trees, thrashing and twisting in the wind.

When Gonzalez was building his store, a two-room *adobe* rectangle with a pitched roof, he had envisioned a thriving village, bustling with children, family, and neighbors. "A good place to settle," he had told his wife. And so, she, Ninfa, put names to the places. *Los Alamitos* for the village, which was no more than a wide flat meadow at the base of the foothills. One day, she pointed to a stand of pine trees. *"La Casa del Sol,"* she said, "will be our home."

But there are no children, there are no families at *Los Alamitos*. There are a few scattered buildings, the crumbling foundation of a house not built, a fence unfinished, the small squat store, and in a clearing scattered with Cottonwood saplings at the base of the foothills, a grave. Sometimes, when the wind is right and the shadows long, there is Ninfa, a spirit wandering among the whispering pines, caught for a moment in silhouette at the top of the ridge, her skirts billowing.

Porfirio turned, and holding SeánFlannery's box under his arm, disappeared behind the curtain and entered the back room, his *casita*. Because there was but one small window high on the east wall, the space was dim from noon to sunset and remained cool during the heat of the day. The room was sparsely furnished with a

1

narrow cot, a chest of drawers, a small round table, two wooden chairs, and a turquoise blue *trastero* that Ninfa painted and trimmed with rosebuds. A woven blanket lay on the hard-packed dirt floor, and unlike the store, the room was neat and clean of the relentless prairie dust. Against the south wall, above the iron cook stove hung an ornately framed photograph of a wedding couple. The woman wears a long, lacey dress and a gossamer veil that floats around her like a cloud. Porfirio had worn his only suit that day and a freshly laundered white shirt buttoned to the top.

After sliding the box into a small *nicho* carved into the *adobe* behind the photograph, Gonzalez returned to the store and took up his place behind the counter. Most travelers and the nearby ranchers skirted Los Alamitos. They preferred the excitement of Loma Parda with its bawdy houses and gambling halls, the variety of the Las Vegas shops and public halls, or the exotic, tinned delicacies at the Fort Union Trader's Store. Porfirio stared at the square of sunlight bursting in through the window, and when he heard the hoof beats of several horses entering *la placita,* he knew it to be his most frequent customer.

"*Buenos días, Porfirio Gonzalez,*" said Vicente Silva, entering the store and scanning the dark corners of the dusty room. As he did on most days, Silva engaged the shopkeeper in a brief conversation about the dry devil-winds and the absence of rain. He bought a pouch of tobacco and dropped more coins than necessary on the counter. Ignoring his change, Silva nodded, turned, and approached the door. He pulled on the heavy metal latch, and without looking back, asked, "Have you seen a lone rider—a stranger on a badly groomed buckskin—pass here?"

"*No, señor,*" answered Porfirio.

Silva yanked the door open and passed silently across the threshold, like the spirit he was often said to be. Listening to the slow, measured hoof beats as the men rode away, Gonzalez pondered the vagaries of life that had brought Mr. Silva and his associates from their Las Vegas enterprises to the little settlement of Los Alamitos. In the months since they arrived, Silva had not opened a gambling hall or drinking establishment, none of the poor farmers had been plundered or murdered, and none of the daughters stolen although one of the sons of Juan Diego Cabeza de Baca deserted his elderly parents to ride with Silva.

As the sun passed, stretching the tree shadows into long awkward angles, Gonzalez again heard hoof beats—a single horse, an uneven step. He pulled on his hat and walked out of the store. From the east, SeánFlannery's horse, Rosie, limped into the clearing, blood trickling from a gash on her right foreleg. Head hanging, reins trailing in the dust, the mare approached her former home, the corral on the north side of the store.

"Whoa, whoa, *yegua*," said Gonzalez and spoke low to the quivering horse. He grabbed the loose reins, caressed her mud-streaked neck, and led her into the corral. After quickly treating the superficial cuts, Porfirio saddled his own horse and rode east. Within minutes, they reached the ridge and halted. If Gonzalez had lifted his gaze, he would have seen the flags and chimneys of Fort Union, but instead he stared down at Los Alamitos Lake, rippling in the wind, surrounded by sparse, bent reeds and crusty grey mud. It was then that he saw the body, lying face down at the edge of the pond, arms and legs spread as if in flight.

Gonzalez urged his horse down the slope. She snorted uneasily but did not shy or offer to bolt. A few feet from the body, he dismounted, dropped the reins to the ground, and with a heavy feeling of futility, knelt beside the body, gently turned it over, and searched for a pulse. "*Díos mio,*" he whispered. Removing his hat, Porfirio made the sign of the cross and bowed his head. Then he mounted his horse and rode at a steady gallop for Fort Union.

Chapter 1: In which an announcement is made.

Outside the Fort Union Opera House, at the northern edge of the Post Trader's Compound, the prairie winds howled, shoving dust and grit through the hairsbreadth between window frame and sill, door and threshold. With the exception of a few early morning and late evening hours, each day the wind thundered across the prairie, bending the delicate grasses and snapping young green trees as if they were old dry twigs. Some nights, the winds picked up again after midnight. The old-timers shook their heads and said the Spring winds carried drought, plague, and Prairie Madness, the incurable, untreatable, and perhaps mythical disease of the plains that diminished the minds of human beings.

Inside the Opera House, the Fort Union Dramatic Society was rehearsing for its premier production. The actors, enlisted men all, were edgy and irritable, their skin taut from the relentless, desiccating winds and the nearly constant sun, their voices sometimes cracking like the boys they used to be.

It was the day before opening night—dress rehearsal—as Private Harlan Davies, the director, called it. These men who spent their precious recreation time as would-be performers had but a few hours until Retreat sounded and they reverted to soldiering. On stage, P. J. Washington was practicing his Indian club swinging to the loud cheers of the actors in costume for *The Irish Attorney of Ireland, 1770.* Davies believed he had scored a coupe when he enticed Seán Flannery away from the Comedy Company to play the lead in this new melo-drama. Only last month, First Sergeant Clooney's correspondence in the *Las Vegas Daily Optic* extolled Flannery's virtues, dubbing him "the very life and soul of the Comedy Company." Davies is betting that without its life and soul, the Comedy Company will falter and his Dramatic Society will become the focus of entertainment at Fort Union.

"Okay, P.J., that looks good," shouted Davies. "Let's get the first act underway. Cast, please. May I have the cast onstage, please," and Davies clapped his hands together.

First Sergeant Jud Clooney entered the Opera House and took a seat in the back row beside Timmy Sullivan. "Where in hell is Flannery?" whispered Clooney.

Irritable and itchy in a gown of thick rough wool, a wig, feathered hat, and an oversized bustle and bosom, Timmy shrugged and rose from his seat. "How in hell should I be knowing that?" Then he moved to join the other cast members assembling onstage.

"Harlan will have his head if he doesn't show up soon," mumbled Clooney, turning to look at the closed doors behind him. "Seán's been off-duty for hours."

At the Post Trader's Store, a few yards south of the Opera House, Josiah Foote stepped out and surveyed the small group of women and old men approaching the *portal*. He stood a moment, hands on hips, frock coat flapping in the wind. Then he shouted, "Closed! We're closed I say! Come back tomorrow." Damn Injuns, he thought, never have a thing of value to trade. Nothing but beads and blankets and baskets. And without a care for what distances they may have traveled, Foote turned his back to them, closed the heavy double doors with a loud bang, then chained and padlocked the handles. Waving the group away, he stepped off the boardwalk. Bent forward against the ferocious wind and holding his hat on his head, he made his way across the grounds toward his home and his wife, the great disappointment of his life—not even a good breeder—he thought.

As her husband approached, Olivia dropped the lace curtain she had been clutching. It billowed softly, fell against the window, then shivered as the wind roared and rattled the glass. Through the pink gauze, she watched the man she had married, hunched over like an enormous mythical beast, approach the house. Olivia hoped the fresh blossoms from the garden—a treat so early in the spring—might lend some gaiety to the evening meal. She sighed as she recalled the early days of their life together, entertaining merchants and travelers, and how she had thrilled to see Mr. Foote leaning against the fireplace mantel, quoting the famous bards.

Has it been but a year, she thought. Like a burr beneath a horse's saddle, her husband's impending nearness made her skittish.

She turned away from the window and walked to the table, her taffeta skirt rustling as it brushed against a chair. She scrutinized the set of the silver, the china, and the linen. She smoothed a wrinkle in the tablecloth. As she adjusted one of the drooping wildflowers in the cut-glass vase, the front door flew open and slammed against the wall of the foyer, loosening several flakes of plaster.

"Oh, dear," Olivia murmured as her hand slipped and she jostled the vase, spilling a few drops of water.

"Oh dear oh dear oh dear," mimicked her husband. "Can't you think of anything more clever than that!" He stood in the arched entrance to the dining room. "I suppose dinner will be late again."

"Good afternoon, Mr. Foote. You are home early. Are you not?" Olivia adjusted her bodice and walked toward her husband.

"Don't simper, woman. It doesn't suit you." And as she reached him, he turned and called out, "O'Brien! O'Brien! Where is that dimwit of a striker! O'Brien, come pull off my boots."

Olivia slipped past her husband to close the front door, but she stopped at the thunder of a galloping horse.

"Bloody hell," shouted Josiah Foote as the horse and rider passed. "Who in the name of all that's holy is that?" Foote jammed his hat onto his head and stomped past Olivia and out through the open door.

Olivia stood in the doorway, watching her husband struggle against the mad prairie winds. "Why it is Private Jameson," she said. Then she closed the door and rested her forehead against the smooth solid wood.

"Ma'am," said Private O'Brien, coming up behind her. "Wouldja be needing something?"

"No," she replied without turning. "Nothing. Thank you, Patrick. But do not go to your quarters just yet. Mr. Foote may have need of you before Retreat."

"Ma'am. I am expected at rehearsal this very minute. Mr. Davies said . . . ."

"Yes, yes of course, Patrick. Go. I'll take care of Mr. Foote."

Olivia returned to the dining room and walked past the festive table to the kitchen. Its warmth and food odors felt as comforting as an old worn blanket. She recalled times with her mother and sisters, washing vegetables, baking bread, and laughing, always laughing. She covered the platter of cold ham with a muslin cloth, moved the pot of potatoes and carrots to the warming box, and banked the fire.

At the Company B laundress' quarters, Mary Margaret O'Keenan was rinsing the last of the day's wash. As she worked, she hummed a tune from her childhood. It seemed like she was always smiling or humming somethin' these days, thought Lulu, working beside her. Lulu pulled up and wrung out a bed sheet, then pushed it down into the tub of rinse water.

"You been a smilin' like ya can't stop," said Lulu. "What's your secret, Miss Mary Margaret? You look almost . . ."

"Pretty?" asked Mary Margaret.

Lulu frowned, "You twist my meaning."

Mary Margaret said, "Me Da always told me, 'You're a wild thing you are, but not a pretty one, I fear.'"

"Well, what a thing to say to a little girl!" Though Mary Margaret was by no means an ugly woman, thought Lulu, her weathered and freckled skin, her broad flat nose and strong chin did not make for picture-perfect prettiness. But she's a lovely smile and she's been smiling more these days, and her step is lighter and freer. Before Lulu had a chance to respond, Miguel tromped in with two buckets of fresh water.

"Rider coming," he said as he set the buckets down on the large wide-plank table.

"It's Jameson," said Lulu, looking out the window. Mary Margaret turned and caught a glimpse of the familiar silhouette rushing past.

"Ah, 'tis," she said. "The Fort Union Courier, as Seán named him. In a bit of a rush, he is."

"He's turning at the end of Company Quarters," said Lulu. "Headed toward Quartermaster's . . . looks like."

Mary Margaret opened the door and looked out at the garrison and the hills to the west. Shielding her eyes from the afternoon sun, she recalled her arrival at Fort Union after traveling for months with a straggling wagon train of small freighters, leftovers from the days of the Santa Fe Trail.

"Dusty, on the edge of starving, and smelling like an ox, I was."

"Huh?"

"Oh, Lulu, the day I first saw Fort Union. Just another immigrant I was, survived the Fort Union and Granada Roads, I did. When I saw the garrison, all laid out in long straight rows, with columns of white, and windows, trimmed in white. The flagstaff pointing to heaven, and the bustlin' soldiers, wagons, animals, children, and women everywhere. I said to meself, 'Mary Margaret me girl,' 'tis home y'are at last.'"

"Well, I never heard sech a pretty picture of this ole army garrison, never in my life," said Lulu.

Mary Margaret returned to the rinse tub. "'Twas Jameson on Shanty, that pure peach of a horse—an' they be approaching Quartermaster's."

"Seeking the Commanding Officer no doubt," said Lulu, pulling up another bedsheet, twisting and squeezing until the drops of grey water ceased. She turned to Mary Margaret, "I'll do the cleaning up. You go and help that fine Sergeant of yours with his lines or his costume or whatever he needs."

"Ah, you're a dear, Lulu. I do like to help him though he don't need it, not a bit. Truly, couldja' be managing the toobs and the last of the laundry? 'Tis a fair amount of work to be done yet."

As a response, Lulu stretched her thick, strong arms up into a V shape exposing a bit of muscle and a bit more of loose pink flesh.

Mary Margaret smiled. "An' where be young Micah?"

"Miguel ya mean? He jes' run out. Finished haulin' the last of the rinse water and off he run. To th' Opera House I 'spect. He loves that play-actin.'"

Mary Margaret went to the washstand and rinsed off the day's dust and sweat. She hung her apron on the bedstead and fussed

9

with her uncontrollable curls, then squashed them into her best bonnet. Then she nodded to Lulu and stepped outside. The afternoon wind yanked her bonnet awry and loosened her black curls, whipping several strands of hair across her face. After a brief struggle, she secured the ties into a large tight bow beneath her chin.

"Mary Margaret," called Lulu. "You forgot your stick. Not safe to be walking about without it." Lulu held out a shiny blackthorn longstick.

"Ah," said Mary Margaret. "Me *shillelagh*. I do fear the sting of that beautiful snake of the Americas."

"A rattler is not a beautiful thing, darlin.' It's a killer."

"'Tis only defending itself, an' it do hiss a warning."

Lulu snorted. "Jes' you be careful, missy."

Mary Margaret took the *shillelagh* and thanked Lulu. The stick had belonged to her Da, the only thing she had that he had touched. She clutched the smooth, worn handle and set off north along Suds Row at a smart-paced walk. As she passed their quarters, a few laundresses nodded a greeting, but most turned away or became suddenly intent on their duties. Mary Margaret tilted her head and walked more briskly. She knew the talk— 'uppity Irish bitch,' she'd been called by some and more often— 'Cold-hearted O'Keenan.' She straightened her shoulders and focused her thoughts on Seán, which brought the smile to her face again. He'll not be nervous, she thought, loves the attention and the dressing up, he does. An' to be playing a smart Irish attorney, smart enough to trick the English landlord. At the end of Suds Row, she turned left and proceeded west along the wide thoroughfare dividing the garrison from the Quartermaster's Depot—No Man's Land the soldiers call it. She passed the commander's office and noticed Shanty, breathing heavy at the hitching post. In no time at all, Mary Margaret reached the edge of Fort Union, where the land slopes gently toward the Post Trader's Compound.

She paused at the rim of the hill. The new Compound was made up of several buildings of various designs and material grouped around an asymmetrical dusty square lined with a few struggling saplings and clumps of tenacious prairie weeds. To Mary Margaret's right, at the northern end of the Compound, stood the newly erected, two-storey Opera House—bright yellow with purple trim, it was cheerful, but she thought it looked like a painted cat. In front of her, at an off-kilter angle to the Opera House, towered the red brick hotel with its four floors of accommodations, white shutters, balconies, and two chimneys. Next door to the hotel stretched a long low building—part *adobe*, part stone, part timber—that housed the saloon, gambling rooms, and store. Enclosing the southern edge of the area was a pole barn and fenced corral. A few horses milled about, raising dust. To the north of the stable squatted a low, flat-roofed, *adobe hacienda,* its white-washed walls glaring in the afternoon sun. The home of the Post Trader and his wife Olivia.

Behind Mary Margaret, Jameson dashed out of the post commander's office, mounted Shanty, and galloped past her without a glance or a greeting. Within minutes he reached the Opera House, halted, and dismounted in one seamless movement. He dropped the reins, yanked off his hat, and burst into the midst of dress rehearsal. She picked up her skirts and ran, wondering what news Private Jameson had brought.

When he entered the dim auditorium, Jameson paused. "Dead!" he panted. "Seán Flannery is dead." Jameson bent forward, hands on thighs, and gulped a breath or two then repeated. "Seán Flannery is dead."

Everything stopped. Washington dropped his clubs, Harlan Davies paused in mid-shout, his mouth hanging open, and Jud Clooney whispered, "Oh my God. God no." The actors on stage turned slowly and faced Jameson, as if accusing him of something.

Jameson straightened up. "I'm sorry to say, Sergeant Seán Flannery is dead."

Clooney stood and turned toward Jameson. "Are you certain? What happened?"

"I come straight from the colonel. Gonzalez, shopkeeper over at Los Alamitos, found the body. Colonel dispatched a patrol."

Jameson took a few breaths while the entire company stood in silence. Then suddenly, as if awakening from a deep sleep,

11

everyone talked at once, first murmurings, then excited questions, and finally, curses and oaths. Davies tried to restore order, but the soldiers ignored him and stripped away their costumes.

Behind the heavy stage curtain, Miguel whispered a prayer, made the sign of the cross, then turned and rushed toward the rear entrance, crashing into Mary Margaret.

"Miguel, me boy, slow down."

"*Lo siento*," he mumbled over and over. "*Lo siento mucho.*" Then he doubled over into a ball of tears and sobs.

Mary Margaret bent and grasped him by the shoulders. "Stop yer bawlin' boy and talk to me."

"It's . . . it's Sergeant Seán."

And then she heard Jameson shout an exasperated answer to the questions of disbelief, "I'm tellin' you, it's Seán Flannery. He's dead."

"No." She said firmly. "No. It canna' be." And her *shillelagh* clattered to the floor.

". . . at Los Alamitos," repeated Jameson.

Mary Margaret let go of Miguel so sharply that he fell backward against the wall. She picked up her skirts and ran across the Compound to the home of Olivia Foote.

"Olivia. Olivia," called Mary Margaret, pounding at the front door.

Olivia roused herself and opened the door. "Mary Margaret, good Lord!"

Her bonnet askew, her curls bouncing in all directions, Mary Margaret rushed into the foyer. Then she stopped suddenly and leaned against the wall, taking in a few painful breaths. "Can ye be helping me? Please, Miss Olivia. I be needin' the use of a fast horse."

"A horse?"

"Olivia, please. I need a feckin' horse. I must . . ."

"Mary Margaret! Mind your language. You are slipping into your brogue, and for what purpose do you need a horse?"

"No time to explain. Ah, Olivia, 'tis me man! 'Tis Seán. Jameson said it. Seán be dead. Jaysus, Mary, an' Joseph! No. It canna' be but he said it. At Los Alamitos, the lake. I'm after . . . sweet mother of God, Olivia Foote, I need to go to him."

"Oh my Lord in heaven," said Olivia. "The village is a good three miles. The only horse available is Tamany, Mr. Foote's Thoroughbred." Surely, she thought, Mr. Foote could not object to the loan of his horse for such a crisis. "But, Mary Margaret, Tamany is not a gentlewoman's horse, not a horse for a jog in the country—though he does well in the traces."

"Olivia, please," urged Mary Margaret.

"Yes. He is just the animal for such urgency, a handful, I'm told. Stubborn in the mouth. I'll tell Mr. Foote . . . well, never you mind what I shall tell Mr. Foote. Come, we must arrange for the buggy. Patrick! Where is that boy? Oh dear, gone to rehearsal."

"No time for a feckin' wagon . . . a saddle an' bridle is enoof."

"Come," said Olivia, closing the door. Together they ran to the stable.

At the corral, Mary Margaret stopped, staring at the small group of startled mounts. She lifted the latch, but Olivia said, "No, Mary Margaret. Go round to the other side, the small pen . . . the blue gate."

The women stepped inside the barn and stared at a row of eight, narrow stalls. Only the near stall was occupied.

"That is Tamany," said Olivia, pointing to the big bay, prancing and blowing air through his nostrils.

Mary Margaret swallowed. "'Tis no surprise the horse be trouble. He canna' turn nor stretch those anxious muscles. An' that be his bridle hanging there?" she cried. "Wouldja' ever look at the bit! Saints preserve us." Olivia backed away as Mary Margaret put thoughts of Seán out of her head and focused on calming the horse. She reached in between the bars, gently stroked his back, and crooned in Gaelic to the wild-eyed Thoroughbred.

Once Tamany had settled some, Mary Margaret inched her way between the horse and the side of the stall until she reached the animal's head. She stroked his neck and hummed low and soft. Tamany's ears twitched as he listened and his breathing slowed. Mary Margaret grabbed the bridle, then reached up and rested her right forearm on top of the horse's head. She shifted the top of the

13

bridle to her dangling right hand, and with her left hand, offered him the bit. He shook his head and pulled back as far as he could, his velvety lips quivering.

"Donchoo worry, Tamany, m'boy, I'll not hurt you," Mary Margaret said. "I'll not hurt you." And with the thumb and first finger of her left hand, she gently massaged his jaws until his trembling lips parted and he took the bit. She secured the bridle, buckled the throatlatch, and carefully backed him out of the stall. Once outside the barn, Tamany pranced in place and flared his nostrils, sucking in the sweet grass smells of the prairie. Mary Margaret held the bridle, firm but not mean, and talked slow and steady, saying things that Olivia did not understand, but the gelding twitched his ears and snorted in recognition. Then his head relaxed ever so slightly and he sighed.

"Ah, that's me brave boyo," she crooned. "Olivia, hold him whilst I find a saddle."

"I cannot. I . . . I'm afraid. Mr. Foote says the horse is unruly, too much for a gentlewoman."

Stroking Tamany's sleek, sweating neck, Mary Margaret drew her eyes away from the horse. She saw in Olivia's creamy white face the stark look of fear and the glint of moisture at the corner of Olivia's eye.

"I'm after riding bareback since I were a slip of a girl, though it be some time ago." Mary Margaret said as she led Tamany to a low pile of lumber so that she could mount.

"Oh. Oh no. You'll be killed! Take the gig," said Olivia with some urgency. "Between the two of us, if you handle the horse, we can . . . ."

"Has he been ridden?" asked Mary Margaret as she slid the reins over Tamany's head and down his neck to the withers.

"Oh, yes. He's broke."

"Broke?" Mary Margaret looked at Olivia.

"That's what Mr. Foote said, 'He's broke good.'"

"Well let us hope he ain't broken permanent."

Olivia backed away as Mary Margaret hitched up her skirts and swung a leg across Tamany's back. The horse danced a few steps to the side but settled when she leaned forward and whispered into his ear. Then she adjusted her body and sunk her weight into the slight curve of his back.

"There's a fine boyo," she said. "You're a fine one, y'are." She dropped her legs and carefully pressed his sides but held the reins steady. Tamany rushed forward and halted when his mouth engaged with the bit and the strength of Mary Margaret's sure hands. "Back boyo, back," she said, and Tamany stepped back three strides. She tried a few more movements—halts, half-halts, and circles. "'Tis a fine horse, Olivia. I dinna know about broken. Wouldja ever be openin' the gate?"

Olivia swung open the gate, and Mary Margaret urged Tamany into a trot, then an easy canter. As she watched Mary Margaret ride off, low and forward, Olivia wondered what she would tell Mr. Foote.

Chapter 2: In which Mary Margaret arrives at Los Alamitos Lake, gazes on the lifeless face of Seán Flannery, and finds a clue.

As they topped Robins' Ridge, the horse slowed to an awkward, jerky walk. All Mary Margaret's urging and squeezing and rump-slapping did not affect Tamany's stride. His nostrils flared as he inhaled the odor of death. He blinked at the scene below, the eerie bobbing and swaying of dark figures against the setting sun. At Mary Margaret's persistent urging, he backed down the hill in avoidance, his ears twitching with the shouts and groans of men, the nervous whinny of a horse.

Mary Margaret sighed and dismounted. She spoke soothingly to the horse and led him up the rise again. At the rim of the hill, she stopped abruptly and stared at the swinging lanterns and darting shadows. Tamany inhaled deeply, snorted, and pulled back against the reins. Mary Margaret stood tall and straight, her silhouette, with its crushed bustle, hanging bonnet, and wild curls, outlined against the fading light of day. Snatches of conversation rose on the erratic winds.

"That's right. Now lift. Lift him!"

"I got 'im. I got 'im."

"Ah God. You're dragging 'is foot. Lift 'is foot someone. Ah, for the love of God!"

Mary Margaret dropped the reins and covered her mouth with both hands. Sensing freedom, Tamany spun and galloped down the slope. Mary Margaret rushed forward a few steps, then stopped and took in a deep, burning breath. The wind whipped her skirt into a frenzy of calico, but she forced herself to straighten her back, square her shoulders, and walk down the hill toward Los Alamitos Lake, a lake that would in Ireland be but a mud-bog. Tears blurred her vision, and at the bottom of the hill, she stumbled and fell to her hands and knees. She swallowed a cry, righted herself, and brushing bits of dirt and small stones from her hands. She walked on along the shore toward the gathering of shadow men settling a motionless body onto a stretcher. They pulled a blanket up and covered the face.

16

Mary Margaret arrived as two soldiers lifted the stretcher. She whispered, "Hail Mary full of grace . . ." and reached out her hand toward the inert body. First Sergeant John Jay Holloway gently grabbed her elbow.

"Uh, Miss O'Keenan, I do not think it would be advisable to . . . um . . . to look at . . . ." He paused, swallowed, and said, "It is my sad duty to inform you, that is to say, I'm sorry, Miss Mary Margaret. It is Seán. You do not want to look."

"'Tis certain y'are, Jack?"

Holloway nodded.

"So I must then. I must look upon his face," she whispered. Wrenching herself free of Jack's hold, she took a step toward the stretcher.

Holloway nodded to the stretcher-bearers. "Leave it," he ordered. The soldiers lowered the stretcher to the earth, stepped back, and stood at attention.

Mary Margaret dropped to her knees and bent over the corpse. She lowered the blanket and looked upon the motionless white face of the man she had hoped to marry. In the lantern light, Seán's eyes sparkled with false life. She touched his mud-caked cheek, drew her fingers along the jawbone and down the neck, clearing the dirt from an angry bruise. The collar of his undergarments protruded from the edge of the blanket. Mary Margaret slid the blanket down to his ankles, then removed it with a sharp, quick gesture.

When first I laid eyes on you, Seán Flannery, you be dancing a jig on that old wagon in back of the Guardhouse. Whistlin' and dancin' for the joy of it. An' when you seen me, you tipped yer old forage cap like it was the king's own crown an' winked at me, you did—as if I'd be so low as to show me interest. An' you looked me full in the face. An' 'twas then I knew. Oh I knew, in spite of meself, I knew you was me man. An' I walked on, proud in me back, me head high . . . but that never stopped yourself, not you, Seán Flannery. You dropped to the ground, spraying dust upon me best dress. Seán Flannery's me name, an' yourself?

17

Well, I wasn't having none of your pattyfingers, so I strode ahead as fast and strong and straight as me dear mother would have me. Not a word passed me lips. Into the chapel I walked. An' you, Seán Flannery, proud as a lord, walked beside me as if we be steppin' out. The cheek of you. Sat yourself down beside me, you did, that day, an' every Sunday since. An' prayed louder than a whisper, you did, loud enough for all to hear yer bog-trottin' brogue, you're singing words. Ashamed of that Irish lilt I was . . . me tryin' so hard to be American.

"Miss Mary Margaret. Come away now. Leave him be," said Holloway, bending to grasp her arm. "He's gone." To the attendants he said, "Cover his face."

Mary Margaret looked up at Holloway. "Where be his uniform?" She said then turned back to Seán. She looked at the full length of him. "His boots? Where be his boots? An' his weapon?"

Without a tear and only a bit of a catch in her voice, Mary Margaret said, "I be wantin' to know, Jack, where be Seán's things . . . an' Rosie? Where be his horse?"

"This is how we found him. Now, come away please," was Jack's reply.

But Mary Margaret steadfastly remained on her knees in the mud. She pulled free of Jack's hold and placed one hand firmly on Seán's chest. From behind her, a gentlemanly voice said, *"Por favor,* Ma'am, may I be of assistance?"

Without removing her eyes from Seán's, Mary Margaret said, "Miss O'Keenan, Company B Laundress, at your service. And who be yourself?" Then she turned and saw a short, well-built man tipping a wide-brimmed, grey hat as soft and smooth as the skin of a faun.

"Allow me, at this most inopportune of moments, to introduce myself. I am Juan Garcia Otero, Sheriff of San Miguel County. May I ask, Miss O'Keenan, are you acquainted with the deceased?"

18

It took all of her strength to hold back the tears. It took all of her will power not to deny everything. She wanted desperately to say, No I do not know him and walk away and be done with the sorrow. Her words came out in a low, steady tone, "Yes, Sheriff O'Tero." Mary Margaret rose from her knees, lifted her chin, and facing the Sheriff, said, "Sergeant Seán Padraic Flannery, Company B, 23rd Infantry."

Not a pretty woman, thought the Sheriff, not in the popular fashion of the day. Her face is not soft and round. The high prominent cheekbones and wide nose give an odd look to the eyes, as if she were staring off in the wrong direction. Not curvaceous. Not wearing stays he observed. Angular, bony shoulders, rough, big-knuckled hands. That would be from the work, he deduced. But, he thought, there is determination, pride, strength, or perhaps it is the look of survival in the set of her mouth. Not a pretty woman, but certainly, compelling.

The sheriff had seen such strength once before, in the face of his mother, when they brought home the mangled body of his father hanging from the back of a burro. The *banditos* had taken everything—beaten his father and stolen his horse, the stud that was meant to improve the bloodline. They left his father's body in a ditch. The sheriff, then a boy of twelve, had cried unashamed tears, but his mother, standing taller than her five feet and straighter than the rifle in the crook of her arm, spoke loud and strong for all to hear. '*Este es Juan Pablo Otero, mi esposo.*'

"*Lo siento,*" said Sheriff Otero. "Please accept my sincerest sympathies, Miss O'Keenan." He spoke each word carefully and individually, attempting to gain her full attention. "But, if you please, a moment of your time. Might you be aware of a person, or persons, who would perhaps have cause to bring harm to Sergeant Flannery?"

"Harm?" she said.

"Yes. It appears Sergeant Flannery was attacked. And that he was, perhaps, in some way acquainted with his attacker."

"Well now," interrupted Holloway. "We do not know that, Sheriff."

19

Mary Margaret watched as each man took the measure of the other. Her thoughts turned on the sheriff's question. She thought of Private Shiner and how he hated Seán for calling his bluff, for boxing him and winning fair and square. She thought of the rivalry at the garrison between the Comedy Company and the Dramatic Society. She remembered Timmy Sullivan's anger when Seán got the lead role in the new theatrical. She recalled stories Seán had told her of chasing down and recapturing an outlaw who had sworn revenge.

Mary Margaret stepped in front of First Sergeant Holloway and looked directly into the dark eyes of the sheriff. "No," she said. "Not a livin' soul. An' sir, where be his clothes, his boots, his cap? An' wouldja' ever be knowing how it is he got here? Where be his horse? These be the questions you must be askin', are they not? An' didja ever read the footprints?" Mary Margaret pointed in the direction of the muddy mess at the edge of the pond that she herself had trudged through unstopped.

His face hidden in the shadow of his hat brim, Sheriff Otero said quietly, "*Con permiso*, Miss O'Keenan. It is true. Sergeant Flannery was found within my jurisdiction, but my deputy and I arrived some time after the American soldiers had secured the area."

"Well now," said Jack Holloway. "We are not anticipating an investigation. No foul play."

Mary Margaret turned and looked squarely at Jack. "No foul play?"

"At this time, Miss Mary Margaret, we . . . ."

"Ah, Jack, 'tis clear as the nose on your face. Didja not see the bruise?" Her voice cracked. She sighed as she stepped away from the two men, and then she knelt again at the side of the stretcher. She leaned over Seán's body, caressed his upper arm, and drew her hand down to the crook of the elbow and along the forearm to his cold wet hand. Holloway approached the Sheriff, and they walked a few paces north of the kneeling woman. The two men talked in low whispers. Mary Margaret unclenched Seán's hand, lay it flat, and felt something as soft and spidery as a web slip from his dead grasp.

Holloway appeared at her side. "Well now, Mary Margaret, it is time to go."

Mary Margaret stiffened, "A moment alone with him, please." When Holloway hesitated, she whispered, "Please, Jack. You be his friend. Give me this time with him while his spirit still hovers."

"Very well then. A moment." Holloway dismissed the attendants and moved off to join them, a few paces beyond the ambulance wagon.

Mary Margaret looked up and across Seán's body into the eyes of the Sheriff. "Please sir," she said. "A moment alone with me man."

Recalling his mother's angry pride and silent anguish, Sheriff Otero nodded and walked off toward the last of a warm orange sunset. Mary Margaret watched him climb the mound and stand against the prairie winds. In spite of her grief and anger, she could not stop herself from wondering how he kept his hat from flying away. As she watched, three riders approached the Sheriff and halted. Mary Margaret looked down at Seán, the length of him, the wet long johns clinging to the body she'd not feel against her, the manhood she'd never know.

"Ah, Seán," she whispered, glimpsing his bowed leg, the tortured ankle for which he could not find a truly good-fitting boot.

An' how is it you can run and march and dance with that crippled foot? Practice, me girl. Practice. An' don't you be calling me that. I ain't yer girl, Seán Flannery. An' how did it happen? I sensed your hesitation, I did, but the question had been put out there, not to be taken back. An' you told me, slow at first, then relaxing in the telling of it. Yer old drunk Da, the cart careening down the hill, out of control, the wild-eyed pony, the catch, the tumble—arse over tea kettle—an' findin' yerself, a slip of a boy, tangled in the harness and braces. Your foot trapped beneath a wheel. . . lying there the whole of the night. Waiting for your Da to wake, an' he never. An' the knowing of it become something we shared.

21

Mary Margaret stuffed the small spidery thing into the pocket of her skirt. "I'll find out who done this. That I will," she whispered. She lightly touched his cold wet lips with her own then sat back on her heels, bowed her head and made the sign of the cross. Then she looked into Seán's still eyes and said in a low hoarse whisper, "In life I never told ya'. Seán Padraic Flannery, I tell you now. I love you. And I swear by the saints in heaven, I will find the bastid who done this if it be the last thing I ever do on God's good earth. That I will."

Chapter 3: In which Mary Margaret goes on the stage.

The sun slipped behind the *Sangre de Cristo* mountain range, streaking the sky with brilliant clouds of pink, purple, and orange. As Mary Margaret shakily rose to her feet, First Sergeant Holloway covered Seán's body with the rough army blanket. In unison, the bearers lifted the stretcher and slid it into the Rucker ambulance. Before anyone could move to stop her, Mary Margaret climbed in and settled herself on the floor with her back against the spring seat. She reached over, folded down the blanket, revealing Seán's face, and rested her hand on his shoulder. The wind plucked and flipped the edges of the blanket, but Mary Margaret stared straight ahead at the rear of the wagon.

"Sir?" questioned the young driver.

Holloway approached the side of the ambulance and said in a low, sympathetic tone, "It is, as I am certain you are aware, Miss Mary Margaret, against regulations. Come now."

Mary Margaret first felt a rush of intense anger, then haughtiness, but she settled on desperation. "Please, Jack. 'Tis to be me final ride with 'im. Please."

Holloway winced and looked around at the small detail of soldiers—privates all. He turned back to Mary Margaret. "So be it," he said. And he motioned for his horse, mounted, and ordered the ambulance driver to move out.

As one of the soldiers began lowering the canvas sides, Mary Margaret said, "Ah, please, don't be shutting us in. 'Tis a grand and glorious evening." The soldier looked at Holloway who nodded assent. The driver flapped the reins, and the wagon jolted forward then stopped abruptly, the wheels deep in the grey mud. The driver clucked and slapped the reins again, but the ambulance did not move. Then he cursed and shouted obscenities, expressions Mary Margaret had not heard since her days and nights at the Five Points. Holloway rode ahead, grabbed the harness, and encouraged the animals to pull harder.

Lord Jaysus, Mary Margaret prayed, you'll be after havin' a good place in heaven for Seán Padraic Flannery who always did right, never hurt no one what dinna' deserve it, and loved me in spite of m'self. Then, with a sudden violent jolt, the ambulance lurched forward and out of the mud.

> *'Tis naught but a wagon, Seán darlin'. . . fit for feed and flour and hay. Not for a lady an' gent to be travelin' the countryside. 'Tis, you said, an' you smiled your smile that put the teasin' playful spark in your eyes. An' didn't we set out early that morning for the grand city of Las Vegas Grandes. . . me in me best dress an' you be wearin' your old brown suit that you coom to this country in . . . a bit short in the sleeves an' britches . . . tight across the chest. 'Twas a stiff an' boompy ride, but your broad smile shaded me from the roysin' sun. Never did I feel so safe as when yer eyes smiled upon me, Seán Flannery.*

Holloway released the harness and slowed his horse until he was riding alongside Mary Margaret.

He said. "Can you abide my presence a few paces? A question or two?"

She nodded.

"Seán's Rosie, did you ever know her to spook?"

"Never." The ambulance swayed, hesitated, then shot ahead once more.

"Wonder what would make her spook," said Holloway.

"The assassin."

"Well now, Mary Margaret," said Jack. He cleared his throat several times before continuing. "You need not concern yourself with thoughts of murder. The sheriff's a good enough man, if a bit over zealous. It is most likely Seán broke his neck when he fell."

"Fell? Never." Mary Margaret whispered harshly. "Seán Flannery rode as one with that mare, an' you be knowin' that, you do, Jack Holloway. You be ridin' with him for nearly a year. Seán couldna' fall if he tried. An' wouldja' be sayin' you dinna' see the marks of murder on his neck! An' where be his uniform? Are you after thinking he be going in for a swim?"

24

Holloway was given to believe that a woman, in such circumstances as these, might tend toward hysteria, so he rode in silence for a few minutes.

John Jay Holloway, a gentleman from an old Baltimore family, had been taught good manners should prevail in all situations. He had attended college for two years, hoping to become a surgeon, when abruptly, he proposed marriage to his second cousin Flora, and within a month, he enlisted, expecting an assignment in Maryland. When orders came for the frontier and Indian wars, Jack dutifully released Flora from her promise, but she refused. They married without family approval. Flora remains in her parents' home awaiting his return.

John Jay Holloway believes that he follows the proper course in all things, but some at the garrison say his ambitions get the better of him. On this evening, Holloway attributed Mary Margaret's statements to grief, so he did not say that soldiers' uniforms, weapons, and boots are commodities and as such, often stolen. He did not say that no matter how good a horseman, every rider can be unseated by surprise or misadventure.

After several moments of silence, he said, "Mary Margaret, may I intrude upon your sadness further?" When she did not respond, he continued. "As you are aware, it is my duty to settle such matters as these. After being ordered to the site by the commander, my patrol found Seán's body partially submerged in the pond and . . . ."

"The mud doncha' mean," quipped Mary Margaret. "Didja ever look on his face, Jack Holloway? Didja?"

"Well now, Miss Mary Margaret . . . ."

"Donchyou 'well now Miss Mary Margaret' me, Jack Holloway. This be your friend layin' here in death. An' you being in charge of investigating 'such matters,' as you say, didja' ever . . . ," she paused and then said, "An' where would we be going? Should we not be heading toward Las Vegas an' Doc Stern's for the post mortem?"

"The Army takes care of its own. We are taking the deceased to the Dead House at the garrison hospital."

"The deceased?" Mary Margaret searched Holloway's expressionless face. "This be the man you rode beside. The man you called your friend. The *deceased* be Sergeant Seán Padraic Flannery!"

"Please do not make this more difficult than it need be. Seán was my friend, yes. But I must perform my duty as I see fit."

To the driver, Mary Margaret said, "Take us to Las Vegas, please." Then, "Sheriff. . . Sheriff O'Tero."

Sheriff Otero was kneeling at the north edge of Los Alamitos Lake, holding up a lantern and examining the mess of footprints, hoofprints, and wheel ruts. He had knelt to pull at a small, shiney thread stuck in the mud, but at the sound of his name, he looked up at the retreating ambulance. He freed the threads, stuffed them into one of his pockets, and handed the lantern to Deputy Lucero, a good man although they did not always agree when it came to politics.

"*Espéreme,*" said the sheriff to Lucero and ran to catch the slowly departing wagon.

"Please stop," asked Mary Margaret. Then raising her voice to a command, she said, "Stop the wagon."

"Halt," said Holloway as the sheriff reached the rear of the ambulance.

Mary Margaret pled her case to the sheriff—a full investigation, a post mortem examination. Sheriff Otero looked intently at the pleading woman. He was impressed by her logic, her determination, and her passion. He explained again about jurisdictions, cooperation among agencies, and the power of the American Army. He told her that Dr. Williamson at the Fort was well trained in the art of autopsy. Holloway said nothing. Mary Margaret looked from one man to the other, then suddenly she relented and slumped back against the seat. The ambulance moved forward. As the sheriff watched it depart, he recalled his mother's long futile battle to clear his father's name and thought, this will not end here.

The Rucker ambulance, its yellow paint glowing in the fading light, climbed to the top of Robins' Ridge then descended the eastern slope. At the base, the small patrol encountered Tamany, grazing peacefully. Holloway approached the horse, captured the reins, and led him toward the wagon. Once again, Tamany shied and reared at the smell of death, so Holloway moved ahead, upwind, leaving Mary Margaret alone with her thoughts. She set her eyes on the black profile of the *Sangre de Cristo* mountain range as the wagon, with its sad cargo and somber detail of horsemen, proceeded. From Fort Union, the wind carried the plaintive sound of "Taps," signaling the end of the military day. Mary Margaret closed her eyes, shutting out the undulating line of the mountains and the final gloaming of what she thought was the worst day of her life.

Fort Union seemed to erupt from beneath the earth like a series of brown, flat-topped volcanoes. Constructed on the floor of a wide flat valley, the garrison and depot buildings formed elongated rectangles with jutting chimneys. Built near the junction of the Turkey Mountains and the Cimarron branch of the Santa Fe Trail, Fort Union was at nearly 6,700 feet above the level of the sea and 2,000 miles from the nearest shore, yet it appeared to rest on an ocean floor—a grassy prairie cut by the scars of wagon trails and *arroyos,* dry stream beds where water occasionally and violently cascaded from the nearby hills.

Soon after arriving at the post in the Spring of 1880, Assistant Surgeon Williamson wrote a detailed report of what he saw: "Bordered on the east by the Turkey Mountains and on the west by a range of the *Sangre de Cristo* Mountains—odd name that, it means the blood of Christ—Fort Union is situated latitude 350 degrees 54' 21" north; longitude, 27 degrees 54' 15" west, and lies in a broad valley, seemingly five and a half miles in width.

"The closest major settlements include Mora, 18 miles to the west, and about 28 miles south, the Town of Las Vegas Grandes, the San Miguel County seat. In addition, there are several small outposts nearby, such as, Loma Parda, a favorite among the men due to its various and unseemly inducements, is but a few miles southwest. Many of my treatments result from sexual indiscretions and violence at this village. Los Alamitos, a small settlement, a scattering of native buildings and a limited general store, is nearby.

La Junta, a lovely, forested spot, where the Mora and the Sapello Rivers intersect, and Tiptonville, where some of the garrison horses are stabled, lie barely six miles due south. Less than a mile west of the garrison is a Post Trader's Compound, providing goods, accommodations, and entertainment.

"Although its supply duties have been greatly diminished since the arrival of the Achison, Topeka, and Santa Fe Rail service, the Fort is busy and well-populated with intelligent and gentlemanly officers. The Quartermaster Depot, located a few hundred yards north of the garrison, maintains excellent storehouses and cellars as well as a fine herd of mules and a multitude of repair shops and blacksmithing facilities. With all the comings and goings of soldiers, families, day-laborers, and merchants, the Fort resembles a small but prosperous community, and there are often theatricals, hops, afternoon teas, and other diversions.

"As for the hospital and its environs, it is one of the very finest I have seen to date. It is situated approximately 300 paces east of the garrison proper and is comprised of a large central building, 13 feet wide and 130 feet long. The outbuildings include a fully-equipped Dead House, two storage sheds, and an enclosed garden for the purpose of growing healthful vegetables. The hospital is constructed of what are called "adobe bricks," formed by mixing the local, clay-like mud with straw for stabilization, pouring the mixture into twelve by twelve inch frames, and laying them in the open air to dry. The walls are a full three-feet thick and continually weep fine dust. A wide central hall with wooden floor runs the length of the building from north to south and separates the six wards, each containing six beds. The hospital is unique in that its roof is pitched—unlike the flat roofs of the garrison buildings, which, I am told, require constant care. Although there are flaws from an hygienic perspective, nonetheless, the building is more than adequate and surpasses all of the post hospitals I have encountered since arriving in this country."

In that first communiqué, Williamson recorded observable details and geographical facts. However, a year later, in a letter to a colleague, the doctor offered a more emotional description: "The weather turned fierce with snow and mud. Spring and Summer plagued by constant, ferocious Winds swirling in all directions, rattling windows, and battering buildings, fences, and those brave souls who must venture out. The soil, being light and sandy, is blown about in clouds of blinding, suffocating dust that irritates the air passages and is the prevalent cause of catarrh, bronchitis, and an unnamed disease with symptoms inclusive of hysteria, depression, and, at times, irrational violence. In my several notes, I refer to this condition as 'Prairie Madness.' It attacks men and women alike—even the animals exhibit signs of uneasiness. Perhaps, one day, when I find myself in better spirits, I shall compose an article on this phenomenon. Perhaps not. With the exception of a few windless, sun-filled days, and the immense night skies—when the air is calm and conducive to pursuing astronomical studies—all is Wind and Desiccation."

The cortege passed north of the Trader's Compound, along the backside of the opera house, and entered Fort Union at the thoroughfare between the Depot and the garrison. Mary Margaret heard hushed voices, a whinny, and the rustle of a woman's skirts. Bodies ebbed and flowed around her like miasmic creatures in a nightmare. She looked at Seán's cold, white features and gently closed his eyes, her hand lingering a moment. Then Mary Margaret pulled the blanket up and covered his face. She straightened her back and folded her hands in her lap.

For you, Seán. I made these for you. An' you smiled, knowing what I be thinking, that there's no a boot made to fit yer damaged ankle, but here's a pair of fine soft socks. An' you put them on, there and then. Sat on me floor, yanked and yanked 'til yer boots and old wooly socks be strewn about. On with the new ones. Mary Margaret me girl . . . an' don't be frownin. . . your m'girl now you made me a pair o' socks. An' didn't I laugh at the cheek of you, Seán Flannery.

As the ambulance lumbered past the parade grounds. Mary Margaret reached into her pocket and clutched the small spidery thing. Feels like a tiny nest, she thought. The ambulance stopped with a sudden jolt, and she knew they must be at the Dead House, though she had never been there herself. Standing outside the double doors were the members of the Fort Union Dramatic Society.

First Sergeant Judson Clooney separated himself from the group and approached the side of the wagon. "Miss O'Keenan," he said. "Please accept my sincere condolences. And if it please you, allow me to help." He offered his arm.

All her instincts urged her to lean upon his kindness. She made no reply but grasped the bench and pulled herself upright. She walked to the rear of the wagon and jumped to the ground, the thud of her boots startling the assembled group. Clooney appeared and stood silently. He did not offer his arm again.

The large double doors of the Dead House swung open, and Assistant Surgeon Lt. Williamson appeared, wearing a soiled white coat and holding up a lantern. Mary Margaret looked at him and understood that her journey with Seán had come to an end. She squared her shoulders and strode toward the doctor.

"O'Keenan, sir," she said with a slight curtsey. "May I have a word? If you be so kind." And quickly, before he could protest, she stepped into the dark corridor. Everyone watched them move off together as Olivia Foote arrived in her husband's gig. No one spoke. They heard whispering and saw the laundress gesture toward the ambulance. They watched the surgeon nod as the bearers carried the body into the Dead House. When the stretcher passed her, Mary Margaret reached out and rested her fingers lightly and quickly on Seán's ankle, then she backed away into the darkening night.

Olivia descended her carriage and rushed forward. "Oh Mary Margaret," she said, "I'm so sorry, so sorry. Come with me."

Mary Margaret relaxed and leaned on Olivia's arm. Together they took a few steps. Then she halted abruptly.

"No." She said, confused and shamed at letting down her guard. She struggled free of Olivia. "Where be the sheriff? An'Jack. Jack Holloway!"

"I'm here, Miss Mary Margaret," said Jack as he dismounted. "Rest assured, we shall do what needs to be done."

"'Twere no accident, Jack Holloway. Mind me, now. No accident."

Jack approached Mary Margaret and gently took hold of her shoulders. "We'll take care of things now. This is no work for a woman."

She shrugged off Jack's hold and searched the dark faces silhouetted by the glow of the lanterns.

"No work for a woman! I wash yer dirty linen, yer stained and bloodied uniforms. No work for a woman indeed!" She turned her back to Holloway and stared at the crowd until she found the man she wanted. Mary Margaret walked up to Harlan Davies. "I be taking Sgt. Flannery's role in the theatrical, I will. I know the lines and the movements. Tomorrow night, eight sharp?"

"But . . ." protested Davies.

"Mary Margaret O'Keenan!" gasped Olivia.

31

Chapter 4: In which Mary Margaret and Olivia discuss important matters, and Dr. Williamson performs his duty

"I cannot imagine what you could be thinking. Why on earth would you want to go on the stage?"

They sat in Olivia's parlour, cups of tea in hand. Mary Margaret welcomed Olivia's kindness and warmth but was puzzled and cautious. Although for the past year, she had spent nearly an hour each week in diction lessons with Olivia, Mary Margaret would not have counted the woman as a friend. They were close in age, but their relationship was that of teacher and pupil, and Mary Margaret was ever conscious of their different stations in society. As the wife of the Post Trader, Olivia was, though not among the society of the officers and their wives, a lady. As a Company Laundress, Mary Margaret occupied the lowest level of the military. She did not reply. She sipped her tea.

"Mary Margaret? Are you all right? Well now, of course you are not all right. Good Lord, how insensitive I am! Forgive me. How can I be of help? Would you like me to write to your family?"

"For the love of God, Olivia, I kin read 'n write well enoof. Sure you be knowing that." Mary Margaret paused and glanced about the room at the flickering shadows, the soft folds of the lace curtains. "An' there be no one. Me Ma dead these seven years, Da gone for . . . I'm sure I dinna know how long. Not long. An' me brother be working at the big English house. He were always good with the horses, was our Bill." Mary Margaret stopped abruptly, suddenly feeling as though she had exposed herself. She looked at Olivia. "No, ma'am. 'Tis nothin' you can be doing for me. Tho' I do thank you for your kindness."

"Well, if you should need, that is, if I can be of help, call upon me. But please do not call me ma'am, makes me sound like an old dowager or a governess." Olivia sipped her tea, then continued, "I shall call you Mary Margaret and you shall call me Olivia. And that is that."

A small smile tickled Mary Margaret's lips. "Well and good," she murmured, not yet comfortable with the idea but willing to give it her best.

"Well, Mary Margaret, and what was it you said to fine young Dr. Williamson? I must say, it did my heart good to see the man so flustered. I'll wager a mere woman never addressed him so directly."

Mary Margaret nodded but said nothing. They sat in silence for a few minutes, listening to the winds batter the walls and rattle the windows.

"Mary Margaret?"

Mary Margaret roused herself from the sweet languor of tea in a lady's parlour and set her cup and saucer down on the small round table to her right. She looked at Olivia and asked, "How did you coome to be at the hospital, tonight?"

Olivia was brought up short by the question. It seemed to carry more weight than its mere words. She too set down her cup and saucer.

"I waited and watched. Mr. Foote, well, he keeps late hours at the saloon. After you rode for Los Alamitos, I stitched a bit, but my mind was not on it. From this window," she nodded toward the tall, double windows facing the compound, and Mary Margaret shifted her gaze. Through the filmy gauze of the curtains, she saw the glow of the hotel lights. "I saw the ambulance pass," continued Olivia, "and the patrol approach, and then First Sergeant Holloway returning Tamany to the corral. Sergeant Holloway stopped and told me what happened, and Old Sam at the stable hitched the buggy for me. Good Lord, Mary Margaret, I thought you might need a woman's help."

Recalling Olivia's fear at holding Tamany, Mary Margaret wondered how it came about that Olivia arrived with Tamany in the traces. She asked quietly, "You drive a carriage?"

"Oh, yes. My father ensured we girls could handle a light carriage, for Sunday visiting and such. But we had grooms, you see.

33

Mary Margaret nodded. "'Tis proper no doubt." Then after a pause, she said, "He's after helping me, he is. Dr. Williamson. He'll be examining Seán's body for evidence."

"Evidence?"

"Sure, he kin say how Seán died." The strain of the past hours showed in Mary Margaret's dull eyes, puffy lids, and the streak of mud across her cheek. "I promised Seán, I did. I be finding his killer, I will."

"Killer? Killer! Oh good Lord. But Jack said . . ."

"Oh, 'twere no accident. Seán never fell from no horse, an' surely not Rosie. An' why would he be taking off his clothes out there? No. 'Twere no accident. Something happened today, sometime in the mornin' perhaps, after . . . ."

"The Store! Oh, Mary Margaret, I saw him, Sergeant Flannery, in the store this very morning. He bought . . . uh, well, it was meant to be a surprise, of that I am certain, although I suppose it does not matter now. Oh, I am so sorry."

"'Tis important," said Mary Margaret, straightening her back and lifting her chin. A spate of coughing overtook her, masking the crack in her voice. "Please, Olivia, tell me."

With her hands, Olivia pressed out a wrinkle down the front of her dress. "As you wish. They had words, Mr. Foote and Sergeant Flannery. He . . . ." Olivia clamped her hands over her mouth when she heard the heavy footsteps on the front porch. 'Mr. Foote,' she said. "Mary Margaret, you shall stay the night, of course, in our extra bedroom."

The front door swung open and Josiah Foote entered, carrying with him the smell of dust, hard liquor, and cigars. He appeared in the open archway and stood with his feet apart, as if striking a pose. In one hand he held a riding crop, tapping it against his tall, black boot, and with the other hand, he removed his hat. Dust greyed his black trousers and frock coat. Mary Margaret thought him to be frightening with his long sharp nose, high cheekbones, and white white skin. *'Tis something menancing in the pale eyes, an emptiness.*

"Miss O'Keenan," said Josiah Foote. "May I offer my condolences. Mrs. Foote is correct. You must stay the night. If it

34

suits you, of course." The crop slid gently up and down against the side of his boot. "Olivia, a word, please."

"Yes, Mr. Foote. I'll be but a moment, Mary Margaret." Olivia unfolded herself from her place on the sofa.

Josiah Foote gestured for his wife to precede him. As Olivia passed, Foote turned back to Mary Margaret and said, "You are welcome to the use of my fine Thoroughbred," in a tone that clearly indicated displeasure.

> *Mr. Foote, indeed. Ah, Seán. There be somethin'* *unsettling about the man. 'Tis true, he be many times older* *than Olivia . . . twelve year I do believe. Ah but never* *would I be calling you Mr. Flannery. Never in all me born* *days. 'Tis afraid of him she is. I feel it.*

Mary Margaret thought she heard Seán's soft chuckle, but it could have been the wind rattling a pane or disturbing the bushes. She sipped the barely warm tea and tried to block the image of Seán's dead eyes. Her thoughts raced through the things she must do to find the assassin. Her first step would be to determine where and when Seán died. She expected Dr. Williamson would provide the necessary details. Her mind darted from thought to thought. She recalled Timmy Sullivan's envy when Seán was drafted from the Comedy Company to play the lawyer Connelly for the Dramatic Society, a role that Timmy coveted. Although Mary Margaret did not believe such a thing to be a sound reason to kill a man, she could not know what was in Timmy's heart. But this new possibility, the thought of Seán having words with Josiah Foote.

> *An' there be Shiney—'tis a fair bully he is. An' he be* *the one swore revenge on you? Who be the outlaw swore* *to kill you and Jack? I be needin' to know the why, an' the* *how, an' the who. What's that you say?*

Olivia reentered the room carrying a pile of folded linens. "I'll just make up the bed, Mary Margaret. You finish your tea. And have a bit of nourishment, try to nibble a biscuit. I am certain you have not eaten since Lord knows when. You will need every ounce of strength you can muster."

"Ah, donchyou be going to all that trouble. I be wantin' to sleep in me own bed this night, I do."

"Nonsense," boomed Mr. Foote, who followed Olivia into the room and stood close behind her.

"It is no trouble, dear," said Olivia, and Mary Margaret thought she heard a plea in the woman's voice.

"Mr. Foote, Olivia, I thank you, I do, for the kindness you be showing me. But I do so wish to be alone this night. I'm that weary, I am."

Olivia opened her mouth to speak, but Josiah Foote said, "Well, Miss O'Keenan, since you are determined, I shall see you to your quarters." As Mary Margaret mentally prepared a protest, Josiah Foote continued, "It is too late for an unattended lady such as yourself—though to be sure, I have encountered a laundress or two about the premises of an evening. However, it is too late and dangerous, for you, Miss O'Keenan, to walk to Suds Row. And, furthermore, it appears the buggy is already hitched for some reason." And he flashed a steely glance at Olivia.

"Thank you, sir," said Mary Margaret.

"I need a moment," said Foote and left the room abruptly. Olivia set her burden down on a trunk behind the sofa and settled herself beside Mary Margaret, grasping both her hands. "We shall get through this tragedy together. The coming days will be difficult . . . hard, very hard. The funeral. I will accompany you in everything, that is, if you wish it, Mary Margaret, if you feel the want of my support."

Wondering if this woman who was teaching her the American ways could be havin' her on, Mary Margaret studied Olivia's bright green eyes and saw only sincerity and concern.

Olivia rushed on, her words spilling out in a hurried whisper, "I shall not forget that, here on a post where gossip is a major form of entertainment, and where, as the wife of the Post Trader, I am shunned by the officers' ladies, you Mary Margaret, befriended me."

"Hush, Olivia, 'tis no cause to be thanking me. 'Tis not my place to judge nor to talk. An' where would I be without your fine lessons? Just another Irish washerwoman is what I'd be."

Olivia smiled thinly. "Be that as it may, although I am not certain that Sgt. Flannery was murdered, I will help you, Mary Margaret, in any way that I am able." Olivia paused then said, "Except I will not go on the stage."

Tired and sad as she was, Mary Margaret smiled. "I dinna think it be necessary. I thank you for allowing me the loan of Tamany, an' 'tis true, I may be needing your help. Seán was murdered. There's no doubt in me mind. I saw the marks on his neck, and I found this clutched in his fist." Mary Margaret recaptured her hands from Olivia's and withdrew the bit of fluff from her pocket. She opened her hand and held it out flat.

"What is it?" asked Olivia.

Mary Margaret poked it. "Why, 'tis hair, I think. A clump of red hair with a bit of mud and grass."

"Hide it away. Mr. Foote returns," whispered Olivia as she rose and walked around behind the sofa, her wide skirts obscuring Mary Margaret. "Mr. Foote," said Olivia. "I shall fetch a shawl." Olivia turned her head slightly to be certain Mary Margaret had secured the hair, and then said, "The wind is fierce tonight."

Josiah Foote said nothing as he stepped into the parlour. His wife passed him and swished along the hallway connecting the front rooms to the rear bedrooms. Mary Margaret smoothed her skirt as Mr. Foote approached the divan. She stood and faced him. He opened his mouth and seemed about to speak when Olivia returned, and draped a thick wool shawl around Mary Margaret's shoulders. For a moment, the three stood in silence as if they were players in a tableau.

"Are you quite certain you want to go to your quarters, Mary Margaret?" asked Olivia, breaking the stillness. "You are most welcome to be our guest."

"I thank you, I do," said Mary Margaret. "'Tis a night to be alone with me thoughts. But I do 'preciate your kindness." Mr. Foote walked out of the parlour and opened the front door. Mary Margaret pulled the shawl around her, straightened her back, and followed Mr. Foote out to the buggy. As she passed Tamany, she stroked his neck in gratitude. She nodded to the striker, Private Patrick O'Brien, who held the horse steady. Then, quickly, before Mr. Foote could offer his arm, she climbed in and settled herself. Josiah Foote climbed in and took up the reins. Olivia walked out onto the covered porch and stood, bathed in the pearl gray light of the rising full moon. A few large drops of rain fell with a splat upon the tin roof, and in the distant north, lightening flashed.

In the Dead House, Dr. Williamson lit the gas lamps and cursed the architect for not providing enough illumination for such delicate and important procedures. As a young intern, he had been fortunate to observe Sir William Osler perform several autopsies, but on this night, in a musty, dimly lit morgue on a God-forsaken United States Army post, those days of his youth seemed far away.

Williamson, once the darling of Montreal Memorial Hospital, recalled the vicious intensity of the unfounded accusations that drove him from his country and landed him in New Mexico Territory. He had never touched any of his patients inappropriately. "Indeed," he said to the corpse, "what can be inappropriate for a surgeon? Damned women!"

He grabbed a notebook, inkwell, and quill, from the cabinet and set them on the desk. Then he turned and uncovered the corpse, dropping the blanket to the wide-plank, floor. He slowly circled the table observing the condition of the body.

Not caring to master thinking in any language other than English, Williamson spoke his thoughts aloud in the vernacular, but he recorded his notes in Latin. "The body is clothed in a long cotton under garment. Mud spatters the garment. Along the left side of the face—a long smear of mud. No foam is present at or in the mouth."

He turned the body on its side, and stood, for close to a minute, observing. He noted additional mud splatters on the back. The wind whistled through a sliver of a crack somewhere. He returned the corpse to its original position.

"Let us determine the tale your body has to tell, Sergeant Seán Flannery."

Williamson called for an orderly as he began cutting away the garment. He stepped back and circled the table again. "Can't see a damned, not a God-damned, thing. Private Jones," he called. "Fresh water please."

Williamson sighed and left the room. In a few minutes, he returned with a bucket of cold water and three towels. He washed the body and continued. "The face is swollen, veins distended, bruising about the neck, seems to be impressions of fingers, a deep bruise the size and shape of a man's thumb. Damned woman! She may be correct." In his notebook, he recorded the information and sketched a representation of the bruise, then continued his examination. "Small bruise in the area of the left kidney. Rigor mortis commencing. Body temperature 92.8. Dead approximately five hours, no more than seven."

Williamson recorded the slight bow in the right ankle. "That's been there awhile," he said, wondering about this enlisted man. "'Free use of all his limbs,' state the requirements for service, though you and I know enforcement is lax. Well, you managed your training. Done well enough these past years to make sergeant. Not many do, Sergeant Mister Flannery. Not many do," said Williamson as he proceeded to surgically open the chest.

Chapter 5: In which Mary Margaret falters, and Miguel reveals important information.

When the buggy halted in front of her quarters, Mary Margaret thanked Josiah Foote and quickly stepped down.

"I shall see you to your door, Miss O'Keenan," he said.

"Ah no, 'tis not necessary, sir. 'Tis but a step or two."

"Very well. Good night then."

The man had said nothing during their short ride together and never laid a finger on her, nonetheless, Mary Margaret felt as though, in some subtle way, she had been compromised. As her mind registered the departing hoof beats, she slid her key into the lock and turned it. There was no click. She pushed the door open and stood on the threshold. Thinking that Lulu forgot to lock up, Mary Margaret entered the main room, still warm and moist from the day's labor with steaming vats of hot water. The fresh, soapy odors comforted her as she reached for the lamp on the table just inside the door. Finding the box of matches, she struck one and lit the wick. As the flame rose, the room took shape before her eyes.

"Jaysus, Mary, and Joseph, and all the saints in heaven," she said. At the far end of the room, the tubs and laundry table had been upended. Her bed-linens were strewn across the floor, the mattress was twisted, the drawers of the old chiffonier yanked open with her personal things—knickers and all—draping the edges. Flour, molasses, and spices had been pulled from the cupboard and piled in a heap on the floor. As Mary Margaret righted the rocking chair, the one she had hauled across the plains, she saw that one of the armrests had been chipped. The raw wood glared like an open wound. She sighed and slumped onto the chair. She closed her eyes and rocked slowly.

Ah, Seán. I'm that weary, I am. I feel my bones break and my heart falter without your smile, your strong right arm. An' who be doing such a thing as this to me quarters? An' for what purpose? Searching for somethin' but, I swear, I dinna know what it could be.

Could it be the tangled nest of red hair you be clutching? Could be your assassin knows I have it? I fear 'tis all too much for me muddled brain. I dinna know what to do, how to begin. Indeed, Seán, what is this but a bit of red hair clasped in your fist. 'Tis the hair of your killer? Ah Seán, there be a hundred redheads on the post. 'Tis a worthless clue. What's that you say? 'Tis so, I be needing to investigate their whereabouts, yes, the duty rosters.

Even though she felt despair gnawing at her heart, Mary Margaret did not cry. She had not shed tears or sobbed since the nights she spent at the Old Brewery in New York—awake and huddled beneath vermin infested blankets, her hand clutching the knife.

'Tis not a thing I want to recall, Seán Flannery, not atall. Waking to find the filthy mitts of a toothless old drunk pawing me clothes . . . sure I never undressed in that place. An' didn't me days on the farm teach me that I dinna' want to breed, and handlin' the cows and horses give me the strength an' skills to protect m'self, but 'twas a nasty, boggin' place, that, the Five Point of New York City, with nothin' but a sluggish ditch for to be doing one's business.

An' I recollect clearly, not a smile passed your lips, Seán Flannery. An' you said, to be sure, them days is passed, passed like the clouds of yesterday. You have a way with the words, you do.

Mary Margaret returned the tiny nest of hair to her pocket. As the chair creaked back and forth, she relaxed into a semi-sleep until startled by a thud and a footstep. She stopped the chair, held her breath, and listened, but heard only the ever present wuthering of the wind. In the uneven glow of the lamp flame, shadows danced across the mud walls. "'Tis nothing," she said aloud. Then a soft thud made her jump to her feet. She grabbed the lamp from the

41

table and crept to the door. She grasped the door handle, and in one fast motion, turned the knob and yanked the door wide.

"Who be there?" she shouted, thrusting the lantern out in front of her.

A young voice whimpered, "Ouch."

"Micah?" she called.

"*Sí*. Yes, Ma'am. It is Miguel."

Mary Margaret sighed in relief and collapsed against the door frame. "What are you doing here? 'Tis late, is it not?"

"I do not know the time."

Mary Margaret saw by the streaks on his dirty face that Miguel had been crying. "Come here, boyo. 'Tis sad days indeed and more to come, more to come, I fear," and she hugged him. Too young to be embarrassed, the boy cried heavily in her arms. "Hush now," Mary Margaret crooned. "Come in why doncha'?" and she pulled the boy inside, closing the door behind him. She dampened a soft cloth and wiped his face, revealing the smooth young skin.

"'Tis a ladykiller you'll be one day, with those deep brown eyes and thick black hair."

Miguel straightened up and shrugged away from Mary Margaret. "I saw something, Ma'am. I saw someone, tonight, going into . . . ." He paused as he looked around the room. "*Que pasó?* What happened, Ma'am?"

"Sure I dinna know. I only just arrived on the scene m'self, now didn't I? But what did you see, Micah me boy?"

Miguel took another look around the quarters. "Someone's been looking for something, Ma'am."

"God in heaven, I do believe you are correct in that deduction. Now what did you see?"

"I saw someone, a man, going into the opera house."

"Sure there's lots of people, actors an' . . . ."

"No. I do not think it was one of the Company. I saw him only from the back. A big man, bigger than Mr. Foote. Big as Shiney, and carrying a bundle."

"Shiney? Private Walter Shiner? That works at the Trader's Saloon? Pr'aps he had some business. A bundle, you say?"

"*Sí*. Like the bundles that come here. But I do not know who it was."

"Like a bundle of clothes?" Mary Margaret felt a sudden rush of badness come over her, a feeling like fear, a feeling she did not like at all. "When, Micah?"

"This night, sometime after Private Jameson . . . after . . . ."

"Ah hush now . . . hush," she whispered and looking at Miguel, she wondered, not for the first time, about the boy's life. He seemed to be his own little man—coming and going as he pleased. She knew he had a home in Loma Parda, and she had heard the gossip as well. Some said his Da killed his Mum, others that she died of the consumption, still others that she run off with a tinker. His Da, Mary Margaret knew, drank more than he should and gambled away his earnings and got into many a brawl over the cards. Some said Miguel slept on the floor of one of the bawdy houses, others that he crawled into one of the harlots' caves in the nearby hills. Mary Margaret had seen him riding a burro and sometimes in Lulu's wagon. There was goodness and compassion in him yet, she thought, but the hardness of too much knowin' too early in life will soon be showing in his eyes.

"Micah. Sergeant Seán were murdered. Strangled, p'rhaps, and his clothes and rifle stolen."

Miguel roughly swiped at his tears. "I will go now and find the bundle."

"No. Stay with me this night. 'Tis too late for you to be travelin' about and searching in dark places or trudging home to Loma Parda." As he opened his mouth to protest, she said, "Please, Micah. 'Tis a comfort y'are."

Miguel smiled, "*Pero,* first we clean up. *Sí?*"

Chapter 6: In which Mary Margaret talks to Dr. Williamson.

By 10:00 am, while Lulu took over the washing duties, Mary Margaret sat on the wooden bench in front of Assistant Surgeon Williamson's office at the northeast end of the hospital. Odors of sickness and disinfectant and something foul floated on the sun-filled air. Mary Margaret waited with apparent patience, hands folded in her lap. Without wanting to, she imagined the dimly lit Dead House, bare and cold, where she last saw Seán's body.

"Miss . . . .um . . . Miss O'Keenan," the soft, childlike voice of a young civilian nurse shook Mary Margaret from her sad reverie. "Dr. Williamson will see you now." She led Mary Margaret to a door marked Assistant Surgeon and left her standing alone in the corridor. Mary Margaret knocked, waited a few seconds, and then entered. Immediately, Dr. Williamson rose from his chair behind a large oak table strewn with papers, open books, and a dusty vase of dead flowers. He gestured to a chair facing his desk but she remained standing.

"Yes, yes. What is it?" he said, impatience lacing his words.

"'Tis but a moment of yer. . . your time, sir, that I be after. That is, I will need to be getting back to me tubes. But could you ever please tell me how Sergeant Flannery died?"

Williamson looked at this woman who refused to sit, this woman who all but ordered him to perform an autopsy, which, of course, he would have done anyway. He felt a sudden desire to shake her. He turned his back to her and from the cabinet behind him, withdrew a sheaf of papers.

"I think it will be no surprise to you Miss O'Keenan to know that Sergeant Flannery died of asphyxia due to strangulation." Mary Margaret's gasp was so slight that the doctor, standing no more than four feet away from her, did not take notice. Without looking up from his report, he turned and faced her. "Strangulation, confirmed by the fracture of the hyoid bone. Contusions on the throat indicate strangulation by hand. No ligature marks, that is, no evidence that a rope or belt was used, as

44

in most of these cases. Some bruising in the area of the left kidney. Dirt, skin, and blood under the fingernails," the doctor looked up, "infer a struggle."

"Pardon me, sir?"

"A struggle. He fought his attacker, or attackers."

Mary Margaret swallowed hard. "I mean sir . . . that is . . . what do you mean by 'these cases?'"

"Murders, that is. Two thus far. One in 1880, enlisted men all. Strangled with what appears to be a belt, probably their own. Appears they were murdered for their uniforms and weapons. More likely the cause is a woman or a gambling debt."

"Excuse me sir. Sergeant Seán Flannery were not a man to be killed over such things as these you mention. He were a honest, a good soldier. 'Twas not a day went by he did not do his duty as ordered."

"Yes, yes." Williamson waved his free hand at Mary Margaret and almost shouted, "Examples, Miss. They were examples of what we see here."

"I'm after thinking they were not appropriate examples, sir." Silently, Mary Margaret thanked Olivia for the words and the confidence to say them.

Dr. Williamson grunted and returned the papers to the cabinet. "In any case, Sgt. Flannery was clearly strangled by hand."

"What do you make of the bruise in the area of the left kidney?" asked Mary Margaret.

"A punch . . . debilitating I should think."

"Sir?"

"A good punch or two to the kidney is extremely painful and debil . . . well, it would render a man quite helpless."

"Oh," said Mary Margaret. "He did not drown then?"

"No, he did not," replied Dr. Williamson with a bit of sympathy as he noticed Mary Margaret's pale face and the intensity of her posture. No, Miss O'Keenan. There was no foam present. As in cases of drowning."

"He did not fall from his horse?"

"If he fell from his mount, it appears to have been due to a struggle."

45

"Then sir, 'twere. . . to your mind. . . no accident?"

"No."

"May I see him?"

"The body is being embalmed as we speak. He will be buried this day."

"Embalmed?"

"Miss O'Keenan," Williamson's impatience returned. "I need not explain every detail of an Army Surgeon's tasks to you—a company laundress."

Mary Margaret opened her mouth to retort, then heard Olivia's warning, 'be—or at least—appear to be respectful.' "Please sir, I am but an ignorant immigrant to this grand country and grateful for the work as laundress. I am not familiar with the word 'embalmed.'"

"Embalming is the process of ridding the body of its deadly organisms, bacteria, and the like. Introduced by Dr. Thomas Holmes," Williamson warmed to his subject and the opportunity to educate. "During the recent rebellion, the American Civil War, embalming became necessary due to the large numbers of corpses lying about on the battlefields. Bodily fluids are drained. A mixture of arsenic and water is injected and . . . ."

Mary Margaret stopped the cruel flow of his words with, "Thank you, Dr. Williamson. 'Tis a comfort to have such a knowledgeable surgeon as yourself here at Fort Union. 'Tis necessary? This embalming?"

"Army regulations. That is all I have for you."

"But sir, if you please, Sergeant Flannery needs a proper burial."

Williamson said, "It is being arranged. They are building the coffin now. If you listen . . . ." The doctor paused, as they heard the banging hammers. "Catholic, I believe. A priest from Mora."

As the doctor intended, Mary Margaret felt like a child dismissed for bad behavior. She wished she had allowed Olivia to accompany her. "Thank you," she murmured and forced herself to walk slowly out of the office. Once outside, she rushed along the corridor, her hand grazing the wall for support, and escaped the suffocating hospital in time to vomit behind the juniper berry bushes alongside the wide veranda. As she wiped her mouth with a handkerchief, Mary Margaret looked up to see First Sergeant Jack Holloway walking up the stairs to the hospital entrance.

Chapter 7: Seán Flannery is laid to rest, and Private Shiner makes an appearance.

Mary Margaret placed her hair brush face up on top of the chest of drawers next to her cot. She looked in the mirror and made a final, futile adjustment to her hair, patting and pinning the errant curls into place. She did not want to bury Seán, did not want to walk in the dust behind the wagon, did not want to slap the plain pine box in a traditional farewell. She did not want to be the focus of anyone's good intentions, not those of the Colonel and his wife, nor Jack Holloway, nor Olivia Foote. Mary Margaret wanted to crawl into bed under fresh sheets and hide like a rabbit in its hole, but she pulled on her grey bonnet and tied the purplish black ribbons into a large bow beneath her chin.

With her hands, she smoothed and brushed dust from her grey paletot and her brown serge travel skirt, both faded by the New Mexico sun. As she pulled on her gloves, three quick raps at the door startled her, and she jumped involuntarily before opening it.

"Miss O'Keenan, ma'am," said a young soldier, removing his forage cap. "My condolences to you, if I may intrude, I am Private Shephard, sent by Commander Winters to escort you to the burial," and the commanding officer's striker offered his arm.

"Escort me?"

"The commander sends his regards and a buggy, ma'am. It is a fair distance to the graveyard. Could be six miles or more."

Mary Margaret nodded but said nothing. She feared that too much talk might loosen the welling tears and muffled sobs. She did not take the young soldier's arm. She crossed the threshold, turned and locked the door, then waited. Private Shephard moved quickly ahead of her and opened the door of the smart new trap hitched to a sleek grey mare. Wishing she had a grand lady's veil to hide her reddening face, Mary Margaret allowed the soldier to help her into the carriage. In silence and a bit too slowly for her liking, they proceeded to the Dead House, where the ambulance, with its escort of six mounted soldiers, a bugler, and First Sergeant Holloway in dress uniform, prepared to move out. The canvas sides were tied up, exposing the long box, draped with the Union flag. Private Shephard neatly turned the covered buggy and fell in behind the ambulance. With her back as straight as she could muster and her gloved hands folded in her lap, Mary Margaret stared ahead, training her eyes slightly above the level of the coffin.

Then they waited. The soldiers at attention did not speak or joke or chuckle. It was the first calm day in more than a month, and in the absence of a howling wind, the sounds of horses shuffling and tack clinking filled the air—then hoof beats, as two carriages approached. She did not turn to see Colonel Winters and his family in their official carriage or the Foote's buggy.

> *'Tis a sorry-looking troupe Seán Flannery, six guards, Holloway, a bugler, a young recruit drivin' your wagon . . . not a black plume nor a black drape. Most of the companies be on maneuvers I'm told. Solemn, yes, an' in parade dress . . . sabers and clean white gloves, brushed caps. Buttons and brass glintin' in the sun. Sure they was ordered to be here.*

Holloway lifted his arm and gave the command to move out. The ambulance jolted forward. From somewhere behind Mary Margaret, a horse whinnied and the sound of two horses galloping filled the air.

Shephard leaned over and whispered, "For your solace and perhaps curiosity, Miss O'Keenan, the sounds you hear are the honorable Mr. Gonzalez of Los Alamitos leading a *pinto* horse with a riderless saddle."

She nodded acknowledgment but did not turn her head. She inhaled the warm sweet smell of grass, horse sweat, and leather as she swallowed the hard lump in her throat. The patrol turned slowly and moved northwest toward the garrison burial grounds at the foothills of the *Sangre de Cristo* mountains.

> *Ah, Seán. 'Tis sorry I am.*

'Tis sorry I am for the precious moments lost when I wasn't payin' attention.

'Tis sorry I am for not cherishing every time you spoke or laughed or sang me a tune.

'Tis sorry I am for me fierce temper an' words spoken in haste.

'Tis sorry y'are fer livin' still? you may ask.

Aye, 'tis sorry I am.

The procession moved at a slow, measured pace and within the hour reached the grave yard, a collection of unmarked graves surrounded by a white wooden fence. As they passed through the open gates, Mary Margaret found it difficult to breathe. She thought she could not bury her man. She drew in a breath.

As he reined in the horse, Private Shephard said, "Miss O'Keenan, do you need a moment to compose yourself?"

It was the right question, a question Mary Margaret would never answer in the affirmative. "No, private, thank you. I be well. Quite well." And she slowed her breathing.

When she moved to exit, Shephard said, "A few minutes yet, Miss. They're getting into position."

Mary Margaret stared forward. A few paces ahead, she watched six soldiers dismount and position the green-wood casket on a set of cross-boards. When they slid the ropes under the coffin, she closed her eyes.

Aye, 'tis sorry I am, Seán, that I never . . . that I couldna' declare me love for you. Tho' in spite o' me self, I did an' I do. Ah, you charmed me, you did, with your warmth and carin,' your devilish smile. But 'tis not the charm nor the Blarney. 'Tis the carin' and the honest, uprightness of yourself. An' oh you made me laugh, you did. But why you loved me I dinna know.

50

Later and mercifully, Mary Margaret would recall little of the ceremony, only that the sun was warm, the breeze soft, and the hole deep. Small bits of images will come to her as in dreams . . . a bunch of white daisies clasped in Olivia's hands, a pile of earth and stone beside the long, deep hole, soldiers at attention, a fidgeting horse, an unknown priest in a long black robe. She would recall the members of both performing companies, and the dark silhouette of a large man standing on the periphery with the sun behind him. Mary Margaret felt certain that Seán's murderer was among the mourners. She did not search the faces, but she hoped that Lulu and Miguel stood among the civilians scattered at the edges of the military. It gave her comfort to think so.

It was a brief, simple ceremony, punctuated by the mournful sound of taps. But as the soldiers mounted up and the drivers positioned their animals and carriages, Mary Margaret thought she heard a familiar tune, played soft and low on a penny whistle.

Sure, it canna be, Seán.

As she climbed into the Colonel's gig, she heard the bugle join in, picking up a marching tempo. She turned her head, searching for the whistle-player.

It canna be, but 'tis.

"'Tis," she murmured, "'Tis 'Peggy and the Soldier.'"
"Pardon, Ma'am," said the driver.
"The tune," she said. And in the Irish way of celebrating the dead, she sang softly.

> *And when he saw she was so true, he could not stay*
> *hard hearted.*
> *He said, "My darling, I'll marry you, and none but*
> *death shall part us,*
> *And when we're in some foreign land, I'll guard you,*
> *my darling, with my right hand.*

And pray that God a friend might stand to Peggy
and her gallant soldier."

Ah Seán, sure I could use your good right hand.

As they neared the garrison, the Foote carriage pulled up beside Mary Margaret, and Olivia extended an invitation for tea and cakes. Mary Margaret declined. Then Olivia said, "The Commander will be there." Through her grief, Mary Margaret realized that Olivia was suggesting more than a reception. Perhaps an opportunity to learn something about Seán's death.

"Ah yes," said Mary Margaret, "'Tis an honor for me man." And she thought, will this pain in my heart never cease?

And so, it was in Olivia's parlour, once again sipping tea, where Mary Margaret overheard Private Gus Peterson, 'the champ of the Comedy Company,' as Seán called him. She thought, the private has had a bit too much of Josiah Foote's fine Kentucky bourbon.

"No sprize, no sprize at all the man's been murdered. Sgt. Flannery made too many enemies."

"Take care, Gus," said First Sgt. Holloway. "Flannery was a good soldier. He did not deserve such treatment. And who calls himself the enemy of Seán Flannery? You?"

Mary Margaret heard a mumbled reply that could have been anything and tried to sidle up closer to the small group of men.

"Flannery had enemies," said Peterson, "And you know who they are, Holloway."

"My condolences Miss O'Keenan," Harlan Davies said, laying his warm moist hand on Mary Margaret's forearm.

She withdrew discreetly and said, "I thank you for your sympathy, Private Davies. I'll be seeing you tonight then? Opening night?"

"No, Ma'am. The house will be dark. Respect for the dead."

"But Seán would . . . ."

"No one has the heart, nor the sober constitution, to perform adequately. Opening night performance will take place tomorrow night. Are you certain you are up to it?"

"Yes, sir," said Mary Margaret.

"But," Harlan paused as a small commotion broke out at the front door. Mary Margaret turned to see First Sgt. Holloway approaching the only man on the post bigger than himself, Private Walter Shiner, called "Shiney" when he was not within hearing distance.

"You are not welcome here," said Holloway.

"Come to pay moy respects. I got a right," shouted Shiney and puffed up his chest like a barnyard rooster.

Walter Shiner was a thick, square man, over six feet tall, with fists like anvils and eyes like dark blue storms, hooded by bushy red brows. His broken and bent nose shone angrily in the afternoon sun. Seán had often remarked, 'Sure, 'tis the face of a man that's stopped many a blow.' Born in America to a brutal father and a gentle, ineffective mother—Shiner was seven when she died and his father put him in an orphanage, telling the good sisters that he didn't know the boy. 'Found him stealing and fighting on the streets I did.' Shiney ran away regularly and worked at living up to his father's lies. The nuns, strict as the Lord allowed, had no effect on his nature. As soon as he was old enough, he joined the Army. Sister Catharine Elizabeth prayed for the miserable boy until the end of her life.

After close to ten years, Shiney, who made sergeant twice but was busted down regularly, wore the stripes of the private and the insignia of the 10th Infantry. The talk on the post was that he supplemented his meager military pay by doing "odd jobs" for Josiah Foote and exacting a tribute from each member of the Shiney Boys, his motley gang of petty thieves. Most people believed Shiney was responsible for the odd fires and brawls that broke out at the Fort as well as in Loma Parda and Tiptonville. Some even thought he killed a fellow soldier last year. Once, Shiney and his stragglers appeared at Los Alamitos, shoving and threatening Porfirio Gonzalez, but Vicente Silva happened by that day. Silva is said to have spoken a few, low words in Shiner's ear,

53

and none of the Shiney Boys were ever seen there again. At the garrison, the only man who stood up to Walter Shiner, blow for blow, had been Sgt. Flannery. First Sergeant Holloway preferred diplomacy.

Jack Holloway said, "Well now, Private Shiner. You must know that you are not welcome. You were no friend to Sgt. Flannery."

Mary Margaret left Harlan and approached the First Sergeant. "Sure, anyone as wishes to mourn be welcome, First Sergeant Holloway."

"But, Miss Mary Margaret, I do not think . . . ."

"Shoosht, Jack," she whispered and held his forearm. Shiney strutted into the room, brushing past Mary Margaret without a word of condolence, and walking directly to Josiah Foote. Mary Margaret watched as he doffed his forage cap to Olivia and exposed his bald head rimmed with fuzzy red hair. She watched Shiney and Foote engage in conversation. She saw Olivia move closer to Mr. Foote and hoped that the movement allowed her friend to hear their words.

What am I to make of all this, Seán? Enemies. Gus Peterson says you have enemies. Who might he be referring to? Timmy Sullivan? The outlaw—what was his name—the horse thief you and Jack brought in? An' Shiney, who never had a good word for you? Specially not after the fair beatin' you gave him. What's that you say, Seán? Stay outta Shiney's way. I dinna think I kin keep it all straight. Who be your enemies? P'rhaps Peterson himself? Who, Seán, who?

"My condolences, Miss O'Keenan," said Colonel Winters, brushing his thick grey mustache. "A terrible, untimely occurrence."

"You poor, poor dear," said Mrs. Winters, fluttering like a sparrow and lightly grazing Mary Margaret's hand. "I expect you will be leaving us soon, what with the Army mustering out the laundresses."

"Charlotte," interrupted the Colonel, his face reddening slightly, "Not a decision that needs to be made on this day."

"Oh. Of course not dear," said Mrs. Winters, taking a short step backwards.

"Thank you sir," said Mary Margaret, addressing the commander. "Tomorrow will be soon enough to think about me future." And as the Colonel turned to walk away, Mary Margaret said, "But you are mistaken sir. 'Twere no 'untimely occurrence.' Sergeant Flannery were murdered."

Colonel Winters turned and looked evenly into Mary Margaret's eyes. Being a few inches taller than she, the commander bent forward slightly and said in a voice just above a whisper, "I believe it is you who are mistaken, Miss O'Keenan. I bid you good evening." He took his wife by the elbow and guided her through the gathering and out of the house.

Soon after the commander departed, people began drifting out, expressing condolences to Mary Margaret and thank yous to Mr. and Mrs. Foote. Olivia stood beside her husband and Shiney stood slightly behind and to the left of Josiah Foote. First Sgt. Holloway took a place beside Mary Margaret who was trying to figure out a way to be alone with Olivia.

"Olivia, 'tis a good time to clean up," and Mary Margaret reached for two glasses on a nearby table.

"Nonsense," said Mr. Foote. "O'Brien will take care of things. Where is that lazy striker?"

Mary Margaret opened her mouth to protest, but Olivia gave a subtle shake as Judson Clooney approached the group. He took hold of Mary Margaret's hand and expressed his sympathy. Then he leaned forward and whispered, "Be careful who you put your trust in Miss O'Keenan." He straightened abruptly and said aloud, "If I can be of any help—any help at all—please do not hesitate to call upon me. I enjoyed many a long talk with Sergeant Flannery. I am saddened to lose such a companion."

"Ah, Mr. Clooney," she said. "'Tis in your debt I'd be if you'd see me to me quarters."

Mr. Foote, standing close by, offered to take Mary Margaret in the buggy. But she claimed the need of a breath of air and a bit of

55

a stretch, "'Tis not often we have a windless afternoon. Mr. Foote, wouldja ever release the Commander's striker—the kind Private Shepard—for me?"

Josiah Foote nodded in reply, and Olivia offered to help Mary Margaret in the morning with costume adjustments and practicing lines.

"Bright and early," said Olivia. "I shall come to your quarters. I have just the right bit of cloth for a cummerbund."

The evening air proved refreshing. Gentle breezes ruffled the brown grasses and early spring weeds. There was a kiss of moisture in the air although no clouds were visible.

"Sure it feels like a bit of rain on its way," said Mary Margaret.

"Could be," replied Clooney, "drifting down from the Turkey Mountains."

Mary Margaret stopped suddenly, turned, and looked into Jud's green eyes. "What is it you know, Mr. Clooney? Who be Seán's enemies?"

"As you are yourself, Miss O'Keenan, I shall be direct, but I have no hard facts, no evidence, nothing to point to. I cannot say, there, that is why I feel this way."

"'Tis intuition then?"

"Perhaps. We men find the notion a difficult one, but it could be just that, intuition. News—or rather gossip—moves through the garrison like a wildfire. It is said that Seán Flannery was murdered—strangled."

"'Tis true," said Mary Margaret. "An' who be his enemies, Mr. Clooney?"

"Let us walk on," replied Clooney as he nodded to a soldier crossing the thoroughfare. They approached the rear of the Officers' Quarters, and Jud stopped and faced Mary Margaret, gently grasping her forearm. Not a tall man, he met her eye to eye. His sandy brown hair, green eyes, and tendency to pudginess, gave him an air of the average and ineffectual. Judson Clooney was the garrison "egghead," and many soldiers poked fun at him. But Mary Margaret knew a bit of his history—a sniper in the recent rebellion, earning him two medals for bravery. He was promoted in the field to brevet First Sergeant. A solitary soldier, who did more reading and writing than drilling and riding, Jud Clooney was never seen without his notebook. "I am certain Seán told you to be careful of Shiney—that would not be news. I believe Peterson is harmless even though he gossips like an old woman. Outright enemies. I know of no one in particular. However, the patrol he was attached to encountered many hard types. I do not trust Josiah Foote, nor the commander."

"Colonel Winters? 'Tis the Commanding Officer of Fort Union you suspect?"

"I would not go so far as to use the word, 'suspect.' As I said, Miss O'Keenan, I have nothing to point to."

"No evidence. 'Tis so. I thank you, Mr. Clooney, for your kindness and your honesty. And your friendship. Sergeant Flannery valued your opinion in many things." They continued in silence across the parade grounds. As they passed Company B Quarters, the sounds of men joking and laughing, the scraping of chairs, and the thuds of boots punctuated the silence.

Clooney said, "Miss Mary Margaret, there's talk that you've been snooping around, accusing a soldier."

"I'm after accusing no man," cut in Mary Margaret. " Soldier or otherwise. But I promised Seán Flannery I would find his killer, and I intend to do just that. An'what of First Sergeant Holloway?"

The question took Clooney by surprise. "Holloway? Uh, he seems straight enough. A Baltimore gentleman, family money. Honest, if a bit ambitious. Keeps to himself. Considers himself a friend to Sgt. Flannery, does he not?"

Mary Margaret nodded. As they arrived at her quarters, they heard the bugle call for Parade Dress. She took the key from her reticule, turned to Jud and said, "'Tis the sad truth. Seán Flannery were strangled by the bare hands of a man. A man who was known to him, thinks the Sheriff of San Miguel. Doctor Williamson, himself, told me of the marks of strangulation. I'll find Seán's killer, I will."

As she unlocked her door, Jud said, "I counted Seán Flannery as my friend. I shall keep his murder in the newspaper, before the eyes of the public, for as long as I can. I am at your service, Mary Margaret, any time you need help," and he bowed slightly from the waist. "But please be careful. I believe, or perhaps intuit, that there is more to this than the murder of a fine soldier."

"'Tis right you are in that." She unlocked and pushed open her door then inclined her head in Jud's direction. "An' if you please, Mr. Clooney, wouldja ever be addressin' me as Miss O'Keenan. 'Tisn't proper, I be thinking, for an unattached gentleman such as yourself to be addressing me by my given name."

Chapter 8: In which the show goes on.

The day dawned calm and bright with a clear sky unrelieved by a single wisp of cloud. But Mary Margaret awoke in turmoil—images of big rough hands closed around Seán's throat, Seán's dead-bright eyes staring into the night, and Laya—Layla, *haven't thought of you in many a day,* Layla in her violet silk gown, swinging from the beam. As Mary Margaret sat up, she recalled the Commander's words, 'I believe it is you who are mistaken, Miss O'Keenan.' She rubbed her eyes and shook herself free of the night's torments. She drew on her shawl, set a fire in the cookstove, poured water from the pitcher into the basin, and splashed its coolness on her face and neck. Then Mary Margaret undressed and standing before the tall mirror, soaped herself, rinsed, and wrapped herself in a clean rough towel. As she stood in the middle of her quarters, considering her nightmares, she heard a soft tap on the door. Peeking through the window, she saw Olivia standing outside and looking around curiously.

Mary Margaret took note of her cramped and messy quarters. Can't be helped, she thought, as she shrugged into her nightdress and wrapped a shawl around her shoulders. "'Tis welcome y'are to me humble home, Olivia," said Mary Margaret, opening the door.

Olivia smiled in response then told striker O'Brien to set the trunk inside Mary Margaret's quarters and return in two hours time. Olivia thanked him as he completed his task, and she watched as he drove the buggy toward the Trader's Compound.

"Patrick and I gathered Sergeant Flannery's costume and brought it. With a nod, Olivia indicated the trunk. It would have been sheer madness for you to cart everything all about, now, would it not?"

Mary Margaret nodded, grateful for the practicality and the consideration of the woman. "'Twould—I mean—it would have been sheer madness. A cuppa coffee? A biscuit? Some eggs?"

Olivia's shook her head. "A cup of tea would be most welcome, Mary Margaret. No sugar, no milk. But I shall make it while you put on your costume." Olivia turned her back to Mary

Margaret and set about the familiar and comforting business of making tea.

Minutes later, dressed as the Lawyer Connelly, Mary Margaret sat at the table sipping tea while Olivia fussed with Mary Margaret's thick black curls, pressing the hair down and pinning it flat.

"Let me see," said Olivia. She placed the black Derby on Mary Margaret's head, stepped back, and looked with a critical eye. The hat fell down below Mary Margaret's eyebrows, coming to rest on her nose, and both women laughed. "A bit more height on the top." Olivia removed the hat and rearranged the pile of curls.

"Olivia, what did Seán buy that morning? At the Trader's Store?"

"Oh, my dear Lord! I never did tell you. He bought a locket, a pretty little thing, heart-shaped, gold, with a lovely *fleur de lis* pattern on the front side and rosettes and ribbons on the back. It came with a fine gold chain. Very delicate."

Mary Margaret squeezed her eyes shut at the vision of Seán considering the purchase, deciding among the store's offerings. Then she winced as Olivia pulled out all the hairpins and brushed Mary Margaret's hair up on top of her head, twisting it into a thick bun.

"'Twas no locket on his body," said Mary Margaret, forcing herself to recall the dark scene at the edge of Los Alamitos Lake. "Or thereabouts as I could see. Though 'tis true I had little time or ability to search. Perhaps, Sheriff O'Tero found something."

"Let's have a look at you." Olivia replaced the hat and took a step backward. Then she leaned forward, scrunched the hat down, and angled it to the right. "Jaunty," she proclaimed. "Look for yourself," she said, holding up a hand mirror.

"'Tis no disguise, but it will do. Do you suppose the locket was stolen? Or lost in the struggle, buried in the mud?"

Olivia frowned. "Mr. Davies will surely have some makeup to thicken your eyebrows and darken your skin. Now, would not the locket likely be in his quarters or in his haversack? Stand up now."

"Might I finish me tay?"

"Of course." Olivia sat and took a sip of the barely warm tea, set down the cup, and looked straight at Mary Margaret. "Let me think. I had just entered the store and was examining some new fabrics that arrived from Boston. Sgt. Flannery was completing his purchase. That new clerk, what is his name? Joseph, I believe, was behind the counter. He placed the locket in a small, red velvet sack, pulled the golden strings, and handed it to the Sgt. When suddenly, there was a loud, thunderous crack, and the entire fireplace mantel groaned and fell in a heap upon the floor."

"What?"

"Please, Mary Margaret, let me think. Yes. The fireplace mantel collapsed, they do that from time to time, ceilings as well, moisture collects and . . . anyway, many of the *adobes* from the surrounding wall tumbled down as well. Sgt. Flannery secured the area, and Joseph began sweeping, trying to capture that horrid fine dust. Sgt. Flannery was piling up the bricks when he found something stuck in a crevice in the wall. It was then that Mr. Foote entered, cursing the fireplace, the builder, the prairie, and, I think, God himself. Now, let us have a look at the fit of your jacket."

Mary Margaret rose and stepped away from the table. "What happened next, Olivia?"

"Let me think. I believe Mr. Foote thanked Sergeant Flannery for helping to clear away the debris. Oh, this will not do! Your bosoms stand out like *cerritos*. You must remove your corset."

"*Cerr-ee . . . ?*"

"It is a lovely Spanish word for little hills—*cerr-i-tos*. Now then, turn around, remove the corset, or Bust Improver, or whatever it is makes you so buxom, and put on a short chemise. I shall need a thin towel, perhaps a few flour sacks?" Mary Margaret pointed to the bottom drawer of the chiffonier where Olivia found three old flour sacks, worn soft by washing and use, and set about ripping them apart and re-sewing them into a long, winding cloth.

"An' 'twas all that was said between them, Olivia?"

"No. Oh no, indeed. They exchanged angry words, at least, I heard anger, although restrained, in my husband's voice. But, the oddest thing, as the sergeant turned to leave, I noticed he was smiling, so I thought all was well. I watched him mount and ride away."

"What direction?" asked Mary Margaret, steadying her voice as she imagined Seán and Rosie riding out that morning—when all was still well and there was a future. Olivia did not respond immediately. She took a few more stitches. "Olivia! Which way did Seán ride?"

"I am thinking, if you will just have a bit of patience. North, I think. Seems to me there was something else said between them." Olivia finished the seam, knotted the thread, and held up her creation. "We shall bind them. Wrap you like an ancient Egyptian mummy." Then she saw Mary Margaret's crestfallen expression. "Oh, my dear Lord. It must have been to Los Alamitos he rode. If he did not go to his quarters, why then, the locket would likely be in his haversack. Oh, my dear, this must be so difficult for you."

Mary Margaret stiffened at what she saw as sympathy in Olivia's eyes. "An' the time o' day?" she asked.

"I did not look at my time piece, but in my memory, the wind was up but the sun was not yet high. Mid-morning, perhaps."

In silence, Olivia tightly wrapped Mary Margaret's breasts and secured the cloth with four small stitches. "Can you breathe? You look a bit pale."

"'Tis fine," said Mary Margaret and put on the white, man's shirt that smelled faintly of Seán. "But, Seán would have been on duty at that time." She readjusted the trousers and secured the braces, then shrugged into the gold and black brocade vest and the long black frock coat.

"I wouldn't know about that," said Olivia. "Let me see the length on the pants." She knelt and pinned up the pants so that they brushed the top of Mary Margaret's instep. "The locket was meant for you. There is no doubt."

"'Tis so, an' I mean to have it. 'Tis me present."

Olivia said nothing. She scrutinized Mary Margaret's appearance. A sudden devil wind slammed against the west wall, showering the window with a cloud of fine sand. "10:00 o'clock in the morning and the wind is up. I fear this will be a fierce, dry spring. Summer as well, no doubt." Olivia sat back onto her heels. "If I could only remember. I am certain there was something more said between them. Oh, what was it? Turn around now."

Mary Margaret rotated slowly as Olivia pinned up the trousers.

"And, what do you make of the ball of red hair you found?" asked Olivia.

"'Twas clutched in Seán's fist, it was. I believe, in his struggle for his life, me man yanked the hair from the head of his killer. Ah, but, there be a hundred redheads at Fort Union . . . or more."

"We only need to know which redheads were not accounted for at the time of Sergeant Flannery's death. As volunteer at the hospital, I have access to the daily duty roster."

"Of course," said Mary Margaret. "Didn't Seán himself say that?"

"What?"

"I mean, sure, he <u>would</u> say it. If I were to ask, that is, if he were . . . ."

"Of course he would. Sergeant Flannery was a good soldier— a tracker of villains along with First Sergeant Holloway. Oh how things improved here at the post once the commander assigned them to the protection patrol—well, that is the name I'd give to their duty. Guarding the shipments and our homes. Bringing in rustlers and murderers." Olivia stood, staggered slightly, and clutched the table for support.

"Olivia? Are you ill?"

"Oh, it is nothing, a bit of lightheadedness. Now, take off the britches and I shall put in a hem. Then we must press the creases again, so please warm the iron."

Mary Margaret studied Olivia's face. It had paled suddenly as she rose, and dark circles curled beneath her eyes. She asked, "Guardin' our homes?"

"Oh, yes," replied Olivia. "There was a time—it seemed every day—rowdy young men, soldiers I suppose, just walked into quarters without so much as a 'by your leave.' Just walked right in . . . in the light of day and stole whatever it was caught their fancy. Such thievery! Didn't seem to matter if people were at home. I lost an entire silver tea-serving set. Mrs. Winters was robbed of . . . ."

"The commanding officer's quarters was robbed?"

"<u>Were</u> robbed. No, wait. The word <u>quarters</u> might just be one of those persnickety collective nouns. I shall have to . . . ."

"Olivia!"

"Yes? Oh yes, they ran off with cash dollars and a very elegant pocket watch. Never to be found. Is the iron hot? The post gossip assigned guilt to Private Shiner, but I do not believe it. Oh, he bullies the new recruits and brawls whenever he can arrange an altercation, and it may be that he did set those fires, but, robbery, no, and not murder. No, I do not believe it. He's not a bad sort, not really."

"Murder?"

As Olivia quick-hemmed the trousers, she recounted the tale of a murdered soldier, Private Abreu, whose father had been a commander in the militia. "A brave young man—quiet, reserved, thoughtful. He disappeared earlier this year. His body was discovered about a mile east of the Fort, just paces north of the Santa Fe Trail, naked. Mutilated." Olivia paused. "I assisted Dr. Williamson. Sad. His family is devastated."

Olivia sighed and passed the britches to Mary Margaret. "Now I think on it, Private Abreu was in the very same patrol with Sergeant Flannery and First Sergeant Holloway."

Mary Margaret looked up from pressing the new crease. "How was he killed?"

"Strangled, poor soul."

Mary Margaret paused. "Strangled? By human hand?"

"Good Lord, Mary Margaret! You're scorching the trousers!"

Mary Margaret lifted the iron and set it on the brick. "Ah 'tis nothing. Will not show," she said. "Was he strangled by human hand or with a belt or rope?"

64

Olivia thought for a moment, "No indications of a ligature. Perhaps, I hope, that these investigations will reveal his murderer as well."

"An' what was it you learned from Shiney and Mr. Foote? After Seán's burial?"

"Oh, yes. I'm afraid I did not learn a thing. They seemed to be talking of the work of the store or the saloon. Walter said something like, let me think now. He said, 'it's done,' and Mr. Foote smiled, but when our eyes met, his smile turned to a frown, and he told Walter—most inappropriately I thought—to keep his yip shut."

Mary Margaret smiled at the odd combination of Olivia's stately appearance and the street language. "Wouldja be meaning to say—*yap*? Keep your yap shut?"

"Yes, that sounds right. Are you familiar with this expression?"

"Ah yes. 'Tis common enough. He be telling Shiney to keep the information close to the breast . . . to say nothing of it. But I do not think 'twas work they spoke of—'It's done' could be referring to Seán. To his murder."

"It could refer to anything."

At dusk, Mary Margaret stood at the rear entrance to the Opera House. She had come early to be backstage when the actors entered and began dressing and gossiping. She ran her hands down along the dove grey trousers, thinking she had not felt so free since she was a 'wild thing' running with the goats in the fields. She shrugged her shoulders, then pulled the hat down tighter.

> *Ah, Seán, look at your Mary Margaret now. Will she pass for a gentl'man? An' will it be she learns something of your murderer? Be with me, Seán.*

Mary Margaret lifted the latch, pushed open the heavy wooden door, and walked into the dimly lit backstage area, expecting the soldier-actors to stare, but as her eyes adjusted, she saw but a few shapes. From the outline of the gown and the roll in his walk, she recognized Timmy Sullivan in the costume of the young heroine, making his way across the stage and bent in conversation with the English Landlord whom she knew to be played by Bill Casey. She approached as quietly as she was able and caught snippets of their conversation.

Shaking a finger in Sullivan's face, Casey said, "'Tis Davies' call, not yours. If he thinks she can . . ." He stopped in mid-sentence when Harlan Davies appeared, as if on cue, from behind a thick, black curtain strung across the rear of the stage.

"That's right," said Davies.

Sullivan shouted, "But does she know how to move? Be upstagin' me she will. An' I be thinking she canna' be strutting 'cross the stage like a man would!"

"Well," replied Davies. "Can you be mincing across the stage like a young coquette?"

Casey laughed and slapped Sullivan on the shoulder.

Davies was not convinced that Mary Margaret was the best choice to replace Flannery, but it was his decision to make, he made it, and by God, everyone had better follow suit. He knew that Sullivan had expected to move into the role. He knew, also, that here in this God-forsaken outpost, far from civilized, forward thinking cities, it was still considered scandalous for a woman to be wearing men's trousers and strutting in front of an audience, especially with these brutal murders. But Davies also knew that these very facts would bring a bigger audience. A full house, perhaps as from as far away as Las Vegas.

"Standing Room Only," he said aloud.

"But she's . . ." Sullivan did not finish his sentence as Mary Margaret bumped a chair and sent it skidding several inches before hitting one of the prop walls.

"Ah, evening gent'lmen," she said, with more confidence than she felt, and touched two fingers to her hat.

"Evening," said Davies. Sullivan turned and stalked away, disappearing into the darkness of stage left.

"He'll come 'round," Casey said. Then he called out, "Ah, fer the love of God, Timmy!" and followed.

"Come into the light Miss O'Keenan. Let me look at you." Davies scrutinized Mary Margaret's costume and appearance. "You look fine, fine. With that flat wide nose and high hollow cheeks, you'll pass nicely. But a moustache will help. Follow me." And he strode across the stage in the same direction that Timmy and Casey went. Mary Margaret ran to keep up and found herself tripping down a narrow, twisty stairway, then along a short, dark passageway until they were underneath the stage. They entered a large, windowless room, hung with mirrors, and hooks, and costumes—feathers, furs, silks, and bombazine. The dull orange glow of several kerosene lamps illuminated a long wooden table littered with rags and brushes and cans of assorted grease paint. At intervals on the table, stood a few framed mirrors with shielded candles set into their sides. Mary Margaret saw Timmy spreading rouge on his cheeks, Bill Casey waxing his red moustache, and Patrick O'Brien, Mr. Foote's young striker, in gown and gray wig, making some adjustments to his bustle. She was forced to cover her mouth and swallow her laughter.

Ah Seán, didja not have some trouble to maintain a serious demeanor? Demeanor, tis a word Olivia taught me. Didja not balk, yourself, at the costuming and the posturing? An' who will I be sharing a laugh with now?

Davies reached for a small round can and gestured. "Here, come here, Miss O'Keenan. If you please."

At his words, all of the actors stopped what they are doing and turned to stare, with undisguised curiosity, at Mary Margaret, in the costume of Mr. Michael Thomas Connolly, the Irish Attorney.

Someone whose voice was familiar but whose face was unrecognizable in a cap and false beard, said, "Ah, O'Keenan, you're as welcome as the flo'ers in May. Break a leg."

"I surely hope not, sir!" She replied.

"'Tis a phrase—an expression of good will and good fortune, my dear. No harm meant," and when he raised his cap, Mary Margaret recognized young Ben Bolton in the costume and make-up of old Mr. Fielding.

"Miss O'Keenan," said Davies. "Would you be so kind as to come here? Come come." And he gestured for her to approach the far end of the table.

As she moved to join him, Timmy Sullivan suddenly shoved his chair back, blocking her way. And without looking at her, he said, "You'd best be careful Miss O'Keenan. Acting can be a dangerous occupation."

Mary Margaret felt chilled by his statement. "Wouldja be after referring to me man? Are you sayin' 'tis the acting got him killed, Private Sullivan?"

"I ain't saying no such thing. I'm saying *you* best be careful, Miss O'Keenan." Sullivan stood and pushed past Mary Margaret, leaving her to negotiate the chair as best she could.

Ah, Seán, what am I to make of Timmy Sullivan? Sure he's jealous an' angry. Always was a bit of a lig, cutting up and playin' the fool. An' he be havin' the red hair. But murder? What's that you say? Sure, 'tis as you say. Olivia be after checking the duty rosters. I shall hold me thoughts 'til I be knowing more.

At the Foote home, Olivia was pinning up her hair. Tall and slim, with fair skin and eyes, Olivia had been blessed with thick auburn locks that shone with health and curled easily.

Entering the bedroom, Mr. Foote said, "Where do you think you're going?"

"Why, to the Opera House, Mr. Foote."

"Disgraceful! A woman on stage, and a laundress at that! And at least two soldiers of this garrison murdered, barely cold in their graves. No, Mrs. Foote, you are decidedly not going to the Opera House this night."

"But . . ."

"There'll be no more talk of it!" He shouted and slammed the dressing table with his open hand, rattling the bottles and startling Olivia. She dropped her brush and looked at her husband's face in the mirror. A few strands of her hair escaped the tight bun she had been forming.

"But Mary Margaret will be expecting us."

He bent and whispered harshly in her ear, "No more talk of it." He grabbed the brush and raised it above her head. "Now, I'll brush those pretty locks for you." He yanked at the remaining hairpins and roughly stroked her hair with the brush. Olivia watched in the mirror, recalling the days of courtship. She wondered if she may have imagined those times, saw more in the man than there was or could be, for, she thought, he never speaks of poetry now and seldom smiles. Olivia chided herself, remembering how good he had been to her father, lending him money. She vowed to be less demanding, more accommodating. In the mirror, her eyes met his. She saw barely controlled anger, but she could not decipher a reason for it.

She took a deep breath and said, "Why do you hate me so?"

"Hate you? You are not important enough to hate. You are useless and insignificant, like the small heaps of dust blown in from the prairie—a nuisance." He set the brush down on the table and stepped back. Then, in a voice as cold and as hard as winter, he said, "Can't even produce an heir," and stalked out of the bedroom.

Mary Margaret peeked out from behind the main curtain, searching the audience for Olivia, Lulu, or someone she knew, but she saw only strangers. Except for a few of the Company B officers and their wives, she recognized no one. Ladies in fancy dress and gentlemen in top hats filled the seats and chatted comfortably. The room was noisy with their talk and easy laughter. Then she saw Colonel Winters, his wife, and young daughter enter and take the spaces reserved for them in the front row. Following behind the commanding officer, First Sergeant Jud Clooney made his slow, deliberate way along the left aisle and behind him appeared Miguel, then Lulu.

No, Seán darlin', that's not how the line goes. Ah, Mary Margaret m'dear, but that's how it should go. Sure, you can hear 'tis better this way. But 'tis not how the good Mr. Carleton wrote it. An' you laughed, you did, and

69

called me—me—a bogtrotter an' said, Well, we'll change it, then. And 'twas not the only line we changed.

"Miss O'Keenan. Backstage please. Curtain's going up," whispered Harlan. Startled out of her reverie, Mary Margaret blinked and hurried to take her opening-scene position.

Ah Seán, 'tis your voice they be wantin' to hear singing these lines. 'Tis your strut and carriage they want to see--spite of the crooked leg--swaggering 'cross the stage, you with your straight shoulders, your tilted Derby, an' broad smile. You are the Irish attorney.

Chapter 9: In which Mary Margaret visits Seán's quarters.

As the bugler sounded Drill Mount, Mary Margaret knocked on the door to Seán's quarters. First Sergeant Holloway opened it immediately.

"Mary Margaret. How may I be of assistance?"

"May I come in, Jack?"

Jack retreated a few steps and Mary Margaret entered the quarters that until two days ago, he had shared with Seán. Because of the special patrol they were assigned to, they were housed in one of the newly renovated supply depot warehouses.   She surveyed the square room, with its white-washed walls and wooden floor, strewn with Indian and Mexican rugs in faded reds, blues, and blacks.

> *So this be where you slept and read and shined your boots and cleaned your weapons. 'Tis your looking glass on that near wall? Does it hold your image still? And below, on the table, your brush, and yes, a few strands of your light brown hair. The window where you glanced out to see the weather, and 'tis your boot-blacking rag laying on the floor where you dropped it? 'Tis your painting on that far wall? The poor cold horses with their rumps turned 'gainst the storm an' their tails flyin' out like flags.*

Mary Margaret took a step toward the painting.

"Mary Margaret. How may I be of assistance to you? It is true I am off duty, but I am not without duties."

"'Tis a shame, those lovely horses, such a terrible storm."

"Yes, I suppose," said Jack fixing his gaze on Mary Margaret.

"I be after taking Seán's things, his personals. But as for the uniforms and such, give 'em to a needy soldier."

"Well now," Jack said in an official manner. "We shall need to separate what belongs to the army first."

"Ah, 'tis so. Of course. Thank you for allowing me presence here this day."

Jack did not reply. Mary Margaret looked at the two narrow cots, separated by the width of a window with a small, rough-made washstand beneath it. She knew Seán's bed by the white and green quilt he purchased when last they visited Las Vegas, the day he borrowed the old feed wagon and mule team from the Quartermaster.

An' 'twas a grand day, Seán. I fear I dinna' tell you what a grand time it was. The lovely lunch at the Wagner's Hotel, the stroll 'round the new park--me on your arm as proud as a lady, an' you tall and straight as a lord. An' the shops! Mr. Graaf's delightful bakery and the Great Emporium of Mr. Charles Ilfeld. I never seen the like. An' to be sure, the grand halls and saloons with their noise and music and laughter. The train depot, an' weren't we just in time to see the Santa Fe come puffin' in an' the fine ladies in their peacock colors and gents in top hats making their slow, graceful way to the waitin' hacks—those nobby riggs—carrying them off west of the river to the fancy Hotels? 'Twas a grand day.

"Miss Mary Margaret?"

"Ah, Jack, I be rememberin'. 'Tis a wondrous thing, the memory. Now, where would he be keeping his personal belongings, his valuables?"

"Perhaps the crate under his bed. But items of importance and value we keep with us at all times. Thieving remains prevalent on the post."

Jack stooped, his sabre scraping along the floor, and dragged a low wooden box from beneath Seán's cot. He lifted the lid and Mary Margaret peeked in. She poked and shifted the contents. "'Tis nothin' but old bits, an' hobbles, a bottle of Bears Oil, a broken belt."

Jack rose to his feet and pointing to a small tintype hanging on the wall above Seán's bed, said, "That would be his family."

Mary Margaret rushed to the framed image and took it down, staring into the serious faces of a handsome man—a bit like Seán around the eyes—a weary-looking woman, and three children whose faces were blurred for their wiggling. Mary Margaret held the photograph against her breast. "But where be his diary an' letters from home? His pocket watch."

"Diary? Do you mean his log? He was often jotting things down in a small, leather-bound notebook he tied up with a strip of hide. Referred to it as a diary? I shall need to see that. Could be here." Jack walked to the washstand and pulled out the center drawer. "I do not recall that he received any letters."

"May I see, Jack?" Mary Margaret placed the photograph on the cot and quickly moved to put herself between Jack Holloway and the washstand. Without waiting for an answer, she peered into the drawer and rummaged around in the contents. Among pieces of broken metal, old buttons, and scraps of cloth and leather, Mary Margaret found a two-shot Derringer pistol. "'Tis nothing here," she said, turning her body so that she was able to take the gun and three loose bullets and slip them into her pocket. "Where wouldja be keeping your precious things, Jack Holloway?"

"As I said, I keep the things I value on my person, or when on patrol, in my saddle bags."

Mary Margaret surveyed the room and spotted the large clothing rack beside the entrance door, crowded with uniforms, sabres, carbines, bridles, and a stable frock. One wooden peg at the far end was empty amidst the jumble of two men's goods.

"As you know, 'twas nothing on his body," she said, approaching the long stable coat and reaching out to search the pockets.

Grabbing Mary Margaret's forearm, Jack quickly intercepted her. "That one is mine."

"I do apologize. Where be Seán's coat? An' his tack an' haversack?"

"Why, with Rosie, I suspect." Jack made a mental note to visit Los Alamitos. "Well now, just what is it you are looking for?"

"Jack, 'tis brilliant, y'are," she said without answering his question. "Ah, 'tis getting late an' no doubt, you be having some reporting or other such duty. I best be gettin' on." Mary Margaret picked up the photograph. "I dinna think you'll be needing this?" Jack shook his head. Then she walked to the washstand and picked up Seán's hairbrush. She held it up to Jack as a question.

"Take it. It will be stolen otherwise." After a moment of silence, Jack said, "Are you happy, or perhaps I should say pleased, you did it? Going on the stage, I mean. In front of the whole post and folks from Grandes—not your gentlemanly types— and from Tiptonville?"

"Oh yes, Jack. I did it for me man." She did not tell him about Timmy Sullivan. "Didja ever find Seán's uniform an' boots an' weapons?"

"Now, I cannot be telling you things about an open investigation."

"Investigation is it? 'Twould be your patrol handling such things. So there is an investigation?"

Holloway saw the error of mentioning the word *investigation.* "I cannot say."

"You already said, Jack. I suggest you search the Opera House an' the Comedy Company headquarters. Talk to Dr. Williamson an' Timmy Sullivan an' the entire cast. . . ." Mary Margaret spoke calmly and evenly in an attempt to control the turmoil within. She desperately wanted to do it all—the searching, the investigating, the interrogating. She wanted to study the footprints at the lake's edge, and find out who these enemies were that Peterson spoke of, and to question Shiney.

"Well now, I do know how to perform my duty."

As her foot grazed the threshold, Mary Margaret stopped and turned. She looked up at Jack. "Of course you do, Jack. An' who be the outlaw, the nasty boyo your patrol encountered in Loma Parda?"

"Our patrol often encounters the criminal element—'nasty boyos'—as you say. And at Loma Parda there's nothing but gambling, and bars, and houses of . . . ."

"Sure I know all about such things, Jack. I be meaning the horse thief your patrol tracked from Robbers' Roost over to Rayado. Captured him, did you not? An' he . . . ."

"That would be Fancy Frank Cole," interrupted Jack Holloway. "Though I see no earthly reason why he earned the epithet—*fancy*. Stole five United States Army mules and two horses. We caught him at Rayado, trying to sell the whole herd—with their brands as plain as the nose on your face. Captured him and brought him in for trial. He escaped though."

"Sure, 'twould be the one I speak of, Jack."

"A few weeks later, Seán and I were down at Tiptonville to retrieve a new mare for the Commander's daughter, and we spotted Cole coming round the corner from the livery and heading, no doubt, to the Happy Cock, one of his favorite watering holes. Smilin' Seán, he called 'your man.' We captured him then, just the two of us."

"Smilin' Seán. . . ."

"Well now, Mary Margaret, if you'll allow me to finish my narrative. As I was completing the equine transaction, Seán entered the Happy Cock saloon, stood at the bar, and—I make an assumption here as I was not present at the time—ordered a drink. Cole comes in and Seán ignores him. But the bartender looks up and says, 'Well, if it ain't Fancy Frank Cole?' Seán, with full knowledge of the horse-thief, smiles and says, 'An' who be Fancy Frank Cole?' Cole himself answers with, 'Well, I ain't a-wearing no monkey suit.' He struts up to the bar and stands next to Seán—elbow to elbow—as it were. Well now, this is when I entered the saloon. Seán turns, as slow and as calm as a lord, smiling all the while, and engages Cole in discourse, which allows me to slip around and crouch behind the bar. 'Tis me uniform you be calling a monkey suit, sir?' says Seán. Cole brings his face up close to Seán's and says, 'Got no use fer the uniform or the man in it.' And Seán just keeps smiling. The bartender acts nervous and says how he's wantin' no trouble, and Seán says, 'Tis no trouble you'll be getting, sir. Likely our friend Mr. Cole be getting the trouble,' and that smile never left Seán's face. Cole takes the bait, and steps back a few paces, his hand on his gun handle. Well now, that's when,

75

with a signal from the bartender, I stand up from behind the bar, and Fancy Frank Cole is suddenly staring down the barrel of my model 1873."

"'Tis quite a story, Jack. An' Mr. Cole? He be serving his time in the American prison?"

"Well now, he <u>was</u>. Escaped again . . . about three weeks ago. And swore revenge."

"Ah," said Mary Margaret. "I be thanking you for your time." She turned and took a few brisk steps in the direction of her quarters. Jack watched. Her steps were heavy, careful, or maybe determined, he thought. When she passed Suds Row then Company Quarters and approached the flagstaff, Jack thought he should follow her, but after checking his timepiece, he realized he was expected at Colonel Winters' quarters.

Holloway stepped back inside his quarters, pulled on his hat, adjusted his belt, and buttoned the top button of his sacque coat. He picked up his gloves and stepped outside, closing and locking the door. Then he struck out at a brisk walk in the same direction Mary Margaret had taken, catching sight of her distant figure as it approached the Trader's Compound. Jack proceeded directly to the Post Commander's quarters.

As he approached the door and raised his fist to knock, Colonel Winters' daughter Victoria opened the door and ushered him into the building.

"Pappa is most anxious to see you, First Sergeant Holloway," she said, looking up at Jack through her thick dark lashes. She showed him to a small front room, knocked, and announced his presence to the Colonel.

"Enter," called Colonel Winters. Then, after Holloway saluted, "At ease. Explain."

Jack took an uneasy 'at ease' position. "Well now, sir. I, uh, have not yet found the papers in question. I . . . ."

"I know that. Explain."

Jack went into an elaborate explanation of his attempts— subsequent to the murder of Sergeant Flannery—to determine the whereabouts of the documents said to be in Flannery's possession.

As Jack completed his evasions, Colonel Winters abruptly shoved his chair back and stood. Jack blinked.

"Enough," said Winters. "Your explanation is unacceptable. You did not find the papers on Flannery's person. You were ordered to retrace his movements, secure the papers, and deliver them to me. I will not have scandal in the final months of my military service. I intend to retire with full honors. Do you understand?"

"Yes sir. I shall interrogate Porfirio Gonzalez tomorrow . . . ."

"Gonzalez?"

"Yes sir. He owns and operates a small mercantile business in Los Alamitos. It is quite possible that Sergeant Flannery was coming from the store when . . . ."

"Yes, yes. Why not today?"

"Well now, sir, today being Sunday, well, these people observe the Lord's day."

"Quite. I expect a full report—with the documents intact—immediately after Retreat tomorrow. Dismissed."

Jack came to attention, saluted, executed an elegant about face, and left the study as quickly as possible. In the wide hall running the length of the quarters, he encountered Mrs. Winters. Somewhat surprised, he nodded solemnly. Mrs. Winters smiled, made a slight curtsey, and saw him to the door.

Chapter 10: In which Mary Margaret and Olivia go on an outing.

After leaving Seán's quarters, Mary Margaret walked directly to the Foote home. She knew she should not involve Olivia, but she had no one else to turn to. She was not certain who else she could trust. As she lifted the knocker, the door swung inward and Mr. Foote spoke in surprise, "Miss O'Keenan. Most irregular to come calling on a Sunday, the Lord's day."

"Mr. Foote, sir. Good day. Wouldja ever be meaning, since 'tis the Lord's day, the saloon be closed as well as your own front room?" said Mary Margaret.

Foote frowned. "Come in," he said, standing aside to let her pass. "May we help you in some way?"

"I'm after seeing Olivia, I am."

"Oh, Mary Margaret. Do come in," said Olivia. "You poor dear. You've been through so much—have you dined? I shall make tea and we shall have a nice talk." Mr. Foote squinted but said nothing more. He departed the house, pulling the door closed with a dull thud.

"Olivia, I be . . . ."

"Hush," said Olivia as she rushed from the foyer into the parlor and crossed quickly to one of the windows. She peered out through the filmy curtains and watched Mr. Foote cross the road and enter the saloon. Then she turned to Mary Margaret. "Now, how can I be of assistance?"

"I be needin' to go to the store at Los Alamitos. P'rhaps, I mean, is it possible that I could have the loan of Tamany?"

"Not Tamany, not riding him. Mr. Foote was not happy about that. Sit down Mary Margaret and tell me why you need to go to Los Alamitos."

"Sure some things be missing from Seán's quarters. An' Jack says Seán would likely keep such things on his person or in his haversack. 'Twould be with Rosie at Los Alamitos I be thinking. The locket . . ." Mary Margaret stopped when she saw the puzzled look on Olivia's face. "The locket you saw Seán buy. 'Twas not in his room, nor his diary, an' nary a letter from home. 'Tis an oddity—no letters. Is it not?"

"But Mary Margaret, surely, the store at Los Alamitos will be closed on Sunday."

"Does not Mr. Gonzalez live there as well?"

"Indeed he does," said Olivia. "I think what you need, Mary Margaret, in your sorrow, is an outing, a ride in the country. 'Tis good for the sool," she said in a fair imitation of the Irish brogue. "Patrick may still be here. Patrick," Olivia called. When he appeared, she said, "Would you be so kind, just now, before you leave for the day, Patrick, to hitch the phaeton." Then, knowing her husband would inquire concerning her whereabouts, she said, "I shall be taking Miss O'Keenan on a much-needed outing, a refreshing drive in the countryside."

After Olivia changed from her church dress, she and Mary Margaret made their way to the stables. In a smart burgundy traveling suit, veiled hat, and black leather gloves, Olivia drove the gig out of the corral and negotiated the narrow passage between the corral and the hotel, avoiding the windows of the saloon. Mary Margaret was impressed by Olivia's dexterity, but Olivia dismissed the skill as just another 'ladies talent,' like painting and piano and arranging flowers. "Now, if I could ride like you, Mary Margaret . . . you ride like you are one with the animal."

"Sure in Ireland, the horse is something special, it is. 'An' God took a handful of the southerly wind, blew his breath over it, and created the horse.'"

"An old Gaelic saying?"

"Sure I dinna know. Somethin' me Da used to say at many a derby. But, tell me, how is it you come to handle Tamany and a gig an' still be afraid to hold the horse, to ride?"

"The Winfield family, my family, own a large ranch near La Junta. Sheltered by sturdy young cottonwood trees, lush fields, apple and plum orchards, my youth was spent in frivolities— dances, visiting, sketching parties. I did not learn one practical skill except driving a buggy and that, only so I could take my mother, whose hands had become horribly disfigured from the ravages of time and arthritis, on her visiting rounds. She was never without black lace gloves."

Olivia paused and a small sigh escaped her lips. "But, to the business at hand, Mary Margaret. We shall ride the Granada Road south. It'll take us a bit longer, but that way, should anyone be watching, and they are always watching, it will appear as if we are just ambling. The road dips below a small ridge. After we pass the hill, we shall turn northwest onto the old Star Fort Road. It passes just this side of Los Alamitos Lake."

Mary Margaret was doubly impressed by Olivia's skills at deception. "How is it you come to be knowing these things? An' will we have time? I be thinking it will be dark afore we return."

"Do not say 'I be.' You are using the first person pronoun with the infinitive. Say simply, 'I think.' And to answer your questions—remember, this countryside is my home. Our ranch is not far. Of course, no one has lived there for several years now. Once mother died," Olivia hesitated. "Well, our lives changed. But when I lived there, when I was young, we often visited Los Alamitos. We shall be there and back before the sun sets."

Mary Margaret realized that she had underestimated Olivia. They rode in silence for several miles, the increasing afternoon winds provided ample sound as they howled and battered the small, covered carriage. Occasionally interrupted by Olivia's gentle clicks and slapping of the reins, Mary Margaret's mind jumped from images of Seán's cold blank stare to his warm smile. The prairie was ablaze with sun and buzzing insects, lulling Mary Margaret into a mild, drowsy stupor.

Olivia said, "I am sorry that I could not attend the play last evening. Did it go well?"

Startled for a moment, Mary Margaret opened her eyes. "Timmy Sullivan be very angry."

"Is angry," replied Olivia.

"Timmy Sullivan is angry," repeated Mary Margaret. "P'rhaps he be angry enough to kill."

Olivia sighed, "Perhaps he is angry enough. In any event, I was inquiring after the performance."

80

"Ah yes. I remembered me lines. Mr. Davies says I be—am—a natural. 'Twas a full house."

Olivia pulled back carefully on the reins and turned Tamany onto the rutted, rocky, and overgrown Star Fort Road, seldom used since the railroad arrived and the Santa Fe Trail business began trickling away. "Why is Private Sullivan angry?" she asked.

"He be thinking shoulda been him taking Seán's role. He threatened me, he did, he's that angry."

"Oh, Mary Margaret. Do be careful. Some of these young soldiers are not gentlemen. And remember . . . ."

"I'm be learning, that I am, Olivia. I mean . . . ah, for the love o' God, let us do forget the lessons for the day."

Olivia smiled and said, "Yes, good Lord, what am I thinking? No lessons today. Maybe you should allow First Sergeant Holloway to handle this investigation. Did you show him the ball of hair?"

"'Tis three days, Olivia, three days and nights an' I see no results. I be thinking nobody cares. Sure, if it was Jack Holloway killed, Seán would be beating the bushes, he would. No. I did not show him the hair."

Further conversation was inhibited by the bumps and deep ruts and Olivia's need to concentrate. Indeed, Mary Margaret thought the swaying and jostling must be affecting Olivia, for she appeared a bit poorly. The two-seater swung and jolted along, and after little less than an hour of torturous bouncing, they arrived at the rise on the east side of the lake. Mary Margaret gasped when she recalled the night, and the lanterns, and Seán's body. Olivia said nothing but took both reins in her left hand, and with her right, held Mary Margaret's forearm in a gesture of comfort and encouragement.

Olivia turned the buggy onto Gonzalez' narrow road, circled the lake, and entered the settlement, which had changed little since Olivia's youth. The cottonwood trees had grown, and their fresh buds promised summer shade. A new, flat-roofed *adobe* building neatly trimmed in bright blue faced the Gonzalez store. The relentless dust swirled in small devil winds, and not a dog nor a child was visible. Somewhere above them, a raven called as Olivia halted the buggy in front of a small, rectangular building, its pitched, tin roof glinting in the daylight. One shutter hung by a hinge, and on the side wall was painted one word—Gonzalez.

Olivia settled the gig in front of the building's wooden bar, and the women descended. Mary Margaret loosely wrapped the reins few times around the post. She patted Tamany's neck and whispered a quick thank you. Then she turned toward the building.

"'Tis a store?" she asked.

"Indeed," laughed Olivia, "well, partly." She knocked on a window. "*Señor* Gonzalez," she called. "May we have a word?"

After a few minutes, a short bearded man with black eyes as bright as river-washed pebbles, pulled open the door. He squinted, shaded his eyes with his hand, and said, "*Sí?*"

Olivia said, "*Buenos días, señor* Gonzalez. Perhaps you remember me. *La jita de* Walter Winfield. Winfield Ranch?"

"*Sí.* Elizabeth."

"That would be my older sister. I am Olivia, *la media.*"

"Oh yes, the middle child." As he gestured the women to enter, he said, "*Come esta su familia? Su* Pappa?"

Inside, hand-hewn wooden tables bore piles of dusty blankets, bolts of faded calico, and boots of various sizes. Bridles and halters and cinches hung from pegs on one wall. Behind the glass and oak counter, shelves held a jumble of boxes, cloth sacks, and small metal objects that Mary Margaret could not identify. She bent forward to examine the contents of the display case and saw pieces of exotic jewelry—a necklace of silver and opal, long shiny jet earrings, a lady's comb studded with turquoise stones, and two pocket watches. Olivia whispered in her ear, "He buys things, well, tenders loans, I believe, when people get into trouble and need money."

As Olivia conversed in Spanish with the shopkeeper, for Mary Margaret, it continued to be a day of surprises. She listened to the foreign words and sensed respect and concern between the two. She saw sorrow in the man's eyes as, no doubt, Olivia told him of her mother's passing. Then suddenly they both turned and looked at Mary Margaret as Olivia introduced her to Mr. Gonzalez. He welcomed Mary Margaret in English.

"SeánFlannery," he pronounced the name as if it were one word, "was my friend. We enjoyed many interesting talks. He was a good man, an honest soldier. *Lo siento mucho.* I am so very sorry, a most unfortunate accident."

The sadness and anger and suspicion Mary Margaret had been holding close to her heart rushed forward toward this soft-spoken, gracious man. "'Twere no accident, Mr. Gonzalez. Sergeant Flannery was murdered. An' I mean to find his killer."

Without responding, Mr. Gonzalez turned and retreated behind the curtain. Mary Margaret and Olivia exchanged questioning glances. He returned in a few seconds with a long, flat cedar box and placed it on the counter. In response to their questioning looks, Mr. Gonzalez said to Mary Margaret, "Do you have the locket and the key?"

"Ah, no. I do not know what you mean," she replied.

Gonzalez explained. "On the day of his death, SeánFlannery arrived sometime after noon. He rushed into the store and purchased this safe-box, then pulled a packet of papers and a small book from inside his uniform coat and placed them in the box. He purchased a lock and sealed the box. He told me to give the box only to the one who comes with both the locket and the key."

"I dinna know a thing about a box nor a key." Mary Margaret paused. "But sir, the locket you speak of I believe 'tis me own, ah, 'twas intended for me. An' I come for Sgt. Flannery's things—his saddle, haversack, an' saddle bags. Were they not with Rosie?"

Mr. Gonzalez retrieved the box and withdrew behind the curtain.

Olivia whispered to Mary Margaret, "The papers. From the fireplace wall?"

Gonzalez returned empty-handed and said, "Please, come with me."

The women followed him out of the store and around to a corral on the north side of the building, sparsely shaded by budding trees and a low *portal.*

"Rosie," said Mary Margaret, "Rosie dear." The *pinto* lifted her delicate head, snorted, and stared.

"*La yegua,*" said Gonzalez, "came limping into *la placita* no more than twenty minutes after SeánFlannery left. The cuts are healing well." He opened the gate, and Mary Margaret followed him into the corral. Olivia waited outside the fence. The mare backed up two steps then halted as Gonzalez spoke softly in Spanish holding out his hand. Rosie stretched her head forward, sniffed, and nuzzled his empty hand. Mary Margaret stood aside and with her eyes, examined the horse. She saw the scab of a three-inch cut on the mare's foreleg and several scratches on both knees. Gonzalez haltered Rosie and led her to Mary Margaret who reached out and caressed the gold and white neck. Rosie shivered as Mary Margaret's hand encountered a welt beneath the rich orange mane.

"*Mira,*" said Gonzalez. "It is possibly from a whip or a stick. And here, *mira,* small scratches and swelling around the mouth. Someone pulled her, yanked her by the bridle, back and down to her knees."

"I be thinking 'twas a very strong man," said Mary Margaret as she examined the rest of the horse, crooning in the Gaelic and running her hands along the warm, smooth body. "Where be the saddle an' bridle an' such?"

"*Aquí,*" said Gonzalez. He tied Rosie to a post and led Mary Margaret to a grey wooden shed leaning against the wall of the main building. Inside, it was dark and musty, and something small skittered away as they entered. From several of the large wooden pegs on the wall, Gonzalez withdrew a United States Army saddle and blanket, a haversack, knapsack, bedroll, and bridle and placed them on the dirt floor. Mary Margaret dropped to her knees and lightly ran her hand along the saddle, then untied and opened the knapsack, spreading it flat. She sorted the contents—a copy of *The Soldier's Handbook,* Seán's scratched old pocket watch, a tin cup. In the haversack, she found three extra uniform buttons, Rosie's spare bit, some short leather straps, and—at the very bottom, wrapped in a clean scrap of blanketing—a small red velvet bag.

She picked up the red bag and sat back on her heels. Out of the corner of her eye, she watched Olivia edge closer to Rosie and stretch out a tentative hand. Except for the occasional swish of her honey colored tail, the horse stood still, dozing. Olivia stroked the *pinto*'s neck and fingered the fine red-orange mane.

> *Ah Seán, your gentle Rosie, a southerly wind, that'll blow courage on Olivia.*

Mary Margaret untied the gold strings and opened the bag. She pulled out a cloud of cotton and spread it on the open haversack, exposing a gold, heart-shaped locket engraved with a *fleur de lis* on the front side.

Olivia came up behind her and said, "Open it."

Mary Margaret pressed one side, and the heart swung open revealing a small bronze key. She picked it out and held it up to the sun. "Mr. Gonzalez," she said. "'Tis the very key?"

Back in the store, Mr. Gonzalez retrieved the box and slid it across the counter to Mary Margaret. As she was about to unlock it, he said, "*Por favor, no.* SeánFlannery told me to give it to the one with the locket and the key, but not to open it. Please take it away. Take everything."

Mary Margaret paused, then, said, "Tell me how he were that day? Angry? Sad?"

"In a hurry. Usually, we talk, we smoke. Not that day. *Como un hombre de negocios.*"

"All business," said Olivia.

Mary Margaret tried to imagine the two men talking animatedly, perhaps by a warm stove. To see Seán smiling and the stoic Mr. Gonzales speaking more than three words. But she knew the magic of Seán Flannery. Had he not worked it on herself?

> *Were you after charmin' Mr. Gonzalez with your Donegal stories of turbulent seas and rich, dark peat, and magical creatures? An' didja ever tell him of the acid hunger, the lice, and the bone-breaking cold?*

After securing the key inside the locket, Mary Margaret placed the delicate chain around her neck and fastened the clasp.

Olivia said, "Perhaps it would be best to hide the locket for a time."

Mary Margaret slid the locket inside the collar of her dress and said, "Sure we can be taking the saddle an' . . . ."

"No," interrupted Olivia. Turning to Gonzalez, she said, "You will likely receive another visitor from Fort Union, perhaps, First Sergeant Holloway. He will, no doubt, be conducting an investigation and searching for evidence. *Señor* Gonzalez, *por favor*, allow us to leave the tack as we found it. We shall, however, take the locket and the box. Now, as to Rosie?"

"Ah, Mr. Gonzalez," Mary Margaret said, "Wouldja be after caring for Seán Flannery's Rosie?"

"I cared for her from the day she was born until the day SeánFlannery bought her. I will care for her until you are ready to take her."

"Me?"

"*Sí*. She is your horse now."

"I suppose she is, Mr. Gonzalez. 'Tis so—until we find Seán Flannery's family."

As Mary Margaret and Olivia bid farewell and climbed into the buggy, three men on horses entered the small *plaza*. Mary Margaret wondered if they were the same men who had stopped to talk with the Sheriff on the night of Seán's death, for there was something familiar about the leader. She stared openly, fixing their handsome weathered faces into her memory, until Olivia whispered, "Do not stare Mary Margaret. That is Mr. Vicente Silva, the one on the black horse, and two of his associates. There is talk he does more than sell liquor in his Las Vegas Grandes establishment."

"Ah, yes, 'tis the owner of the Imperial Hall," said Mary Margaret, sitting back as Olivia slapped the reins and Tamany trotted smartly forward. As the phaeton passed the riders, all three men lifted and tipped their hats to the women. "'Twould it be that Mr. Silva frequents Loma Parda?"

"Loma Parda? I am sure I do not know. Why?"

"I be traveling to Loma Parda as soon as Lulu makes the arrangements. Sure, I be learning something there, picking up a bit of the gossip."

"It is dangerous, going to Loma Parda, even with Lulu. A young lady . . . ."

"Ah no, 'tis Lulu and her nephew visiting from Kansas City, stepping out for a fine dinner and a game or two of poker. I be wearing the costume of the Irish Attorney, I will."

"Oh, Mary Margaret," Olivia sighed. "Tell me you do not play poker."

"I do, Olivia. That I do."

"Surely, it would be best if you let Sergeant Holloway take charge of this situation."

"'Tis right y'are," said Mary Margaret. "Jack Holloway be a good man, but not the brightest. Maybe it be his own ambition gets in his way. Overlooks things he does. It may be you did not notice. Least, seems that way to me."

"Now Mary Margaret, you are forgetting that First Sergeant Holloway is Sgt. Flannery's friend as well as superior officer. He will do his best."

Mary Margaret did not reply. She leaned back against the plush seat, and they rode in silence until they reached the juncture of the Star Fort and Granada Roads. Then Mary Margaret asked Olivia what she and Mr. Gonzalez discussed in Spanish.

"He told me, as he told you, Sgt. Flannery was in a hurry that morning—abrupt and business-like, that the sergeant selected the box, then removed a packet of papers and a notebook from inside his sacque, and secured all in the box. He said that Sgt. Flannery told him it would be best if he did not know anything about the contents of the box, that it was military business. And, Sergeant Flannery instructed him, "in the event that he did not return for the box to give it only to the one with the locket and the key."

Ah, 'tis a burden they are, these papers. Would they belong to Mr. Foote? An' what am I to do with them? An' 'twere they meant for my eyes? Sure, if the locket were

87

intended for me . . . but was it? An' Jack, what is it makes him drag his feet?

As if hearing Mary Margaret's thoughts, Olivia said, "Clearly, the locket and, therefore, the key, were meant for you. And no one else. While we are out here, away from prying eyes, let us open the box."

Mary Margaret did so, and withdrew a thick, leather-bound notebook, softened and shined with use, its corners curled at the edges. She immediately clutched it to her chest. It seemed to burn with Seán's heat, and she had to remind herself that she must not indulge her sorrow. "Ah," she said, "'Tis Seán's diary." When she opened it, the whiff of himself, that particular combination of tobacco, leather, and the scent of the man, overwhelmed her. She closed the notebook, rested it on her lap, and reached into the box. As she pulled out a leather pouch, the carriage wheel hit a rut, and the box tumbled to the floor, spilling its contents--two brown envelopes and a thick set of folded papers. Olivia halted Tamany, rested the reins, and helped gather the papers.

"Why, this pouch belongs to Mr. Foote. There are his initials burned into the corner, JJF in a circle, like a brand. He puts it on everything."

Mary Margaret opened one envelope and unfolded its contents. "'Tis a letter to Mr. Foote from Mrs. William W. Belknap." She handed it to Olivia who carefully read it, folded it, placed it on her lap, then unfolded it and read it again.

"It is dated January 13, 1875," said Olivia, "and it confirms Mr. Foote's appointment to the position of Fort Union Post Trader." When Mary Margaret said nothing, Olivia continued, "From the wife of then Secretary of War William Belknap. But, embedded in the language of the letter is—what I would only call—a receipt."

"A receipt?" asked Mary Margaret as she laid Seán's diary in the box and reached for the other envelope.

"Well, perhaps, it is better said . . . an acknowledgment. Yes. Do you not know of Secretary Belknap? Of the scandal?" asked Olivia. Mary Margaret did not respond, not wanting to seem ignorant, and Olivia continued. "He resigned, some say so as not to be impeached before the United States Senate for fraud, specifically that he had awarded a military trading establishment to a gentleman, a civilian, at Fort Sill in return for a sum of money. He resigned before the articles of impeachment were drawn. It is believed that many of the Post Trader appointments under Belknap were fraudulent, that is, Secretary Belknap was paid to favor certain contracts. Once he resigned, however, the Senate had no jurisdiction. No criminal charges of any sort were brought against him. The matter just went away."

"'Twere true—the charges?" asked Mary Margaret.

"I do not know. There was no resolution. Most assuredly, it was some years past."

"Would such a receipt be from Mrs. Belknap—not Mr.?" asked Mary Margaret as she opened the second envelope and unfolded two onionskin sheaves. "'Tis another letter, or receipt, for—Jaysus, Mary, and Joseph—for the sum of $20,000 dollars!"

"Mrs. Belknap took care of her husband's personal correspondence, I am certain, but," began Olivia. Then she paused. "Uh, and what of the packet of papers?"

Mary Margaret unfolded the packet which contained several sheets of long, slightly yellowed paper. "'Tis a deed . . . ah no . . . a contract, somethin' relatin' to," and she looked at Olivia, "to the Fort Union Post Trader Complex."

Knowing that the language of the papers in her hands was beyond her reading skills, Mary Margaret was relieved when Olivia said, "If you please, may I see them?"

Olivia read silently for several minutes. Mary Margaret stared ahead at the windswept prairie and flattened grasses. In contrast to the scene before her, she recalled her early days in service. A cold afternoon in the classroom on the upper floor of the O'Connell home. She and the children puzzling over pages in books. She had raised her eyes and gazed at the window. Outside, a grey, rainy day, and she—wishing to be in the stable with the steamy horses and the sweet smell of fresh-cut hay. When suddenly, as if he were beside her in the buggy, Mary Margaret jumped to hear the tutor's words, 'ignorant country lout,' and the giggles of the children.

"Do you know what this means? Mary Margaret?" Olivia's voice cut through the bitter memory, but Mary Margaret did not respond.

Olivia opened her mouth to speak but closed it again. Then she said, her voice so low Mary Margaret barely heard, "It means that Mr. Foote is, or perhaps may be, a criminal."

Chapter 11: In which Mary Margaret learns the difference between a diary and a log.

In the privacy of her quarters, Mary Margaret closed the thick woolen curtains, turned up the kerosene lamp, and locked the door. She placed Seán's box on the table.

> *Sure, 'tis a reason to kill a man—incriminatin' papers—an' you took them, Seán. An' I be wondering what it was you planned an' why you dinna go to the commander. Mr. Foote is not a redhead, but Shiney is and Shiney does whatever Mr. Foote tells him to do.*

Withdrawing the key from the locket, she sat at the table, unlocked the padlock, and opened the box. She removed the contents and spread them before her—the envelopes, the packet of papers, and Seán's notebook. Her eyes and thoughts were drawn to the diary. *'Twas one of the last things you touched.* Across the front of the book, Seán had scratched with a knife, "Flannery 23rd Infantry." With her finger, Mary Margaret traced the words. Then she laid both hands on the surface of the book, covering it entirely. She fancied she felt heat and a slight tremble.

> *Sure, you're a fine figure of a woman, Mary Margaret O'Keenan. An' Mr. Flannery, you be a fair judge o' that wouldja'? I may not have seen many, but I do know quality when I meet it. Ah the cheek o' you, Seán Flannery!*

> *Me Da always said, Mary Margaret, me girl, you're no beauty, still, you're fit and strong y'are, and a good worker.*

> *Mary Margaret, you said to me, you're a beauty in my eyes, y'are--with your raven curls, an' flashin' eyes the color of the Irish sea—an' as changeable. An' what wouldja Da be knowin' about beauty? Sold that excellent black mare for pennies, did he not?*

91

"Seán," she whispered, *"Seán Flannery, I do miss you."*

She opened the notebook and caught her breath when she saw his bold, childish printing. She imagined him, one leg crossed over the saddle, sitting atop Rosie in the shade of a tree. Perhaps he wet the pencil on his tongue before scribbling his notes.

Mary Margaret blinked to clear the image then read aloud, following the writing with her finger. 12 JAN MORN, RAIN, WIND. RR BY NOON. COLE GONE. She turned page after page and realized that Seán's entries were all in a code of his own making, filled with abbreviations and symbols that she could not decipher except for dates and a word or a name here and there. She surmised that the notes related to the work of the patrol—RR she thought. . . not rail road but Robbers' Roost! Mary Margaret turned to the final entry: 14 AP, MORN, FT DOCS. LA. JJH. NOT CO.

'Tis mysterious writings. Whatever does it mean? JJH? COLE be Fancy Frank, the horse thief no doubt. An' LA be Los Alamitos? Whatever does FT refer to? Fort? Father? An' DOCS . . . DOCS . . . doctors? Documents! FT . . . fort trader? Josiah Foote's documents? An' sure as the bloom on a rose, CO be Commanding Officer. See JJH you write, not the Colonel. Or wouldja be meanin' CO for Cole? What's that you say, Seán? Sure JJH be John Jay Holloway—so I must trust someone.

But, Seán, 'tis a bad feelin' I have.

Mary Margaret inched forward and turned the pages, searching for the entry for the day they met. Nothing, not a mention of her name, nor the meeting, not even the date was entered. She turned more pages looking for her name or initials or anything that could refer to their life together. Not a mention. Nothing at all. Mary Margaret leaned back in the chair, trying to recall the date of the day they traveled to Las Vegas. She found only this: 6 AP COLE. JGO.

> *'Twas the fight? 'Twas Cole you had the altercation with at the Imperial? The man who made the rude remarks? I dinna recall the look of the man. 'Twas Mr. Silva interfered, of that I'm certain. And the officer of the law that day be, sure, 'twas himself, Sheriff O'tero—JGO. Ah, Seán, 'tis no mention of our lovely waltz.*

Heavy footsteps thudded on the stone pathway of Suds Row. The sound of them dwindled as they passed her door, then increased again as the walker returned and stopped outside her quarters. The door handle rattled, the door shuddered. In a series of quick, instinctive moves, Mary Margaret jumped up and gathered the papers, stuffing them into the pocket of her skirt, then carefully closed and locked the box. From the top drawer of her chiffonier, she pulled out Seán's Derringer pistol. She extinguished the lamp and slipped into the space between the dish cupboard and one of the laundry tubs just as she heard the click of a key in the lock.

> *A key, Seán. Sure 'tis how he searched me quarters on the night you died. But who be having a key to me quarters? Anyone, you say, 'tis as easy as fallin' out of bed.*

The door banged open and on the threshold stood a tall, broad-shouldered man, a lantern hanging from his left hand revealed scruffy, mud-encrusted Jefferson shoes and deep blue infantry trousers, splattered with mud. With the waning moon behind him, Mary Margaret saw only a silhouette. Unfettered by manners or fear, the man stomped into her quarters. He held up and swung the lantern. Mary Margaret squeezed herself flat against the wall and slid down to the floor, grateful she still wore mourning. Holding the pistol steady with both hands, she aimed it at the widest part of the man. As the lantern swung from left to right, she glimpsed the broken nose and glaring eyes of Walter Shiner, his head turning in unison with the lantern.

He saw the empty bed, the chair pushed back, the locked box on the table. He rushed forward, grabbed the box, and left, leaving the door ajar to the night winds. Mary Margaret lowered the pistol and dropped it into her lap, a trickle of sweat slid down the side of her face and along her neck.

Chapter 12: In which Olivia makes a decision, and Josiah Foote shows his hand.

<u>Monday, April 18</u>

It was afternoon at Fort Union, the day's drilling temporarily ended. It was the time of day when those who were not on duty engaged in a bit of recreation. Olivia set down her needlework and walked to the parlor window. She peered through lace curtains and saw Jack Holloway tie his horse to the hitching post in front of the saloon and approach her front porch. She admired his tall, broad figure, his well-groomed and smart-fitting uniform. She thought of Jack as a 'good man.' She wanted to love a good man and to be loved and cared for by a good man. She admired Jack, she liked him, but she did not love him.

At his knock, Olivia turned and walked slowly to the door. She did not want to do this. She thought and thought but could not come up with any other way to proceed. She opened the door, looked up into his clear blue eyes, then looked down at his cleaned and waxed boots, supple with wear and care.

"Good afternoon, Olivia, I trust you are keeping quite well," said Jack with a slightly affected bow.

"Good afternoon, First Sergeant Holloway. Come in," she replied and stepped back.

Oh, it's <u>First Sergeant</u> is it? Well now." He looked down at the top of Olivia's head, the straight part, the sheen of her hair. He reached out but withdrew his hand without touching her.

"Come in, Jack. There is something I must say to you. But I swear I do not know how to begin."

"Then you best begin," he said abruptly, commandingly. Then, in a softer tone, "Just begin, Olivia."

Olivia leaned against the open door, then straightened, raised her head, and looked beyond Jack's shoulder at the saloon, the hotel, and the brilliant, cloudless sky above. The odor of dust rose to her nostrils. She met Jack's eyes, saw the anticipation on his face.

"Oh Jack, come in."

"No. There'll be no sitting on the divan, no tea, no lessons. Say what it is you feel the need to say, Olivia, and say it here and say it straight."

"Very well. I can no longer spend time with you. Here or anywhere." She stared at the buttons of his uniform.

"Well now," said Jack. "I understand most clearly, Mrs. Foote. You need say no more, nor do I desire it. Most assuredly, we are, neither of us, free to . . . ." Jack faltered, searching for a word, a word he hoped Olivia would supply. She remained silent, staring at his buttons. Then he cleared his throat unnecessarily and said, "Good day to you, Mrs. Foote." He bowed slightly, turned and strode briskly across the flat open space to the saloon. Olivia wanted to cry. She had anticipated some sort of emotion from the man—anger, resentment, sorrow. She closed the door, returned to the barrel-backed wing chair, and took up the shirt she had been mending. She took no more than six stitches in the collar before the deep sobs shook her body and she buried her face in the shirt to hold back the tears.

At the saloon, Jack walked up to the bar, adjusted his saber, and ordered bourbon. The barkeep was a somber man, not given to small talk or jokes. He poured a healthy shot and slid it across the bar into Jack's waiting hand. Jack downed it and indicated another.

"What do you know, Amos?" asked Jack, not in the way of preamble or conversation or passing the time. A genuine inquiry.

Amos shrugged and served Jack another drink.

"Sergeant Seán Flannery was murdered," Jack said.

"None o' my business. That's army business. Your business."

Jack fiddled with his glass and forced himself to smile. "That is precisely the reason I am asking."

"Don't know a thing," said Amos and wiped down the bar.

"Where's Foote?"

"Don't . . . ."

"Yeah, Yeah," said Jack, losing his patience. "Don't know nuthin'. Would you like to look in his office?"

Amos leaned across the bar and said in a low, harsh whisper, "Look yourself."

Jack picked up his glass and spilled the contents across the bar, splashing a few drops on Amos' forearm. "Well now. I'll just do that while you clean up." Then he headed toward the Post Trader's office at the far end of the bar. Rapping on the door, he shouted, "Josiah Foote. First Sergeant Holloway here. May I have a word?"

Jack heard a rumbling sound and a man's low curse, then footsteps, and the door swung open. He expected to see Josiah Foote, a man he felt some guilt toward, but it was a woman who opened the door and stood before him. A woman Jack had seen in Loma Parda, Miss Chela Chavez. His surprise was so obvious, she smiled.

"Afternoon, First Sergeant Holloway," she said, then turned and dropped a quick, half-curtsy in Foote's direction. "Thank you sir, a pleasure doing business with you." She breezed past Jack, her silken skirts swishing and a trail of heavy perfume wafting in the air.

"Come in, come in," said Foote with impatience as he slammed shut a drawer of his desk.

The office was small and crowded with an oversized desk, three chairs, and a large ornate coat rack topped by a mirror. Crates of whiskey and bourbon lined one wall, covering the window and making the room so dark a lantern was lit. A layer of fine dust coated most surfaces. On the wall behind Foote, a few inches above his head, hung a painting of a man and woman fornicating in the woods. The woman's long blonde hair trailed across the scene as if they were underwater. Jack drew his eyes away from the picture and looked directly at Josiah Foote.

Noting the flush of blood in Holloway's cheeks, Foote said with a smirk, "Impressive, ain't it?"

"Where were you on the morning of April 14? That would be last Thursday."

"Ah, I see. We shall dispense with the amenities. No foreplay for you, eh, Sergeant?" Foote opened a cigar box on his desk, removed two, and offered one to Jack who refused. Foote unwrapped the cigar, bit off the tip, moistened it, and twisted it in his mouth. As he struck a Lucifer match, he said, "I was here, young sir." He lit the cigar, took a few puffs, and said, "Right here, doing my books. But I do not know why that should concern you, Sergeant Holloway."

"First Sergeant, if you please. I was promoted three months ago. I am inquiring into the murder of Sergeant Seán Flannery. There's talk you and Flannery had heated words in the store that morning."

"Let me think." Foote took two more puffs, filling the room with smoke. "It seems to me, early in the day, Flannery stopped at the store. Bought something, a trinket of some sort, I believe."

Jack waited.

"You are welcome to sit, Mr. Holloway," said Foote, indicating one of the empty chairs.

"No thank you, sir." Jack ignored Foote's game—the use of the title mister being only appropriate to officers. Jack knew Foote was goading him. "What was the fight about?"

"Oh, not a fight. I would not call it a fight. All ended congenially. Can't say as I recall the actual topic under discussion that morning. Could be it was the price of flour in Mora . . . been going up steadily, you know, or perhaps the weather. . . dry, very dry. Is it not?"

"And Shiney? Can you recall where he was?"

"Oh, I could not answer for Private Shiner's whereabouts, now could I?"

"He works for you, does he not?"

"Yes. Shiner does odd jobs from time to time. Cleans up, repairs, weeding in Mrs. Foote's kitchen garden . . . things of that nature . . . when he's off duty, of course. I do not recall seeing him that day. Perhaps you saw him, Sergeant, as you were leaving my home."

Jack remained cool externally, not showing the turmoil this question aroused. "No, Mr. Foote, I do not take piano lessons in the morning. I was on duty that morning. I take my lessons in the afternoons, as you know."

"My wife plays prettily. Does she not?"

"Yes. Mrs. Foote is an accomplished pianist." Jack felt he had lost control of the interview. He adjusted his sabre and straightened his belt.

"Yes, quite prettily. And the diction lessons. Mrs. Foote is a credit to her sex, is she not, Sergeant?"

Jack nodded and said, "First Sergeant, if you please. I do not take diction lessons. Thank you for your cooperation, Mr. Foote," and turned to leave. Facing the door, with his hand on the handle, he said, "You were seen. Did you know that? Leaving the store in a bit of rush right after Flannery left." He turned to see Foote's reaction.

"Yes, I recall now. The fireplace mantel had collapsed, crashed to the floor. Rubble everywhere. I went in search of someone to repair it."

"Well now, that would be Private Shiner, no doubt," said Jack, "That'll be all, for the moment, sir." Jack left the stuffy office and closed the door slowly and softly behind him, but not before glimpsing Josiah Foote, tilting back in his chair and puffing his cigar.

Olivia dropped the shirt and rose from the chair. She circled the parlor several times then approached the windows just as Jack stormed out of the saloon. She watched him stand on the covered boardwalk and remove a small notebook and pencil from inside his uniform jacket. He wrote something then slipped the items back inside. She backed away from the window as he stepped off the boardwalk and approached his horse. Jack mounted and rode toward the Opera House at a slow jog then sharply turned his horse west toward Los Alamitos and urged him into an easy canter. Olivia returned to the shirt she had been mending, but before she had completed more than a few stitches, the front door burst open and Mr. Foote entered.

Olivia looked up and was surprised to see him without his jacket or hat, with a cruel—but not unfamiliar—expression of malevolence in his flashing eyes. She stopped in mid-stitch and opened her mouth to form a greeting.

"What have you done? With your socializing and flirting, piano lessons and such—drawing attention to yourself! Putting me under scrutiny!" In three strides, Josiah Foote reached the chair. He leaned both hands on the armrests and pushed his face so close to Olivia's she smelled the cigar on his breath. He grabbed her by the upper arm and wrenched her from the chair. The white shirt flew out of her hands and settled on the floor, the needle stuck into Foote's hand. He pulled it out, and tossed it across the room. Olivia shrunk back from him, but he held her tightly.

"Please," she cried. "You are hurting me."

He shoved her across the room and down onto the green velvet sofa. "You will make a child, woman. You will."

As he yanked at her skirts, Olivia shouted, "Stop! Let us at least go to the bedroom."

"Bedroom! You're nothing but a fancy whore." He pulled her from the sofa and threw her to the wood floor. A fine cloud of dust rose around her.

Olivia cried now, sobbing with no attempt to control the tears or the hoarse guttural sounds erupting from her throat. She slapped at her husband, hitting his face and throat. He hit her hard across the cheek, his ring making a bloody scratch, then pulled her skirts and petticoats up and over her face, pinning her to the floor. Olivia struggled, and her muffled voice cried out, "No. Not here!"

Foote leaned in close to her ear and through the cloth of her skirt, whispered harshly, "You are my wife. You have no right to refuse." Olivia went silent, feeling the sting of truth in his statement. With one strong, violent movement, Josiah Foote forced his wife's legs apart and clawed at the opening in her pantaloons. She offered no resistance. A muffled whimper escaped her lips. He spread her tense, unwilling thighs, then unbuttoned his pants, and roughly entered her, thrusting again and again, tearing and bruising the soft, dry flesh. Olivia remained as still as death, trying to absorb the pain. She thought of other things—the soft gold of prairie grass, the pure white of summer clouds, and for a few blessed moments, she left the room, tossing and dipping above the earth on the constant winds. Then suddenly, she was thrust back

100

into reality as her husband arched against her and shuddered with a hoarse moan.

When he finished, he withdrew abruptly, stood, and buttoned his pants. Olivia did not move. Without another word, Josiah Foote stalked out of the house, slamming the door behind him.

For several seconds, Olivia lay stiff and cold and incredibly still. Then with sudden frantic fury, she yanked and pulled at her skirts, trying to free her face. She heard a soft ripping sound when, caught on her hairpins, her hair came undone and her skirts fell free. She saw light again and was surprised that the crisp sunlight was unchanged by the violence it had witnessed. She pulled the petticoats down to cover her exposed limbs and cried out as her back and shoulder muscles tightened. She grasped the settee and pulled herself up to a sitting position, wincing as a sharp pain like a knife cut shot from the apex of her thighs to the middle of her abdomen. Her hair fell around her like a rich red blanket. She rose to her feet, slowly, like an aged warrior. As she bent to remove her stained and torn undergarments, cold, wet semen slid along the inside of one thigh. She stood as still as a rabbit. Then she yanked off her pantaloons and stuffed them into the mending basket, burying them amid socks and linens and spools of thread. She smoothed her skirts, spread her fingers, and ran them through her hair again and again.

Olivia did not search for the needle, she did not resume her mending. She walked past the white shirt, lying grotesquely, like a broken body, on the Oriental rug. At the small writing table in the corner of the room, she winced as she sat. She reached for a piece of writing paper and thought, *Dear Father,* and it was then, as she thought of her father placing her hand into that of Josiah Foote, that the horror and despair of her life overtook her. Olivia crossed her forearms on the desk and rested her head.

"Dear Father," she said in a low voice filled with defeat.

Blinking away the image of Seán Flannery lying cold and still, First Sergeant Holloway arrived at Los Alamitos Lake. He rode along the edge, where the mud had dried into white, crusty lumps. He halted his horse and dismounted. Dropping the reins, Jack stared intently at the small ridges where the brown, wind-rippled waters had lapped the earth. With the toe of his boot, he dug into the mud a few inches, then smoothed out the indentations and repeated the process several times in the area where Seán's body had been found. He widened the arch of his search, knowing how the wind and the receding waters often reveal things previously hidden. It was as he turned to go that Jack caught the flash of light, a sparkle, like the glint of a firefly. He carefully moved toward the shimmer, stooped, and pulled at a gold thread wedged in the mud. When it came free, he recognized it as the thread used to form a soldier's sleeve insignia.

Jack stuffed the thread into his pocket, and after completing his search of the area, mounted, and urged his horse up the slope and on to the village. At the store, he tied his horse to the hitching post and entered. Porfirio Gonzalez nodded as the First Sergeant introduced himself and explained the reason for the visit. Mr. Gonzalez had been expecting a soldier—as Miss Olivia had said.

Jack asked to see Sergeant Flannery's horse and tack, and Mr. Gonzalez led him to the corral where Rosie was nibbling at a few new shoots poking up through the dry earth. As Jack approached to examine her, Rosie flared her nostrils, shook her head, and backed away.

"Well now," said Jack. "Easy there girl. Skittish she is."

Mr. Gonzalez, mentally noting the unusual behavior of the horse, haltered Rosie and held her. When Jack examined the healing lacerations, she danced away from his touch.

"Most unusual," said Gonzalez as he stroked her head and spoke softly to her.

"Horses are unpredictable creatures," said Jack. "Thank you for caring for this animal."

Mr. Gonzalez nodded, and Jack asked to see the tack, and Gonzalez obliged.

In the shed, Jack untied the sacks and spread the contents out before him. "Mr. Gonzalez," he said, "I am looking for Sergeant Flannery's log book." And when Jack described the notebook, Mr. Gonzalez shrugged. "Would you have anything else belonging to

Sergeant Flannery? Perhaps he left something with you? Asked you to hold something for him?"

Mr. Gonzalez considered the question. He considered lying to this soldier. And, as if reading his thoughts, Jack said, "Please sir. If you are holding something for Sergeant Flannery, or you know something, well now, it would be of much assistance. That is, I am investigating Sergeant Flannery's death. He rode with me." Jack paused. "He was my friend."

Gonzalez told Jack about the box. "But I do not know what was inside. SeánFlannery warned that it would be best if I did not know."

Jack said, "May I see it, please."

"No sir, that is, the ladies took it with them. *La amiga de* SeánFlannery and *la Señora* Foote."

Less than an hour later, First Sergeant Holloway paced up and down in the corridor of Colonel Winters' home quarters. Waiting made Jack worry, and the movement relieved some of his anxiety. He heard muffled, low talking, punctuated by an occasional raised syllable, not quite a shout. From across the Parade Ground, the bugler blew Stable Call, then suddenly the Colonel's daughter, Victoria, with a small tea tray, appeared from the far end of the long dark hallway.

She smiled as she looked up at Jack Holloway. "You must join us for tea, First Sergeant Holloway."

With formal apologies, Holloway declined. Victoria pouted— she was not accustomed to being denied what she wanted.

"Very well then," she said with a haughty toss of her curls.

The door opened and Josiah Foote said, "And here is your lovely daughter, sir, and she has brought a tempting tray." When Josiah saw Jack, he said, "Sergeant . . . excuse me . . . First Sergeant Holloway, how fortunate a day it is—to encounter one another yet again. The gods smile upon me."

Jack nodded, ignoring Foote's sarcasm.

"Miss Victoria," said Foote. "Would you have a cup of your delicately brewed tea on that tray? I would dearly love a cup of your tea."

"Why yes, Mr. Foote," said Victoria with a smirk at Jack.

Josiah Foote backed away with a flourish, making space for Victoria to pass.

"Good day to you, First Sergeant Holloway," she called as the door closed behind her.

After several minutes and more pacing, the door re-opened. "You may go as well, Victoria," said Colonel Winters, his voice on the edge of irritation. Josiah Foote and Victoria left the drawing room. Foote bowed to her and left the building without a word to Jack.

"Holloway. Enter," shouted the commander. "At ease. What news?"

Jack recounted in detail, with many a 'well now,' his visit to Los Alamitos as Colonel Winters tapped a pencil rhythmically on the top of the mahogany desk. As Jack continued, the colonel shifted his position several times in the way of a person who cannot endure sitting for very long. He crossed then uncrossed his legs. Finally, exasperated, he jumped to his feet.

"And you think the documents are in the box? What would the women want with them, I ask you, Holloway? More than likely, they could not make head nor tails of such papers."

"Well now, sir, I . . . ." Jack hesitated as his commanding officer's cloud-grey eyes locked his own.

"Yes, Holloway? What?"

"I do not know, sir, what the women would want with such documents. I do not know what these papers represent."

Winters threw the pencil across the desk. It skittered, fell off the edge, and rolled to a stop at the tip of Jack's boot. Winters said, "The laundress's quarters have been searched without success. And Mrs. Foote has been taken care of. One of these women has the documents and has cleverly hidden them. As for the contents of the documents, First Sergeant Holloway, it is neither prudent nor necessary that you be privy to such knowledge. By way of carrying out your orders, all you need know is that the leather pouch has the initials JJF burned into one corner."

"Understood, sir," said Jack, as he retrieved the pencil and placed it on the desk.

"And?"

"And? Well now, my next step . . . uh . . . ."

"Holloway," and the commander's voice took on the low measured tones that Holloway had come to fear. "Additional sources." When Jack showed no signs of comprehension, Winters said, "Were there not others at the site where Flannery's body was found?"

"Ah, yes sir," replied Holloway, recalling the faces at the scene. "Well now, I shall investigate additional sources."

Winters stood abruptly, scraping his chair along the floor. "Find the papers in question. That is an order." Holloway came smartly to attention, saluted, and executed a perfect about face. With some trepidation, the Colonel watched him depart.

Mary Margaret sat with her back to the light. She opened the newspaper, flipped to page three, and read.

Las Vegas Daily Optic
Death of a Sergeant—The Garrison Theatricals—A New
Organ for The Post Chapel

Regular Correspondence of the Optic. Fort Union, April 18, 1881. On Thursday inst., Ap. 14, as all was in preparation for the pending Dramatic Society offerings, a startling report spread through the garrison. The lifeless body of one Sgt. Seán Padraic Flannery of the 23rd Infantry, a fine soldier, had been discovered, lying face-down in the mud at nearby Los Alamitos Lake. It happened that your correspondent was in attendance at the Opera House when the death was reported. The entire company had assembled there for dress rehearsal when Private Jameson burst into the proceedings and breathlessly announced the sad news. Sgt. Flannery had been slated to perform, with the company, on the very next night. The news was shocking to all assembled, and the company dispersed immediately. However, a more distressing report yet awaited the post. It was revealed on the next day, by Asst.

Surgeon Williamson, that Sgt. Flannery had been strangled by the hand of a strong, albeit, brutal man. Indications of a struggle were also visible. Furthermore, Flannery had been stripped of his uniform, his weapons stolen, and his horse, which had bolted and fled to the village of Los Alamitos, had been injured. Sgt. Flannery was a man of prepossessing appearance and not a man to be trifled with. He was five feet eight inches in height with a fit and strong physique, and he served with honor in the Special Patrol, created by previous Commanding Officer Caldwell for the protection of U. S. Army property as well as the soldiers and their families. He was laid to rest with military honors on Friday in the post cemetery. Your correspondent was privileged to have attended one of Sgt. Flannery's estimable performances and had greatly anticipated seeing him light up the boards once again. Your correspondent is most saddened to report that Sgt. Flannery is not the first soldier to be mistreated in this dastardly manner—murdered. Earlier in this year, the body of Pvt. Francisco Abreu of the 10th Infantry was found on the open prairie northeast of the Quartermaster's Depot. He had been strangled by hand and stripped of his uniform and weapons. Abreu had been reported missing in the pages of this correspondence by his parents, residents of Rayado.

In remembrance of Sgt. Flannery, the Fort Union Opera House was dark on Friday, April 15. On the subsequent evening, the Dramatic Society opened the new season with an evening of skits, Indian club swinging, a solo performance of "The Girl He Left Behind Him" rendered by Professor Anton Chappa, and the play, *The Irish Attorney of Ireland, 1770.*

Major La Tourrette, Chaplain, was pleased to welcome a new addition to his congregation—a lovely pipe organ built and shipped by train from the Bannock Company of St Louis, Missouri. A celebratory tea was hosted by Miss Victoria Winters, daughter of the Commanding Officer.

J. Clooney, Regimental Correspondent

Mary Margaret folded the newspaper, folded it again, and again. She made it as small as she could then threw it to the floor and stomped on it. She picked up the flattened packet, and tossed it into the fire.

Chapter 13: In which the drama is reviewed; Mary Margaret talks to Gus Peterson.

<u>Tuesday, April 19</u>

At the Company B laundry, while the linens were soaking in the rinse tubs, Lulu searched through the *Las Vegas Daily Optic* for a review of the Dramatic Society's production.

"It may be Clooney's correspondence hasn't reached the *Optic* yet. Or it may be it's in the *Gazette*," said Lulu, turning the pages.

"Ah no. 'Tis only for the *Optic* he writes."

"Well, lemme try them society pages," said Lulu. "And here it is." Lulu's mouth moved silently as she read through Jud Clooney's correspondence.

With a long wooden paddle, Mary Margaret stirred the soaking sheets. "Today you be reading it aloud, Miss Lulu?"

"Oh yeah, sure," replied Lulu, coming to the end of the correspondence's report. "Here we are."

> . . . *The Irish Attorney of Ireland, 1770,* a most interesting entertainment, played to a full house on Saturday last. Every seat in the Opera House was occupied and many theatre-goers stood in the aisles. The Commanding Officer, Colonel Winters, and his family were in attendance, also Mr. Edward Friend of the *Las Vegas Daily Optic*, Mr. Robert Alvey of the *Mora County Pioneer*, and theatrical patrons Mr. and Mrs. Dunlap and their charming daughter Helena, who presented young Master Bolton, who portrayed Mr. Fielding with much emotional flare, a lovely floral tribute. Mr. Washington's Indian club swinging—always a treat—was outstanding. He performed thirty distinct maneuvers without a single slip. Master Willie Kerwin's clog ended to loud applause and calls for "more." Professor Chappa's heartfelt rendition of "The Girl He Left Behind Him" brought more than a few tears to sober eyes. But the drama was the height of the evening. The performers showed a certain brilliance, as there were no unseemly pauses. Miss O'Keenan

performed the role of the Irish attorney with reserved exuberance, and Timothy Sullivan did well as the lovely heroine. However, although the play was a good one, it suffered two major disasters. The neglects of the drop curtain at the end of Act I left the performers in a very embarrassing predicament, and there were a few blunders by some of the less seasoned players in very unseasonable places.

"Compliments of First Sergeant Clooney. And jest what does he mean by blunders?"

Mary Margaret looked up and paused. "Ah, 'twould be Timmy Sullivan—that is, the lovely Miss Fielding—he were making his exit in Act Two an' tripped, he did, the poor mite. He saved himself a bit of embarrassment—quick thinking—by turning the trip into a fair jig."

"Oh yeah, I thought that was part of the play. Didn't you Miguel."

"No. I was at all the rehearsals," said Miguel disparagingly. "I knew better."

"Well la dee da. Pardon my ignorance," said Lulu.

"Nary a mention of Seán Flannery?" murmured Mary Margaret.

"Well, uh, no, Mary Margaret. Not this day. Yesterday . . . ."

"Read it. I did, Lulu. No need to be sparing me. But, 'tis most thoughtful, considerate and I thank you. What else does the fine First Sergeant Clooney tell?" Mary Margaret returned with more vigor to stirring the sheets.

Lulu ducked behind the newspaper. "Well, he sez how chapel got a new organ and Miss Winters had a cel-e-bra-tory tea. Wonder what ole Sour Puss Peterson has to say?"

"Peterson's? It would be in the *Gazette,*" said Mary Margaret.

Miguel stepped forward and offered a battered, rolled-up edition of the *Las Vegas Gazette.*

"Thank you," said Mary Margaret as she rested the wooden paddle against the side of the tub and took the paper. "An' here it be. Well!" she said with indignation. "The eejit, the lig."

"What?" said Lulu, squeezing and wringing out the sheets.

Mary Margaret read silently for a few minutes, then blurted out, "'A ridiculous, disgraceful failure. They made complete dupes of themselves . . . take the whole lot of them and dump them in the nearest refuse heap.'"

"Well well, ain't he the intellictial!"

"Lulu, what means this: 'Jud, you ignorant dupe . . . to throw stones others moulded but dare not toss.' I dinna understand. And this . . . 'not old enough or wise enough in the ways of the Army . . . curry favor with the wrong crowd.'"

"Oh, that Gus. He's got it in for the drama boys, ya know, ever since Sgt. Flannery, God rest his soul, left the Comedy Company."

Mary Margaret set the papers down on the large laundry table. "I dinna understand?"

"Well, there's been bad blood 'tween them since your man left the Comedy Company. Remember as how Sergeant Flannery, God rest his soul, shone in their one big performance? Then took the leadin' role—the Irish Attorney—with the Drama Society. Well, Gus been a staunch supporter—charter member I believe—with the Comedy Company and always lambasting, so to speak, the new Drama Society, calling 'em names and writin' disparagin' words 'bout them in the newspaper. They 'most come to blows once— him and your Sergeant. Least that's what I heard."

"Sure, it canna be, Lulu. 'Tis only entertainment, a diversion."

"There's some don't look on it that way. I heard there was harsh words 'tween 'em, threats mebbe. Peterson accuzin' Sgt. Flannery of deceitful ways and calling him a opportunist. And Gus accusing First Sergeant Clooney of . . . of, well, you know— licking boots, so to speak."

Miguel laughed and Mary Margaret said, "An' what be the meaning of this saying?"

Lulu opened her mouth, but Miguel answered. "It means someone is trying to get favors by doing someone else's bidding."

"Ah, yes? 'Twould apply to Sergeant Seán Flannery, as well?"

"Don't know nothing 'bout that, Miss Mary Margaret," said Lulu. "And it's certain you wouldn't notice anything amiss, with eyes only for your Sergeant. And for good reason, a fine figure of man he was, in spite of the limp." Then when she saw Mary Margaret's face turn to stone and the faint smile dissolve, Lulu said, "I am sorry," and came quickly around the tub and gave Mary Margaret a strong sweaty hug.

"Tis fine I am, Lulu. Fine," said Mary Margaret, stiffening at the sudden closeness. Lulu realized that she had overstepped some invisible boundary and abruptly withdrew. Lulu wondered what hurt the girl so bad that she withdrew from sympathy and friendship. She recalled how close Mary Margaret had come to happiness. The happiness of a few days ago turned now to careful steps and brittle posture.

"'Tis no apology needed. He was a fine . . . ." began Mary Margaret. She hesitated then said, "Ah, but now I think on it, Gus Peterson did say something about me Seán having enemies." Mary Margaret paused and the newspaper slipped out of her hands. "Lulu, do you think there be enough hatred between them for murder?"

"Murder? Oh, murder don't require no hatred, jest enough likker, a good weapon, and a small, very small spark. Sometimes a reckoned threat or 'bad look,' as they say. I recall a youngun,' his body found over at Mora—nekkid as the day he were born. Beat bloody. Couldn't hardly recognize him," said Lulu.

Mary Margaret shuddered. "'Tis time we be hanging the sheets," she said. "This boy, he were strangled?"

"Naw, beat to death," murmured Lulu.

Mary Margaret said, "Miguel, fetch the fresh water, please."

Lulu set about wringing out the rest of the sheets of the first rinse then dumped them into the tub that Miguel was filling with fresh water from the cistern. Mary Margaret grasped a pile of unwashed linens and pushed it down into the steaming soap-water, pushing and kneading until the water turned grey. The room steamed with simmering water, damp wooden tubs, and the wetness of nine sets of bed sheets. Delicate drops of moisture slid down the darkened *adobe* walls, and steam clouded the few windows. Mary Margaret's curls twisted into tight ringlets, and her face reddened with heat and exertion. They worked in silence until all the sheets were washed, rinsed twice, and hung on the ropes to dry.

As they were cleaning up the laundry tubs and table, Mary Margaret suddenly asked, as if they had still been talking, "Where is it you be hearing all this, ah, news?"

"Gossip doncha mean? Loma Parda mostly. When people's gamblin' and drinkin' and lovin', they's usually talkin' too. Why jes t'other day . . . ."

Mary Margaret interrupted, "Excuse my impoliteness, but I be askin' in particular about the murders an' this altercation between the acting companies."

"Altercation . . . damnation, Miss Mary Margaret, next you'll be lecturin' at the school." Lulu laughed but sobered when she saw the seriousness in Mary Margaret's eyes. "Uh, well, it's Loma Parda where I hear most ever'thing as happens hereabouts, 'cept for some things from th'other laundresses and they hear 'em from the soldiers what work in the officers' quarters, ya know, the strikers."

Mary Margaret dried her hands on her apron, removed it, and moved to the other side of the room, her living quarters. She wiped steam from the small mirrored glass on top of the dresser and tried to capture her rebellious curls. "Thank you, Lulu, 'tis certain it is I be needing to make that trip to Loma Parda like we planned."

Lulu opened her mouth to protest, for although Mary Margaret was but another laundress and her manner of speech not elegant, Lulu found something ladylike in the woman's carriage. Not a delicate frame, even when corseted, but—it's the walk, thought Lulu. She walks like she deserves to be treated like a lady. Lulu could not abide the thought of the pawing and the leering of the rowdies and 'young sports' as they thought of themselves.

"Oh, No, Miss Mary Margaret. Mebbe we shouln't. Loma Parda is not . . . well, it's a bad place. There's many call it 'Sodom on the Mora!'"

Mary Margaret continued as if she had not heard Lulu. "Micah me boy, I thank you for followin' Shiney as you did, though 'twere a foolish thing. An' I be needin' another favor. Wouldja ever hang about the Comedy Company headquarters— behind the Opera House—an' see what you see an' hear what you hear, an' . . . ."

"And report to you. Yes, Miss Mary Margaret," said Miguel, and although he did not salute, he stood tall, as if at attention. She thought the boy was too young to shoulder such responsibilities. She reached out her hand and caressed his cheek. Miguel turned and dashed out of the laundry.

"Lulu, can you be managing alone here for a few hours? 'Tis just the cleaning up to finish."

"Don't you worry 'bout me. Do what you need to do, Missy. But if you must make this visit to Loma Parda, and I caution you not to, we best do it together. It is my home after all. We'll work up a story to go with your disguise."

"The Irish attorney," said Mary Margaret. "Seán's costume. I be wearin' the fine suit of the lawyer Connelly. Introduce me as your nephew from New York."

"Nah! Nobody'll believe that! Kansas City. I got a sister there. We'll plan and plot when you get back."

Mary Margaret shoved a final pin into her curls and pulled on her bonnet. As she reached for the doorknob, she turned and, without a thought, closed the space between them and gave Lulu a quick, light hug then turned and ran out in search of Gus Peterson. It being afternoon, when most soldiers are hanging about, she went directly to the enlisted men's quarters where she learned that Peterson had just left in search of a game of poker more than likely at the Post Trader's Saloon. So she set out for the Trader's Compound. The winds were tolerable and the walk easy. She thought it could have been a purely pleasant stroll if Seán be biding with her.

When she entered the saloon, a few men looked up from their cards and quickly returned to their games. Gus was not among the players at the occupied tables. He was not at the bar.

"Didja' ever see Pvt. Peterson today," she asked Amos.

113

"You want a drink?"

"I be looking for Pvt. Peterson," she repeated.

"Heardja the first time. You want a drink?"

Mary Margaret sighed and turned to survey the room again, thinking she may have missed him. The men lay down cards and made bets. No one looked up. As she reached the door, a voice behind her said, "Try the Comedy Company." She turned and said a thank you to the room then hurried to the Comedy Company headquarters in the storage shed behind the Opera House. She did not see Miguel, but she was certain he would be lurking somewhere—watching and listening.

As she raised her hand to knock on the door, she heard voices raised in anger. "Goddammit! Peterson . . . ." She put her ear to the door and heard shuffling and thumping, as if something heavy and awkward were being moved about. "Toldja to keep yer damn mouff shut din't I?" Mary Margaret shoved open the door, and as the dust settled, she saw Gus Peterson and Walter Shiner shoving an old oak chifforobe into place in front of a large, amoeba-shaped hole in one of the mud walls. They settled the piece of furniture and stood back, admiring their work.

"Good day to you Private Peterson, Private Shiner," she said.

Both men turned. Shiney said nothing. He brushed past her, bumping her shoulder, as he stomped out. Mary Margaret righted herself, tilted her chin up, and walked into the room.

"'Tis true we have not been formerly introduced, sir. I be Miss O'Keenan, Company B laundress. I believe you were acquainted with Sergeant Seán Flannery." Peterson said nothing so she continued. "Might I have a few moments of your time, sir? 'Tis important to me."

Peterson shrugged and indicated a dusty chair, but Mary Margaret remained standing. She felt stronger and more confident on her feet. "After Sergeant Flannery's funeral, you came to the home of Mr. and Mrs. Foote, to pay yer respects I have no doubt. An' you spoke of enemies. Did you not, sir?" Peterson did not reply. "Ah now, I believe you said you were not surprised—I think those are the very words you spoke—that Seán Flannery were murdered. Can you be telling me more about that Private Peterson?"

"Nothing to tell. I was drunk. Upset at the death of a fellow soldier. That is all."

"Enemies be a word you spoke that day. I believe you said Sergeant Flannery had enemies. Wouldja ever be one of them enemies?"

"Aren't you the brazen one, coming in here—alone—accusing me of murder!" Peterson walked up close to Mary Margaret, close enough for her to smell a trace of whiskey on his breath. She fingered Seán's pistol in her pocket.

"Brave? No sir. I be desperate. I promised me man I would find his assassin, I would, and bring the man to justice. 'Twould be one of his enemies I be thinking."

"And you 'be thinking' that I am one of those enemies? That I am implicated in the killing of Seán Flannery?" interrupted Peterson. Mary Margaret flinched as he suddenly raised his arm. Peterson smiled as he removed his cap, and she noted the sandy brown, close-cropped hair. "Yeah," he continued, "I bashed him and the Drama Society in the newspaper. Yes, I was angry at the man for deserting us—we worked hard to develop a following among the soldiers. But I am not a killer. There is no circumstance—none—that I can think in which I would take the life of a fellow soldier. Flannery should not have deserted the Comedy Company like that, but that is no reason to kill a man, Miss O'Keenan."

Mary Margaret felt as though she had been put in her place. Peterson was a smart soldier, too smart to be a private, but he had a temper and he drank too much. "Then who, Private Peterson, do you think killed Sgt. Flannery?"

"It does not matter who I think killed Flannery. The enemies I was referring to are as follows," and he ticked them each off on his fingers. "One, Walter Shiner, who Flannery exposed many times as a vandal, arsonist, and thief. Two, Frank Cole, who Flannery infuriated and helped capture—twice. And then there's Josiah Foote—for what reasons, I do not know."

115

As Peterson listed the men, an image of each floated into Mary Margaret's consciousness. She recalled Shiney's tangled red-orange hair.

"Josiah Foote?" she said.

"I do not know for certain. But Foote was forever taunting Flannery. And of course Flannery give it right back to 'im."

"What of Timmy Sullivan?" she asked.

"Sullivan?" Peterson laughed. "That whiney, snively boy? He hated Flannery and that's a fact. Had a bit of a tussle—wouldn't call it a proper fight—out behind the Opera House when Flannery took the lawyer's role. Shiney was there, and me, and Clooney. Sullivan hates everyone on the damn post. But not much of a killer. Not even much of a pugilist! Got a right hook like a little girl."

Mary Margaret asked, "Just to ease me mind, Private Peterson, where were you the morning Seán Flannery were murdered? 'Twould be . . . ."

This time Peterson's laugh was genuine. "I have to admire your tenacity and forthrightness, Miss O'Keenan. Of course, I might answer 'none of your damn business' to such a question, but I will not. I reckon that you are intent upon a worthy mission and I wish you well in its pursuit. I was on guard duty. And if I were you—a company laundress—I'd be careful where and when and whom I question."

"I thank you for your time, sir—an' the warning—kindly meant and kindly taken. I'll be on me way." Mary Margaret turned, opened the door, and stepped outside, but before closing it, she looked back at Peterson and said, "Sure, 'tis quite a bit o' damage the Comedy Company sustained behind that chifforobe."

Peterson nodded and said, "Right you are, Miss O'Keenan. Damn rats!"

Bridget Molloy, Company B Laundress

Ft. Union Cavalry Soldier and Mount

Hilario Romero, San Miguel County Sheriff, 1881-82
(New Mexico State University Library, RG83-108)

Enlisted Men's Quarters

Officer's Quarters, Fort Union, N.M.

Officer's Quarters Front Porch

Officer's Quarters - Interior

Office of the Quartermaster and of the Commanding Officer

A Favorite at Ft. Union Performances

Fort Union Hospital with Dead House

Hospital Courtyard

Native Americans in Front of Post Trader's Store

Post Trader Buildings

Mechanic's Corral

23rd U.S. Infantry Band

Retreat Parade Ceremony on Parade Grounds

Buffalo Hall, Las Vegas, NM (Denver Public Library, F14748)

Jackson Street Boarding House, Las Vegas, NM, 1898
(Rex Studios, NMHM/DCA, 088159)

Chapter 14: In which Mary Margaret and Lulu visit Loma Parda

<u>Tuesday, April 19</u>

As the aging Dougherty wagon tilted and bumped its descent toward Loma Parda, Mary Margaret peeked from beneath the black derby. "'Tis a grand slope and rocky. Would the town be trying to keep people away?" she said, lightly applying the brake and urging Lulu's mule forward slowly. "'Tis a sensible gal y'are, Sally. Walk on."

"Age and experience," laughed Lulu. "This here mule's walked this here road more'n any pilgrim. She done 'er twice a day, six days to the week, for I don't know how long—mebbe a year or two. 'Fore I worked for you I was helper to that thievin' witch, Angela Gabriela Smith, huh! Named for a angel and she's got the temperament of a gargoyle. Then there was . . . ."

Mary Margaret half listened as she concentrated on descending the long hill and taking in the village, spread out beneath them. Two rows of low stone buildings capped by pitched roofs reached out like long fingers toward the huge grey hill for which the village had been named. To her right, a sprinkling of small, square *adobe* houses dotted the sprawling valley bottom. In the warm light of the setting sun, she saw no signs of gambling halls or saloons. All looked peaceful. Several tethered horses snuffled in a corral, and on the far side of the village, a line of cottonwood trees marked the course of the Mora River. The wind rushed among the buildings and bare branches, swirling dust and dried leaves into tiny cyclones.

"'Tis a lush an' fertile valley. A fair paradise."

"Well, wha'dja 'spect?" said Lulu. "The jaws of hell? And don't be so limp at the wrist. Nobody'd believe yer a nephew a mine with them hands. Oh, they're big and strong enough, and a bit rough, but women's hands all the same."

When they reached level ground, Mary Margaret halted the mule and pulled on Seán's white cotton gloves, then grasped the reins with a firm hold, snapped the leathers, and spread her legs wide, propping one foot against the front of the wagon.

"Better," said Lulu. "Now, Miss Mary Margaret . . . ."

"Ah, for the love of God, Lulu, don't be calling me that!"

"Johnnie, I mean, Johnnie." Lulu was interrupted by the sudden appearance of an uncovered wagon pulled by four mules as it came crashing out from behind one of the long houses on the left. "Pull to the side! Move! That'll be the Black Mariah off to pick up the boys. Them's that have the dollar, and it don't stop fer nothing."

Mary Margaret slapped the reins and urged Sally to the side, but the oncoming wagon was the better motivator, and Sally nearly tipped the Dougherty in her anxiety to get out of the way. After Mary Margaret caught her breath and the wagon brushed past, she said, "Black Mariah? Wouldja be meaning the Sheriff?"

"Nah," laughed Lulu. "Jes' what we call it, is all. Coupla' the saloon keepers formed a group, so to speak, and fitted out an ole feed wagon to carry the boys back and forth 'tween Loma Parda and the Fort."

Mary Margaret recalled the small groups of soldiers they had passed on the trail. "'Tis a waste of money and mule I be thinking. Infantry be walkin' everywhere."

"The most use it gits is after a night of heavy drinking and whoring. Stop first at the hotel, Johnnie," and Lulu gestured ahead and to the right. "So's we kin get a decent meal. I'm hungry enough to eat a half-dead mule."

"Hotel?"

"Yeah, that's it, yonder, b'side that big cottonwood." Lulu pointed to a two-storey square building with a small upper balcony. Dim light flowed from the six-paned windows on either side of a green door above which, hand-painted in black, read the word 'Hotel.' Mary Margaret directed Sally and settled the wagon along one side of the building where a mud-spattered buckskin stood quietly at the hitching post.

As they entered, a man shouted from behind the bar, "Well if ain't Big Lu. And got yourself a fella, I see."

Mary Margaret said nothing and kept her eyes downcast. Lulu puffed out her ample bosom and said, "This here's my nephew from the East. My sister's young'un. Studying to be a lawyer

131

man. And we'll take supper." Lulu straightened her shoulders and cocked her head toward the tables and chairs in the small front room that served as bar, lobby, restaurant, and gambling hall.

"Pleased to meet you . . . uh . . ." The bartender extended his hand.

"Johnnie," said Lulu, "Johnnie Williams." Mary Margaret offered her gloved right hand.

The bartender nodded, grabbed her hand, and shook it vigorously. "Will Price at your service. Don't stand on ceremony. Set yourselves down. Got stew tonight . . . lamb . . . mebbe. Cain't really be certain a that."

They sat at a greasy table in the corner near a closed door. Dimly lit by four gas lamps, the room held three round tables and assorted chairs. The once red and gold wallpaper was blighted by soot and peeling in a few places, and soiled gold draperies obscured the waning daylight. Mary Margaret leaned over and whispered to Lulu that Will Price seemed artificially cordial, but Lulu told her, it's just his way.

A woman with a round, undefined body and wispy black hair approached the table, wiping her hands on a smudged apron. "Evenin' Wisteria," said Lulu. This here's my nephew from out East, Mr. Johnnie Williams. Gonna be a lawyer."

Wisteria nodded without expression, her face was smudged and sullen. Mary Margaret smiled from beneath her hat and nodded a greeting.

Wisteria opened her mouth, revealing jagged grey teeth. "Watcha wan?"

"We'll be dining tonight," said Lulu.

"Stew's what we got."

"Be fine. Jes fine. And two whiskies?" Lulu looked at Mary Margaret who nodded assent.

As the woman departed, Lulu whispered, "She's a little tetched in the head. Nobody'll have her at any of the houses since the night she went berserk and cut old man Fernandez who never hurt a living soul. So she works here, lives in the shed out back. I'm scared of her myself."

Mary Margaret swallowed. "She killed a man?"

"Naw. He survived. Has a nasty scar on the neck though."

As Mary Margaret asked why Wisteria stabbed him, the woman herself reappeared with two glasses of whisky. She pulled two forks, two knives, and two squares of fairly clean cloth from her apron and set them on the table, then trudged back into the kitchen.

"Why'd she stab him?" Lulu repeated. "That's a damn fine inquisition, Mr. Johnnie." And Lulu chuckled. "Damned if I—or anyone outsida' Wisteria's head—knows the answer to that one."

As they ate their meal, a hot, floury soup with bits of tough meat and grainy potatoes—the fresh *tortillas* being the best part of it—no one entered the hotel.

> *Ah, Seán, 'tis a beautiful valley. Has the look of Erin, it does. But the village seems a dreary, sad place, and a trifle fearful I am. 'Tis a mistake, no doubt, coming here. What's that you say? I'm here now. See what I see, hear what I hear. That I will.*

"Pie," said Wisteria as she cleared away the empty dishes.

Mary Margaret shook her head no, but Lulu said, "That'll be jes fine, Wisteria. Best part a any meal, I say. Didja make it?"

Wisteria burst into a harsh cackle. "Naw," she croaked. "Naw," shaking her head as if Lulu had said the funniest thing ever.

After finishing her piece of pie, Lulu said, "Things don't get started 'round here 'til, oh, 'bout nine or ten o'clock. Course they go on all the night. We'll go to my place, put up ole' Sally, and I'll get all gussied up. They'd 'spect it, company an' all."

Mary Margaret raised her eyebrows but said nothing. She paid for their dinner, and they left the hotel. In the somber, grey light that hung in the sky as night claimed the day, Mary Margaret followed Lulu's directions to one of the smaller homes close by the river. As she drove the main thoroughfare of Loma Parda, she saw the village coming to life. Light flowed from most windows now, a piano tinkled, cigar smoke drifted on the wind, and an occasional shout reached her ears.

"Over there," pointed Lulu. "T'other side of the river." Recognizing home and anxious to reach rest and feed, Sally strained against the reins. "Giv'er her head," said Lulu. "She knows the way." Mary Margaret loosened her hold and Sally broke into a light trot then came to a halt in front of a square, white-washed structure with a steeply pitched roof and covered front porch. The rough-hewn posts, low fence, and window framing were painted crisp white and shone like bones in the pale light. "Wouldja' mind settlin' Sally for me? Corral's b'side the house. She's an easy keeper—like me," and Lulu patted her own belly. "Jes' give her a few good flakes o' hay from the shed and fresh water. Probably wouldn't mind a bit of a brushin.' Then come on in."

"'Tis your very own place, Lulu?" Mary Margaret asked, not hiding her astonishment.

"Yes. I was not always alone, once. My husband and me. We was jes' kids when we married. Anyway, we come west from Kansas City. Looking fer cheap land to start a home and family." Lulu jumped down from the wagon and approached the porch. Without turning back, she said, "He was a good man, my Bill, a honest man, but no farmer. Killt' in the rebellion."

Without another word, Lulu stepped up onto the wooden porch, unlocked the door, and disappeared into the dark house. Mary Margaret sat a moment, taking in the whistling wind, the rushing of the river water, and Lulu's trim little home. A warm glow emanated from one of the windows as Lulu lit a lamp.

While Mary Margaret was seeing to the mule and Lulu lighting the lamps, a tall man with a black beard and green eyes, dressed in a dusty longcoat, entered the hotel restaurant from the kitchen door and passed the table where the two women had dined. He strolled up to the bar. His holster and gun bulged at his right hip. He set a foot on the brassy rail and leaned on the rough wooden bar.

"Whisky," he said. "And donchyou slip me none o' that Loma Lightning."

"Right you are, Mr. Cole, sir."

"No need to be so God damn cow-towin', Price. I ain't after you. Who're them two?"

"Well sir, hospitality, that's my business. And I guess you didn't recognize the lovely Miss Lulu. I believe she caught your fancy, once or twice? At the Palace?"

Price set a single shot of whisky on the bar in front of Cole, who looked at the meager amount and snapped, "Hospitality?" Cole picked up the glass, downed it, and slammed it onto the bar. Ignoring Price's questions, he said, "Another. Now, go on."

"Go on? Oh yeah, Lulu and her nephew, Johnnie something, Wilmore or something, visiting from the East, her sister's . . ."

Cole held up one hand in a gesture that clearly meant stop and drank his second shot. "Enough information. Give me another," he said and pushed his glass toward Price. Cole threw a few coins on the bar and took the third glass with him. He sat at a table in the corner and took a deck of well-worn cards out of his coat pocket. He shuffled, spread the cards, gathered them, and shuffled again. He downed his third whisky, then shuffled again, tapped the deck on the table, shoved it back into his pocket, and rose. As he passed the bar, Cole said, "You better not be lying, Price. 'Bout them two."

After she stroked Sally's neck and turned her loose, Mary Margaret entered Lulu's home through the back door, arriving in a small, neat cooking area and moved throughout the home in search of her hostess. In the parlour, she found sparse, unmatched furnishings—a round table, a settee, and two rocking chairs. Red organza hung at the tall windows. There was nothing hanging on the walls.

"In here," called Lulu from the other room. Mary Margaret passed through a small hallway connecting the two rooms and stepped into a cheerfully crowded bedroom. A cherry wood four-poster bed, matching chiffonier, and full-length mirror on a stand had somehow been crammed into the small space. In one corner a low table held a basin, water pitcher, and towels, above which hung a portrait in shades of white, black, and grey. A plump young girl with a round face and a big, open-mouthed smile sat straight and tall, in a long sleeved dress. She held a bouquet in her lap, and a wreath of small white blossoms crowned her wild hair. Beside her stood a handsome, unsmiling man, his hair parted in the middle and slicked tight to his head. He wore a dark suit that bulged at the buttons and a collarless shirt buttoned to the neck.

There'll be no wedding portrait for you nor for me, Seán luv. No four-poster, no babbies, no cozy kitchen, nor steaming kettle.

Lulu knelt at the foot of the bed, rummaging through an open trunk. "Whadda' ya' think?" she asked and pulled out a bright red, shimmery gown with crushed white flowers at the shoulders. "Don't get company much." Then, as she noticed Mary Margaret's gaze, she said, "That's me and Bill." She rose to her feet and stood so close Mary Margaret smelled rice powder, sweat, and a bit of dust. "We was full of hope in them days."

Mary Margaret swallowed her sadness and said, "A handsome couple y'are." Then, in answer to Lulu's question, "An' 'tis a beauty of a dress."

In front of Mary Margaret's eyes, Lulu transformed herself from a drab laundress into a lovely, rose-colored bird with green plumes in her grey-blonde hair. Her cheeks glowed like apples after she applied a bit of the Bloom of Youth, creating a sharp contrast to her white *décolletage*. As she worked, Lulu peered into the mirror and gave instruction. "Keep yer mouth shut, yer hands out of sight, and yer hat on. Remember, yer my nephew, you ain't no gent with fancy manners, and don't ferget to gawk at the gals! If you need to talk, mumble and cough a lot. But mostly jes lissen. I'll do the talkin.'"

Mary Margaret said nothing. She watched, mesmerized, as Lulu put the finishing touches on her hair, fluffing it out in places, smashing it down in others.

"Johnnie," said Lulu. "Johnnie!"

"Ah, yes . . . ah. Pardon Ma'am?" Mary Margaret croaked, lowering her voice to a harsh whisper but projecting, as Harlan had taught her.

136

"Good," said Lulu and twirled to face Mary Margaret. "Well?"

The corset and basque slimmed Lulu's middle pushing it all up into her breasts. The red of the dress and the rouge brightened her green eyes. And Mary Margaret caught a glimpse of the smile from the picture hanging above the basin. "Lulu, you are beautiful."

"Yeah? Well, I usta' be a looker," she said, pulling at the white silk gardenias at her shoulder.

"Ah, Lulu. Sure you be a beautiful woman, still. You look like a cardinal."

"Heh," Lulu croaked, "Ya mean the bird or the priest? Now, flattery, that's good. A young gent such as yerself would prob'ly employ the fine art of the compliment."

Mary Margaret offered her arm, "The bird of course. Wouldja ever be giving me the pleasure of your company?"

"Let's away then," said Lulu, taking Johnnie's arm. Outside, the wind had ceased its battering and howling, and as they approached a low stone building that now seemed on fire with light, noise, and smoke, a gentle breeze fluttered Lulu's feathers and playfully rustled her skirts.

"We'll go to the Palace of Passion, my former place of employment. Hope you ain't put off by the smell of sex, Master Johnnie."

Mary Margaret coughed and said, "'Tis no'a thing to a young man from the great and wondrous Kansas City."

As Mary Margaret, trying to walk and feel like a man, and Lulu approached the Palace of Passion, two riders jogged into Loma Parda from the south road and dismounted at the hotel. They positioned their horses on either side of the buckskin, tied them to the hitching post, and entered the lobby. The tables were filled with men. Steam and the odor of old potatoes thickened the air. Wisteria hurried to and fro, carrying bowls of stew and clearing tables as men shoved back their chairs, departed, and were replaced by remarkably similar-looking men.

"Good evening, Mr. Silva and company," said Price with a smile. "How're things at the Imperial?"

Vicente Silva leaned across the bar. He was not enamored of Price's pretense at *amistad*. He grabbed the barkeep by the shirt and said, "Cole." Then he let go so sharply Price lost his balance and fell backward against the bottles. He smoothed his shirt and keeping out of reach said, "He was here earlier. But he ain't here now."

"I can see that," said Silva, then turned and said something in Spanish to his companions who smiled unpleasantly. To Price he said, "I seen his damn ugly *caballo* outside. Where is he now?"

"I believe he's looking for a game. Mebbe the Emporium, or Chela's place. Mebbe the Palace."

Silva turned and spoke softly to his companion. Then they left. Outside, Silva rummaged through Cole's saddlebags. The horse pricked up its ears but did not otherwise move.

"Nada," called Silva. *"Vamos."*

The two men strolled across the thoroughfare and entered a low, flat-roofed *adobe* building. Inside were three round tables, a small bar, and Chela Chavez, the best Monte player in New Mexico Territory. It had been said that she won more than three hundred dollars from Doc Holliday one night in Las Vegas Grandes, but that had not been proven. Three clean-shaven, young soldiers and Mr. Josiah Foote sat with Chela at one of the tables. As Silva and *El Lechuza* entered, she looked up briefly then returned her attention to the cards.

"Still winning?" asked Silva with a laugh. Then, as he reached the bar, "Seen Cole?"

"Nope," said the barkeep and poured two shots of tequila. "On the house."

Almost in unison, the men drank, set their glasses down, and departed

Johnnie and Lulu entered the main parlor of the Palace of Passion. Three walls were painted dull red while faded black draperies covered the fourth. A thin layer of dust shrouded the floor. Overstuffed divans and velvet settees in various colors and styles stood in odd places as if a giant hand had sprinkled the furnishings about the room like seasoning in a stew. A long wooden bar, with a portrait of a reclining nude hanging overhead, clung to one wall. After introducing her nephew to some of the young ladies, Lulu guided Johnnie to the bar and ordered two whiskies. Johnnie rested one foot on the brass rail and an elbow on the bar, shoving the other hand into the pocket of the britches. When drinks arrived, like her Da, she downed it. The hot burning liquid made her eyes water, but she showed no distaste. She did not cough.

Lulu whispered, "Loma Lightening."

Mary Margaret set the glass down on the bar and motioned for another. Around her, the room vibrated with heat, smoke, and raucous laughter. From a far corner, a piano player tinkled out familiar tunes, and the high-pitched giggles of the girls cut into and overpowered the male voices.

As Lulu suggested, Johnnie leaned back against the bar and gawked at the girls. She saw undernourished children who looked perpetually startled and a few sweaty old women--tired and bored. These were no fancy women like the ones she had seen decorating the halls and hotels of New York and Dublin. These girls were dirty, their clothing soiled and frayed, their hair straggly and snarly, their complexions dull grey. Sprinkled among them, Johnnie saw a few enlisted men in uniform and two older men who appeared to be prosperous—maybe professional gamblers. Phrases carried on the thick smoke-filled air—'done for,' 'a soldier's life!' and 'Killt is what I heard.' Johnnie searched the crowd but could not detect the sources. Everyone seemed to be speaking at once.

Ah, Seán, tell me what I be doing here? Can I hope to learn anything a'tall in this din. 'Tis louder than Dublin on a Saturday night. 'Tis a mistake I be thinking, Seán Flannery. But, as you say, I'll wait and watch and listen.

"This here's my nephew," said Lulu. "From Kansas City. My sister's young'un." Lulu was introducing Johnnie to Mrs. Eisely who stood behind the bar smoking a freshly rolled cigarette.

"Johnnie, this here's the proprietress of the Palace of Passion, the best bawdy house west of the Mississippi." Johnnie turned to the bar and nodded, touching her fingers to her hat.

"Well then, a celebration. Drinks are on me," said Mrs. Eisely. "Didn't know you to have a sister, Miss Lulabelle."

Before Lulu had a chance to respond, the front door opened and a breeze ruffled her feathers, sending a tiny chill along her spine. The room went quiet for a few seconds, and Johnnie watched a tall man with a curly black beard approach the bar. He wore a long dusty black coat. Standing on the far side of Lulu, he ordered whisky.

As Cole drank the shot, Lulu said, "Why, it's Frank Cole, ain't it?"

Fancy Frank Cole turned his head slightly in Lulu's direction and nodded. Johnnie stared, taking in the bulk of the man and the thick black hair hanging below his hat. Must be over six feet, she thought, and built like a buffalo—big enough to pull a horse to its knees.

"This here's my ne . . ." began Lulu.

Cole waved an impatient hand at Lulu. "Take care, Miss Lulabelle. Take care," he said, not as a parting nicety, more like a warning. Then he tossed a coin on the bar, tipped his hat to Lulu, turned, and strolled out of the building. It seemed to Mary Margaret that his sole reason for coming had been to give Lulu a warning.

Sure, 'tis the man you and Jack caught and arrested and recaptured. The man who named you 'Smilin Seán.' Big enough and, sure as I stand here, mean enough to kill you. Maybe 'tweren't your killer's hair in your hand atall. What's that you say? Sure, you be correct in that. I do jump to conclusions. But this Fancy Frank Cole. 'Tis a man with a reason for killing you.

"Johnnie. The lady's talkin' to ya.'" Lulu's voice cut into Mary Margaret's thoughts. And Johnnie turned to see a skinny, pale girl, with eyes the color of wild asters, flat of chest and

140

shivering in a skimpy, peach-colored nightdress. Could not have been more than fourteen.

"I . . .uh . . .evening, Ma'am."

The girl touched Johnnie's forearm and said, "Evnin' sir. They call me Lotus. Wouldja want to dance with me?" When Johnnie hesitated, the girl said, "Please."

> *If you please, Miss O'Keenan of Fort Union, formerly of County Clare in the great homeland of Ireland, wouldja ever care to dance with me?*

> *Ah Seán, you asked so proper even me Ma could not object. An' the piano player struck up that lovely American waltz I dinna know the name of. An' dance we did round an' round the grand Imperial Hall. An' for the time of the dance, the world went away and we be the only two people. An' seemed your leg was whole an' me mind was calm. 'Twas the day I knew I loved you. 'Tis sorry I am I did not say it.*

"Be pleased to," said Johnnie. Holding the girl at arm's distance and not knowing how to lead, they stumbled through a waltz while Lulu leaned over the bar and chatted with Mrs. Eisely. The girl talked without stopping about unfamiliar people and events. So, tilting her head downward and talking in her lawyer's whisper, Johnnie asked, "I hear there are lots of murders out here in the west. Heard of any?"

The girl hesitated, missing a step and bumping into Johnnie, who pulled back quickly. "Oh, yes," said Lotus picking up the waltz moves again. "Lots o' murders hereabouts."

"Soldiers too?" croaked Johnnie.

The girl nodded, "One fella got his head split open with a axe for steppin' out with the wrong gal. Not none of us, mind you. One of them *ladies* from a fine family in Mora."

"And 'twere a soldier?"

"A soldier? No. Leastways I don't think so. But a couple of soldiers was kilt right here in Loma Parda. When was that?"

Lotus' eyes glazed over as she puzzled through the muddle in her mind. They danced on, circling the edge of the room.

Finally, the girl said, "Tell me 'bout Kansas City. Fancy ain't it?"

Mary Margaret cleared her throat and spoke of the new Cosby Hotel, the only one Lulu had mentioned, with water pumped up to all five floors, heavy satin draperies, and thickly stuffed velvet chairs scattered among potted palms. She described stately, corseted women wearing diamond necklaces as bright as new snow. The girl's eyes widened with each new treasure.

"'Tis your turn," said Johnnie. "Tell me of the murders."

Lotus hesitated then said, "T'aint fair. You know my name. What's yers?"

"John, but most call me Johnnie." Mary Margaret coughed roughly keeping her voice hoarse and low. "About the murders, Lotus?"

"Well, Johnnie, lemme think. Last year? Mebbe, not that long ago. A nice man with nice manners. No roughing about. A general mebbe or a private—anyway, he were a soldier, I think."

"Johnnie," Lulu grabbed Mary Margaret's elbow. "Time we was leaving. Promised your Ma I wouldn't keep you out late."

"But we . . . uh . . . yes, of course, Aunt Lucinda," whispered Johnnie. When she saw the look of fear in Lulu's eyes, she stopped, stepped back, and bowed from the waist.

"Lucinda!" squealed the girl in delight. "Yer called Lucinda?"

Lulu turned a piercing look on Lotus and said, "And <u>yer name</u>, little one?

The girl clamped both hands over her mouth. then clasped them in front of her chest as if in prayer. "Don't tell, oh please don't tell. Don't mean no harm." Lotus turned and ran to a nearby settee, squeezing herself in between two of the older girls.

"Well I'll be," said Lulu. "What's got into her?"

Mary Margaret said, "Poor lil' ejit. She be as futtery as the *deenee shee*."

Lulu lean over and whispered in Mary Margaret's ear, "I don't know what in hell you're sayin', but if you mean she's scart of somethin', I agree. Now let's get outta here. I got something to tell ya."

As they approached the door, it swung open, and two men dressed in trim brownish suits and barely dusty boots met Mary Margaret's startled gaze. "Good evening," the taller man said directing his eyes at Lulu and touching the brim of his hat with two fingers. Lulu made a quick courtesy. The piano hesitated for a beat then the player banged out a loud polka.

"Evenin' sir," said Lulu. "Come now, Johnnie." And as the men passed by them, she slipped her arm through Johnnie's and tugged her out into the night. "That is Mr. Vicente Silva," whispered Lulu. "Owns the Imperial Hall in Las Vegas Grandes and his friend, more like his shadow. Don't know his name, ever'one calls him *Lechuzo*, the owl, 'cause seems like he kin see in the dark."

"Ah, yes. I have encountered Mr. Silva and his owl at the Imperial Hall an' in the village of Los Alamitos. I dinna think he recognized me."

Seán, didja ever notice the color of his hair . . . that deep auburn . . . as close to red as hair can be. But Mr. Silva? Sure you be acquainted with Mr. Silva, traveling' the countryside as you did. 'Could he have a reason to kill you? Sure he's just a saloon keeper. What's that you say? I'm trying to keep it all straight in me head, that I am, though me thoughts do wander. The fight? A bit of a tussle it was to be sure, but 'twas proud I were of you—defending me honor. Mother o' God, Seán! Now I've seen him, 'twas Mr. Frank Cole himself threw that punch? Come outta nowhere it did. An' Mr. Silva be the man interrupted the altercation.

Chapter 15: In which Mary Margaret learns what 'they say.'

"C'mon," said Lulu pulling Johnnie across the narrow boardwalk and into the dusty road. "The Imperial? In Las Vegas Grandes? You're quite the travelin' lady," whispered Lulu.

"Hang on, Lulu, you're taking me breath away, y'are. An' what be that place there, that low dim building off to itself."

Lulu turned, "Chela's Place. Let's go. I got somethin' ta tell ya and I'd ruther be home to do it."

Mary Margaret pulled free from Lulu's grasp and stopped dead. "That be Mr. Foote's Tamany, tied there, waitin,' an' not too patiently I see."

"Huh?" said Lulu, following Mary Margaret's gaze. "Don't know nuthin' 'bout that and don't care. Com'on." And she grabbed Johnnie's hand and pulled.

Still Mary Margaret hung back, "'Tis odd, Lulu. Seems Mr. Foote be a traveling man."

Lulu gave Mary Margaret a strong tug and hurried her along the thoroughfare. They passed two drunken soldiers, a loose horse trailing its reins, and a fancy gal strolling on the arm of an officer. Mary Margaret strained to look at the soldiers, but Lulu was insistent, and as soon as they got to her house, she dragged Mary Margaret inside and bolted the door.

"Now, Mary Margaret, you set down and listen. This is dangerous business you're messing with. The good dame Eisley may exaggerate a mite, but she don't lie outright. Set down and listen, please."

Mary Margaret sat on one of the straight-backed kitchen chairs.

"Hush and listen," continued Lulu as she lit a kerosene lamp and brought it to the table. "Soldiers—men who fought in wars mind you—murdered, disarmed, stripped nekkid and you think yer tough enough to catch this killer?"

"But surely. . . ."

"But surely nuthin' Missy." Lulu sighed deeply. "Eisley says least three . . . ."

"Three? Another?"

"Don't know 'bout no numbers!" Lulu's voice rose to a shout. Then she took a deep breath and continued in a more even tone. "The talk in Loma Parda is someone jes' don't like soldiers. Eisley thinks it's for the valuables—uniforms, rifles, and sech— anything they kin sell. But, trouble is, none of the goods turn up nowheres. So I says to her, 'well then, it ain't fer the profit.' So then she owns, could be someone jes' hates soldiers."

"Strangled all? By hand? Any be murdered by axe?"

"Axe! No. Leastways, she never said. But I heard one poor boy had his head beat to jelly."

"Sure, he be a nasty *quilt*," said Mary Margaret.

"Huh? For God's sake! What does bedding have to do with anything?"

"Excuse me use of the Irish. 'Tis a bad person—mean and low, you might say."

"Oh. Despicable—I'd say. So what I'm tellin' ya is this. Leave this here investigatin' to them that knows. Now, you stay the night here. Come early morning, 'fore light, we'll sneak you back to . . . ."

"Could be Frank Cole," interrupted Margaret.

"Huh? Cole? Naw, don't think so. He hates soldiers, to be sure, and the law, but he ain't no killer, leastways, not unless he hasta,' never in cold blood."

"Cold blood?"

"Cold blood. Means just that—killing someone without heat, without passion or anger. Cold and calculatin.'" Lulu stopped abruptly at the sound of hoof beats. "A burro," she whispered. Then two thuds at the door as if someone was trying to kick it in. "Yes?" she called as she rummaged in her gown then pulled out a small pistol. "Who's there?"

"*Señora?* It is Miguel."

"Come in, come in," said Lulu, pocketing the gun and unbolting the door.

"*Lo siento,* Ma'am," said Miguel. He stood in the open doorway, a round blue bundle slung over one shoulder. "I did not know you have company, Miss Lulu."

145

"Ah, Micah, me boy. 'Tis me. 'Tis Mary Margaret," and she removed the mustache.

Miguel stared for a minute before he recognized the costume then the woman. He smiled. "I found a bundle." He pulled it around in front of himself and dropped it on the floor. A fine cloud of dust rose in the dim lamp light.

"Wherever did you find this?" asked Lulu. Mary Margaret remained quiet and still, staring at the bundle wrapped in a soldier's sacque coat, belted with a soldier's belt, and tied with thick rough rope. What looked like a wooden cane protruded from beneath the rope.

"The Opera House. I followed Private Shiner, watched him hide it under the stairs. I waited until dark. Now I bring it here, to *la señora*, for keeping safe."

The two women stared at the bundle.

Mary Margaret spoke first. She squared her shoulders and said, "'Tis the belongings of Sergeant Flannery?"

"I did not open it."

Lulu asked, "There was only this bundle? Nothing more?"

"*Sí. Es todo,*" said Miguel. "Only the one bundle, and the shilla. . . ."

"Me shillelagh. I thank you, Micah me boy."

Let me look on you, Seán Flannery. 'Tis a good soldier y'are, but not so neat and trim as the First Sergeant, I fear. An' didn't I brush the dust from your shoulders, an' didn't you offer me yer cap to clean? What cheek! But didn't I brush it and shine the emblem?

Lulu knelt on the floor, untied the ropes, and unbuckled the belt. Mary Margaret suppressed a gasp. The lamp flickered in the soft flow of air as she lifted and separated the items. A coarse dirty rag, an old pair of large cavalry britches, torn hickory shirt, and a few dirty socks.

Laughing heartily, Lulu said, "Well, certainly not the uniform of Sergeant Flannery."

146

And Mary Margaret laughed out loud. "No, 'tis not. 'Tis nothin' but a pile of soiled rags. Micah, 'tis certain y'are this be the bundle you saw Private Shiner hide?"

Miguel nodded. *"Sí."*

"You followed Private Shiner. From where? Where did you first see him?" asked Mary Margaret.

"I followed your instructions. But as I came near the Comedy Company quarters, I saw Private Shiner come riding in hard. His horse, as the soldiers say, was lathered up."

"Ah no, Shiney has no horse," said Mary Margaret.

Miguel was silent. He looked at Mary Margaret then at Lulu. *"Pero,* he was riding a horse, *una grulla,* you know, the color of the big bird."

"A crane?" asked Lulu.

"Sí. The crane. The bundle on the saddle in front of him, like a body. He dismounted and tied the horse. I offered to brush her but he shoved me aside. He grabbed the bundle, and ran into the Opera House. So I followed. I saw him shove the bundle into a hole, like a closet, under the back stair. He left through the rear entrance."

It was silent a few minutes, then, "Ah, a grey mare. With one white sock?" When Miguel nodded, Mary Margaret continued, "'That of the Colonel's daughter?"

"Now that makes no sense at all," said Lulu.

Mary Margaret said to Miguel, "An' from what direction did he ride?"

"Direction?"

"North? West?"

"From where the sun rises."

"From the plains," said Lulu, "the Turkey Mountains. Nuthin' but prairie out there."

"An' you saw him hide this very bundle and leave? An' not another soul about?"

"No. Not even a spirit."

Mary Margaret knelt to eye level with the boy and gently took hold of his shoulders.

"What do you hear of the murders?" she asked.

Miguel looked into her eyes then shifted his gaze to the ceiling, "Talk is there's a crazy man," he said. "A big crazy man, kills for pleasure. Hates soldiers. Steals their clothes *y todo.* Kills with his hands, s*e dice.* It is what they say." Miguel shrugged his shoulders and looked down at the floor.

"But who?" asked Mary Margaret. "Who be doing such things?"

"A crazy man," said Lulu. "A very big crazy man."

In his quarters, Jack Holloway mulled over his recent discussion with Colonel Winters. "Additional sources," he said aloud as he paced the length of the room, passing Flannery's empty cot. In his mind, Jack envisioned the scene at the edge of Los Alamitos Lake. Yes, he thought, I followed orders to the letter. Gathered the patrol, rode for the Lake, investigated the news Jameson brought. Yes, found Flannery's body.

Additional sources, wondered Jack. What does he mean? Others who were there? The patrol—four men—new replacements all, just arrived from Fort Larned. So, not additional sources. The men did not know Flannery. The ambulance drivers, veterans both. Additional sources? Sheriff Otero and his deputy. Why were they there? How did they learn of the death so soon? Three riders on the perimeter—a coincidence? And, of course, O'Keenan.

"Additional sources?" Jack shouted to the walls.

Chapter 16: In which Mary Margaret receives a message, and Olivia remembers.

<u>Wednesday, April 20</u>

The sun topped the Turkey Mountains and filled the sky with the promise of spring as Mary Margaret, Lulu, and Miguel returned to the post. The air was windless and fresh, and a few, brave dandelions dotted the landscape. Sally picked up a lively walk as she approached the stables, and behind the wagon, Miguel's *burro* broke into a trot. Keeping her face hidden in the shadow of the hat brim, Mary Margaret, still in costume, jumped down and opened the gate, Lulu drove into the corral. A private, just relieved of duty, was grooming a horse, and three soldiers were cleaning tack. Lulu greeted all with a wave.

"I'll take care of Sally," Lulu shouted as the private made to take the reins. "Go on now, Johnnie. Meet me later at Company B laundry."

Mary Margaret nodded, and Lulu's nephew strutted across the corral toward Suds Row. Miguel untied his *burro*.

> *Seán me man, 'tis a heart-rousing sight—Fort Union in the early morning—before the wind is up. Clean and fresh as the Irish mist, open as the Burren of County Clare. An' the lovely American flag—risen' and flyin' proud. I luv this country, I do, though I be feeling alone without you.*

Mary Margaret passed the guardhouse and approached her quarters. The rising sun cast a long, man's shadow ahead of her. Although the garrison was bursting with soldiers reporting for duty, patrols mounting and riding out, Suds Row waited silently for its day to begin. Mary Margaret approached her quarters fearing she might encounter another upturned room. She turned the key and was relieved to hear the click of the lock. She swung open the door. All seemed secure and as she left it the day before. She lit the laundry fire and changed into a work dress, folding and stowing the Lawyer Connelly's costume in her trunk. Then she shoved the trunk beneath her cot and set about making coffee and

149

frying potatoes. It was not until she laid plates and forks on the table that she discovered the slip of paper, sticking out from under the oil lamp.

She sucked in her breath as she recalled the great hulking image of Shiney entering her quarters with a key. Mary Margaret yanked the paper and unfolded it. She trembled as she read the hand-printed note,

TO MIZ OKEENAN THE LONDRESS—
PAY STHRICT ATTINSHUN TO DIS HERE
WERNING. STOP YER MEDDLIN OR YOO DIE.

She re-read the note as she remembered Seán's warning— *He's not kind to the ladies.* At the sounds of Lulu and Miguel approaching, she stuffed the note into her pocket, and from the top drawer of the chiffonier, she retrieved the small pistol she had taken from Seán's quarters. She made certain it was loaded, pocketed it, and then rushed to the stove to turn the smoking potatoes.

As Miguel entered, just a few steps ahead of Lulu, he shouted, "Another performance, Miss Mary Margaret, in Las Vegas Grandes. Mister Davies says it will be the best ever. Sunday at the Exchange Hotel."

"On the *plaza*," interjected Lulu. "And the band'll give a performance and street parade. Miss Mary Margaret, didja hear?"

"Sure, I did. Heardja both, I did. One would need be deef not to. But sit now and take some breakfast."

Lulu began serving a plate. "Ain't ya excited Miss Mary Margaret? Performin' at the Exchange?"

"A hotel ya say? Sure, they can perform without O'Keenan. Timmy Sullivan will be only too happy to oblige."

Miguel and Lulu exchanged a questioning look. Mary Margaret set a plate of potatoes and eggs in front of Miguel then served herself. They ate in silence.

"Could be something is amiss?" asked Lulu as she finished her breakfast.

Mary Margaret looked at her. "An' why ever wouldja be saying such a thing as that?"

Lulu stood and began clearing away the empty dishes. "Oh, only yer awful quiet. And, what, if I may ask is wrong with a hotel?"

"Ah well. 'Tis no proper stage I be thinking."

"Oh, donchyou worry 'bout that none. There's a stage and seats in Felix Papa Hall. More'n a hundred seats," said Lulu.

"Sure y'are on that?"

"Oh, yes. I bin to the doin's lots of times. Always a good time," said Lulu.

"Sure I be thinking on it, but just now I need to talk with Mrs. Foote, I do."

"Well then, off you go then. Donchyou worry. Me and Miguel, we know our jobs. We'll get to them."

Mary Margaret looked at each in turn and thanked them. Miguel went for water, and Lulu lit the big laundry room fireplace. Mary Margaret freshened up and departed.

Mary Margaret approached Olivia's home from the rear, brushing the new green shoots of herbs and flowers that made up the kitchen garden. The house seemed eerily quiet—dark and solemn. She knocked on the window of the rear door. Then knocked again. It was unlike Olivia to be so long answering. Mary Margaret banged on the door again, and waited. Just as she turned to leave, Olivia opened the door. Her appearance was greatly changed from the day before. Although she was clean, her dress was wrinkled and one sleeve was crushed, her normally bright hair hung loose and tangled, falling forward and obscuring parts of her face. What was visible of Olivia's face was as white and expressionless as bones dried by the desert winds. There was no color except for the wild feverish brilliance of her eyes—a sheen that Mary Margaret had seen before in Layla's eyes and in the eyes of many a street urchin.

"Come in," Olivia whispered and stepped backward, staggering and falling against the pie chest. The kitchen was cold. Crumbs, a half-empty cup of tea, and dirty linen littered the table.

"Olivia, are you unwell?"

It was a simple question, but it seemed to confuse Olivia. She looked distractedly around the room as if the answer could be found on a shelf or in a cupboard. She fingered her hair. Touched her mouth. "Ill?" she said, "Tired. So tired."

"'Tis more than tired I wager. 'Tis a mite of the Prairie Madness come upon you, Olivia Foote." As if to emphasize Mary Margaret's words, a sudden wind howled from the southwest. "Prairie Madness," said Olivia, staring at something beyond Mary Margaret's left shoulder.

"Let us have a cuppa," said Mary Margaret, summoning up courage and good feelings. "I'll just put the kettle on an' you, ah, wouldja ever like to tidy yourself, Olivia?"

Oliva gave a slight nod and walked slowly out of the kitchen. Mary Margaret lit the fire and cleaned the table. When she turned to fill the kettle from the pump, she felt a presence in the room. It was Olivia, holding a corset loosely against her body, with a confused expression on her face.

"Olivia?"

"I need help."

Mary Margaret set down the kettle, "Mother of God. What is it? Are you injured?"

"He has done it again," murmured Olivia. "Mr. Foote fired my maid. I cannot lace my corset."

"'Tis only that? I be helping you. Though I dinna' see the need of a corset to have tea. An' I be fixing you up with one that laces up the sides, so you won't be depending on a flighty gal. Turn round now. An' what did Maria do wrong?"

"Hm?" asked Olivia.

Mary Margaret opened her mouth then closed it again as she stared at the bruises.

"Olivia, whatever happened to your back?"

"I fell," said Olivia.

Mary Margaret said nothing. She tightened the corset, and Olivia glided from the room as if sleepwalking. Mary Margaret filled the kettle and set it on the stove, then set out a pretty table with fresh linen and china. She found a few unbroken biscuits in a tin and was placing them on plate when Olivia returned wearing a fresh cotton dress. She had brushed her hair, but it hung forward, shielding her face.

"Sure you're as fancy as the queen, y'are. Now let's arrange that pretty hair of yours." Mary Margaret walked around the table and stood behind Olivia. "You'll be needin' a tidy bun at the nape of your neck, I'm thinkin.'"

"No!" shouted Olivia and pulled away. And as she shook her head, Mary Margaret saw a bruise and the long angry scratch on Olivia's cheek.

Mary Margaret did not comment. Olivia pulled her hair forward, covering the injuries. "I . . . oh, dear Lord, I cannot . . . I can not!" A fierce gust of wind slammed against the side of the house, rattling the windows.

"'Tis herself, at your service," said Mary Margaret. "We'll be having our tay. You can tell me when, or if, you've a mind to Olivia. It canna' be anything I've not heard nor seen." Olivia sat at the table and rearranged the spoons and napkins. When the kettle came to a boil, Mary Margaret busied herself preparing the tea.

"Now, Olivia, what did you find on the duty rosters?"

Olivia did not immediately answer. Again, she rearranged the spoons. Mary Margaret sipped her tea and looked out the window at three crows darting and diving against the wind, their black wings shimmering in the sunlight. After a few minutes, Mary Margaret turned her gaze expectantly to Olivia.

"Olivia," she said. "Drink yer tay."

Olivia straightened up in her chair and took a sip.

"The duty rosters? Whatever didja find?"

"Duty rosters," repeated Olivia. She stared off again. Mary Margaret looked about to see what could be distracting Olivia. She saw nothing but the empty parlour beyond, dust motes lazily falling upon the green velvet divan.

"Olivia. The duty rosters? For the red-headed soldiers on the day Seán were killed? Did you learn anything?"

Slowly, Olivia trained her eyes on Mary Margaret. "Oh, yes," she said. "Yes. The red-haired soldiers." She set down her cup. "They were on duty. All of them, that day. Every soldier at the garrison was on duty!" She almost shouted with jubilation. As if she were delivering exciting news. Then she sat quietly. She appeared to be thinking. "But I did find a few anomalies for the day of Sgt. Flannery's death."

"Anoma . . . ?"

Olivia smiled. "Odd, very odd, occurences," said Olivia, in her teacher voice. "Walter Shiner was on fatigue duty at the cemetery, painting the fence, but according to the sergeant in charge—it happens the sergeant is one of my piano students—Walter reported two and a half hours late."

"Ah, sure, he . . . ."

"And Private Sullivan was assigned to guard a shipment of flour from Mora, but First Sergeant Holloway told me that Sullivan did not report for duty. Later, when Jack questioned him, Sullivan claimed illness, but there is no record of it at the infirmary." Olivia fingered the corners of the napkin beside her cup as if trying to pick up a loose thread.

"So, they were officially on duty but not seen carrying out their duties." Mary Margaret paused. Then said, "Ah, Loma Parda. 'Tis a sorrowful, evil place."

Olivia sipped her tea. "It is merely a place. A place where people try to make the best of their lives. One finds evil in the most unlikely places."

"No, I think you be wrong in that, Olivia," and Mary Margaret told her of the other murders, the skinny little girl she danced with, Mr. Cole, and Mr. Silva. "Sure, you knew Mr. Silva be a redhead?"

Olivia said nothing. She seemed to be studying something on the wall.

"Olivia!"

"Well, yes. I suppose, but his hair is dark, more like auburn, not the bright orange-red of the fluff you found."

"'Tis true," continued Mary Margaret, trying to keep Olivia focused. "An' Mr. Cole be no redhead atall. His hair be as black as jet. Olivia, I fear I am lost. Cole has reason—revenge—to kill me man. But Silva—I dinna see no reason, no reason atall to kill me Seán."

154

"A reason to a kill a man," said Olivia. "A man seems to need no reason to kill. Or to do whatever he does."

Mary Margaret stared at Olivia.

"Oh, dear Lord," said Olivia and set down her teacup. "I remember now." She sat up straight. "Words between Mr. Foote and Sergeant Flannery, that morning. Mr. Foote was not at the store when the fireplace collapsed, nor for the cleaning up. When he arrived, he thanked Sergeant Flannery for helping to clear away the rubble. Then, as the sergeant was leaving, Mr. Foote said, 'And did you find something of interest, Sergeant Flannery?' 'To what wouldja be referring?' asked the sergeant. 'Oh, anything,' said Mr. Foote, looking around at the mess of dust and crumbled mud bricks, kicking aside pieces of the broken mantel. 'Anything at all. Sometimes folks hide things in these old fireplaces—treasures—gold, jewelry, money, important papers, between the bricks, you know.' And Sergeant Flannery turned and walked toward Mr. Foote who was standing behind the counter. Sergeant Flannery leaned on his elbows and smiled. 'Sure, if I were to come across a thing of importance, Mr. Foote, 'twould find itself in the rightful hands, it would.' That is what he said, 'the rightful hands.' What do you make of that Mary Margaret?"

"I'm sure I dinna know."

The two women sat in silence, sipping tea and thinking their own thoughts.

Mary Margaret ate a biscuit, but Olivia seemed irritated, uneasy. She raised her cup, then set it down without drinking. She smoothed her skirt. Finally she said, "Sounds like a threat, Mary Margaret. I think Sergeant Flannery found those papers—the papers he hid away in the box at Los Alamitos—that very morning. When the fireplace collapsed."

"An' sure the rightful hands would not be Mr. Foote's. But whose then?"

Olivia did not answer.

"Look at this Olivia. Found it on me kitchen table, I did. This very morning. Inside me quarters—with doors and windows locked." Mary Margaret withdrew the note from her apron, unfolded it, and spread it flat on the table in front of Olivia. Olivia leaned forward. In less than a second, she pulled back as if burned by a sudden flash of fire.

"I know this hand. Walter Shiner wrote this note." Olivia seemed to open her eyes wider. "Mary Margaret, it is time you stopped this investigating business. Some men are . . . well. . . ." Olivia looked directly into Mary Margaret's eyes. "Some men are not gentlemen."

"An' don't I know that to be true. Didn't I live in dangerous places, dangerous times? Didn't I dig and lug turf, carry water in dripping wooden buckets as heavy as boulders. Didn't I see women, girls, little boys thieving and murdering? Carried a knife m'self, slept with it in me digs at th' Old Brewery. You know of the Old Brewery? In the Five Points? New York City? Worse than starving in a cave. A place you do not want to visit. I am not afraid Olivia. There be nuthin' can hurt me more than comin' home to me flat and finding Layla . . . though 'twas not her legal name, 'twas fitting for her . . . hanging she were . . . from the rafter. Seven months gone, she were, an' couldna' work and her man thought she be fit for a punching bag. Prettiest little thing I seen, she were, with golden ringlets round her face." Mary Margaret stopped abruptly, unable to say another word for fear she would scream or blubber like a babe.

"She was pregnant," whispered Olivia.

Mary Margaret was caught up in the memories. In a low sad voice, she continued, "Her note said, 'Maggie me friend, bury me in the lavender silk an' black stockings.' I come home that night after two shifts o' charrin' at the Astor House. We was savin' to move west, me and Layla." Mary Margaret paused, looked down at her rough, big-knuckled hands. "An' wasn't the saddest thing, the very saddest thing of all, that silk dress were gone. Stolen. With all our goods. But not our money—sewed it into me hems and sleeves, I did."

"I. I'm so sorry."

"No need of your pity. I survived, Olivia Foote, I did, and so will you. Whatever be your troubles. An' never did I kill no soul, not even me own. An' didn't I gaze on me Seán's cold face? An' don't I need a reason to go on? An' if 'tis nuthin' but vengeance . .

. . ." Mary Margaret went silent, her shoulders sloped, her eyes closed.

Olivia reached across the table and grasped Mary Margaret's hands.

"Miss Olivia, I only be needin' your help." Mary Margaret withdrew her hands and smoothed her hair. "Excuse me tirade. I do have the fierceness in me at times. I be naught but a wild thing in a dress. The army laundressing is comin' to an end. Seán Flannery and me, sure, 'twas to be a new start if only I'd . . . ."

"Hush, someone's in the garden," whispered Olivia.

The silhouette of a man in a wide flaring cape and Kussuth hat passed across the window then came to stop at the door. Someone knocked.

"Mrs. Foote? Are you there?"

"'Tis Private Davies," whispered Mary Margaret.

Olivia rose, smoothed her dress, and opened the door. Harlan Davies rushed into the kitchen and with a theatrical gesture, swept past Olivia who could not hold back a startled 'Oh!'

"Ah, wonderful, glorious! Miss O'Keenan, you are here. Miss Lulu thought you might be. We need you, I implore you, that is, the Dramatic Society requests. . . ." He stopped, cleared his throat and continued, "As you know, I have arranged for a majestic performance in Las Vegas Grandes. The band will play, a full complement of performers. You must join us as the lawyer Connelly, the audience anticipates you on stage. We shall trip the light fantastic on the stage at Felix Papa's."

"Felix Papa's!" exclaimed Olivia.

Davies paused and turned to Olivia. "Well, it was good enough for Miss Grace Hawthorne."

"But sir, she walked off the stage in the middle of her performance . . . calamitous rough-housing I think she called it."

"Oh, tut tut, Mrs. Foote. Please do not be discouraging."

"Mr. Davies," interjected Mary Margaret. "I thank you, but I dinna think . . . ."

"No, no, no, Miss O'Keenan, do not think. Emote. Commit yourself to our worthy endeavor. There is not a thespian in the

157

entire garrison to portray the Lawyer Connolly. You must, Miss O'Keenan, Mr. Papa is expecting the lady actor."

"Ah," said Mary Margaret, "it be at the insistence of Mr. Papa?"

"Yes, yes, it is part of the agreement, a codicil as it were, but a worthy, very worthy cause. A portion of the house is to be donated to assist in the education of the Fort Union children. You must not, you cannot, refuse us, Miss O'Keenan."

Olivia bent and whispered, "You may learn something."

"Ah, yes, a truly worthy cause. Very well, Mr. Davies," said Mary Margaret.

"Wunderbar!" And Harlan clapped his hands together several times. "So much to do! So much to do! Rehearsals, costume repairs . . . . Miss O'Keenan, dress rehearsal Friday, rest Saturday, and we reunite, *ala* costumes, Sunday, 0600 hours, at the parade grounds. Matinee immediately follows the grand street parade, our own 23rd Infantry Band, all the members of the production—Mr. Washington, Professor Chappa, the cast—of course some of the band members must make quick, quick changes. Oh dear, oh dear, so much to do." And flinging his cape aside, Harlan swept out of the kitchen.

"Oh dear oh dear. So much to do," mimicked Mary Margaret, and the two women enjoyed a few moment of genuine laughter.

"Oh Mary Margaret, you heal my heart," said Olivia.

Las Vegas Daily Optic
Our Fort Union Letter

Regular Correspondent to the Optic. Fort Union, April 20.—
In the *Gazette* of the 15th last, there appeared an unsigned news item in which a tale of murder—indeed a tale of two murders—at Fort Union was construed, or rather, more accurately—misconstrued. As the official Fort Union Correspondent, it is my duty to clarify said information. It is true that thus far in this year of 1881, the bodies of two deceased Soldiers were discovered in suspicious circumstances. However, it is premature to shout

Murder! from the rooftops or to divulge details and information which may be entered as evidence should an investigation become necessary. It appears there are un-named and un-authorized correspondents who attempt to undermine my letters from the Fort and, thereby, impune my character. Indeed, Mr. Anonymous accuses me of championing the wrong crowd. Let it be known that I do not champion any crowd or any individual in my dispatches. I attempt, with honesty and objectivity, to report events at Fort Union.

J. Clooney, Regimental Correspondent

Chapter 17: In which Shiner does what he's told.

As the final notes of "Taps" sounded throughout the garrison, Walter Shiner stomped across the parade ground, and when he reached the thoroughfare between the garrison and the Quartermaster's Depot, he turned west. His huge bulk did not bend against the wind but remained as upright and nearly as wide as a California redwood as he plodded toward the Post Trader's Compound. Shiney approached the Opera House, circled it, then went to the back door on the north side of the building. He pulled the handle, knowing it was not locked, and plunged into the dimness of backstage. He heard the muffled voices of the players in their dressing rooms beneath the stage as they prepared for their second dress rehearsal.

As he approached the stage, Shiner muttered, *"Gotta get dem rags an' stuff, you cretin' he sezz ta me. And that's and order!"*

Shiney headed for the cubbyhole and its barely visible door. He stooped and yanked at the latch. Inside, all was black. He reached in and stretched forward as far as his arm reached. He groped in all directions, withdrew his arm, and thrust his head in, but it was too dark to make out any shapes. He knew he had put the bundle inside the cubbyhole.

"What are you doing there, Shiney?" It was Timmy Sullivan arriving with his costume over his arm.

From underneath the stage, Pvt. Shiner shouted, "Chasin' rats. An' don't call me Shiney!"

"Aye, searchin' for your family, ya'r?"

Fists drawn, Shiner withdrew and stood to face Timmy, who was a full head shorter.

"Sure, I'm just havin' you on, I am," said Timmy and hurried up the steps and across the stage. Shiner heard Timmy's retreating footsteps.

Shiner stood motionless, listening to the voice inside his head. Then he searched the Opera House, and in a trunk behind the stage, he found some soiled rags, a discarded lady's gown, and a few feathers. He grabbed the stuff, shoved it into the cubbyhole, and set the pile afire. It took four of his ration of safety matches to get it going. As soon as a few flames and puffs of smoke squeezed up between the floorboards of the stage, he yelled, "Fire!" and ran from the building. After passing the Foote home, he stopped and turned. He watched soldiers flee the burning building. He watched the wind whip flames up and twist them into devilish shapes as they blistered and melted the paint. He watched the fire completely engulf the Opera House. He watched, unaware that he himself was being watched.

From the window of her parlor, Olivia saw Walter Shiner, illuminated grotesquely by the leaping flames. She saw the smile and the strange expression, like excitement or joy, on his normally bland face, as she heard calls of Fire! Buckets! Help! When she realized that Mary Margaret may be at the Opera House, Olivia hiked up her skirts and ran out of her home toward the gathering crowd.

In the thickening smoke, Olivia crashed into Timmy Sullivan in a soiled and torn gown. "Mary Margaret?"

"Tweren't there, Ma'am," he said in answer to Olivia's question. "'Least I never seen her. Wouldja' ever be havin' a bucket Mrs. Foote?"

"Oh, yes, yes, of course. Come with me." Olivia led Timmy to the pump beside her house, where two buckets sat. "There's another pump behind the hotel," she shouted above the roar of the fire. Timmy grabbed the buckets, filled them, and ran, his skirts flapping and flying behind him.

"Olivia. Olivia, over here."

Olivia turned at the sound of Mary Margaret's voice. "Oh, thank God, you're all right, but where are you?"

The wind blew smoke and dirt across the road, and Olivia's eyes burned as she wondered if she really heard Mary Margaret or if it were the scream of the wind. "Where are you?" she called again.

"I'm here, woman," shouted Josiah Foote from the darkness. "What in the devil are you doing out here? Get inside!" And he roughly shoved Olivia. "Get in the house and stay out of the way you damn fool!" Olivia stumbled then spread her arms out in front of her, reaching for something familiar. Mr. Foote ran toward his Opera House.

"Here, Olivia, here I be," whispered Mary Margaret as she caught Olivia's forearm.

Between coughs, Olivia said, "The fire . . . I thought you . . . . "

"'Tis all right, I am. Was changin' for dress rehearsal. Hadn't arrived yet. I be helpin' the brigade. Maybe you should go inside."

"No. Why does everyone think I'm an invalid! Let us gather pots from the kitchen and help put out that damn fire. I told the Commander months ago to run that water pipe down here from the garrison. First thing tomorrow, I shall call a meeting of the Post Council. These senseless fires must cease."

Mary Margaret smiled. "You be a *sauncy* gal, Olivia. *Sauncy* as they come."

"I do not know what that means, but I do not have time to discuss vocabulary." And as the smoke thickened and ebbed with the fitful whirling of the wind, Olivia and Mary Margaret ran to the kitchen door, gathered the large cooking pots, and joined the bucket line.

Fed by dry winds and the flammable stuff of theatre, the fire raged for hours. The water wagon arrived from the garrison, horses galloping and bells clanging. Soldiers, families, and civilian workers and nurses lined up and passed buckets of water from the nearest pumps. Others tossed dirt on the flames. Everyone worked well into the night, the wind thrusting smoke into their burning eyes and shooting sparks in all directions like a crazed fireworks display. Sometime after midnight, the wind calmed, and by twos and threes, the weary fire-fighters changed shifts.

"That'll be the end of play-acting. The end of performing," said Timmy Sullivan to the small group gathered on Olivia's front porch.

The darkness and the sooty faces and clothing made it difficult to determine who stood among the gathering, but it was clear that all had been struggling to save the Opera House. Timmy recognized Mrs. Foote by her wide skirt, knew Jack Holloway by his voice, and was certain the Foote's striker, Paddy O'Brien, stood in the road beside the porch rail. But there was another young man on the porch proper, standing in front of one of the tall windows, his features undetectable with the house light behind him and his hat pulled down low.

Olivia responded with a long sad sigh, and Timmy said, "I be thinking 'twere deliberate."

"The fire?" asked Olivia.

"Sure the fire, Mrs. Foote. I be thinking someone set that fire, like the others, you know, Templar's Hall, the bakery, an' that nasty stable fire over Tiptonville way."

"But who, Private Sullivan? Who would do such a thing?" said Olivia.

Mary Margaret leaned back against the window frame, pursed her lips, and from beneath the brim of her hat, stared at Timmy. She was determined to say nothing, to listen, and to learn what the men knew.

"'Twas, himself, Shiney, no doubt," said Timmy rearranging the tattered remains of his gown. "I seen him under the stage, I did. Lookin' for something he were. Or 'tis what he said."

"I cannot think what purpose Walter would have in doing such a thing," Olivia said, half to herself. She harbored pity for the large, inarticulate man. When he worked in the kitchen garden, Olivia had often and unsuccessfully tried to engage Private Shiner in conversation.

"Well now," said Jack Holloway, clearing his throat, "The man needs no purpose, Olivia. He does what he is told."

Ah Seán, I be learnin' all sorts of things this night. 'Tis certain Olivia has a soft spot in her heart for Shiney— Walter she calls him. But 'twere Shiney himself set the fire? Saw him I did, running just two steps ahead of the smoke. Sure, he needs no purpose, as Jack says, Shiney does what he's told. What's that you say? Right y'are, Shiney works for Mr. Foote.

Olivia said, "And what are you implying, First Sergeant Holloway?"

Mary Margaret took note of the edge to Olivia's tone and her use of the formal address, and she thought Olivia's manner was more lively than yesterday.

Holloway did not respond to Olivia's question. He turned to Timmy, "We best leave Mrs. Foote to her home duties." And as if by command, Sullivan straightened up and walked to the edge of the wooden porch. The two men bid their good nights to Olivia and stepped from the porch to the road.

"Would you be walking to the post, young sir?" said Holloway from the road.

Olivia laughed. "Why Jack, that is Mary Margaret O'Keenan in the costume of the lawyer Connelly."

Sullivan hooted loudly, "Fine investigator you make, *Sir.*"

Holloway chuckled without mirth and the darkness hid the scowl on his face.

Olivia turned to Mary Margaret, "Oh, stay a bit, I fancy a cup of tea and feel the need of company this night. Mr. Foote will work well into the morning I fear. Private O'Brien will see you to your quarters."

Holloway and Sullivan wished the women a pleasant evening and made their slow, weary way along the lane, passing the pile of charred wood and smoke that was once the Post Trader's Opera House. Mary Margaret and Olivia entered the house, and Private O'Brien sat on a bench beside the door, unbuttoned his jacket, and stared at the glowing embers.

After she closed the door behind them, Olivia said, "What earthly purpose would Pvt. Shiner have in setting fire to the opera house?"

"Sure, I dinna know, Olivia. Maybe he needs no purpose, as Jack says. Maybe he were ordered to. But I did see him. I did. He be running from the building just as the fire broke out," said Mary Margaret.

"Yes, I saw him too," Olivia sighed. She walked about the room, lighting lamps and candles. "But Walter is not a bad man. He's brutish, but harmless, I think."

"Do you know him that well, Olivia?"

"Oh, Lord no. We have talked, that is, I have talked to him. He is rather taciturn. But he has been nothing but a gentleman in my presence. He does a bit of weeding and watering for me. Mary Margaret, I feel certain that this fire is in some way connected to Sgt. Flannery's death."

"Indeed. I do m'self." The weariness and sadness in Mary Margaret's voice broke Olivia's heart, she impulsively reached out and hugged her, a touch from which Mary Margaret stiffened slightly but did not recoil.

"Come," said Olivia, "I need a good strong cup of tea, and a bit of brandy." She picked up a candle and led the way to the kitchen. "Good Lord, I'm forgetting my manners. Mary Margaret, would you like to wash up a bit? There's fresh water and soap on the washstand in my bedroom." Olivia showed Mary Margaret to the bedroom. "Mr. Foote says," but Olivia paused. "Uh, well, some day, I suppose, we shall have water piped into every house at the garrison. As soon as all the pipes are laid. But this will do." She set the candle on the washstand, closed the door, and returned to the kitchen.

Mary Margaret looked around. She never could resist a bit of snooping. Her eyes slid across the fine cherry wood finishes. She ran her fingers along the cool, silver roses embossed on the back of Olivia's hand mirror. She poured water from the fine porcelain pitcher into the generous basin, and soaped up. Mary Margaret removed the lawyer's hat and her head wrap, loosened her hair, and quickly washed her face and hands. The soft white towel felt like a touch of the clouds. Retrieving the candle, she made her way along the hall to the kitchen.

Olivia had set out two glasses of brandy and a flowered plate with thick slices of bread and cheese. The small square room, unlike the tidy bedroom, was warm and crammed with furnishings. A work-table and four sturdy chairs filled the room. Two cupboards trimmed with hand-painted grapes on the vine shared one wall, and a black and silver cook stove, where the kettle steamed, stood at an angle beside the tub and pump.

"Here, drink this," and Olivia offered a glass of brandy. "I had to restart a fire, so the kettle will take some time to boil."

They touched glasses in a silent toast. The brandy warmed Mary Margaret's insides and relaxed her tense muscles, recalling her childhood when a toddy was the cure for everything, except the consumption that took her Ma. Her shoulders slumped as she loosened her cravat and unbuttoned the vest.

"Mary Margaret, I fear your costume is in need of repair."

Mary Margaret looked down at the soot-encrusted suit. She noticed a small tear in the shirt sleeve and brushed ash from the lapel of the jacket, then she said, "'Tis no matter. There'll be no further performances for the Irish attorney."

"Perhaps not. Well, there is the one in Las Vegas Grandes."

Mary Margaret said nothing, recalling her promise to Harlan. The kettle spit out bubbling water, and Olivia wrapped a towel around her hand, lifted the kettle, and poured the boiling water into the teapot. Mary Margaret inhaled the soothing steam and closed her eyes in weariness.

Olivia set the kettle down on the warmer, absently caressing the scratch on her cheek. "So, what more have you learned? I'm afraid I was a bit, well, under the weather when you called last."

Mary Margaret sighed, reluctant to break the spell of warmth and safety.

"I mean about the sergeant's death."

"Ah, yes."

"Would you like another brandy?"

"No. No thank you." Mary Margaret shook herself and straightened in her chair. "Miguel saw someone, Shiney he thinks, hide a bundle in the Opera House on the very night of Seán's murder. 'Twere Seán's uniform I be thinking but . . . ."

"Of course! The evidence was destroyed in the fire!"

"Well, no. Miguel retrieved the bundle and brought it to Lulu's house, but 'twas nothin' but bit of rags and discarded uniforms."

Olivia poured a bit of tea—too weak she decided—and set the teapot down. "A bit more steeping. Please, have a bite to eat."

Mary Margaret looked at the cheese and brown bread, but her stomach turned at the thought of food. "In a bit, thank you." After a few minutes, she said. "'Tis known among the ladies at Loma Parda that several soldiers, as many as three p'rhaps, have been murdered and stripped of all they were wearin.'"

"Oh, dear Lord. This is horrifying," said Olivia, testing the tea again.

Mary Margaret watched the red-brown liquid fill the cups. "Olivia, what do you make of the papers we found at Los Alamitos?"

"Mind the tea, now. It'll be hot. Dear Lord, the wind has returned with a vengeance," she said, worrying about the dying embers. "I hope they posted guards at the Opera House."

Finally, Olivia sat, and the two women sat in silence, listening to the great gusts sweeping in from the open prairie and rumbling through the flat valley. Occasionally, a series of thunderous, pounding, damaging blasts flung dust and pebbles against windows.

Olivia said, "Things improved here at the post when the Protection Patrol got underway. Sergeant Holloway was assigned to lead it, and one additional soldier. Sgt. Holloway requested Sergeant Flannery."

Mary Margaret sat up.

"It may be you did not know this. It was a bit before you arrived."

"What wouldja' be referring to? What things improved?"

"The thievery mostly. Dr. Williamson offered a $1,000 for the return of his mare, stolen with five army mules. They never did find her. He had a bit of an altercation with First Sergeant Holloway about it. When weeks passed and they didn't find the mare, Dr. Williamson accused the patrol of dragging its heels. Said outright that the First Sergeant was lax in performing his duties."

"Do you think Jack be lax?"

"Well, I do not think it so, but . . . ." Olivia sipped her tea. "Yes, it is a very different post."

"'Tis as you say," said Mary Margaret. "'Twere some incidents at Suds Row. Haddie Wilson's fine parasol from England went missing, and Abelina Lourdes received some sort of nasty letter. Didja' ever get a letter yourself, Olivia?"

Olivia set her cup and saucer down gently before answering. The wind suddenly roared and somewhere an unlatched shutter banged against a wall.

"I did," said Olivia.

Mary Margaret waited, but Olivia offered nothing more.

"An' the papers we found at Los Alamitos? You said they showed Mr. Foote to be a thief?"

"Papers? Perhaps I made too much of them. Nothing stated outright. Only my opinion. Could be Mr. Foote paid something extra—a fee or perhaps a debt owed to the Secretary of War." Olivia set her gaze on Mary Margaret and said, "I am with child."

"Ah!" But the fear in Olivia's eyes halted any jubilation that might have arisen.

"But," said Olivia, "the father may not be Mr. Foote, and if it is Mr. Foote, I do not want to bear such a child."

"Olivia!"

"If the father is—well—another, I want the child with every bit of my being, but I am afraid. Mr. Foote is," Olivia paused, "well, he can be rigid and cruel. Mary Margaret, do you have knowledge of midwifery skills? I have heard that the laundresses know things. Even perhaps the knowledge of how to end such pregnancies."

Mary Margaret looked at the scratch on Olivia's cheek. "'Tis true. Some laundresses have such knowledge and practice such skills. But with little success and oftentimes bad outcomes. 'Tis a babe, Olivia, just a babe."

Olivia turned toward the window and gazed out at the blackness. "In any event, it is my problem. I apologize. I shall not burden you with it. You have too much to bear already."

"But Olivia . . . ."

168

"Hush now, Mary Margaret. No more talk of it tonight. Please."

"'Tis Jack Holloway the father?" asked Mary Margaret, recalling the time she came to Olivia's for a lesson and Jack was buttoning his uniform as he departed the Foote house. Olivia's expression softened.

"'Tis. Sure you know Jack be married? Sure it musta been the Prairie Madness come upon you."

Olivia blinked then said, "Mary Margaret, in America we do not say 'tis or 'twas. Remember? We say, 'it is,' or 'it was.'" Olivia reached across the table and took Mary Margaret's hands in her own. "I thank you for your concern. There is no such thing as Prairie Madness. That is nonsense. Tales invented by old bored men to scare little children." But hearing the wind's low rumble, Olivia felt what she would have described as an irritation in the heart, a vague sense of unrest.

Chapter 18: In which Sheriff Otero ruminates on corruption.

At straight-up noon, Juan Garcia Otero, the Sheriff of San Miguel County, considered the news his deputy had brought. The Fort Union Opera House burned to the ground. The Sheriff did not believe in coincidence. If it were his decision, the word should be stricken from all lexicons. He also questioned the idea of "God's will." He had been a boy when his mother spat on the floor of the *Capilla de la Cruz* as Father Ignacio tried to comfort her. "God's will be done," the old priest had intoned. "That is what I think of God's will," she replied with a lift of her chin as if daring God to strike her. "Come Juanito," and they left the chapel never to return, not even to the *camposanto* where his father's body lay. Some years later, Juan Otero, by himself, dug the grave and buried his mother at the ranch. Her body, but not her spirit, as the sheriff often said, lay alone on a windy knoll.

Until the day his mother spat on God's floor, Juan had studied with Father Ignacio every afternoon. Everyone in the village of Mora was certain that one day Juan Garcia Otero would make a fine priest, a religious leader, maybe a bishop. 'Juan has a vocation and a hunger for knowledge,' the old priest had often said. But after the day his mother spat on the floor of the chapel, Juan no longer read Latin at the priest's house, no longer served at morning mass. He lay his bible on a shelf in the back of the hay barn, he roamed the roads and fields of Mora with a small group of boys—*los perdidos* his mother called them—throwing stones into the river, chasing cows, and making mischief. Juan's mother warned him that those lost boys were heading for trouble. And when *los perdidos* turned to stealing vegetables and chickens, Juan retreated to his home, farm work, and reading what books he found. The skinny solitary boy grew into a man much like his father—short and strong, with thick arms and legs, eyes and hair as black as jet, skin the color of wet adobe. The books became his companions. When Fort Union opened its library, he spent his stolen hours there, reading novels, manuals, and newspapers from as far away as Chicago and Boston.

After his mother died, and after four years of drought, he reasoned that a small farm, so dependent on the natural elements, was best abandoned. He sold the cows, chickens, goats, workhorses, and farm equipment. He draped sheets and blankets over the hand-hewn furnishings and boarded up the *casita* his father and mother had built with their love and labor. He packed his books and clothes into his saddle bags, mounted his horse, and rode to the growing town of Las Vegas Grandes. He made a home on Pacific Street, and for a while, just living was enough. He read, dozed in the sun, walked *la plaza* and the dusty roads. Evenings he passed rowdy dance halls, gambling rooms, and hotels. He nodded greetings to townspeople and immigrant merchants. He usually took his meals at Tremble's, and occasionally, he stopped at the Imperial Hall to have a whisky and a talk with Mister Silva. Throughout his ramblings, Juan listened for word of his father's murderers. Once he thought he saw *el Negro,* his father's horse, tied to a hitching post on the west side of *la plaza,* and ran towards him. But as Juan closed in on the animal, a man in a long brown coat came out of the Exchange Hotel, mounted, and galloped away.

After a summer of this aimless life, Juan became disenchanted with the ruffians and the gunshots in the night, with the look of fear on the faces of the women. People who remembered Juan's father with respect came to him, urged him to help. So, in 1880, at the age of twenty-two, he offered his name on the ballot for Sheriff of San Miguel County. He won the election, defeating and therefore making a lasting enemy of Martín Lopez, who the following year became Mayor of the newly incorporated township. The young sheriff took his duties seriously. He hired honest deputies, defied the vigilante rule, studied the laws of the Territory, and he adamantly but diplomatically refused all bribes.

When his duties allowed, Juan Otero rode out to Fort Union Library to borrow the newest arrivals. He read philosophy, he read new ideas about the mind and spiritualism, and he read stories about a detective, not an officer of the law, but a private citizen,

Claude Dupin, who used reasoning based on data and facts to solve mysteries. Juan Otero embraced Dupin's notion of 'ratiocination' and forgot about "God's will." For this, he lost the woman he loved, Anna Maria Valdez. They had walked out together on sunny afternoons when the wind was a soft breeze. Some of his new ideas frightened her, but it was his lack of faith that she would not abide.

So once again, Juan Otero walked alone. Sometimes he caught a glimpse of Anna's lavender skirts and brown curls as she turned a corner. Whenever she saw the sheriff, she smiled with warmth and nodded acknowledgement. He, in turn, raised his hat in respect.

When Deputy Lucero burst into the sheriff's office and breathlessly spilled out the news of a fire at the Fort, Juan Otero was not surprised. The news fit into the puzzle of Sergeant Flannery's death. It was but one piece and the sheriff was not yet able to determine where it fit. Sheriff Otero was equally certain that one day he would be called upon in the matter of Sergeant Flannery.

When the deputy finished his report and stood, his chest heaving, Juan Otero looked up from his newspaper and said, "Go to the Post Trader's Compound at Fort Union. Find out what you can, and report back as soon as possible."

"But . . . jurisdiction?"

"Inquire as a concerned citizen. Do you not have friends at the Post Trader's Compound?"

Lucero hesitated, surprised that the Sheriff knew. "A friend, yes, sir," he replied. "*Señorita* Armijo. She works at the hotel."

"Which, I believe, is the building just to the south of the Opera House. Was she not in danger?"

Lucero nodded.

"Then it is prudent that you inquire after her safety. Is it not?"

"Yes, sir," said the deputy and departed, leaving the door ajar.

Otero set the *Las Vegas Gazette* down on his desk, stood, and walked to the door. Before closing it, his attention was drawn by the sounds of shouts and thuds. Suddenly, the doors of the Imperial Hall burst open and two men tumbled out, throwing

172

punches unsteadily. A small group of about six men and a few women followed and crowded around the fighters. Otero sighed, stepped outside the office, and pulled the door closed behind him. He wished he had not sent his deputy to the fort.

Otero approached the crowd, which expanded before his eyes. He rested his right hand on his weapon. A few of the onlookers turned in his direction then disappeared inside the dark, smoky hall. But the fight continued, dust floating up around the men like fog on a mountain pond.

The sheriff drew his pistol and fired three shots into the air, dispersing most of the remaining crowd but not affecting the fighting men. Then, as one man staggered backward and slumped against the wall, Otero stepped in front of him, and shouted, "*Alto, alto.* Stop," and again fired his gun into the air. Behind him, the fallen man passed out. In front of the Sheriff, the other man moved to draw.

Otero shot into the air again and said, in a deep, commanding, tone, "Johnson. Jake Johnson. Enough."

Johnson squinted at the Sheriff and considered his situation. He bent forward, reaching for the knife strapped to the inside of his boot.

Juan Otero said, "I'll shoot you if I have to, and my gun is aimed at a part of your body you do not want to lose."

Johnson brushed dust off his pants then straightened up. He smiled and turned away, then strode off to find his horse among the herd tethered in front of the saloon. Otero kept his gun aimed on Johnson until the horse and rider rounded the southeast corner of the *plaza.* The sheriff holstered his weapon and turned to help the fallen man, who staggered to his feet and without a word of gratitude, returned to the saloon, waving away Otero's help.

Sheriff Otero shook his head in a gesture of bewilderment and approached the Imperial. Inside, he paused while his eyes adjusted to the dim, smoky interior. Four long tables, crowded with men and women, filled the center of the hall, and to his left, the bar was three deep with dirty, rough-looking men shouting out their orders. Otero saw Vicente Silva seated at a small round table in the rear, waving to him and holding up a bottle of whiskey. The sheriff joined him.

In Spanish, Silva said, "Good afternoon Sheriff. Please, join me in a salute to the day?" *"Buenos días, Señor* Silva. Thank you."

"I'm looking for Jack Cole," said Silva. "Seen him?"

Otero swallowed the harsh whiskey and said, "He escaped again. But I have not seen him. There is a reward posted."

"It is just a matter of time before he steals every God damned horse and mule in San Miguel. He stole my palomino mare."

"And when did this event occur?"

"Two nights ago. In the morning, my gate was open and the mare's stall empty. I'll kill the bastard!"

"Then you will force me to arrest you for murder," said Otero with a faint smile as he recalled that it was a soldier's patrol that recaptured Cole the first time he escaped.

Silva laughed loudly and slapped the table, sloshing the drinks. "Have another, Juan Otero. You make me laugh and to laugh is always a treat."

Otero downed his second drink then stood. "I will look into this incident that was not so important that you should report it but that now gives you some irritation. Please, do not take the law into your own hands. *Muchas gracias.*"

On the *plaza,* Sheriff Otero did not pause. He circled the area three times as he generally did at least twice daily and returned to his office where he pondered his situation. He paced back and forth considering the advisability of intervening on behalf of Vicente Silva, a man known to have deviant tendencies and to harbor criminals.

Chapter 19: In which Harlan asserts himself, and Deputy Lucero reports.

<u>Saturday Evening, April 23, Fort Union</u>

Discouraged at losing the Opera House to flames, members of the Dramatic Society sat on benches and stools drawn into a circle in the center of one of the quartermaster's unused and echoingly empty warehouses. For most of the evening, rehearsals proceeded in a lackluster, dispirited manner, so Private Harlan Davies decided he must take charge. He rose to his feet and called everyone together. Hoping to mitigate the damage caused by the fire, Davies gave credence to the limited preparation time, he acknowledged the change in venue, and he pointed out the less than ideal rehearsal facilities.

"But," he shouted and paused, "I demand nothing less than perfection. Another run-through, *please.* Everyone, to your places. We must shine. We are the first ever thespian representatives of our garrison to travel to Las Vegas Grandes. We must perfect our Sunday Spectacular. You will need to summon up your powers of concentration and especially voice projection as the town will be experiencing its weekly influx of rough men, cowboys, and possibly bandits." His voice trembled, and his statement received a smattering of nods and gestures. "And so," concluded Davies, his voice rising above the talk, "the show goes on! Opening act— Washington—onstage please."

Private Davies proved to be a tireless taskmaster, clapping hands and shouting, "Move along. Washington, pick up the pace. Swing those clubs with vigor! You look like a little girl. No no no no, NO, Sullivan. Lilting, you are a young lady, not a dowager aunt. Like this . . . ." And Harlan executed a lovely pirouette culminating in a delicate, deep bow.

Timmy pulled a face and mumbled, "'Tis a fair queen he be wanting—Victoria herself."

With everything destroyed in the fire, the cosmetics and costumes were inadequate. Davies borrowed rice powder from a few of the officer's wives and a bit of rouging from one of the laundresses. Costumes consisted of an assortment of discarded

175

gowns and outdated suits. In the general dispirit of things, actors were dropping lines and bumping into each other. As midnight approached, Davies became more frantic, and the performers more irritable.

Jud Clooney, who had hastily offered his services as stage manager, saved the night. "Davies, don't forget the old adage: Bad dress rehearsal, great performance." Then he whispered, "If you keep this up, you'll wear them out."

With a dramatic slump into a nearby chair, Davies raised his arms then let them fall dramatically, in a gesture of 'all is lost.' "Enough!" he shouted. A roaring cheer rose from the actors and everyone scrambled to get out of their costumes.

"Stop people! Wait!" shouted Davies, with more force than he seemed capable of. "Remember Sunday's schedule—parade at 2:00 pm, civilian time. We must meet—in costume—at the Parade Grounds 0600 hours and pile into the wagons. Over the protesting grumbles of the cast, Davies, in a hoarse voice, said, "Be advised that the commanding officer has been most supportive of this event—making special arrangements, and schedules and whatnot. And assuring the *Alcalde* that there will be no rowdiness." The mumbling tapered off into silence. "Now, go," said Davies wearily.

Some actors wandered off to the makeshift changing areas, curtained off by blankets hung hastily over sagging ropes. Some trudged out into the starlit night in full costume. Mary Margaret, on her way to one of the exits, suddenly found herself face to face with Timmy Sullivan, and she accidentally stepped on the hem of his gown.

"Wouldja ever be careful, Miss O'Keenan. You be treading on me costume. Ruin it, and you may find yourself most unhappy!" He scooped up his skirt and petticoats, on loan from the Commander's wife, and stared full at Mary Margaret. She opened her mouth to respond, but Timmy said, "There's been talk that you be saying 'twas a soldier killed Flannery. You be asking for trouble." Then, before she could retort or explain, he made an about face and disappeared behind a curtain.

As she thought of the things she might have said, Mary Margaret was bumped from behind. "Sorry, Miss O'Keenan. I'm looking for Sullivan," said Jud Clooney. "He forgot his boa. Are you all right?"

"'Tis fine I am, Mr. Clooney."

"And how is your investigation proceeding?"

"I thank you for your interest." She paused, recalling the tales of Clooney's bravery during the Great Rebellion, his medal of honor.

'Tis a soldier-journalist, now, Seán. The man you called a sharp-shooter. Sure he's killed men afore, though I cannot think of a reason he'd have for killing you. But is he to be trusted?

"I will find out who killed Sergeant Flannery," said Mary Margaret, looking into Jud's calm eyes.

"I've no doubt you will. I'm putting together another story for my next correspondence to the *Optic*. Might there be something you would like me to muse upon?"

'Muse upon,' thought Mary Margaret, a smile pulling at her lips.

"In regards to the investigation?"

"Only this, Mr. Clooney. Sgt. Seán Padraic Flannery were a good and a brave soldier. A man to be honored, not to be murdered. An' I have evidence, I do, as to who the killer may be. But I would not like to divulge the nature of me evidence, not at this time, sir."

"Miss . . . uh, may I call you Mary Margaret?"

"You may not, Mr. Clooney."

'Of course, as you wish. Miss O'Keenan. Could be dangerous to print such information. Is Colonel Winters aware of this evidence? First Sergeant Holloway?"

"No, Mr. Clooney, only I, and now, you. Good evening to you sir."

"May I accompany you to your quarters?"

"No thank you. 'Tisn't far."

Clooney nodded a slight bow then strolled down the dark corridor formed by billowing blankets, the boa floating behind him like blue smoke. He thought he had not made a good impression on Miss O'Keenan. He wished it were not so.

Mary Margaret made to follow him, but her mind focused on the nature of her evidence and she strayed from the main passageway. She turned and turned, trying to recover her steps but became entangled amidst the maze of hangings and piles of animal pelts. She stopped and lifted the edge of a coarse rug.

'May I call you Mary Margaret?' Indeed, Seán, the cheek of the man. Do you suppose he be having a bit of business with Timmy? Something other than the return of a fine boa. An interview, perhaps, or a clandestine meeting?

Mary Margaret peeked behind the rug to find herself at a dead end—a solid wall in front of her and stacks of full flour sacks. From far off, she heard the sounds of muffled voices, as people bid each other good night and good luck. She turned around and retraced her steps. Where did all this stuff come from, she wondered, when she was suddenly caught from behind around the waist. Involuntarily, she emitted a croaking scream, then pushed and pulled at the thick strong arms surrounding her waist. She felt the heat of a large strong body pressed against her back. She was barely able to breathe when a voice in her ear, expelling hot breath through the blanket said, "Stop dis here meddlin I tellya. Dis here is a wernin. I could kill ya now."

As proof, the man quickly moved his hands from her waist to her throat. The rough fabric scratched her neck. 'Shiney,' she thought. Suddenly he shook her vigorously and tossed her to the floor.

She coughed to get her breath back, then turned on all fours and peeked beneath the blanket. She glimpsed a pair of dusty Jefferson shoes as the man turned a corner and disappeared. Mary Margaret scrambled beneath the curtains and searched in all directions, but saw no one. Then she felt a shift in the air, a freshness, and ahead of her, she saw a door begin to close on the ghostly starlight. She crawled to the door, grabbed the handle, and pulled herself upright and out. She saw no one.

Saturday night in Las Vegas Grandes was not the Sheriff's favorite time. Fights were more vicious, shootings more frequent, and it seemed no one spoke in a normal tone of voice. Otero reasoned that the cause of this phenomenon was the influx of cowhands and day-laborers with their weekly payroll and pent-up frustrations.

He had just completed the tedious task of interviewing and deputizing additional, temporary assistants. He snuffed out the kerosene lamp, retrieved his hat, and just as he was placing it on his head, Deputy Lucero burst into the room. The man was disheveled, sweat running down the sides of his flushed, anxious face, and he was covered head to foot in dust and ash. The odor of smoke permeated the room. In one arm, the deputy clutched a large, round bundle tied with rope, and in the other, a U.S. Army-issue rifle.

Otero smiled, *"Buenos noches,"* he said, tipping his hat in mock formality.

Lucero dumped everything on the floor and gasped, ". . . fire deliberately set, sir. Isabela, *Señorita* Armijo saw it all from the window of the storage room at the Trader's Hotel. She was getting some clean linen and . . . ."

"Is her reason for being there relevant to the investigation at hand?"

"No sir. She observed a soldier whom she described as big, *muy grande.*"

"Details? Height, weight?" The Sheriff rushed to his desk and gathered his stylus and notebook.

"Yes, sir. Big, she said, taller than the top of a horse's head. And *gordo,* she said, wide as a door. She did not see his face clearly, but she saw him run out of the Opera House seconds before the flames erupted. He ran to the Trader's Saloon. So," and Lucero stood a bit taller in his boots, "I snooped around sir, investigating. Found this stuff in a shed—headquarters for the Fort

Union Comedy Company according to my witness, *Señorita* Lopez."

Chapter 20: In which the show goes on again, Mary Margaret talks to Private Sullivan, and Olivia steps out.

Mary Margaret stood among the costumed cast members on the back of the open wagon decorated with red and white bunting, shiny rosettes, and the Union flag. Far ahead, leading the parade, marched the 23rd Infantry Band with pointed helmets and flowing white plumes. The cloggers, jugglers, and short-skit players clowned it up behind the band. Next, riding in a fancy, open carriage pulled by a well-groomed, high-stepping pair of bay geldings, came the duet baritones, Professors Erdman and Chappa. Bringing up the rear of the parade was the bright blue Dougherty wagon, carrying the cast members, waving and shouting to the crowd. Even the mules were festive in red bows and ribbons streaming from their bridles.

The parade circled the *plaza* grounds. Mercifully, it had not rained, for dust was easier to negotiate than mud. It was a warm, windless, cloudless day. Children, dogs, merchants, and finely dressed ladies lined the perimeter. As the procession passed the Plaza Hotel, Mary Margaret could not refrain from thoughts of the oysters she had enjoyed with Seán, as she waved and nodded sedately to the crowd. Timmy Sullivan curtsied and waved a fan in front of his face. The actors played up their characters and shouted lines from the production.

As the parade turned along the southern side of the *plaza*, the onlookers became more vocal. The band was welcomed with cheers from women dress in bright colors and showing a bit of flesh. Groups of boys shouted from the storefronts or ran alongside the wagon. But as the wagon made its slow, lumbering way around the *plaza,* the milling crowd separated and some people drifted off. When the old Dougherty passed the Exchange Hotel, a stout, well-dressed man in striped trousers, cut-away coat, and black top hat rushed forward and climbed up onto the seat. He stood, legs apart, balancing himself like a sailor on a rough sea.

Timmy shouted, "'Tis Sir Felix Papa himself. Ain't he the dandie?"

Papa nodded in Timmy's direction, but pointed at Mary Margaret. "Ladies, gentlemen, children—your attention. If you please, may I present to you," he paused with dramatic flare. "If you please, the lady actor, our own, Miss M. M. O'Keenan. See her perform this very afternoon at my hall inside the Exchange Hotel. Follow the wagon."

Felix Papa indeed, nothing but a huckster, thought Mary Margaret, as she nodded and smiled, but Papa's antics grabbed the attention of the crowd. People returned, several ladies strolled alongside, peeking at the woman in men's clothing. Papa continued his discourse, and the parade bulged with townspeople as well as rowdy lags and painted cats from the nearby halls. Mary Margaret eyed the crowd, reminiscent of her Five Points days.

The parade completed another turn around the *plaza,* gathering more followers, then made its way back toward the Exchange Hotel. *Don* Felix Papa jumped down from the wagon and rushed to the entrance doors. He and an attendant immediately began selling tickets and ushering people into the hall while the parade proceeded around the building and turned into the corral.

The actors descended and rushed into their dressing room, formerly a large storage closet. They did their best to freshen up their appearances. Soon the room was crammed with sweaty bodies. The odors of perspiration and grease paint mingled with the musty smell of the building.

Brushing dust from her trousers, Mary Margaret approached an unoccupied corner of the table. She removed her hat, exposing the black stocking that secured her mass of curls, and searched for some cleaning supplies. She spotted a small red brush and reached for it, but a gloved hand grasped her wrist.

"'Tis me brush," Timmy Sullivan shouted above the din. "Me personal brush. Leave me personals alone." And he flung her hand away. Mary Margaret looked around, but no one seemed to have noticed. Some had already departed for their places backstage, and those remaining were busy with preparations.

As she brushed the hat with one of her gloves, Mary Margaret decided to take on Private Sullivan. She lifted her gaze to meet his and said in an offhand manner, "An' where be you when Seán Flannery were murdered? 'Twould be Thursday last, the fourteenth day of April."

"You be suspecting me? 'Tis none o' yer damn business. But I'll tellya—'cause I got nuthin' to hide. I was on duty. Escortin' two wagons of flour from Mora."

"'Tis said you didn't report. Claimed illness."

"Sick? An' who be saying such a thing as that? I'd like to know. I was on duty and I reported as such. Ask Holloway. He'll tell ya I was there—least 'til La Cueva where himself turned south. Paddy O'Brien and Peterson seen me as well. Rode alongside 'em I did."

Mary Margaret hesitated. She did not know how to respond. She did not want him to know it was Jack Holloway who said Timmy had not reported. She would not take the chance of involving Olivia. "Me apologies, Timmy. 'Tis misinformed I am."

"Didja ever think I killed Seán Flannery? Didja?"

"Ah well, you be fair angry when he took the Lawyer Connelly's role."

"Mother o' God, Mary Margaret O'Keenan! Kill a man over a part in a play?" Timmy shook his head and pushed up his false bosom. "Yoo're cold, a cold, hard woman." He turned and strutted toward the other actors, cueing up for their entrances. The crowd cheered and clapped and whistled as P. J. completed his twenty-ninth, perfectly executed maneuver.

"Stop a bit, Timmy. Didja ever say that First Sergeant Holloway turned south? Departed the patrol did he? An' where did go?"

"Dinno' . . . don't need to be telling me his business. Gives us our orders, he does. The escort and the wagons continued on the Mora Road an' Holloway said he'd rejoin us at the arsenal."

"An' did he?"

"If he did, 'twasn't me that seen him. I dinna' see him again 'til later . . . when he arrived at the Dead House with the ambulance. 'Twas dress rehearsal—if you recall."

"An' who be in charge when the First Sergeant is absent?"

"That woulda been Seán Flannery himself . . . if he'd been on duty. That day . . . ah, 'twas Corporal Peterson."

Alert to the ever-present possibility of disturbances, Sheriff Otero stood at the rear of Papa's Hall watching both the performers and the audience. Something untoward generally happened at these gatherings, but today's crowd was a bit different, he thought. There were the usual riffraff but there were also families, soldiers, and some of the new riffraff arriving daily on the trains. The sheriff was especially vigilant. He posted twelve deputies at pertinent stations around the perimeter—although some of the officers were more intent on the entertainment than their assignments.

As Washington took a deep bow, Felix Papa swept open the drop curtains and stomped noisily onto the stage apron.

"And now ladies and gentleman—and officers of the law," he shouted. "The main attraction. What you've all come here to see. *The Irish Attorney of Ireland, 1770,* the fine dramatic presentation penned by none other than Mr. Harry Carleton, directed by Private Harlan Davies, and performed by the Fort Union Dramatic Society. A drum-roll please." One of the infantry drummers obliged. "And starring—well—I leave it to you," he gestured, a grand sweep with both arms to the audience, "to determine the boys from the girls."

Again forbidden to attend the performance, Olivia sat at her vanity table, staring into the mirror. She turned her face from side to side, swept back her hair, and examined the red line left by the angry cut of her husband's ring. She studied her ears and neck, detecting a purple-yellow bruise. She dropped her hair and leaned forward, peering into her own green eyes.

Then she straightened her back, as she'd seen Mary Margaret do so many times. She paused as, in her mind, she saw the white shirt fly through the air and float down to the carpet.

184

She picked up the brush and began smoothing out her hair to form a bun. But, she found herself forming round fat curls and pinning them into place on the top of her head. She pulled excess hair down into soft waves around her face. It seemed her hands had a will of their own. She wove a bright purple ribbon among the curls and tied a bow in front.

Olivia opened the vial of "The Bloom of Youth," dipped two fingers in, and rubbed the reddish paste in a circle on each cheek. She sat back and surveyed her work. She applied more to her lips. The wind whistling through a crack somewhere in the house mocked her attempts. She laughed, and that felt good, so she laughed again, louder.

She stood and twirled in front of the mirror, stopped and yanked the jabot from the neckline of her gown, exposing firm white décolletage. She shoved the chair back and moved through the house—walking fast, strolling, sauntering, posing . . . dancing.

She sauntered out of the house, leaving the door open behind her, and crossed the Compound to the saloon. The wind tugged at the bow, loosening one side.

Olivia hesitated at the entrance then pushed open the door. She paused, leaned against the frame then hitched up her skirt, exposing her boot and the calf of her leg. Then she sauntered up to the bar. Amos turned from washing glasses, opened his mouth, but said nothing.

Olivia rested one foot on the rail, leaned her elbows on the mahogany, and controlling a tremble, said, "Whiskey, if you please, Amos."

Amos poured a shot and slid the glass across the bar. Olivia took a sip as if it were a fine Bourdeaux, then coughed as the heat grabbed and burned her throat. She set the glass down and looked at Amos.

"On the house, ma'am," he said with a nod.

Olivia left the glass on the bar. She walked to her husband's office, turned the knob, and pushed the door open with both hands, slamming it against the wall. She stood, hands on hips. Mr. Foote lifted his head from his account books.

As soon as the Lawyer Connelly stepped out from behind the curtain, catcalls and shouts rose from different parts of the hall. Startled, Mary Margaret ran through several emotions, including fear, until she passed anger and settled on haughtiness. She stretched herself taller, projected her voice as loudly as possible, and went about the business of portraying the Irish attorney.

The audience quieted, except for the soft sniffle of a young girl. Scowling and shaking his head, a man in one of the front rows gathered his wife and exited noisily. The sheriff tipped his hat to the departing couple.

Backstage, Harlan Davies, for the first time in his entire life, said a prayer, "Please, Thespis, *please.*"

The Sheriff unbuttoned his jacket and rested his hand on the handle of his gun.

When Josiah Foote looked up, he said with a sneer, "What the . . . ? Why in damnation are you all tarted up like a Saturday night whore? A ride in the country? Or could it be you're giving one of your <u>piano</u> lessons?" Foote spoke low and mean so as not to be heard by the employees or customers. "Come inside and close the door."

Olivia stepped into her husband's office. "A Saturday night whore," she said with a tremble in her voice that her husband unaccountably found exciting. "Is that not what you made of me?" She gasped for breath, but it seemed there was no air in the cramped and dusty room. "So be it," she murmured. "Do I gather that I have attracted your attention, Mr. Foote?" She faltered, crumpling against the wall like a bunch of water-starved flowers.

"Close the door, woman. Close it."

Olivia did not move. "You are a thief, Mr. Foote. I have seen the papers, read them."

Foote shoved back his chair, stood, and rushed to close the door. He yanked Olivia by the arm, tearing her dress at the shoulder. "What papers? My God! Look at you!" He shoved her down onto a chair and leaned over her. "Do not play games with me. You will lose. And your family as well."

186

Olivia swallowed hard and blinked back the tears threatening to spill down her cheeks. But his statement turned her fright into cold anger. As she opened her mouth, Foote placed each of his hands on her wrists, holding them tightly, like bindings, against the arms of the chair. In an even, controlled tone, the muscles of his cheeks twitching, Josiah Foote said, "To which papers do you refer, *Mrs.* Foote?"

"Do not threaten my family."

"Your family! The family that sold you like a fat sow? Oh, I see you didn't know. Well truth be told, neither did your father. There are two reasons I married you. First, I knew that once we were betrothed, your father would place his trust in me, would borrow the money for his foolhardy freighting business from me instead of the bank, and ever so gladly offer the deed to his land as collateral. He'd been reluctant to enter into negotiations with me, a Post Trader, until I humbly asked for your hand in marriage." Josiah Foote stopped to watch Olivia take in this news. He saw several emotions play across her painted face but could not identify them. "Yes, *Mrs.* Foote, you were the nail that sealed his coffin. Any fool would have foreseen failure with the railroad coming."

"You knew he would fail. Why then . . . ?"

"The ranch, of course, you dimwit. You force me, over and over again, to speak to you as to a child, a half-wit child."

"And the second reason?" asked Olivia.

"Ah, yes, the second reason. With your broad hips and ample bosom—good breeding stock."

"A brood mare," whispered Olivia.

"Precisely, and a worthless one at that. Now, enough of the niceties. What is it you think you know? And to what papers do you refer?"

Olivia did not reply.

"It would seem the Mrs. Foote is not forthcoming. I shall put it to you as simply and straightforward as befits an idiot. Where are those damnable papers?"

Olivia's face went white, and her eyes closed.

Mr. Foote shook the chair. She opened her eyes, said nothing.

"Ah. The silence of the beleaguered. Shall you play the martyr my dear wife? No matter. I suspect Miss O'Keenan has sequestered my documents."

"You did not find them. Sent your poor lackey to search but found nothing."

Josiah Foote trained his angry eyes on Olivia. "Where are the documents?" he said in a low, threatening tone. "Be aware, Mrs. Foote, that your father is in arrears by several months. I am within my rights to foreclose at any time."

For the remainder of the performance, the audience was restless but not offensive. Yet the Sheriff did not let down his guard, knowing that a tiny spark—an inadvertent shove, a whispered curse—could set off a crowd. He strolled easily from deputy to deputy, reminding each of his purpose. As the performers approached the final scene, a scuffle between two blowzy women broke out in the rear of the hall. Otero and two deputies escorted the women swiftly out of the building. The sheriff ordered the deputies to 'See the ladies home.'

"Yoo're safe enoof now, Miss Nellie," shouted Mary Margaret and spread her arms in mock embrace. The ensemble struck the final tableau. Mary Margaret faced the audience and delivered her final line, "You are a woman more sinned against than sinning."

Before the curtain hit the stage, a man's voice shouted "Indecent! Shameful!" Several voices joined in, shouting curses. The curtain thumped the stage and rose again. The members of the cast, in a row and in unison, bowed to a mixture of 'boos', whistles, applause, and foot-stomping. Someone threw a whole cabbage at the stage. It hit Timmy Sullivan in the stomach, then fell to the stage and rolled off the edge. Sullivan ripped off his wig and feathers, jumped off the stage, and engaged in fisticuffs with a man in the second row. Several actors rushed to Sullivan's aid, and within seconds, the hall was in an uproar—feathers flying, gowns tearing, and chairs overturning. Onstage, Mary Margaret stood apart from the cast and tried not to laugh at the absurd scene in front of her.

Ah Seán, 'tis a fair donnybrook, it is.

The sheriff pushed open the double doors at the rear of the hall and shouted, "Outside. Everyone, outside."

Don Felix Papa took the stage and yelled, "Settle down people. There's women and children present!"

In the melee, families rushed toward the exits, as fist fights broke out among audience members, actors, and deputies. Above the screams of women and the cries of children, Otero shouted orders to his men, forming them into a line, arm over arm at the rear of the hall. With a nod from the sheriff, the line of deputies moved slowly toward the stage, gathering up those members of the audience who had not escaped. As his deputies forced the crowd closer to the stage, Otero suddenly appeared on the proscenium—legs spread, hands on hips.

"That will be enough!" he shouted. "I will have order!"

Mary Margaret covered her smile with both hands as people cursed, shouted, and threw punches. Finally, Otero drew his pistol and fired three shots into the air. The bullets lodged in the tin ceiling where they remained until the day, far in the future, that Felix Papa's Hall was demolished by fire.

Olivia shifted slightly on the chair, sat taller, and said, "I do not have the papers, nor do I know . . . ."

"Oh, you know where they are. Now, you will secure the documents and bring them to me or your Daddy loses Winfield Ranch." He paused then added, "As well as that God forsaken freight company."

Looking into his eyes, Olivia knew that her husband was capable of doing anything to achieve his goals—even, she suddenly thought, murder. "You killed Sergeant Flannery."

Foote abruptly released Olivia's wrists, straightened up, and made several perfunctory adjustments to his vest. "Get those papers," he said, turning his back to her. Then he walked behind his desk, sat, fiddled with the ink well, and said, "And clean yourself up before decent people see you."

Olivia stood. "Decent people . . . like Miss Chela Chavez?"

189

With barely controlled contempt, Foote said, "You had best be careful what you say and how you show yourself in public, Mrs. Foote. You are beginning to appear as mad as I suspect you to be."

Chapter 21: In which Mary Margaret talks to Jack Holloway, Jack talks to Colonel Winters, and Olivia reaches a crisis.

After the door closed behind Olivia, Josiah Foote picked up a pencil and drummed it upon his book of accounts. Then he shoved the chair back against the wall, loosening a few flakes of *adobe,* and stormed out of his office.

"Shiner," he shouted. "Where the hell is that God damned cretin? Shiner!"

Amos did not look up from drying glasses. "Out back," he said.

Josiah Foote turned and strode across the room and along the length of the bar until he reached the back door. Outside he found Shiner and two cronies lounging against a crumbling stone wall, joking and shoving each other like school boys.

"Shiner," shouted Foote. Shiner motioned to the other soldiers to disappear. After the soldiers turned the corner of the building, Foote said, "Get to my house." He paced back and forth in front of Shiner. "Get to my house. Get those God damned papers."

"Dem papers Miz O'Keenan got?" asked Shiney.

Josiah continued pacing. "No. My wife has them . . . of that I am certain. Or she knows where they are. And she understands their implications." He stopped abruptly and faced Shiner. "Go to my home. Secure the documents. Do whatever you must."

Walter Shiner squinted. It was a form of question.

"I said, get those God damned papers by whatever means necessary. Take all necessary actions to keep such information secret." Foote paused. "Do you understand me?"

When Shiner did not move, Foote walked up so close to the man that he could smell Shiner's barely washed body and traces of old liquor. "Get the papers and shut her up," Foote said in a low, calm voice. "Do you understand me?"

Back in the sanctity of her bedroom, Olivia poured lukewarm water into the basin and scrubbed until it shone red. She brushed her hair and pinned it into the customary bun at the base of her neck, then changed into the skirt and blouse of her brown traveling costume. As she buttoned up the skirt, she found herself struggling with one of the waist buttons. It is beginning, she thought, caressing her abdomen. She paused, then stooped and pulled a brown leather satchel from beneath her bed.

Olivia packed methodically—three pairs of under drawers, a chemise, two petticoats. But when she could not fit her favorite silk evening dress into the suitcase, she yanked out one of the petticoats and stuffed in the gown. She stared at the contents, added two pairs of drawers, a long-skirt chemise, and a muslin day dress. She rearranged the contents several times, but no matter how many times she repacked, she could not close the bag. A tear slid down her cheek. Impatiently, she wiped her face and set about repacking again.

When Olivia finished, the silk gown lay in a crumpled mess on the bed. She shrugged into her paletot then grabbed the handles of the bag only to discover that she was unable to lift it. How do these women do it, she wondered, thinking of the mothers with babies crossing the prairie, dragging kitchens and clothing and remedies with them. She pulled and yanked at the case until it fell to the floor, then she dragged it to the door.

"Patrick," she called. Leaving the case in the doorway to the bedroom, she climbed over it and walked through the silent house, calling again for Patrick. As she passed the kitchen, a hard rapid knock at the front door startled her, and expecting Patrick, she rushed to open it.

"Jack!" She said. "I . . . ."

Jack Holloway brushed past her and swept, uninvited, into the parlor. He removed his hat melodramatically and dropped it onto a chair. "I must talk to you, Mrs. Foote. You are in grave danger." He noticed the healing scratch and yellowing bruise on her cheek, but said nothing. Before Olivia was able to reply, Jack continued, "The documents. My apologies at my abruptness. But I must insist that you give to me the papers you found at the Gonzalez place. Give them to me now."

"What documents?"

"Do not play the innocent with me, Olivia. The Post Trader's
. . . ." Olivia's broad smile stopped him. He grabbed her upper
arm. "I must have those documents."

"It seems everyone is looking for some sort of papers
belonging to the Post Trader. I do not have whatever it is you are
looking for, First Sergeant Holloway, but I do wonder why *you*
'must have those documents.'"

"Do not play coy. My commission is at stake."

"Commission?" Olivia barely hid her derision with a half
smile. "Do you really think such papers are worth an officer's
commission? Believe me, they are not."

"Then you have them!" Holloway grabbed her by the upper
arm.

"No, I do not," said Olivia. "And I think you should leave
now. Please remove your hand."

Jack dropped her arm but took a step closer. "Olivia, I must
have those papers. If ever you cared for me or for what we once
meant to each other, ..."

A knock at the kitchen door interrupted him, and Private
O'Brien called, "Mrs. Foote, wouldja be needing me?"

Olivia whispered, "Jack, do not dare to call upon our past."
She crossed swiftly to the kitchen and opened the door. "Yes,
Patrick. I have need of your help. Come into the parlor a
moment."

Patrick followed her. "Good day, sir," said Patrick.

Holloway nodded, replaced his hat, and said to Olivia, "Mrs.
Foote, I shall return after Retreat so that we may continue our
discussion." Then to Patrick he said, "You had best not be absent
from Retreat ceremonies, Private O'Brien."

As she closed the door behind Holloway, Olivia turned to
Patrick. "Please go to the storage shed and bring me a trunk. The
small green one. Set it here in the parlor. Then, please return, as
soon as possible with the buggy."

The cast members, too tired and dirty to chatter or josh with
one another, descended from the wagons and trudged into the
warehouse. In almost complete silence, except for the echoes of

their footfalls and the occasional 'pass me this,' the soldiers found their uniforms and changed behind the curtained off areas.

Mary Margaret did not enter the warehouse. She jumped from the wagon and immediately walked south toward Laundress Row. As she crossed the thoroughfare, she felt a tug at her jacket.

"Miss Mary Margaret," said Micah. "I watched. Like you said. At the Comedy Company quarters. They brought in . . . ."

"Yes," interrupted Mary Margaret. "'Twas Peterson and Shiner I ken. I dinna see their burden, but they hid something in the wall."

"No, Ma'am. The two soldiers from Mr. Seán's patrol. One carried a bundle of clothes. One carried a rifle and boots, and one of the boots was . . . uh . . . bent at the ankle."

> *'Ah Seán. 'Tis a wonder how the boot conforms to fit the leg.' You smiled and said, 'Years of the wearin' an' softenin' with soaps an' grease an' oils, me girl.' An' the ankle, 'tis nothing to be done for it? 'No, 'tis a forever thing,' you said with a sadness that broke me heart. Then you leaned across the table, took me hands, and whispered, 'the bend never stopped the dance.' Ah, Seán, undaunted, y'are. An' you pulled me up from the bench and waltzed me round the Imperial Hall.*

"Miss Mary Margaret?"

"Ah yes, Micah. First Sergeant's patrol, you say?" She stopped so abruptly that Miguel was forced to take a step backward. He nodded assent but he said nothing more. He waited, studying Mary Margaret's face, and for the first time, he saw an expression of puzzlement furrow her brow and a trace of fear creep into her eyes. "When, Micah? When did you see this?"

Miguel shivered slightly at the hard tone in her voice and the absence of any trace of her lilting accents. He thought Miss Mary Margaret sounded very American, abrupt and on the edge of being rude.

194

Shiner crossed the dusty road and passed along the north side of the Foote home. He passed the low stone wall surrounding Olivia's kitchen garden without a glance at the place where he had enjoyed a few brief hours of respite. He seemed to grow taller as he continued toward the enlisted men's quarters. Once he arrived, he silently entered his own quarters, sat on his cot, removed his Jefferson shoes, and retrieved a box of boot-blacking materials from underneath. He brushed savagely, loosening months of hardened prairie dust.

"Well I'll be," said Timmy Sullivan entering the quarters with Mrs. Winters' bedraggled gown over his arm. "'Tis the strangest sight I seen. Wouldja ever look at this?" Sullivan continued, pointing at Shiner. "A monkey polishing his shoes."

Shiner said nothing. He pulled a dirty rag from the box, spit on it several times, and scraped it against a chunk of dried and cracked soap. Then, in a circular motion, he rubbed the thick gooey substance into the leather. After cleaning and polishing his shoes, he set them aside and rummaged in the trunk at the foot of his cot. He pulled out his dress uniform and brushed away the dust and lint. Then he dug out a needle, thread, and his old sergeant's stripes that he'd hidden rather than turn-in. He whipstitched the stripes into place then laid out the clothing on his bed and polished his belt buckle and the buttons of his sacque coat. He brushed his Kossuth hat and shined its curled trumpet insignia of the infantryman. Then Shiney cleaned his weapon, a .36 caliber, Colt Navy revolver.

Soldiers came and went through the quarters. Some took no notice of Shiney, doing what most of the other soldiers were doing, getting ready for Retreat. A few shouted or whistled or commented at Shiner's unusual diligence. He ignored them. He thought no clearly defined thoughts as he performed the routine, readying himself for his final duty of the day. He donned his uniform then sat on the cot and pulled on his shoes, tucking the bottom of his pantaloons into the tops of his socks. He stood and buckled on his belt and holster outside his coat, then he loaded his weapon and slid it into the holster. He looped up the left side brim of his hat and settled it squarely on his head.

Private Walter Shiner turned and surveyed his section of company quarters. He crammed his day clothes and cleaning equipment into the trunk and closed the lid. He circled the cot once, smoothing a few wrinkles in the bedding, adjusting the pillow. He pulled on clean cotton gloves and followed a few paces behind the other soldiers. As the group approached the flag staff and hustled into formation for Dress Parade and Retreat, Shiner dropped further and further behind.

Standing at her window and taking note of the scurrying soldiers, Mary Margaret turned to Miguel and said, "'Tis nearly time for Retreat. I must find First Sergeant Holloway. There's a question or two I be needing to ask him."

"Sergeant Holloway is at the stables. I saw him ride into the corral."

"Micah, me boy, there isn't much you miss, now is there?"

Miguel smiled a quick flash of white. "I shall go with you Miss Mary Margaret.

"No, 'tis late. An' why is it you linger here at the Fort on a Sunday afternoon?"

"Following orders, Ma'am."

"That you be, young sir. Followin' orders. 'Tis a good bit of observation on your part, boyo. Jack will need to know about these men. Can you be describing them?"

"Better, Miss Mary Margaret. I know them. It was Private Wilson and Private Mathison."

"The new recruits. They be reporting directly to Jack." She paused, then said, "Time you were getting to your home and bed." She bid Miguel a good night and turned down the lane toward the stables. But he followed, insisting, then pleading, to accompany her. So the two rose dust as they hurried to catch Holloway before Retreat sounded.

In the thoroughfare bordering the corrals, Mary Margaret and Miguel encountered Jack astride his big bay gelding. He reined in the horse, and Mary Margaret rushed up to him, resting her hand on the animal's neck. She was surprised to feel sweat and grit.

"Been riding out, have ya'?" And in the warm light of the setting sun, she noticed a flush in his cheeks, and dust on his usually well-shined buttons.

"What can I do for you? I have but a few moments to get into formation." Jack's cheek muscle twitched.

"Just a bit of information for your investigation, Jack," and she told him all that Miguel had told her.

Holloway looked at the boy, standing straight and tall beside Mary Margaret. "I know nothing of a bundle of . . . of stuff. He is a boy, Mary Margaret. A Mexican. He's lying."

"Jack Holloway! What a thing to be saying! 'Tis ashamed of you I am. Sure the boy was born in this fine country, same as you Jack Holloway."

"No, Miss O'Keenan. He was born in the territory that we fought for and took in the name of our fine country."

"Jack! Wouldja be saying you dinna trust the word of . . . ."

Mary Margaret stopped in mid-sentence as Miguel stepped forward. Looking up into Jack Holloway's eyes, the boy said, "I am Miguel Pedro Vigil y Gomez. My Pappa is Pedro Juan Vigil, and my Mamma was Luisa Maria Gomez. I was born in Santa Fe, the city of holy faith, New Mexico Territory. I am not blind. I saw Private Wilson and Private Mathison carry a bundle, a rifle, and two boots into the Comedy Company Headquarters behind the ruin of the Opera House."

"Out of my way," Jack commanded.

Mary Margaret said, in a firm, resolute tone, "'Tis a question or two I have for you, Jack Holloway, regarding your whereabouts on the morning Sean Flannery was . . . ."

"My whereabouts!" shouted Jack. Then, with conscious control, he said, "Mary Margaret O'Keenan, allow me to remind you of your position. You have no position. The laundress squad has been dissolved. Your hitch is up in less than a month, and then you will leave the garrison. Now step back before I have you thrown into the brig."

Inwardly, Mary Margaret shuddered. She withdrew her hand from the horse's neck but stood her ground, and with a new hardness in her eyes, said, "Shall I be expecting to hear from you

197

soon, Jack Holloway, regarding the investigation into the murder of Sergeant Seán Flannery?"

Holloway said, "I shall perform my duties to the utmost of my abilities. And report accordingly—to my superior officer." With his back straight and head high, Jack urged his horse into a neat, collected trot. After proceeding a few paces, he halted and turned in the saddle. "Miss O'Keenan. Where are the papers you took from Los Alamitos? The papers Flannery secured with Mr. Gonzalez?"

"I'm sure I do not know to what you be referring."

"Well now, I believe you know exactly 'to what I be referring.' I intend to have those documents—one way or another. I will call on you after Retreat. You had best have the papers ready for me. I mean to have Flannery's log as well."

Jack dug his heels into the horse's sides and they moved off.

At the edge of the Parade Grounds, Private Shiner stood at attention and stared ahead at the regimental soldiers and the American flag, flapping erratically in the swirling winds. When the bugler called for Parade, Shiner saluted, executed a perfect half turn to the left, and marched toward the Trader's Compound. With all eyes on the flag, no one noticed the well turned out soldier as he marched with precision and pride away from the ceremony. No one noticed him, that is, until he passed in front of Olivia's parlor windows at the moment when, tired and frustrated, she looked up from packing the trunk.

She stood, hands on hips, calling for Patrick. "Oh, dear Lord," she said. "He's at Retreat of course. I'd forget my head if it weren't . . . ." But Olivia stopped in mid-sentence when she saw Walter Shiner. She thought he looked unusually well but was marching in the wrong direction. When the bugle call ended, she moved toward her front door. She pulled the door open and stepped out onto the porch as Private Shiner entered the saloon. As she reached the edge of the porch, a gust of wind sprayed grit against her skin and ferociously twirled her skirt and petticoats. It was when she bent to grasp her skirt that Olivia heard the first shot.

Chapter 22: Walter Shiner's shoes; Jack Holloway's dilemma.

"Oh, dear Lord," whispered Olivia and ran across the road, dust rising behind her like a small grey storm. When she reached the door of the saloon, she heard the second shot. "Oh Lord," she repeated as she rushed inside and approached the small group of men gathered at the entrance to her husband's office.

Someone grabbed her and a strange voice said, "You don't want to see this miss."

"I am Mrs. Josiah Foote and this is my husband's office. Please sir, let me pass."

The stranger let go of Olivia's arm. She pushed and shoved her way among the men until she reached the open door and stood beside Amos. Although her eyes took in everything, the first thing Olivia comprehended was Walter Shiner's shoes. Rather small for such a big man, she thought, and cleaner than I've seen them. Within seconds her mind translated the scene before her—the spray of red, like watered-down paint, glistening and dripping in uneven streams down the wall behind her husband's desk. She saw bits of pink jam and shards of porcelain dotting the red blotch. With an inner gasp, not audible even to Amos, Olivia realized it was not jam and porcelain she saw. She shifted her gaze to what she could see of her husband's face. His body had been flung backward against the chair by the force of the bullet that entered through his open mouth. A thin stream of blood gurgled and bubbled from somewhere behind his tongue and slowly slid down his chin, puddling on the bright white shirt. It was the only movement in the room.

"Is he dead, Amos?"

"I'd say so, ma'am."

"If you please, Amos, feel his pulse."

"No pulse that I can detect, Mrs. Foote," said Amos, looking up from the his boss's wrist.

"It seems he was writing something," and she pointed to the pencil clutched between his finger and thumb.

"Yes, ma'am." Amos walked to the other side of the desk, stepping over something on the floor, leaned forward, and said, "Looks like beginning of a letter. To a bank." He picked up the sheet of paper, speckled with red spots, and held it out to Olivia. Without looking at it, she folded the paper and stuffed it into one of her pockets.

"Oh Lord," she cried, noticing that it was the large square body of Private Walter Shiner that Amos had stepped over, sprawled on the dirt floor, a bloody mess where his head used to be, a revolver lying several inches from his right hand. "Amos. Do not touch anything. Remove the onlookers and inform the Commander of what has happened here. Now. Amos. Now please."

Amos pushed and shoved the crowd, shouting, "Nothing to see here. Move along now. Saloon's closed."

Olivia pulled the door shut behind her then knelt beside the body on the floor. She took hold of Shiner's hand and made a silent prayer. Then whispered, "Thank you, Walter." She rose and searched the drawers and cabinets, hoping to find the deed to her family ranch. She found only invoices, ledgers, and correspondence related to the business. She stood and sighed then withdrew from her pocket the scrap of paper Amos had given her.

Mary Margaret and Miguel strolled in silence toward Suds Row, each deep in thought. At the door to her quarters, she insisted that Miguel stay the night with her.

"Miss Mary Margaret," he asked, "Do you think that I do not have a home?"

"Well, I . . . . 'Tis late, an' . . . ."

"You should not believe *el mitote*." Then as he saw Mary Margaret's inquiring expression, "Gossip. My Pappa did not kill Mama. She and my tiny sister died at the hands of *la partera*—the midwife—as you say. Nothing could be done. Even Doctor Williamson, who came later, said so. 'Nothing could have been done.' Pappa does sometimes drink too much, sometimes forgets to come home, but we have a home—Pappa and me."

Mary Margaret apologized for considering the truth of the gossip she had heard. Miguel continued, "Pappa is *triste*, sorrowful you would say, much of the time, but he loves me and he does the best he can. We are a family, and I go home now."

Mary Margaret bent and hugged Miguel tightly. "I am sorry. Truly. 'Tis ashamed I am, for listening to gossip—mee-to-tay, as you say. 'Tis true, it flies about the garrison on these wicked, relentless winds. 'Tis Prairie Madness, of that I be sure."

Surprised by Mary Margaret's sudden warmth, Miguel took a small step backward. "Gossip, yes, is evil. But the winds—they are not bad. They just are."

"Perhaps," said Mary Margaret as she unlocked her door. Miguel bid her good night and walked south along Suds Row.

'Mary Margaret O'Keenan, wouldja' ever believe I be courting you if I be married? Wouldja now?' And so I replied, 'tis said among the laundresses, you be having a wife and babbies in the ould country. 'Tis said you send money. 'Mary Margaret,' you told me, taking both me hands in your own, 'lots o' things be said among the laundresses, the soldiers, the officers, and their wives. 'Tis a place full of things being said. Don't make them true. I send money to me Ma's sister. She's as poor as the sod an' not a soul to help her. She be the last of the family. Makes a bit of a livin' sellin' potions, she does. 'Tis free I am to marry.'

Mary Margaret stole one last peek at Miguel, a skinny whisp of a boy in tattered clothing, then she entered her quarters and looked around for signs of distress. But all was as she had left it. As she changed from Seán's costume to her brown muslin dress, she heard the plaintive notes of "Taps." At the washstand, she rinsed dust from her face, brushed out her curls and confined them as best she could inside her bonnet. Then she set out for the hospital.

Mary Margaret entered by the front doors and walked the length of the central corridor. Dust motes rose and fell in the waning daylight, and she heard an occasional moan as she passed the wards. Her boots made sharp clicking sounds on the bare wooden floor. The doctor's door was open. Wearing his dress uniform, he stood behind his desk. When Mary Margaret appeared in his line of vision, he asked if she were ill. No, she told him and requested a few moments of his time, his expert opinion on a biological matter.

"A biological question, you say? I've but a few minutes before . . . . Intriguing. Come in."

"'Tis a question of biology, I believe, sir. But truly, it may be otherwise."

Williamson smiled and offered her a chair. Mary Margaret thanked him but declined, and quickly drew out the balled up bunch of red-orange hair she had been carrying with her since she released it from Seán's clenched fist. She stepped closer to the desk and held it out to him. "'Tis only this," she said. "Can you tell me if it be human hair?"

Williamson looked into Mary Margaret's clear blue eyes that held no hint of her purpose. Williamson picked up the hair with his thumb and forefinger. He sniffed it. Then placed it onto the green ink blotter on his desk. He bent close, separated the hairs, and fingered the individual strands. Then he straightened up and looked into the intent expression on the laundress' face. He grasped the ball of hair, squeezed it, then opened is hand.

"It is coarse, too coarse to be human. By the color, the thickness, and the length of the strands, I'd guess—and it is only a guess, but an expert one—that this is a clump of horse hair. Perhaps from the mane . . . it does not have the length for tail hairs."

"Ah," she said. Her shoulders slumped, and it appeared she might faint. Williamson rushed from behind his desk, encircled Mary Margaret with his arm, and settled her in a chair.

"Sir?"

"I believe you were about to faint," replied the doctor.

"I have never fainted in me life, sir. Though 'twere a time or two when a bit of the unconscious would have been welcomed."

Williamson leaned back against the edge of his desk and said, "I must say, Miss O'Keenan, this," and he held out the clump of hair, "must be important to you."

"'Twas. At least, I thought it so."

Williamson saw the color drain from her face and offered the woman a brandy.

"Thank you, sir, I believe a small taste of the elixir would . . . ." Her voice trailed off.

Williamson poured a shot and handed the glass to Mary Margaret then poured one for himself. Mary Margaret sipped the fine brandy, swallowed easily, then looked into the doctor's eyes. "This nest of hair," she paused, "'twas clasped in Sergeant Flannery's dead hold. I thought it might identify the murderer. 'Twas me best hope. But 'tis a useless bit of Rosie's mane."

As Williamson finished his drink, a young private burst into the office, barely saluted, then excitedly said, "Sir, sorry sir. A shooting. Perhaps two."

"Outside," said the doctor and followed the soldier out of the office. Williamson closed the door behind him, then the two walked a few paces along the corridor in huddled conversation. In a few minutes, the doctor returned to his office and said, "Miss O'Keenan, you removed evidence from a murder scene. Who is Rosie?"

"Ah, 'twas not considered to be murder at the time, sir. An' Rosie would be Seán's very own personal horse. A grand animal . . . ."

"Yes, the horse," said Williamson. "The only witness. However, Miss O'Keenan, I am called away. An emergency. That ball of hair may be of some use yet. I shall keep it safe until such time as it may be needed." He quickly circled his desk and after rummaging in several drawers, yanked free a small brown envelope. He reached for the ball of tangled mane. It was gone. When he looked up, he saw an empty chair and open door.

Disappointed with the doctor's opinion, Mary Margaret walked the long corridor, barely acknowledging the sounds of the restless bed-ridden. She left the hospital and in the fading light of dusk, slowly and thoughtfully walked the stone path. As she

203

turned toward Suds' Row, she heard the rumbling of a fast-moving wagon and the thunder of hooves behind her. She turned to see the ambulance, its horses galloping, manes flying, burst out of the hospital grounds and gallop across the grasslands towards the Trader's Compound. Seconds later, Dr. Williamson rode past on his mare. Mary Margaret hitched up her skirts and followed at a run.

At the close of Retreat ceremonies, First Sergeant John Holloway approached Colonel Winters. "May I have a word, sir?"

"I certainly hope you have a good word for me, First Sergeant. To my quarters."

Mrs. Winters greeted them at the front porch, but the commander dismissed her with a wave of his hand. As his wife retreated to the parlor, he shouted, "Sarah. Brandy please." Inside the Colonel's study, the two men waited in awkward silence—Jack at attention, Colonel Winters slouching behind his desk. After Mrs. Winters set down a tray with a decanter and two glasses on a low table against the wall and retreated, the Colonel, said "At ease. Report."

"Sir," began Jack, but the Colonel held up his hand, went to the door, and opened it. Once certain nobody was listening, he closed the door, poured himself a brandy, and sat on the edge of his desk. "You have the papers, Holloway?"

Jack cleared his throat. "Well now. No sir. I . . . ."

"Then what the bloody hell are you doing here?"

"Sir. You ordered me to report after Retreat."

"I expected you to have something to report!" The colonel gulped his drink and set down the glass.

"Well now, sir. I questioned Mr. Gonzalez. It appears that Sergeant Flannery secured the documents with Gonzalez. But on . . . ," Jack pulled his notebook from inside his jacket. "On Sunday last, April 17th, Miss O'Keenan and Mrs. Foote visited Los Alamitos and retrieved the papers. I questioned Mrs. Foote. She claims to know nothing. But I think otherwise. And Miss O'Keenan. Well now, Miss O'Keenan is, uh, uncooperative. Always has been. I recommend another search of her quarters."

Loud banging on the front door and raised voices filled the air.

"What now!" shouted the Colonel, yanking open his study door and coming face to face with his wife accompanied by Amos.

"Sir, I . . ." began Mrs. Winters, but Amos interrupted with, "A shooting, sir. At the Trader's Saloon."

"God damn it to hell!" shouted Winters, his face reddening with anger. "Go, Holloway. Find out about this."

Jack and Amos rushed from the Colonel's quarters but encountered young Victoria Winters on the front porch. Dressed in a gauzy lavender frock and matching bonnet, she carried a basket of early daisies and offered a small bunch to Jack. Amos ran off in the direction of the Trader's Compound as Jack tried in vain to circumvent Miss Winters.

She rested a gentle but firm hand on his forearm. "These blooms came early this year, First Sergeant Holloway. It would be most ungracious to the Lord to refuse such a lovely bouquet."

"If you please, Miss Winters, I must go. I've no time . . . ."

"Oh please," said Victoria, reaching down and taking his gloved hand. "For luck, Mr. Holloway. For luck and happiness in love."

Feeling rushed and anxious but not wanting to offend the Colonel's daughter, Jack took the flowers and stuffed them inside his uniform jacket, then mounted, and galloped after Amos. "Close to the heart," whispered Victoria with a wave.

From the doorway, Mrs. Winters, called, "Victoria, come inside at once." And as Victoria approached, a frown on her round, flushed face, her mother said, with unconcealed anger, "Just what do you think you are doing young lady? Flirting with a soldier! Get yourself inside."

"He is not just any soldier," said Victoria with a defiant tilt of her head. "He is First Sergeant Jack Holloway."

Through clenched teeth, Mrs. Winters whispered, "Jack, is it?"

"Yes," taunted Victoria. "Jack. And he loves me."

"Loves you? Loves you! And did he tell you that?"

When Victoria did not reply, her mother said, "I thought not. He is too cunning to make such a declaration."

"He loves me," shouted Victoria. "I know it. In the things he does and the way he looks at me. He loves me!"

"He does not. You are a child. And you are not to be giving flowers to Sergeant Holloway or any other soldier, but especially not to him."

"And why not?" said Victoria.

"He is not worthy of your affections. He is more than twice your age. And he is . . . ."

"What, Mama? What is he," shouted Victoria. "Handsome? Charming?"

"Married!"

Chapter 23: In which the bodies pile up, and Olivia takes charge.

As Mary Margaret descended the hill into the Trader's Compound, she saw running men, heard the shouts of urgent male voices, and instantly recalled that night when she arrived upon the death scene of Sergeant Seán Flannery. Now, as she approached the Compound, she saw the ambulance in front of the saloon, a young boy holding the horses. She stopped, steadying herself against the wind, and watched as the soldiers carried two stretchers out of the saloon and slid them into the back of the wagon. Then she ran down the hill and banged on the door to Olivia's kitchen. When no one answered, she rushed around to the front of the building as the ambulance, lanterns swinging and horses sedately trotting, departed. Not galloping, she thought, 'tis dead they are.

Olivia, Jack Holloway, and Dr. Williamson emerged from the saloon, Olivia talking low but animatedly, and gesturing with her hands. Both Jack and the doctor mounted their horses and followed the ambulance. Olivia stood a moment in the road, looking up at the sky. Mary Margaret followed her gaze but saw only a scattering of light clouds spreading across the darkening sky like smoke.

"Mary Margaret," said Olivia serenely, as if in prayer. "It is good you are here."

Puzzled, Mary Margaret glanced about, following the movements of Amos and Patrick and one of the saloon women as they closed and bolted the doors and shutters. Then she turned to her friend. "What's happened, Olivia?"

"Please come with me."

Olivia's parlor was in disarray with an open trunk in the center of the room and a bulging wicker suitcase beside it. Frocks, under garments, and chemises draped the sofa, and boots littered the carpet. Olivia cleared a place for them to sit. Abruptly and without emotion, she said, "Mr. Foote and Private Shiner are dead. Gunshot wounds to the head."

"Olivia, no. It canna' be."

"It is true. I saw the bodies with my own eyes. Blood and bone and parts of brain splattered on the wall." Olivia paused and looked about the room as if for an answer to some unasked question. "And poor Walter . . . most of his head gone . . . just gone."

"'Tis shock. Olivia, you must be in shock to talk this way."

"No. I am quite calm, if a little sad. Poor Walter. He . . . . Well, what is to be said of the man?" Her voice trailed off as she bent and picked up a blue chemise.

"'Tis a brandy you be needin.'"

"Yes. And pour one for yourself as well."

At the sideboard, Mary Margaret picked up a decanter.

"No. Not that one. We shall have a glass of Mr. Foote's excellent French cognac. Inside the cabinet." Mary Margaret opened the double doors and withdrew a sealed bottle. "Yes, the very one," said Olivia.

In silence, Mary Margaret poured two brandy snifters and offered one to Olivia who held her glass up in the toast position. With surprise and apprehension, thinking Olivia had perhaps lost her mind, Mary Margaret complied. Olivia said softly, "To the future—no matter what it brings." Then Olivia raised the glass to her lips and took a long, warm sip.

"*Sláinte,*" whispered Mary Margaret.

A loud urgent knocking at the front door interrupted them.

"That will be Patrick with the buggy," said Olivia. "I've not finished packing, as you see," and she went to the door. "Uh, good evening, Mrs. Winters. This is indeed a . . . ."

"I will not take much of your time, Mrs. Foote," and the Colonel's wife breezed into the foyer. Seeing Mary Margaret, Mrs. Winters said, "Ah, Miss O'Keenan, the laundress. You are here as well. Good. There is no doubt in my mind that you will both want to hear what I have to say."

Mary Margaret's mouth fell open in surprise, and Olivia said, "May I offer you a brandy, Ma'am?"

"No thank you . . .uh, well, perhaps just a tad, to ward off the vagaries of the wind." And Mrs. Winters stepped into the parlor.

Without a word, Mary Margaret poured another snifter and offered it to the Colonel's wife. The woman took the glass, swirled the deep auburn liquid, and sniffed. "Good. Very good indeed," she said then downed the brandy. Mrs. Winters looked around her at the disarray. "You are taking a trip?"

"No ma'am," Olivia cut in. "I was putting some clothes in storage for the coming summer months. Please have a seat."

"We need not observe formalities. What I have to say is brief so listen, please." Throughout her discourse, Mrs. Winters stood, her hands crossed at her abdomen, looking straight at Olivia. "My husband knew of it. He has known all along. When Sergeant Flannery found the papers, the receipts . . . bribery. And Josiah Foote came running like a scared rabbit, the Colonel sent for First Sergeant Holloway and ordered him to intercept Sergeant Flannery," Mrs. Winters hesitated at the gasp that escaped from Mary Margaret but did not falter. "To intercept Sergeant Flannery, secure the documents, and swear the sergeant to secrecy. 'This must not become a scandal. Do whatever you have to,' were the Colonel's words. That is all I know. The Colonel does not confide in me." She bowed her head, staring at her hands which opened and closed in an involuntary gesture of helplessness.

Then her head came up sharply and she squared her shoulders. "But I have ears, don't I," she said with the slightest trace of a County Cork lilt. "An' a brain. Though some think not. An' I . . . ." She stopped suddenly and looked at each of the women, standing before her in stunned silence. "I bid you Good Evening," she said with a quick nod, turned, and disappeared through the open doorway.

Mary Margaret and Olivia said nothing. Transfixed, they listened to the departing clop of the horse's hooves and the crunch of the carriage wheels. Then Olivia turned to Mary Margaret. "Give me the documents."

Seán. It canna' be. Not Jack. But, sure, he left the patrol that morning, so I'm told. 'Twere his own soldiers brought the bundle of your uniform, your very boots, to the Comedy Company Headquarters. But Jack? Your friend?

It canna' be. Ah, for the love of God, Seán, talk to me. Tell me what to do—what to think.

"Mary Margaret!" said Olivia sharply. "This is not the time for daydreaming! The papers. Jack will be searching everywhere for them. Give them to me. I'll put them in Mr. Foote's safe."

Mary Margaret did not move. She felt as though her boots had been nailed to the floor. Her mind raced as she tried desperately to make sense of what Mrs. Winters had said.

"Now!" Olivia's voice startled Mary Margaret, and she shook with the knowledge of her own mistaken notions. She reluctantly shifted her eyes to look squarely at Olivia. "I dinna know who to trust, Mrs. Foote."

"Did you not suspect Jack? Not at all?"

"No. Not a bit." Then the words came tumbling out in incoherent bursts. "'Twas Shiney . . . 'twas Shiney searched me quarters. "'Twas Shiney, or the redheaded man, or Timmy Sullivan—he dinna report for duty that morning. But not Jack. Not Jack."

Olivia closed the space between them and took a firm hold of Mary Margaret's hands."Look at me. Tonight, Walter Shiner killed Mr. Foote then killed himself. I do not know why. Perhaps we will never know, nor need to. But Walter's acts change everything. Josiah Foote can no longer threaten you or my family. We can expose his fraud except . . . well, it seems Jack and Commander Winters are involved." Olivia dropped Mary Margaret's hands and paced the room, walking faster and faster between the trunk and the sofa. "Truly, I believe we need help."

"'Tis stupid I be," began Mary Margaret in a small soft voice. Then, gathering volume, "Me with me *investigatin,'*" she stressed the word with a bitter sarcasm. "Me clues and suspicions and questionin'—an' not seeing what was in front of me very nose. The ball of hair—nothin' but a bunch of Rosie's mane, clutched, no doubt, as Seán went down. P'rhaps he did fall. Stoopid. I be nothing but a stoopid silly cow, trying to bring back her man."

"You stop feeling sorry for yourself, Mary Margaret." Olivia's voice came harsh and stern with anger, fear, and fatigue.

"There is more here than your attempts—though they are most honorable—to assign guilt to the murderer of Sergeant Seán Flannery. Three men are dead. For what? To hide a scandal?" Olivia paused. "What do you mean—horse hair?"

Startled, Mary Margaret looked into Olivia's eyes. "Dr. Williamson examined it—that puff of red hair clutched in Seán's dead fist. Too coarse to be human hair he said. An' all this time, I be searching for a redhead."

> *Mary Margaret, you're as lovely an' cool as the mist on the moors. And, by God, you've a brain in yer head. You couldna' made it 'cross the ocean an' through the mire of New York an' 'cross this wide country without a good strong mind. 'Tis proud I am to be yer man. Will you be me wife?*

Mary Margaret smiled. "The Sheriff," she said.

"What?"

"Sheriff O'Tero," said Mary Margaret. Suddenly certain of what she must do, she straightened up and squared her shoulders.

"The Sheriff of San Miguel County?" asked Olivia, her mind racing toward the idea. "Indeed, Sgt. Flannery was murdered outside of the military jurisdiction. Truly you are brilliant. We can go to the sheriff in the morning, but what of this moment? We must secure the documents." A gust of wind rushed in through the front door, silencing Olivia. It pushed its way into the foyer, careened around the edge of the arched entry, and dislodged several articles of clothing. Olivia bent and grasped a gown that had fluttered to the floor. "Patrick?" she called.

"Well now, Mrs. Foote," said Jack Holloway, closing the door securely behind him. "And Miss O' Keenan. Good of you to be together."

Sheriff Otero locked the thick metal door to the four-cell block.

"That is the last of them, sir," said his deputy.

"Yes," replied Otero, approaching his desk and flinging down the bunch of keys. "These events, whether they be dancing girls, political speeches, or so-called 'theatrical performances,' inevitably end with several—heretofore upstanding citizens—spending a few nights at the expense of the county. Disorderly, the lot of them."

"Disorderly, the lot of them," repeated the deputy.

This was one of the times when Sheriff Otero questioned his decision to hire Lucero. "Must you repeat everything I say, Pedro? My words are not the words of God." He waited until Lucero looked at him then continued. "Now. I want you to ride to Fort Union."

"At this hour, sir?" asked Lucero, looking out at the fading sunlight.

"Yes, at this hour, *to meet with your sweetheart*," continued the Sheriff with emphasis. Then he paused while confusion spread across Lucero's face. "I received news from a passing trader that Josiah Foote has been murdered. Find out what you can. Report in the morning. I'll bed down here for the night."

Before Lucero could respond, the door swung open and the Mayor entered.

"Evening," he said, not tipping his broad, grey Stetson. "Closing up for the night?"

Otero looked directly at the Mayor but made no response.

Deputy Lucero felt compelled to fill the void. "*Buenas noches, señor alcalde,*" he said. "I bid you Good Night. I'm riding off to the Fort."

"A social visit," concluded Sheriff Otero. "You may go, Pedro." And the deputy left all too willingly.

"Fort Union? I have made it clear, Otero, that you are to keep your investigating nose out of this business at the Fort. My contacts keep me well-informed, and . . . ."

"And your palms well-greased," interrupted Otero. "Now, if you please, I have much work to do, taking care of county criminal activities." The sheriff turned his back to the mayor and shuffled the pile of papers on his desk.

212

"Las Vegas Grandes has an understanding with the garrison commander." The Mayor took a step toward Otero. "And you had best honor it. No snooping on the post grounds. Do you understand?"

"I understand perfectly. But, the county does not have such an agreement, nor is it required that I honor *your agreements*." Otero turned and looked directly into the angry eyes of Mayor Lopez. "Good evening."

The mayor cursed and stomped heavily out of the jail. Sheriff Otero smiled broadly as he closed and barred the thick wooden doors. He returned to his desk and raised the flame on the kerosene lamp. From the top right drawer, he pulled out the copy of *Lady's Companion* which the Fort Union Library had discarded. Otero leaned back in his chair, put his feet up on the desk, and opened it to "The Mystery of Marie Roget."

"Have you forgotten your manners, First Sergeant Holloway? Knocking is customary," said Olivia with an attempt at bravado.

Jack entered the parlor without the slightest hesitation. And ignoring Olivia's statement, said, "Leaving, Mrs. Foote? So soon after your husband's untimely demise. Though I fear you shall not be wearing widow's weeds."

"That, First Sergeant Holloway, is none of your concern," replied Olivia.

"That is where you are wrong, Madam. Anything that may be connected to the murder of Josiah Foote is my concern."

"Jack! How dare you insinuate . . . ," began Mary Margaret.

Jack held his hand up demanding silence and said to Olivia, "Your attempted hasty departure indicates some involvement."

"For the love of God, Jack! You dinna suspect Olivia," Mary Margaret continued, stepping into the small space between Jack and Olivia. "'Twas Private Shiner."

Jack sharply turned to Mary Margaret. "Stay out of this. Everyone knows that—in his odd way—Shiney was devoted to Mrs. Foote, would have done <u>anything</u> for her. Much of what happens next will depend on what is in my report to Colonel Winters."

213

At Jack's words, both women fell silent, imagining the possible consequences.

"Well now," said Jack. "I see that I have gained your attention. Listen and listen well. I want the documents you found at Los Alamitos and Flannery's log as well. Do not play coy or feign innocence. I know you retrieved the papers. Give me the documents—now—and I will see that neither of you is implicated in the death of Josiah Foote."

"I do not have any such documents," said Olivia as Mary Margaret took a small slow step backward and out of the Jack's line of vision. "You may search my home and garden," continued Olivia. "You may search my trunks. I will call Patrick to help you."

"Patrick will not be helping anyone this night. It will go easier for both of you if you just give me the papers."

As the orange glow of the setting sun faded to grey, Deputy Lucero arrived at the Trader's Hotel, tied his horse, and rushed inside. He found Isabela in the upstairs laundry room, folding sheets and towels, her hair in disarray, sweat trickling down the side of her face. When she saw him, she smiled and dropping the linen, held him tightly.

"Oh, Pedro, I am so frightened," she cried into his shoulder and told him of the deaths. "Who will be next?" she whimpered, making the sign of the cross.

Lucero held her close and comforted her then told her of his assignment to observe and gather evidence for the Sheriff. She said, "How can I help?"

"I must examine the saloon."

She turned and rummaged in a cabinet for a lantern. Then, lighting the lantern, Isabela led him out of the hotel and around to the rear entrance of the saloon. She handed the lantern to Pedro and unlocked the door with a key from the ring at her waist.

"*Cuidado,*" she whispered. He turned his head and kissed her lightly on the mouth then assured her he would be careful.

In the glow of the lantern, Lucero watched Isabela run the few paces back to the hotel, then he entered the dark saloon. He examined the room, noting the scattered, dusty footprints and the positions of the furnishings—chairs shoved back from tables, one table pushed against the bar. He set the lantern on a nearby chair and withdrew a small sheaf of crumpled papers and a pencil from his pocket and made note of all he saw. Then he retrieved the lantern and entered Mr. Foote's office. He paused in the open doorway of the small room, wrinkling his nose at the meaty odor of blood. He carefully examined everything, touched nothing, and scribbled a few notes. When he completed his examination of the office, he walked slowly back through the saloon, looking around for anything he may have missed. Then he left the saloon, as he had entered, and shoved the iron lock into place.

Outside, Lucero began his search of the perimeter. He walked slowly southward along the rear wall of the building. Although the wind had settled into a gentle breeze, its earlier ferocity had smoothed out all foot prints and hoof prints. After circling the building and finding nothing, Deputy Lucero stumbled. A root he thought. Upon further inspection, he discovered a body—inert legs stretched forward, back slumped against the wall, head hanging forward. Dark liquid flowed freely from the abdomen, blackening the uniform.

He felt for and found a pulse then removed the man's cap. Pulling a handkerchief from his pocket, the deputy wiped the man's sweating face. "I will go for help," said Lucero.

Slowly, the soldier lifted his eyes. "Holloway," he murmured.

Lucero pressed the handkerchief to the wound and placed both of the man's hands on it. "Press," said Lucero. "Keep pressing. I will find Holloway."

The injured soldier tried to form a word but failed. It was only in his mind that he shouted, *No!*

Deputy Lucero ran to the hotel and found Isabela. "Who is Holloway? I must find him," said Lucero.

"That would be First Sergeant Holloway. I saw him—not long ago—entering the home of *la señora* Foote, *pobrecita.* Across the road." Lucero turned, ran down the stairs, out of the hotel, and across the windswept *placita.*

Jack dumped the contents of Olivia's trunk and suitcase on the floor and rifled through the clothing. He toppled the sideboard. Liquor spewed forth, splashing onto the nearby chair, and puddling on the uneven floor. He yanked cushions from the sofa and chair. Then he grabbed Olivia by the arm and shouted, "Tell me where those damn papers are!" He was silenced by a loud banging on the front door and shouts of "*Ayuda!* Help! Sergeant Holloway?"

Olivia looked into Jack's intense, glittering eyes.

Mary Margaret stepped forward. "Shall we ignore calls for help, Jack me boy? With the lamps blazin'?"

Holloway glared at her then said, "We shall go to the door together." To Mary Margaret he said, "You stay here!" As he yanked Olivia from the room, she looked back over her shoulder and mouthed the word 'Go!'

Mary Margaret hesitated, concerned for Olivia's safety, but thinking it Private O'Brien at the door, she lifted her skirts and ran out of the parlor, across the hallway, and out through the kitchen door. Suddenly plunged into darkness, she stopped to let her eyes adjust then picked her way among the silhouettes of chokecherry and raspberry bushes toward the low white wall, glinting in the reflected light from the open door. She climbed over the wall, snagging her petticoat, then scrambled up the hill toward Fort Union, feeling certain she would at any moment be grabbed from behind.

When Olivia opened her front door, Deputy Lucero, in his excitement, momentarily forgot to address her in English. Instead he spoke in rapid Spanish—introducing himself, his mission, and describing the fallen soldier, and the call for 'Holloway.' Olivia responded in Spanish, excluding Holloway.

Jack said, "What? What is he saying? I heard my name. What is it?"

Olivia wrenched her arm free and faced Jack. "This is Deputy Lucero from Las Vegas Grandes. He says that he needs help. He's found a wounded soldier behind the saloon."

Jack recoiled slightly, enough for Olivia to notice. Then, continuing in Spanish, she explained to the deputy that the man beside her was First Sergeant Holloway, and she quickly asked

Lucero if the soldier had been asking for the First Sergeant or calling out a warning. Lucero raised his eyebrows, but showed no other sign of surprise. He mentally wrote all this in his notebook, then, looking directly at Holloway, said in English, "Sir, there is a wounded soldier behind the Trader's Saloon. He is bleeding from a stomach wound."

"Jack," said Olivia. "We must help. I'll get bandages while you go for the doctor."

Jack considered the situation. Refusing to attend to a wounded soldier as soon as possible would look suspicious, and not allowing Olivia to get medical supplies would be even more suspicious. The muscles in his jaws vibrated with frustration. "Of course," he managed to say between clenched teeth. "Come, Mrs. Foote. I will help you." As they went together to the chifferobe in Olivia's bedroom to gather the necessary supplies, Jack whispered menacingly in Olivia's ear, "Where in hell did that vixen go?"

"I'm sure I have no idea," replied Olivia. "At this moment, I have more important things to attend to, if you please."

"I do not please," said Holloway.

Olivia did not look at him. She spoke evenly and slowly as if to a child or a lunatic. "Jack, fetch a pitcher of water, some soap, and several towels."

Feeling trapped and angry, Holloway did as she instructed and followed closely behind.

When they rejoined the deputy, Olivia said, "First Sergeant Holloway, I really do believe it would be prudent for you to fetch Dr. Williamson."

Jack Holloway squinted his eyes in irritation. "Mrs. Foote, it is I who knows what is most prudent for a First Sergeant. My place is always and foremost with my soldiers."

Olivia nodded, and they followed Deputy Lucero. When they arrived at the rear of the saloon, the deputy set his lantern beside the body, and Olivia immediately knelt and began preparing the bandages. Holloway felt the soldier's neck for a pulse then abruptly rose and said, "I shall find Williamson."

As Holloway crossed the road to his horse, Olivia leaned forward and began ripping open the uniform, but as she wrung the water from a towel to clean the wound, Lucero's hand on her forearm stopped her. "*Está muerto.* He has passed." Olivia looked up into the smooth young face and blank blue eyes of Private Patrick O'Brien.

Mary Margaret ran to her quarters and quickly lit a lantern, then gathered the packet of documents and Seán's diary. She stuffed the papers into several of her skirt pockets, stuffed the log book inside her jacket, and buttoned all of the buttons. She grabbed the lantern and dashed out, but once outside, she stopped dead in her tracks. Standing in the middle of Suds Row, looking at the garrison, the quartermaster's depot, and the soldiers' quarters, Mary Margaret realized there was no place where she could hide the papers from Jack Holloway. Then she turned and ran along the path to the hospital. She entered at the rear, through the double doors where last she saw Seán's body—the Dead House—and found Dr. Williamson about to perform a post mortem examination on the body of Josiah Foote.

Williamson looked up. "Miss O'Keenan. We meet again. Do you have more instructions for me on how to perform my duties? Or perhaps a question of biology?" he asked with a smile to soften the sarcasm. In spite of himself, he admired the woman.

Mary Margaret executed an awkward curtsy. "No sir," she said. "'Tis clear as rainwater you be knowin' your business." She looked around the room—two long tables with their cargo of the dead. Against one wall a counter strewn with instruments, a rough-hewn washstand with basin and pitcher, and a white cabinet with glass doors. No place to hide a packet of papers and a diary, she thought.

"Well, is there some way I may be of assistance?" asked Williamson.

"I . . . I, uh . . . yes," said Mary Margaret. "If you will, Sir."

"Well?"

"Couldja be hiding something for me? An' asking no questions about it?"

"I am a bit busy, Miss O'Keenan, if you had not noticed," said the doctor, returning to his examination.

Mary Margaret walked to the other table and lifted the sheet. She stared, at first unable to identify what she saw. One side of Shiney's face was as complete and ugly as ever, but the other half was a mass of blood, and tissue, and shattered bone. Mary Margaret dropped the sheet and performed a perfectly executed swoon, collapsing slowly onto her side.

"Good Lord!" shouted the doctor, rinsing his hands in the basin. "Are you all right, Miss O'Keenan?" Williamson reached out and lifted her to a seated position. "Head forward now," and he gently pushed her head down between her knees. "So you never faint?"

"Grand, just grand, I am," whispered Mary Margaret, her voice muffled by her skirts.

The doctor released her and helped her to her feet. "Perhaps a bit of fresh air," he said. "I'll see you to your quarters."

"No . . . thank you, Doctor. 'Tis only your attention I be needing," and she pulled the papers from various sections of her person. "These are important, very important, papers, evidence, sir, in the murder of Sergeant Flannery. And, bribery, sir, at the highest level. Couldja be keeping them for me."

"I am constantly and consistently amazed by your audacity, Miss O'Keenan. You barge into my Dead House, interrupt my work, and then perform a neat bit of acting—as if you were the great Sarah Bernhardt herself."

"If you please, Doctor Williamson. Let no one—no one—know that you have these," and Mary Margaret held out the documents. Williamson did not immediately move, and for a moment, she thought he would refuse. She waited in silence.

Dr. Williamson cleared his throat. "I will not aid your cause unless you explain to me the nature of this evidence."

"'Tis proof, sir. The Post Trader, under the very nose of—and perhaps with the knowledge of the commanding officer—Josiah Foote paid a large sum of money to the United States Secretary of War in return for the position of Post Trader. 'Tis these papers Seán Flannery be murdered for," and she thrust them into the doctor's hands. Then she unbuttoned her sacque and removed the notebook. "An' this be Seán's diary—his log—explaining things."

Mary Margaret concentrated to overcome her brogue and continued. "Please, sir, if you will but secure these documents for the night. In the early morning, I shall retrieve the packet and . . . ," she hesitated, then out of desperation decided to trust Williamson, "and take the papers to Sheriff O'Tero."

"And why, might I ask, have you chosen me for this task?"

"You be one of the few people at Fort Union that Jack Holloway would not dare to search."

"Holloway?"

Yes, sir. We do believe he is involved."

"We?"

"Mrs. Foote and meself."

"Mrs. Foote. Very well. But only until morning." For the first time, the doctor looked at the bundle of papers then slid them into a pocket somewhere deep inside his long, blood-splattered coat. At the sound of hoof beats, Mary Margaret shoved the diary into the doctor's hands and shrank back against the wall behind the open door.

Jack Holloway galloped his horse up to the doors. "Doc," he shouted, halting his horse. "Need your help at the Trader's Saloon. A wounded soldier."

"Very well, First Sergeant."

"I fear you will need the wagon," said Jack.

Chapter 24: Prairie Madness.

Olivia sat back on her heels and cried for Private O'Brien. "A pleasant young man, honest and trustworthy," she mumbled. 'Ah no, no family at'all, ma'am,' she recalled him saying. No one to come asking questions, she thought, no one to speak for this dead boy. She leaned forward and closed his eyes with her hand.

"He was a friend?" asked Lucero.

Olivia nodded. She said a silent prayer, then looked at the deputy

"Perhaps you may need to make a report, Deputy Lucero. The ambulance will be here soon. Those poor horses must be tired with all this back and forth."

"*Con permiso, señora.* The Trader's Compound lies outside the jurisdiction of the garrison, does it not? It may be best if I remain. And if you please, the name of the young soldier?"

"Very well," murmured Olivia. She did not want to be alone in the dark with Patrick's cold body. She felt tired and wished she could lie her head down amidst the sweet, dry grasses and sleep for a week. "Private Patrick Michael O'Brien." Olivia bunched the wet towel she held and leaned forward to wipe Patrick's face, but the deputy informed her that in all probability, this was now a murder investigation and she should not touch a thing.

"Oh," said Olivia as the surety of that statement entered her consciousness.

"Next of kin?" he asked.

"None, that is, I know of no family. Perhaps the garrison records," she said as she heard approaching hoof beats. She turned to see the ambulance, its lanterns swinging, its horses heaving. "Deputy Lucero, are you certain that Patrick asked you to find First Sergeant Holloway?"

"No, ma'am, I am not certain." Lucero consulted his notes and said, "Private O' Brien merely called out the name Holloway, and I ran for help."

"Please say nothing of this in the presence of the First Sergeant. I have reason to believe, he is, that is, he may not be forthright in this matter." Olivia paused. "I . . . ," and her final words were swallowed up in the approach of the wagon.

Doctor Williamson arrived before the ambulance, dismounted, removed his black satchel, and rushed to the small group. The doctor knelt, made a cursory examination, and pronounced Sergeant O'Brien dead.

"Well now," said Holloway, dismounting and joining them. "The bodies are piling up."

"Holloway," said the doctor in a stern voice. "That is an extremely inappropriate remark."

Within seconds, Olivia stood and closed the space between Jack and herself. And without a word, she slapped him hard across the cheek.

Jack grabbed her hand and said, "You are distraught, Mrs. Foote. And it is no small wonder. I shall escort you to your home."

Dr. Williamson rose and looked at Olivia Foote. Her hair had come loose and several strands flew about her flushed and sweaty face. Her eyes glowed unhealthily in the lantern's light. "Yes," he said. "Perhaps you should rest, Mrs. Foote." He rummaged in his medicine bag and brought out a small green bottle with a cork stopper. "Mix one teaspoon of these powders in a glass of water. It will help you sleep."

"I am quite all right," said Olivia, trying in vain to wrest her hand from Holloway.

"Well now, Doctor, I'll see to it," said Jack, taking the bottle and securing it in the pocket of his trousers. "I shall see the lady home and ensure that she is cared for properly."

As he saw that she was preparing to protest, he whispered in her ear, "I've a pistol at your back, Mrs. Foote." Olivia jumped slightly as Holloway grabbed his horse's reigns, and they all walked toward the Foote house. Deputy Lucero rose and bid good night to the doctor, then mounted and rode for the Sheriff's office.

Once inside her home, Olivia wrenched free and backed away from the man she had once embraced. He was every bit as handsome, she realized, but his face was distorted by the hateful emotions he could not conceal. "Well now, Mrs. Foote. You may be seated while I continue my search."

Olivia moved behind the sofa and remained standing. She watched Jack rip through her flimsy dresses and petticoats, flinging aside the remnants. "I had always thought the sword was ceremonial and nothing more," she said. "I see, however, that it has a most practical use." She thought of the gash in Patrick's abdomen and almost swooned.

Jack stopped abruptly and turned to look at Olivia. "Oh, most definitely, Mrs. Foote. It has many uses of a practical nature." He raised his sabre in a mock salute. As it caught the pale yellow glow of the gas lights, the sword twinkled like crystal, and Olivia stared, mesmerized, until she saw a small puddle of dark red lying in the crevice of the handle.

Jack resumed his search, but not finding the documents among her clothing and trunks, he grabbed Olivia and dragged her throughout the house. In his frenzy, he yanked the drawers from the chiffonier, pulled sheets and blankets from the bed, towels from the shelves, he tipped over furnishings, knick-knacks, and food storage bins. He became increasingly irritated and frantic, almost hysterical.

"Jack," she said evenly and calmly. "As you see, there is nothing here. Mr. Foote kept all his important papers in his safe. In the office."

Jack turned on her. The fierce anger and a trace of fear, thought Olivia, on his face made her shrink back against the chill of the *adobe* wall. They stood facing each other in the kitchen. "Well now, Mrs. Foote, it would be my considered opinion that you must have hidden them on your person."

"Jack, I . . ."

"Remove your garments."

"I will not!"

"Remove that fine silk dress, the delicate lace undergarments, one by one, as you so lovingly have done in the past, Olivia my love." Olivia did not move. She felt as if she were paralyzed. "Now!" he shouted. "Or I shall be forced to do it for you. And I will not be as gentle as I once was."

Olivia did not move.

"Now!" repeated Jack, and in an instant, he closed the gap between them and grasped her bodice.

As if awakened by a nightmare, Olivia came to life. She slapped at his hands. "I will do it," she said. And one by one, she removed her clothing, shaking out the various items to show the absence of papers.

Jack laughed softly, and the softness itself was menacing. "Well now, you make a pretty picture, Mrs. Foote, do you not? Naked amidst the refuse." He lifted his sword and placed the tip between Olivia's breasts then slid it down to the edge of the pubic bone. "And I daresay, you have plumped out a bit since last we . . . ."

"Jack, what has happened to you? You are crazed. I do not know you."

Jack retreated a few steps, sheathed his sword, and said, "Well now, Mrs. Foote, I have no time to debate with you the nature of my sanity. It appears that it is Miss Mary Margaret who holds the documents. I will not be thwarted." He turned quickly and strode out of the house. Olivia hugged herself and wondered if he really thought she would be wearing the papers.

Deputy Lucero pounded on the thick doors of the San Miguel County Jailhouse.

"*Espérame*, I am coming," called Sheriff Otero, rubbing the sleep from his eyes as he emerged from the small room in the rear of the building. He peered through the square cut in the door. "Lucero. Good," he said and unbolted the door.

As soon as the doors closed behind him, Lucero started talking, spilling out all that he had seen at the saloon, Private O'Brien's death, and the strange behavior between Mrs. Foot and First Sergeant Holloway. He was certain that *la señora* Foote knew more than she revealed. He noted that just before he knocked on the door to the Foote home he had heard a man's voice, perhaps, Holloway's, demanding something about "those damn papers."

Sheriff Otero nodded and asked, "Is that everything, Pedro?"

"I think so, sir. Here are my notes."

"You may go. You have served well tonight. I thank you. Go home and rest. Keep your notes and reread them—perhaps your memory will fill in some empty spaces. Tomorrow, I fear, shall be a busy day."

Lucero shook his head. "*Pobrecitos,*" he said thinking of the murders at Fort Union, Isabela's fears, and the sad, frightened Mrs. Foote.

Within minutes of leaving Olivia, Jack Holloway arrived at Mary Margaret's quarters. He tethered his horse. He did not knock but unlocked the door with a passkey and barged in. She was seated at the round, oak table in the center of the living section, writing. She jumped up, knocking the chair over and upsetting a sheaf of papers. One sheet floated to the floor. Jack seized it.

"Jack Holloway," said Mary Margaret, attempting to wrest the paper from him. "What be the meaning of this intrusion? An' where ever didja get a key to me quarters?"

Jack ignored her questions and flapped the paper in her face. "What is this?"

"'Tis none o' your business. That's what it is."

"Sit!"

"I will not."

"You shall," he said between clenched teeth. "I have had enough of your meddling." He righted the chair, grabbed Mary Margaret, and shoved her down onto the seat. "Well now," he said and leaned over her. "Where are the documents Flannery stole from the Post Trader's Store? And do not say 'What documents?' We—you and I and the lovely Olivia—know to what papers I refer."

As Jack read the beginning of the Mary Margaret's letter to President Garfield, she searched his face for a remnant of the man who had been Seán's friend. She saw instead a feverish flush on his skin, darting eyes, and a jaw as set as stone.

"Ah, Jack, what's become of you? Are ya that wracked with ambition?"

He laughed as he shredded the paper. "Where are the documents?" he shouted.

Hearing a slight tremor in his voice, Mary Margaret said, "'Tis a touch of the Prairie Madness I ken."

"I require none of your low Irish *wisdom*. Just give me the God damned papers."

"I do not have any such papers. Search me quarters if you will." Mary Margaret leaned back in the chair, crossed her arms, and watched as Jack turned her meager belongings upside down and inside out. Sweat stained the armpits of his usually immaculate uniform, perspiration and dust lined his face. He mumbled distractedly as he rummaged, and Mary Margaret heard him make a reference to Seán. When Holloway completed his fruitless search, he turned to face her.

"An' what was that you said, Jack? 'Not on his person?' Didja say such a thing? An' was it Seán Flannery you be referring to? Jack?"

Holloway looked squarely at Mary Margaret. "Then you have secured them in the very clothing you wear."

As he approached, Mary Margaret jumped up from the chair and pulled Seán's pistol from the pocket of her apron. She aimed it at Jack's chest. "Leave me be," she said, her heart throbbing and the pulse in her temples pounding.

Jack smiled and took a long step toward her, his hand stretched out to grab the gun. Mary Margaret lowered her aim to the groin and cocked the pistol.

From the open door, Olivia called, "No!"

Mary Margaret started slightly and pulled the trigger. The bullet entered Jack's leg a few inches above the knee. He went down like a felled tree. "How couldja, Jack Holloway!" snarled Mary Margaret. "Seán Flannery be your friend. He rode with you. 'Had yer back,' as the lads say. You murdered him! An' for what, Jack? For what?" She knelt beside him and held the little pistol to his temple. "How couldja?" she whispered, cocking the gun.

"Oh dear Lord," said Olivia. "Mary Margaret!" Olivia rushed into the room and shoved Mary Margaret aside as the gun went off and the remaining bullet lodged in the door. Olivia grabbed a petticoat lying on the bed and ripped it into a makeshift tourniquet. "Bandages Mary Margaret. And get some towels or clean linen." Once again Olivia set about dressing a severe wound.

Mary Margaret lay the gun on the bed and made the sign of the cross. "Ah, sweet Jaysus, Olivia. Sure I would have killed the man. That I would."

"Mary Margaret O'Keenan! Fetch me those sheets! And then fetch the doctor."

Mary Margaret shuddered as if a ghost had crossed her soul. Then she grabbed one of the lanterns and rushed out through the open door. Across the lane, half-dressed soldiers swinging lanterns emerged from the enlisted men's quarters. Mary Margaret paused and looked back at Olivia, tightening the rag around Jack's bloody thigh.

"He'll be passin' out soon," said Mary Margaret. "An' there's many a soldier will be inquiring . . . you'll be safe here." Then she ran, her heavy brogans pounding the stones of Sud's Row. Minutes later, she arrived again at the Dead House. She burst in then stopped just inside the door to catch her breath before explaining the situation to Dr. Williamson.

"For pity's sake," he mumbled. "The man was right—the bodies are piling up. The thigh you say. We'll need the stretcher-bearers." He called out the names of several soldiers but none responded. Standing among the bodies, Mary Margaret heard the doctor snarl, "For the love of God, not an able-bodied man within earshot!" Then, as he once again grabbed his medicine bag, "Come Miss O'Keenan. You had better accompany me. I daresay someone will . . . ." The wind swallowed his final words.

Mary Margaret closed the doors behind her and ran to catch up with the doctor's long strides. He muttered several unheard curses and something about the 'nearness of death' as he went. When they arrived at her quarters, they encountered a small group of enlisted men. One soldier had taken over tending to the First Sergeant, and Olivia, her skin sallow and moist, her dress wet with blood, was leaning against a wall. After examining Holloway, the doctor looked up.

"Will he . . . is he. . . ?" asked Olivia.

227

"He's lost consciousness. The injury requires surgery," Williamson said. "Here, come here you soldiers, carry him to the hospital and be quick about it." As four soldiers lifted Jack's body, the doctor continued. "Lost a considerable amount of blood . . . artery seems intact. Should recover." Then he slammed shut his valise and rose. "Must notify . . . ."

"Please, sir," interrupted May Margaret. "Couldja be delaying such notification . . . ten p'raps twenty minutes? We believe the Colonel to be involved. Just give us a bit of time."

"Miss O'Keenan, what happened here?" He nodded in the direction of the disheveled state of her quarters, then he noted Olivia's condition.

"Mrs. Foote, sit, please," and he gently escorted her to a kitchen chair and felt her pulse then rummaged in his bag.

"Thank you, Dr. Williamson. I'm fine, really. I have no need of smelling salts."

"Tell me—one of you—what happened here, and be quick about it."

"Ah, sir, 'tis a . . . ."

"I'll wager it has something to do with these," he said, and from his inside pocket, Williamson withdrew the documents and threw them on the table.

Mary Margaret nodded. "Thirty minutes," said the doctor. "I do not for one bloody moment believe that Colonel Winters is in any way involved in these dastardly shenanigans, but you have thirty minutes. It will take that and more to staunch the bleeding, which is, of course, the greater necessity. And now, Mrs. Foote, are you well enough?"

"Truly, doctor, I am well," said Olivia, anxious for him to leave.

As the door closed behind Dr. Williamson, Mary Margaret said, "Will it never stop? This killing?" She paced up and down between her cot and the table. "'Tis gone. All is gone—me man, me pretty future."

Olivia reached out and hugged Mary Margaret. For a moment the two women stood in silence. Then Mary Margaret pulled free.

228

"'Tis no time to be wallowing in me own self-pity. You be right in that Olivia."

"Oh Lord, I would not call that wallowing."

"If Colonel Winters is involved, we truly be in grave danger," said Mary Margaret as she picked up the pistol, retrieved the remaining bullet from her top drawer, and loaded the chamber. "We must leave Fort Union immediately." She looked closely at Olivia. "'Tis late an' you be weary. Couldja be handling a buggy ride as far as Loma Parda? 'Tis but a few miles but rough."

"Loma Parda?"

"'Tis nearby but safe, I think. Lulu will take us in for the rest of this wicked, wicked night. Then in the mornin' we'll push on to Las Vegas Grandes and the sheriff."

"But . . . ."

"She'll welcome you she will as you be me friend." Mary Margaret shoved the pistol into her pocket, grabbed a shawl for herself and wrapped a blanket around Olivia's shoulders. "But we'll be needing the trap."

"Of course, of course. We shall use Mr. Foote's, that is to say, *my* gig, as soon as I change my blood-spattered dress."

They traveled slowly and without a lantern, keeping to the edges of the walkways and the thoroughfare. They arrived at the Post Trader's stable but were forced to wait silently until a man finished tending his horse. Then Mary Margaret hitched Tamany, and with the precious packet of evidence stowed beneath the seat, they rode under the silvery glow of a clear sky, a half-moon, and a heaven of stars.

After they passed out of the garrison and turned onto the Loma Parda road, Olivia produced a packet of Lucifers she kept with her, and lit the small side lanterns. The breeze was slight, but it moaned through bare branches, and each tree they passed seemed to reach out long crooked fingers to scratch the horse, snag the women's skirts, or scrape across the top of the gig. The lanterns swung eerily, lighting their eyes like the stars above them. Mary Margaret drove, staring forward into the night, but Olivia looked back, almost constantly, expecting at any moment to see a patrol in pursuit. After nearly two hours, they arrived at Lulu's door, their faces taut and strained.

Chapter 25: In which all is revealed.

<u>Monday, April 25</u>

The morning dawned grey and calm with traces of moisture collecting on the windows, shrouding the landscape, and dripping from the corrugated tin roof of Lulu's home.

"P'rhaps it'll rain," said Lulu. "Coffee? Eggs?"

Olivia's face paled and she shook her head. "No thank you, Mrs. McAdam. I feel . . . ."

"Poorly. And call me Lulu. We spent a night together, Ma'am."

"Then you must call me Olivia, not Ma'am. I am indebted to your kindness. Taking us in without a question. Thank you, Lulu." Olivia smiled.

"That'll be the babe . . . making you ill. When are ya' due?"

"I . . . I'm not . . . ."

"Ah, well. None of my business, right you are. Tea then," said Lulu, turning to the pump.

Mary Margaret entered the kitchen pinning up her hair. The dark circles under her eyes, her wrinkled dress and dusty boots betrayed the strain she tried to hide with a cheerless smile. She leaned against the pie cabinet and sipped the coffee Lulu handed her.

"A thousand blessings," Mary Margaret said holding up her cup in a mock toast. "It is grateful I am for the hospitality of the Mc Adam home, but we must be away early to reach the Grandes this day."

"Las Vegas Grandes, ya' mean?" asked Lulu.

"Yes. I have information and evidence for Sheriff O'Tero."

"And we shall travel together in my horse and carriage." Olivia bowed her head for one second then smiled in the knowledge that she was indeed capable of making such decisions, that it was very much her horse, her gig, her choice. "There is certain testimony concerning the murder of poor Private O'Brien that I must present. Mary Margaret, would you please continue driving as I am feeling a bit poorly this day."

Lulu said, "Yes. O'Brien, and all of them, deserve that much."

Mary Margaret looked into Olivia's eyes. "Yes. 'Tis true. We do this together, and with your help, Lulu."

"Well," said Lulu, looking at the two women. "I'll be damned if I know what you two are about, but take a blanket. I reckon there's weather on the way, and 'bout time too. The dust is as thick as fog."

The ride was long and chilling. A spring storm was descending from the *Sangre de Cristo* range. The countryside lay heavy with thick grey clouds, and splats of water plopped sporadically on the roof of the two-seater. Moisture seeped into the women's clothing and glistened on their hair. With a good rest and a full stomach, Tamany kept a steady trot, and the women rode in silence, Mary Margaret peering ahead at what she could see of the trail through the mist. She prayed they would arrive before the ruts turned to mud. Olivia kept the blanket spread across their knees and was grateful for the loan.

As a gentle but persistent rain fell, they arrived at Las Vegas Grandes and found a dry stall for Tamany in the Mercer Stables behind the jail building. Mary Margaret gathered the papers, and Olivia stowed the blankets under the seat. The two women approached the jailhouse door, and Mary Margaret knocked.

The sheriff opened it immediately. He stepped aside. "Miss O'Keenan, I have been expecting you. And Mrs. Foote I presume? Come in, *por favor*."

"An' just why wouldja be expecting us, sir?" asked Mary Margaret curtly.

"Come in, come in. Let us settle in for a long talk," said the sheriff. "I believe you have information regarding the murder of one Sergeant Seán Flannery." Sheriff Otero poured three tin mugs of coffee, set them on his desk, and said, "If you please, be seated." He indicated the two straight-backed chairs facing his desk.

Mary Margaret sat, removed the packet from her skirt pocket, and placed it on her lap. Olivia settled herself in the remaining chair. Otero answered Mary Margaret's question in detail. He explained that he was following, albeit from a distance, the goings-on at Fort Union and at the Post Trader's Compound. "There is much to be gleaned from the newspaper correspondences of the illustrious First Sergeant Clooney." The sheriff told the women that he too had been ruminating on the bits of information, evidence, and rumors gathered by Deputy Lucero. "But," he said with sincerity, "You, Miss O'Keenan, and you Mrs. Foote, shall provide the missing pieces of this grave and dangerous conundrum. And perhaps together we shall close the door on this criminal activity."

Mary Margaret said, "Conundrum is it? 'Tis a fine fancy word, but, I think *murder* and *evil* be better ones in this instance."

"Perhaps," replied the sheriff. "*Pero,* Mrs. Foote, *lo siento mucho.* May I express my sincere condolences to you on the loss of your husband."

Olivia acknowledged the formality with a nod. Mary Margaret took a sip of the coffee, then, setting down her cup, she began, "Sheriff O'Tero, 'tis grateful I am for your kindness and the genuine concern you showed me on the night of . . . on the night Sergeant Flannery's body was discovered. I was distraught an' may have been remiss in expressing me gratitude." The sheriff nodded and Mary Margaret continued. "'Tis your help we've come for, that is to say, I was not expecting to be helping you, sir."

"Perhaps, we shall help each other," Otero said.

Mary Margaret leaned forward, placed the packet of papers on the sheriff's desk, and crossed her hands on top. After a few seconds, she gently pushed the documents toward the sheriff. Then she told Otero what she knew, what she suspected, and what she wanted. Olivia remained silent, allowing the coffee to cool in her cup. As Sheriff Otero listened, he spread the papers across his desk. He looked up to see Mary Margaret's shining eyes intent upon him. He cleared his throat and carefully separated each sheaf, turning it this way and that, sniffing and inspecting the writing with a magnifier glass. He then picked up the notebook with Seán's name scrawled across the cover and began turning the pages.

Abruptly, Mary Margaret broke the silence, "Well sir?"

After a brief pause in which the three harbored their separate thoughts, Sheriff Otero said, "Miss O'Keenan, Mrs. Foote, if you please. As the esteemed Edgar Poe's great detective, Monsieur Dupin, so eloquently states, 'to calculate is not in itself to analyze.' We have gathered much information as well as evidence through observations—both intentional and random—and now, I suggest, it is time for 'recapitulation, analysis, inference.'" After a few seconds of silence, he asked, "Is it not?"

Mary Margaret said, "'Tis, I suppose. But 'tis also time for action, sir. Is it not?"

"Ah yes. But first analysis," reiterated Otero. "And we must be wary, vigilant. Our analyses and inferences will only be as sound as the quality of our observations and memories."

Mary Margaret nodded.

"*Esta bien,*" said the sheriff, mentally noting Miss O'Keenan's studied immobility and Mrs. Foote's small hand movements.

Sheriff Otero stacked the papers into a neat pile and setting them aside, he leaned to his right and opened one of the large side drawers, from which he withdrew another sheaf of papers, his narrative of the events as he knew them. "I shall share with you my knowledge, and as necessary, please correct me, that is to say, fill in the missing pieces."

"On the morning of April 14, 1881, at approximately 10:00 am, Sergeant Seán P. Flannery entered the Fort Union Post Trader's Store . . . ."

"Excuse me, sir," interrupted Olivia. "It would have been nearer to 10:30. I know this because I entered the store a few paces behind him."

The sheriff made the correction and continued, "at which time, the following occurred: Firstly, the Sergeant purchased a gold, heart-shaped locket with a *fleur de lis* pattern on one side and roses and ribbons on the other. A clerk by the name of Joseph Sanchez served the Sergeant. Secondly, as the two were completing the transaction, the fireplace mantel on the east wall collapsed. Sergeant Flannery secured the area and, with Joseph's help, began clearing away the rubble, at which time the Sergeant came upon a leather packet containing an assortment of documents."

234

When the sheriff paused, Mary Margaret leaned forward and said, "Excuse me, Sheriff O'Tero, but wouldja be telling me how it is you could be knowing what happened in the Post Trader's Store on that morning?"

Somewhat taken aback, Otero replied, "Of course, Miss O'Keenan, I was not present and did not observe the incidents. Eye witness testimony reported to me."

Mary Margaret straightened up. "Spoys? Sheriff, wouldja be havin'—and 'tis no shame in it—spoys at the Fort?"

"Spoys? Uh , oh yes, I understand. I would not say spies. Many of the nearby villagers, some who have known me from the day of my birth, are most fortunately employed at Fort Union, as well as the Post Trader's establishments. As you may know, there is always talk. It is my duty to examine such talk and distinguish that which is sound, that is, probable, from that which is, improbable or unlikely. Perhaps you will correct me should I err in this, Miss O'Keenan?"

"To be sure, sir. If I am able."

"Shall I continue?"

Mary Margaret nodded and leaned back in the chair.

After pausing to sip his coffee, Otero continued. "Fourth, . . ."

"Excuse me, sir," interrupted Mary Margaret with a small smile. "But wouldja be sayin' *fourth?* I be counting three."

Otero lifted his gaze to meet Mary Margaret's wide eyes. "The cleaning of the rubble would be number three." Mary Margaret nodded. Sheriff Otero cleared his throat, and Olivia made a very small sound that could have been the beginnings of a giggle. "Fourth, Mr. Josiah Foote entered the Store and engaged in a heated discussion with Sergeant Flannery, the specific topic of which remains unclear although a few words were distinctly heard: 'fraud, pay-off, and the phrase—"tis a feckin' shame it is'—this last shouted by the Sergeant."

Sheriff Otero paused and looked up.

Olivia said, "Yes. I heard Sergeant Flannery and Mr. Foote. I do not recall the exact words of the exchange, but the Sergeant said something to the effect that Mr. Foote should be ashamed of himself." Olivia paused while the sheriff made additional notes.

235

Then she continued, "Mr. Foote reached out his hand and demanded the papers. 'My documents, if you please,' he said. Sergeant Flannery replied—and this I recall clearly, 'They be your papers, Foote, but due to the nature of the documents, it is my duty to confiscate them and report such to my superior officer. 'Tis certain I am, the documents shall be returned to you in . . . .' The remainder of the sentence was cut off when Mr. Foote shouted, 'The devil take you Flannery.' And," continued Olivia, with a glance at Mary Margaret, "I recall that Sgt. Flannery smiled broadly and tipped his forage cap, which infuriated Mr. Foote. Then Mr. Foote said, 'We shall see what your superior officer thinks,' and stalked out of the store. I peeked out through the side window and saw him, Mr. Foote, climbing the hill to the Quartermaster's Depot."

The sheriff raised his hand. "A moment, please." He scribbled more notes then looked up and asked, "Mrs. Foote, does not the Commanding Officer's duty office lie in that direction?"

"Why, yes. It does," replied Olivia. "His office is in the very same building."

The sheriff wrote a few quick notes. "Proceed, if you please."

"Well, Sgt. Flannery re-folded the papers, slid them into the pouch, and then, he too departed. I was transfixed, as you may well imagine, by these events, but before the door swung shut, I saw the sergeant mount his *pinto* and . . . ." Olivia suddenly stopped.

"And?" Mary Margaret said to Olivia.

"Is there something more, Mrs. Foote?" asked Sheriff Otero.

"Well, only now, in recounting the incident, I recall that the Sergeant rode up the hill. I saw him pass the window, I suspect, following Mr. Foote. But within perhaps ten minutes, yes, as I was completing my transaction, I saw Sergeant Flannery doubled back and rode south and west." After a brief pause, Olivia said softly, "toward Los Alamitos."

"We cannot assume the sergeant's intended destination," said Otero. "We can, however, note that he and his horse did arrive some time shortly thereafter at Los Alamitos."

"So," Mary Margaret said, "Seán spoke with Colonel Winters that very morning. The Colonel knew of the documents."

"Perhaps." The sheriff made a few more notations and said, "But, Miss O'Keenan, we must not engage in—as thrilling as the chase may be—jumping to conclusions. Based on the testimony of Mrs. Foote, we cannot be certain that Sergeant Flannery actually arrived at the Commanding Officer's quarters or that they spoke. We can only know that he rode in that direction. May I continue?"

Olivia smiled and Mary Margaret nodded.

"I have acquired certain additional testimony." And Otero read from his report. "At approximately noon on April 14, 1881, Sergeant Flannery arrived at the village store in Los Alamitos where he conversed briefly with Porfirio Gonzalez before asking him for help. Here I quote *Señor* Gonzalez. 'SeánFlannery requested that I hold some important papers for him. He told me that he had spoken with his commanding officer, but did not feel good about leaving the papers with him. 'Tis a higher authority I must seek' he said.'"

The sheriff looked up. "So you see, we have testimony that Sergeant Flannery arrived at Los Alamitos and further testimony, albeit hearsay, to the effect that the Sergeant had conferred with his commanding officer, Colonel Winters. However, we do not have details of that conference."

"Then," continued Otero, " according to Mr. Gonzalez, Sergeant Flannery entrusted his friend with a leather pouch, a notebook, and a small package."

Sheriff Otero paused, and Mary Margaret took the opportunity to say, "Excuse me, sir, we know this to be true. Did we not ourselves—Olivia and m'self—visit Mr. Gonzalez, an' didn't we find the locket an' the key? Didn't we ourselves secure the papers?"

"Indeed," said Otero. "You agree with my recapitulation?"

As Mary Margaret straightened her back and opened her mouth, Olivia gently rested her hand on Mary Margaret's forearm. The gesture was enough. "Yes," Olivia said to the Sheriff. "It is the time after Mr. Flannery left Mr. Gonzalez that is in question."

Sheriff Otero smiled. "Indeed. After securing the said papers and notebook with Mr. Gonzalez, Sergeant Flannery mounted his horse and rode toward Fort Union, and of course, he would pass the Lake. When the sergeant approached Los Alamitos Lake, we cannot know for certain what transpired. At this point, I wish not to speculate."

Mary Margaret sighed, rhythmically tapping her fingers on her thigh. She said, "Tis p'rhaps so. But I am certain . . . ."

"Indeed, Miss O'Keenan? You are a witness? Can your testimony be soundly supported by evidence?"

"'Tis proof you be needin' and I have it," said Mary Margaret, jumping to her feet. "'Tis known to me that First Sergeant John Holloway departed from his detail—he were leading a patrol guarding a shipment of flour from Mora to the Quartermaster's Depot—but turned off, he did, an' rode south toward Los Alamitos Lake where he caught Seán unawares an' done the deed. Private Sullivan, told me that as the patrol approached La Cueva, the First Sergeant received a dispatch from Colonel Winters, and . . . ."

"Excuse me, please," interrupted Otero, holding up one hand. "Would you be so kind as to speak more slowly so that I may accurately record the details of Private Sullivan's statement?"

"'Tis grateful I am for your care, Sheriff." She paused and repeated the information, adding, "The First Sergeant assured the patrol that he would rejoin them at the arsenal. But Private Sullivan did not see Holloway again until later, Retreat, that evening." Mary Margaret sat down quietly.

"And," said Olivia, "we know that earlier, in the morning, when Mr. Foote left the store he went directly to Colonel Winters' quarters. Clearly, the commanding officer is somehow involved in this conspiracy."

Sheriff Otero blinked. "Conspiracy," he said softly. "How, Mrs. Foote, do you come to such a conclusion?"

"Well, I . . . ."

"'Tis an inference," said Mary Margaret. "Is it not, sir? An inference based on observation an' testimony."

The sheriff smiled broadly to hear his theories mirrored. Then he became too busy trying to keep pace with Mary Margaret as she explained subsequent events—the new recruits with the bundled-up soldier's uniform and Seán's riding boots, the Comedy Company headquarters, Private Peterson, and Private Shiner."

Mary Margaret paused. The room was filled with the sounds of the sheriff scribbling furiously and the incessant drumming of rain drops on the tin roof. Suddenly, Otero stopped in the middle of forming a word and looked at Mary Margaret. "How do you know they were the boots of Sergeant Flannery?"

"Seán's ankle be bowed outward. A childhood accident. It affects the shape of the boot."

"I see," said Otero. "I see that there are many aspects of the situation—or perhaps—conspiracy. At this time, let us please concentrate on what seems to be the beginning, that is, the death of Sergeant Seán flannery. Let us return to the lakeside," he said, picking up his report. "If it is not too painful, Miss O'Keenan."

Mary Margaret nodded, and the sheriff read his report on the condition of the body when discovered which coincided with Mary Margaret's recollections. But when he read the autopsy report, Mary Margaret flinched as she recalled Seán's cold hand and staring eyes. She smoothed her hair. She tidied her skirt. Otero looked up briefly, continued reading to the end of the section, then again leaned down to his right and withdrew something from a lower drawer. As he straightened, he placed on the desk a portion of a sleeve insignia—shredded golden threads clinging to the edges of the chevron and diamond—the symbol of the rank of First Sergeant.

"On the night of April 14, when you, Miss O'Keenan, called me to the ambulance, I had pulled this from the mud close to Sergeant Flannery's body."

Mary Margaret jumped to her feet. "'Tis proof then! 'Twas Jack Holloway killed me man. That be his patch"

"It would seem . . . ."

"'Twould not *seem,* sheriff. '*Tis.* 'Tis the proof we need.

"Certainly, if Holloway is the *only* first sergeant at the garrison."

"No, he is not," said Olivia softly.

Mary Margaret turned to Olivia. "Olivia, for the love o' God, you know . . . *we* know 'twas Jack killed Seán. Didn't he search us, an' Mrs. Winters tell us? An' wouldja be forgetting Private O'Brien's murder? Do you suppose First Sergeant Clooney, or any of the others, be dashing about the Trader's Compound murdering soldiers?"

Olivia stood and gently took hold of Mary Margaret's hands. "We are trying to fit all the pieces together. Perhaps it is time you tell sheriff what you found clutched in Sergeant Flannery's hand."

"Ah no,'tis nuthin.' Discredited, it was, by Doctor Williamson."

"Perhaps Sheriff Otero has another interpretation," said Olivia.

Mary Margaret looked at the expectant face of Sheriff Otero. She rose and in a low deliberate tone, she explained how it was she found the nest of coarse red hair clutched in Seán's hand. Then she dropped it onto the desk.

"Horse hair?" he asked.

"'Tis only that," she said. "Dr. Williamson examined it and confirmed this. We believe it to be the hair of Seán's own horse. 'Tis useless, it is."

"Perhaps not," said Otero. "Nothing is insignificant at this stage of our investigation."

Mary Margaret slapped her hand upon the sheriff's desk. "'Twas Jack Holloway killed me man," she said.

"Miss O'Keenan, do you mean to say that you have some knowledge that unequivocally places Mr. Holloway at the scene?"

"Ah no," she said, "but 'twas Jack." Her voice faltered, and turning her back to the sheriff, she walked to the window. Rain spilled from the *tejado* and coursed in streams down to the board walk. "'Tis a waste of time, this going over and over of things."

"Mary Margaret," said Olivia. "Please tell the Sheriff about Mrs. Winters."

Mary Margaret did not immediately move or respond. Then she turned and walked back to the desk. She looked into Sheriff Otero's inscrutable eyes.

"Mrs. Winters, the Colonel's own wife, came to us. She told us—me and Olivia—that himself did indeed order First Sergeant

240

Holloway to intercept—she said was word he used—Sergeant Flannery, secure the documents, and swear the Sergeant to secrecy."

"Why?" asked Otero.

"Why? Why!" shouted Mary Margaret, confused by the Sheriff's question. "Because Seán . . . Seán would not be sworn to secrecy. And for that he be murdered!"

Olivia said, "If I may explain a bit? It is known at the garrison that the Colonel is adamant there be no scandal associated with his name. After Seán's visit that morning, he became aware of the contents of the documents, which indicate fraud, or bribery, or possibly conspiracy. Mrs. Winters quoted the Colonel as saying to First Sergeant Holloway, 'Do whatever you have to but get those papers.'"

"Hm." Sheriff Otero wrote furiously for a few seconds. Then rose and walked around the edge of his desk. "There are many threads we must weave together. You may be correct Miss O'Keenan. We may be on the verge of arrest. However, we must await the return of my deputy with, I expect, the evidence necessary to confirm your suspicions." He approached Mary Margaret, firmly grasped her elbow, and guided her to the chair. "It should not be long now. Please sit and bear with me as I plod through the twists and turns of these remarkable events. Then, when all is in place, I swear to you, we shall act and act swiftly."

Mary Margaret allowed the Sheriff to guide her. She sat, as a wave of exhaustion crashed over her. To control the sudden feeling of sickness, she concentrated on Otero. His expression betrayed no anxiety, no insecurity, but she thought she detected a trace of sympathy, and she did not like it. She folded her hands in her lap and said, "An' what is it we be waiting for your deputy to bring?"

"Of that I am not certain. He departed early this morning with a civilian search warrant—Colonel Winters refused to issue an Authorization to Search the quarters of First Sergeant Holloway."

"And what is to be found there? Sure, Jack destroyed all bits of evidence. He is no fool."

"Miss O'Keenan, you are the Company B Laundress, are you not? And he is a member of Company B, is he not? Then it follows that during the course of fulfilling his duties, should he have muddied and torn one of his uniforms, he would present it to you for cleaning. Is this not so?"

Mary Margaret nodded and Otero continued, "But should he have muddied and torn a uniform in the act of murdering Sergeant Flannery, that is entirely another matter. Is it not? And if such a uniform exists in his quarters, it may indicate, at the very least, his presence at the location of Sergeant Flannery's murder."

"Sure, there be other laundresses who would . . . ."

"Who would, no doubt, do his laundry." The sheriff completed her statement. "But I suspect that such a laundress may question his reasons and possibly engage in a bit of *mitote*."

"Oh, that is so true, Mary Margaret," said Olivia. "You know how the others would gloat over such a possibility—that your skills are not good enough for the First Sergeant of the Company. First Sergeant Holloway would not take such a chance. Of that I am certain."

"If I may continue?" said Otero, leaning back in his chair and folding his arms across his chest. "Miss O'Keenan, it is my understanding that you have been conducting an investigation of your own in the vicinity of Fort Union. Would you be kind enough to share information that you deem pertinent, that is, for inclusion in my report?"

Before Mary Margaret was able to answer, Olivia said, "If I may, there is also the matter of Private O'Brien. He was murdered last night. Run through by a sabre. Perhaps your deputy has informed you. After we tended to him, I was accosted and searched by First Sergeant Holloway, at which time, I detected blood pooled in the handle of his sword. And furthermore, the First Sergeant indicated that he was indeed responsible for Patrick's death." Olivia provided the necessary but brutal details regarding Holloway's crazed search of both her home and herself. "When satisfied that I did not have the documents he was seeking, he left. I believe he then proceeded directly to Mary Margaret's quarters."

There was a pause while the sheriff completed his writing. The rain remained at a steady drumming.

Mary Margaret swallowed hard then responded. "Jack Holloway did indeed burst into me quarters and tossed me things about. But when he tried to search me person, I shot him. An' as to the investigating sir, 'tis me duty as . . . as I see it. An' I have indeed learned much. 'Twere a number of soldiers murdered during the past six months or so. An' they be stripped of their uniforms and weapons. 'Tis information I gathered at . . . uh . . . on the premises of the Palace of Passion."

"Yes," replied Otero. "I have knowledge of such crimes. You yourself did not observe these bodies?"

"No sir."

Olivia said, "Sheriff, these murders. It is common knowledge at Fort Union, that is, investigations were conducted, reports made. In all instances, an inquest determined that these deaths were unnatural."

"Indeed," said Otero. "Are there any reasons to believe that Sergeant Flannery's murder is *not* the work of the same individual?"

Mary Margaret cleared her throat. "Dr. Williamson told me that ligatures were used in previous strangulations, but Seán was strangled by hand." She sat motionless for a few minutes while the sheriff scribbled.

"Yes," he said. "It is an important difference."

She then reminded the sheriff of the documents, Mrs. Winters' statements, and a note in Seán's log indicating his reluctance to trust the Company B First Sergeant. "His own mate," she concluded.

After a brief pause, she said, "I believe that immediately following the incident at the Trader's Store, Mr. Foote went directly to the Commander and Sergeant Flannery followed him. Perhaps the Commander ordered Seán to hand over the documents, but himself being an investigator an'. . . ."

"Himself? An investigator?" asked Sheriff Otero.

"Yes, himself, didja not know that Sergeant Flannery was an investigator?"

"Uh, begging your pardon, I am not familiar with your particular use of the English reflexive pronoun. So, by *himself* you mean to indicate Sergeant Flannery?"

In spite of her anxiety and frustration, Mary Margaret smiled. "We be having all sorts of troubles communicating, sir. 'Tis a fine group of detectives we be!"

Olivia laughed and the Sheriff smiled although he remained mystified by the term *himself.*

"Ah," said Mary Margaret. "For the love of God, Sheriff O'Tero, with that smile on your face, you be a right good looker."

The sheriff cleared his throat, looked from one woman to the other, then turned his eyes to the narrow, barred window facing *la plaza.* "I fear the storm brings a chill," he said. He crossed the room to the large pot-bellied stove and poked at the embers until they glowed. Then he added several small logs and returned to his chair behind the desk.

Olivia stood and explained about the special patrol that Flannery and Holloway were assigned to.

"An,'" continued Mary Margaret, "*himself,* that is, Sergeant Flannery, being experienced in the ways of interrogating, knowing when someone be putting him on—even if 'twere his very own commanding officer—I believe Seán Flannery refused to give over the papers."

The fire caught and crackled, filling the silence of the jailhouse and sending out tentative waves of warmth that were suddenly fanned by a rush of wind from the open door. Deputy Lucero, hugging a large bundle wrapped in his own oil-skinned long coat and tied with rope, rushed into the room. He dropped his burden on the floor and removed his hat. Water flew from the brim and sprinkled Mary Margaret's back.

244

Chapter 26: In which life goes on.

The Sheriff rose from his chair as Lucero swung the iron-clad door closed. "Come, Pedro, warm yourself by the fire. You have my sincere appreciation and respect for your diligence and your success."

Mary Margaret rose from her chair and stared down at the bundle as the damp chill scuttled off to wait in dark corners. Sheriff Otero came around from behind his desk, knelt, and untied the ropes. He spread First Sergeant Holloway's spare uniform on the floor, then matched the torn insignia patch to a space on the right sleeve. He noted the presence of mud spatters on the front of the trousers and jacket.

"'Tis the evidence we be needing," said Mary Margaret softly. "The proof."

"I believe it is, Miss O'Keenan."

Olivia crossed the room and stood behind Mary Margaret as the sheriff lifted the left sleeve of the uniform.

"It appears there is a tangle of hair, perhaps from that of a horse's mane," said Otero, pointing to several strands of red hair tightly curled among the sleeve buttons.

Mary Margaret did not respond. In that bit of hair, she saw the murder, the struggle with the horse and rider, Rosie falling to her knees, Jack's big hands closing around Seán's neck. She saw the look of sadness and shock of betrayal in the eyes of her man.

"Miss O'Keenan," said Sheriff Otero. "I believe we have the proof we need to charge First Sergeant Holloway with the murder of Sergeant Seán Flannery. As for the other deaths, I do not know. As yet, I have no evidence connecting all four murders. Perhaps, more information will be forthcoming."

Mary Margaret blinked away the image of Jack's hands and the struggle in the mud. "'Tis another uniform discovered. You be aware of that, Sheriff?" When she saw the puzzled look on his face, she explained about Miguel and Jack's new recruits. The Sheriff wrote frantically as she stood and said to Olivia. "We must go. I fear we have much to do."

Deputy Lucero said, "*Con permiso,* the trail is flooded to the north. By now it is impassable."

"Oh good Lord," said Olivia. "We are stranded."

Mary Margaret felt suddenly hopeless and indecisive. She raged inwardly at the elements, at the countryside and its betrayal. For several seconds, no one spoke. They stood as actors in a tableau, and Mary Margaret recalled the final scene of *The Irish Attorney*—all action halted by the last line: "'Tis the work of demons, to be sure. She be a maid more sinned against than sinning."

"Mary Margaret?" said Olivia, gently taking her cold hand. "Are you unwell? May we have some water please, Sheriff. I fear she may faint."

"No. No. Never fainted in all me life," said Mary Margaret.

The sheriff addressed her directly. "Miss O'Keenan, please be assured that as soon as God and the conditions allow, I shall take a small contingent of deputies and arrest First Sergeant Holloway."

"An' I'll be there beside you, I will."

Otero continued, "Your presence is neither necessary nor desirable. Now, with your permission, Deputy Lucero will escort you ladies to the new and most respectable boarding house on Jackson Street."

> *Ah Seán, if only I'd had the courage, sitting there on the stone bench at Mr. Lincoln's Park. You be waitin' for an answer and me be dawdling.' I dinna believe it. You askin' me for my hand in marriage. Oh the regrets I have. You never knew. I kept my love for you hidden like a treasure locked away in me heart. Me with no dowry. An' when the silence become uneasy, you took me hand and said, 'An' that be Jackson Street, newly cut. Sure this be a fine place, surrounded by American presidents.'*

With Deputy Lucero to guide them, Mary Margaret and Olivia arrived at number 1729 Jackson Street, a two-storey, clapboard building on which hung three signs. Two large ones, painted in deep blue on bright white: "Furnished Rooms to Board" and

246

underneath "Livery in Rear." Beside these, a smaller sign, hand-lettered in black on unvarnished wood—"For Sale." While Deputy Lucero made arrangements with the proprietor, Mary Margaret and Olivia took the buggy to the stable. Together they settled Tamany with a good rubbing and brushing, a generous stack of hay, and a bucket of water.

As they approached the open barn doors, they saw a lantern swinging on the back porch of the house. "Come in ladies," called a woman. Through the light mist, they saw her gesturing.

"That'll be the landlady," and Mary Margaret stepped forward.

"A moment," said Olivia, catching her friend's arm and pulling her back into the barn. "You have been true and loyal to me. You never spoke of my . . . my . . . pending confinement. I am grateful for your silence." Mary Margaret opened her mouth but Olivia silenced her. "No, just listen to me, please." She took hold of Mary Margaret's hands. "You have been a friend and a comfort to me—with never a question. Now I shall try to be the same to you."

"Ah, but you are me friend."

"Mary Margaret, if you please," and they both smiled at their recollections of Sheriff Otero. "Let me have my say. This is important—though I fear you will not like to hear it. Only a true friend would say it to you. You have done all you can. You must allow Sheriff Otero to take hold of these matters. He is quite capable—if a bit stodgy—well, perhaps, methodical is a better word."

"'Tis I who must make justice for me man," interrupted Mary Margaret, struggling to escape from Olivia's hold.

"Why? Justice will be done. Why must it be at your hands?"

"Because," Mary Margaret paused, then all in a rush, words tumbling over themselves, she said, "I never told him, Olivia, I never told me man I loved him. 'Twas across the road, there, at the park. They were painting the trim of this very house. 'Twas newly built. And we talked of a future together. He wanted me to be his bride. And I dinna' say a word of encouragement though I loved him—I love him still—his smilin' eyes, the wit and charm, the strength and gentleness of the man. An' didn't he make me

247

laugh? Me Ma always said, 'Marry a man who can make you laugh. All else is naught.' Made me laugh he did, Olivia, made me laugh at meself and me silly, put-on aires and me figurin' he called it. 'Mary Margaret, me darlin' he'd say, 'tis all this figurin' be pollutin' yer humours,' he said."

Mary Margaret's voice faltered, and she coughed to hide a sob. "An' he'd walk me out, or sing me a ditty, or dance a bit of a planxty, an' in no time atall I'd be out of meself. I knew I loved him. I did an' I do. But I never told him. 'Tis I who must do for him. 'Tis me penance."

"Stop it. I will not allow it. Penance, indeed! You must forgive yourself. Seán would—if there were a thing to forgive. Do you not think that he knew? He'd have waited for your answer. I have no doubt he is waiting still."

From the porch came the gentle call again, "Ladies, *señoras*, come in, *por favor*."

"We best be going. Perhaps Timmy Sullivan be right—I am a cold hard woman, but I dinna' want to keep the good lady waiting."

"No. I am not moving," said Olivia. "Not until you forgive yourself—here—now."

Seán Flannery, for the love o' God, what has happened to the Lady Olivia? Makin' demands she is. What's that you say? Ah yes, I do love you. An' I be proud and pleased and excited to be marrying you. Can you forgive me for dawdling?

Mary Margaret turned her head ever so slightly to the right as she heard a whisper carried on the soft wet breeze. And in the mist she saw him—the broad warm smile, the devilish glint in his eyes. She saw him doff his cap and bow, formally, from the waist as if in the presence of the queen. Then the fog swirled in a sudden turmoil of wind and he was gone.

"Seán."

"Mary Margaret?" Olivia's voice seemed to reach her from far away.

Mary Margaret watched the shards of blowing rain, felt moisture sliding down her cheeks and seeping beneath the collar of her dress, and she smelled the sweetness of the fresh hay. Tamany stomped a hoof and blew through his nostrils.

Mary Margaret turned to Olivia and said, "Thank you, Olivia. Shall we go in now lest we perish in this Godforsaken rain?"

Regular Correspondent to the Optic. Fort Union, April 29.—
On Monday last, April 25 last, Colonel Samuel J. Winters, the
Commanding Officer of the Fort Union Garrison, was confined to
quarters pending further investigation into allegations of murder
and conspiracy under his command. The extent of said
wrongdoings is, as yet, not known; however, it is quite possible
that a conspiracy exists that extends beyond the Fort, possibly as
high up the ladder as the U.S. War Department. As the garrison's
appointed correspondent to the *Optic*, I urge the members of the
general public to reserve judgment until the facts are assembled
and criminal charges—if any—are filed. Let me say this, however,
it is true that the unexpected deaths of four soldiers attached to the
23rd Infantry, are currently under investigation. It is yet to be
determined conclusively whether such deaths occurred as a result
of murder, suicide, or accident. At this early stage of the
investigations, I shall not engage in the naming of names nor the
distribution of unsupported accusations. According to San Miguel
County Sheriff Juan Otero, criminal charges are pending. Sheriff
Otero declined to expand. Please be assured that immediately the
facts are known, I shall report them, as is my duty, to the *Las
Vegas Daily Optic*.

It is my pleasure to report that the Japanese Tea Party,
organized and presented for the benefit of the Fort Union School
Fund by Miss Victoria Winters, was by all accounts a smashing
success, no less in the enjoyment of the assembled officers and
their families than in the funds raised. Under Miss Winters' astute
directions, the Quartermaster outdid himself in serving exotic
delicacies and creating beautiful decorations which transported all
those who attended to the Asian continent.

J. Clooney, Regimental Correspondent

Las Vegas Daily Optic
Our Fort Union Letter

Regular Correspondent to the Optic. Fort Union, April 30.—I take no pleasure in fulfilling my duty this day. Indeed, this shall be my final dispatch. The news I am required to report has so shaken my personal beliefs that I am resigning as the Fort Union correspondent, and when my hitch is up, I shall move on. I would that my final dispatch were of another nature.

On April 22 of this year, the Fort Union Commanding Officer, Colonel S. Winters, 10th Infantry, was re-assigned to Fort Larned. Winters was neither absolved of wrong-doing nor charged with offenses. Accusations implicate him in a conspiracy to conceal fraudulent behavior in regards to the Post Trader's assignment—fraud that involves the United States War Department under a previous administration. Col. Winters has not been charged with a crime, and no courts marshal have been announced. Furthermore, it appears that attempts to conceal the nature of this fraud and its perpetrators resulted in the untimely deaths of Sergeant Seán P. Flannery, 23rd Infantry, Private Walter J. Shiner, 23rd Infantry, and Private Patrick M. O'Brien, 23rd Infantry, as well as that of the post trader, Mr. Josiah Foote. Civilian and military charges of obstruction of justice, conspiracy, and murder have been brought against First Sergeant John Jay Holloway, 23rd Infantry. Currently, Holloway is confined to the post guardhouse. It is not my purview to assign guilt, and I shall not indulge in idle or harmful speculation. The process of the law shall determine the outcomes of the charges.

Commendations are the order of the day, however. On behalf of the Fort Union community, I sincerely express gratitude to the following: Sergeant Gustave Peterson, 10th Infantry; Privates Wilson and Mathison, 23rd Infantry; Sheriff Juan Otero of San Miguel County for his relentless pursuit of the truth; Master Miguel Gomez of Loma Parda for providing vital evidence; and, lastly, to the Company B Laundress, Miss Mary Margaret O'Keenan, for tenaciously following the trail of evidence and questioning her superiors.

Would that investigations had shed light on the unnatural deaths of Pvt. Francisco Abreu, Henry Watts, and Jeremiah Hanson, all of the 10th Infantry, soldiers good and true, who died within past several years. Investigations continue.

Finally, I wish to express my sincere and everlasting gratitude to the editors and readers of the *Las Vegas Daily Optic* for their upstanding integrity and loyalty to this correspondent's column.

J. Clooney, Regimental Correspondent

Epilogue
Leaving Fort Union

A light, intermittent snow falls. At the entrance to the Fort Union graveyard, Mary Margaret halts the new carriage, pulled by the unlikely pair of Rosie and Tamany. She wonders if the horses recall their past proud moments under saddle. She pulls back the brake, rests the reins on the seat, and jumps down, raising the light powdery snow. She enters and climbs the small incline to the grave of Seán Padraic Flannery. She lifts her gaze to the *Sangre de Cristo* range, takes in the odor of pine. Then her eyes settle on the hillocks of unmarked graves lying before her like ancient drumlins. September fifteenth, she thinks, early snow, long winter. Her eyes light on Seán's grave, identified by a small pyramid of river rocks, spotted with melting flakes. She kneels and makes the sign of the cross.

> *'Tis sorry I am to be leavin' you, Seán. Though it be but a few hours' ride on Rosie's strong back from Las Vegas. I'll be visiting every Sunday, regular as a bishop for dinner. An' continue the fight I will, until each soldier's end is known and grave has a marker with a name to be spoken in prayer.*

> *I dinna . . . I mean to say, I do not know what the town of Las Vegas Grandes can hold for me or Olivia. Likely she be going to her family after the babe is born . . . though she says no. Says she's her own person now and needs her own home. 'Tis a fine place we be going to, Seán. You'd be proud to live in it, you would. It is but a year old, the very one we watched them paint the day we sat in the Lincoln Park. An' when I sit in me parlor, I see the lovely trees. . . they be growing inch by inch. Number 1729 Jackson Street, if you please, me own home, me own address, with the kind help of Olivia. In the spring, we be planting lilacs in the front, and their perfume be permeating—a word Olivia taught me—the household. The house be Queen*

Anne style, she says. 'Tis grey clapboard siding, neatly trimmed with white, and topped with a real shingle roof, pitched against the snow. There be a long front porch waitin' for a swing, it is. An' a patch of good soil at the rear for planting potatoes and greens. Sure, we be taking in boarders to help with the monthlies. But Olivia and me we makin' a home. Come visit, Seán Flannery.

The wind whips and swirls big fat flakes of snow. Tamany stamps a hoof and Mary Margaret glances back over her shoulder at the waiting horses.

"Right you are, Tam. We best be going."

'Tis time I be departin.' 'Til Sunday then, luv.

Mary Margaret rises to her feet and squinting her eyes, peers up into the sky. Flakes settle softly on her lashes. She looks down again at the grave then turns to the carriage, climbs in, and gathers the reins.

Olivia stands in the center of what was once her favorite room, the parlor, vacant now except for a handful of dust and dry leaves clustered into a small heap. A few dabs of snow drift in through the open door and melt on the blackened floor. Gone are the green velvet sofa, the grey brocade, wing-back chair where she once sat mending a white shirt. Olivia closes her eyes on that moment of brutality then shifts her gaze to the tall frosted windows, the bare walls. The fireplace mantle holds a fine layer of plaster—no candelabra, no crystal decanter. Olivia blinks, closing what she would come to think of as a brief, horrifying chapter in her life.

Leaving, she thinks, is the easy part. It's the arriving I'm uncertain of. Can we make a home—Mary Margaret and me and my baby? Olivia recalls her trepidation as the time of day drew near for Mr. Foote to return—agonizing over the quality of the meal, the cleanliness of the rooms, her dress, and her very smile. She wonders what 1729 Jackson Street can hold for her. One room, she thinks, but my own and my baby's. A room where I can, if I choose, close the door.

Olivia turns and walks out onto the wide front porch. Her gaze takes in what was once her world, the Fort Union Trader's Compound. She sees Mary Margaret bring the horses to a smart, neat halt. "Oh, just one moment please," and she rushes back into the house. At the cold fireplace, she removes her glove and grasps the simple gold ring on the third finger of her left hand. Yanking it free, she tosses it onto the ash pile where it slowly sinks out of sight. "Good bye, Mr. Foote," she says aloud. Then, "Good bye, Mrs. Foote." She turns, her skirt raising a fog of dust, and walks out through the open door. She closes the door and leaves the key in the lock.

Mary Margaret jumps down to help Olivia. Heavy now and awkward, Olivia climbs into the carriage. Mary Margaret tucks two blankets around her friend then climbs in.

"Are you ready, Olivia? Will you not miss Fort Union?" Olivia peers out through the swirling snow at the chimneys of the garrison. "Oh, I'll surely miss the afternoon clouds, the raging purple sunsets, the mournful call of the coyotes, but no, Mary Margaret, I shall not miss Fort Union. I'm ready. Quite ready."

"Then it is time we be departing."

"'Tis," says Olivia.

1729 Jackson Street. Come round anytime, Seán Flannery. Anytime atall.

Glossary

brevet. A commission promoting a military officer to a higher rank without increase of pay and with limited exercise of the higher rank, often granted as an honor.

casita. A small house (Spanish).

Dead House. The morgue.

nicho. A small shelf carved into an adobe wall (Spanish).

paletot. A man's fitted overcoat; also a woman's fitted, sometimes flared, jacket worn especially in the 19th century over a dress with a crinoline or bustle.

portal. A patio attached to a home, covered with a fixed roof, and supported by posts (Spanish).

reticule. A woman's drawstring bag used especially as a carryall.

Sangre de Cristo. Blood of Christ (Spanish); the name of the southern range of the Rocky Mountains in New Mexico.

striker. An enlisted soldier who works as a household servant, usually for an officer.

Suds Row. The area at Fort Union where the laundresses lived and worked; aka, Laundress Row.

sutler. A civilian merchant, usually contracted by the military, who sells provisions to an army in the field, in camp, or in quarters; aka, Post Trader.

throatlatch. The strap on a bridle or halter passing under the horse's throat.

"toobs." The tubs for washing laundry (Irish brogue).

trastero. A free-standing cupboard or cabinet (colloquial Spanish), similar to a "Hoosier" cabinet.

wuthering. From the verb to wuther, to blow with a dull, roaring sound; blustery, turbulent.

yegua. A mare (Spanish).

Author's Notes

*History is a novel that has been lived, a novel is history that
could have been.*
Edmond and Jules de Goncourt

. . . a murder was committed at Loma Parda on Sunday last—
the 9th of October, 1871. The dead man was found, devoid of all
clothing, which seems to have been the motive. The dead man was
named Bergman. He belonged to the Eighth Cavalry band
stationed at the fort [Fort Union]. His head was beaten to jelly by
stones [notice on the post board].

F. Stanley, *Fort Union (New Mexico)*

Prairie Madness, Conspiracy at Fort Union is an historical
novel. So it is a work that both "has been lived" in its historical
sense and "could have been" in its fictional aspects. When *Prairie
Madness* came to fruition, I was fortunate to have a great group of
people willing to read the first galley proof. Those readers wanted
to know which parts of the book are history and which fiction. So,
here goes.

Writing the novel grew from two sources—my Keenan Irish
family roots and my earlier book, *Footlights in the Foothills,
Amateur Theatre of Las Vegas and Fort Union, New Mexico,
1871-1899.* Research on Fort Union revealed that beginning in
1883, at least three amateur acting companies were based at the
garrison, staffed by soldiers, and advised by officers. The names
of the companies and the soldier/performers were often included in
the weekly letter from the post correspondent to the *Las Vegas
Optic.* I used some of the names for characters in *Prairie
Madness.* Sean Flannery, "The very life and soul of the Comedy
Company," is one.

According to census reports, the "Irish" side of my family, that
is, the paternal ancestors of my mother Reta Elizabeth Keenan
Portelle, is made up of Murrays, who emigrated from Ireland and
Scotland before 1880 and Keenans, who emigrated from Ireland in

1881. Family lore centered around hardship—large families supported on laborers' occupations like box handlers, wagon drivers, sometimes "none," until finally, "Stationary Fireman." Regardless of the harsh realities, these stories were lovingly and proudly told. Like the one about when my grandfather, Ladderman William Keenan, Boston Fire Department, chased down a burglar and caught him. By the way, before joining the fire department, my grandfather was employed as a private detective, a fitting model for Mary Margaret O'Keenan. Additionally, O'Keenan (O'Cianain) was the early, Medieval form of Keenan, a name famous for producing important clergymen and/or historians (Edward MacLysaght, *Irish Families: Their Names, Arms, and Origins*).

Research is often self-perpetuating. In addition to research on family and Fort Union acting tropes, I looked at everything related to garrison life and regulations, soldiers, army laundresses, the ethnic make-up of the Frontier Army, social life at Fort Union, the murders of soldiers, and fraud in the Office of the U. S. Secretary of War under President Grant.

ETHNIC MAKEUP—THE IRISH IMMIGRANTS

In the 1880s, the population of the United States Army included an estimated 150,000 Irish men and women. The close of the American Civil War coincided with the onset of Indian wars, and the Army sent its soldiers to its string of southwestern posts. In addition to serving as soldiers, many Irish immigrants participated in the great land rush, became merchants, and, sometimes, their American born children joined the ranks of famous outlaws and/or lawmen of the Western Frontier like Henry McCarty (Billy the Kid), Tom O'Folliard, and Pat Garrett, the grandson of Irish immigrants. Garrett and his deputy went after, arrested, and brought Billy and three additional outlaws through what would become Las Vegas, NM, in December of 1882, where they rested overnight.

Sources agree that from 1802 until at least 1887, women served in the military as laundresses and received housing, food, fuel, and medical treatment as well as fees for their work. Records show the names of many Irish immigrant laundresses at Fort Union; one of them was Bridget Molloy, but she could have been Mary Margaret O'Keenan. There were many Irish immigrant soldiers stationed at the garrison, and one of them was Patrick Cloonan of Company B, who married Bridget Molloy; but he could have been Sergeant Seán Padraic Flannery, who wanted to marry Mary Margaret O'Keenan.

Histories of Fort Union note that from the early to the mid-1880s troops living at the garrison numbered between 200-300. Families, civilian workers (wagon repair, animal care), and the Post Traders' employees likely doubled that number. However, by 1879, the railroad had reached the frontier, making dramatic changes in the economy and population of Fort Union. Its Quartermaster's functions—supplying the southwestern posts—dwindled.

A CONSPIRACY

The characters and events in *Prairie Madness* are fictional although during the novel's time period, at Fort Union, soldiers were murdered, post bullies existed, there was a post trader, there was an excellent hospital, autopsies were performed, Vicente Silva owned the Imperial Hall as well as a "safe house" in Los Alamos (Los Alamitos), and a syndrome called Prairie Madness was recorded in letters and diaries of the time.

Historically, incidents of bribery took place at Fort Sill, ca. 1876. William Worth Belknap, a general in the Union Army, served as Secretary of War from 1869-1876. In 1876, Belknap resigned his cabinet post pending charges of corruption. "He was impeached and tried before the Senate of the United States, the specific charge against him being that he had promised to appoint Caleb P. Marsh of New York to maintain a trading establishment at Fort Sill, Indian Territory, . . on consideration of a certain sum of money to be paid quarterly to Belknap or Belknap's wife." Belknap resigned before the articles of impeachment were drawn up and, therefore, the Senate had no jurisdiction (http://library.morrisville.edu/local_history/sites/gar_post/belknap. html Retrieved 5/16/2007).

In spite of Belknap's resignation, the impeachment trial continued in the Senate for five months. Ultimately, Belknap was not convicted (John W. Dean, "Refocusing the Impeachment Movement on Administration Officials Below the President and Vice-President," *Find Law*, 12/15/2006).

LOCATIONS and DATES

Las Vegas Grandes is my fictional name for the current City of Las Vegas, New Mexico. Los Alamitos is based on the village of Los Alamos eleven miles north of the city. Fort Union, its garrison, Post Trader's Compound, and Quartermaster's Depot are based on what is now the Fort Union National Park, Watrous, New Mexico. Although the Loma Parda village, gambling halls, and hotels are deserted, the ruins remain.

In Chapter 3, the description of Fort Union in Dr. Williamson's letters is based on material quoted from *The Las Vegas Optic* in *Fort Union (New Mexico)* by F. Stanley.

Occasionally, historical dates do not coordinate with the dates in the fiction of *Prairie Madness*. For instance, I found no records or references to theatrical performances at the Fort Union garrison before 1883.

The rich history "that has been lived" at Fort Union and along the Western Frontier, as well as my own genealogical connections to and research findings about immigrant populations in the 1880s Southwest led me to write *Prairie Madness, Conspiracy at Fort Union*—a story "that could have been."

Acknowledgements

Since its inception, July 25, 2006, *Prairie Madness* has been a work of love, frustration, joy, and breakthroughs. To thank everyone who helped with this long, off and on, project is difficult, but I shall try my best. My sincere apologies to anyone whose name I may have accidentally left out.

Great big thank yous to:

Those who assisted at the birth and toddlerhood: Deborah Blanche and Jane Hyatt, fellow writers/conspirators; at Fort Union—Claudette Norman, Mario Medina, Tibur Reminyck; and at Wind River Ranch, Brian Miller.

Those who read, critiqued, proofread, and mused with me through the teen years: Lisa Cron, UCLA Writers Studio; in New Mexico, Joy Alesdatter, Deborah Blanche, Steven Davis, Roy Luján, David Pascale, Lucy Reed, C. W. Riley, Susan Schmidt, and Sara Stevens; in Long Beach, CA, Janet Dignam, Alice Rushdy, Moss Sherian, and Peter Werrenrath; in Shelton, WA, Rachel Romero, horsewoman extraordinaire.

Those who made and performed the theatrical productions of "Who Killed Sean Flannery?": Deborah Blanche, Lisa Cisneros, Joe Cooney, Tim Crofton and the United World College Theatre Program, Hoyle Osborne, Jeremiah Stevens, Mike Trujillo, and Jane Voss.

Those who helped with the photograph section and permissions research: David Pascale, Photographer; Carol Ditmanson, Western National Parks Association; Ranger Mike Weinstein and Volunteer Research Librarian Mitch Barker, Fort Union National Park; and Robert N. Dunnagan.

Those who helped with research: staff members at Carnegie Public Library, The City of Las Vegas Museum and Rough Rider Memorial Collection, Fort Union National Monument, and Donnelly Library, New Mexico Highlands University.

The man behind the book: David Pascale, who believed in its publishability.

The fabulous tech support and publishing skills of Peter Werrenrath.

All the horses I've known and Louie Plagge for teaching me how to listen to them.

About the Author

Born in East Boston, Massachusetts, Edwina Romero started writing by making up stories for her younger siblings and later, her co-workers. Much later, she earned a Bachelor of Arts, Master of Arts, and Ph. D.—all in English. In addition to teaching college-level writing, she published short fiction, poetry, and professional articles. Much much later, Romero set out on her own as a writer and editor. *Prairie Madness* is her first novel. She lives and writes in Las Vegas, NM, and Long Beach, CA.

Made in the USA
Lexington, KY
12 January 2019